Alberensa

AL JONES

For Sally Jeanne Colegrove
熊貓
(Xióng Māo)

*For all have sinned and fall short of the
glory of God.*

Romans 3:10

PROLOGUE

The Auvergne
27 November 1095

RONZIÈRES

The Old One announced that the women of Montjoix would pray the office of Terce even though they were not at the convent. She dragged Sister Barbara into the Ronzières village church and shamed the monks into following them. Julian protested, "Sister Maria Magdalena, we should keep on our way to Clermont, or we might miss the Pope's address."

An ancient face, nearly fifty, glowered at Count Raymond's armorer from within its cowl. "All of us at Montjoix have vowed a life of chastity, poverty and obedience, Master Julian. We must pray the daily offices. If that makes us late for the Holy Father's words, then the Lord did not intend for us to hear them."

Maria Magdalena led the religious into the gloom of the small stone sanctuary, allowing the dampness within to flow out on those left behind. Two slit windows high up on each side wall provided but little illumination for the holy space, but the monks and nuns did not require the morning sunlight brightening the street outside. Day after day, year after year, they prayed the Hours to glorify the True Light that shone in the Darkness, the Light that the Darkness could not overcome.

Julian turned to Raymond's other men and shrugged. They looked upon a handsome man, taller than most, with large arms and shoulders from his heavy work for the Count of Toulouse. He had lighter hair than many in the County. His blue eyes, also unusual, more often found farther north, in the lands of the King of France.

"I suppose we might at least give thanks to the Lord for this sunny day."

Heads nodded in agreement. The Auvergne, in the hilly center of France, could be most unpleasant in November. Rain and cold winds up the Loire River Valley often added misery to the shortening days as winter neared.

Waiting outside the Ronzières church, Julian felt a heavy sameness, the same sameness that hung over every village on the way to Clermont. A single muddy track passed through, lined with the wooden huts of the serfs. A smell of mud and manure and sweat and animal filled the air. These farmers battled nature every day to keep their homes warm and dry, since just one bad storm could wash them away, ruin their crops and bring on starvation. Or one small cooking fire could get out of control and burn down their entire village.

"Let's help them while we wait," said Julian, pointing to a family at work. Flames had escaped from the stone hearth in the center of their dirt floor, igniting the thatch roof and making them homeless as winter approached. The husband and two older boys steadily cut and wove strips of wood through vertical staves while the wife and a small girl followed, daubing a lime and mud cement into the gaps between the wood. A neighbor woman sat in front, plaiting fresh thatch for the roof. Julian and the others sat down beside her and joined in the wood cutting and the thatch plaiting.

The weeks of Pope Urban's Clermont council had provided ample time to experience the worst of the Auvergne. The Count, his family and his most important retainers found lodging in the city. For the rest, including Julian, the Count arranged quarters at Montjoix, an hour's walk to the south.

Generations of benefactors had endowed the monastery and its associated convent with chapels, dormitories, chapter houses and refectories. Covered walkways bridged the space between the buildings, creating cloistered squares with greenswards in the center where the religious might experience the outdoors and yet walk within the sacred confines. A wall pierced by only a single door separated the men from the women. A much higher wall surrounded Montjoix, separating them all from the world and its evils.

Julian and the others often returned late, after Vespers, well after the monks had finished dinner and retired to their cells for prayer. Abbott Sylvestre ordered food saved for them. He asked the sisters from the convent to serve the late meal.

Raymond's retainers quickly grew fond of Sister Barbara, an attractive young nun with captivating hazel eyes. She engaged them pleasantly, unlike many of the women who served the meal and retired back through their wall without speaking. Finally, Julian asked her to "sit with us a moment, Sister Hazel Eyes, and take a cup," and she did. Within minutes, Sister Maria Magdalena chased Hazel Eyes back to her cell.

When Barbara again accepted Julian's offer of "a cup" the following evening, and the Old One again chased her away, the blacksmith sought out Sylvestre. That night, Maria Magdalena and Barbara both sat down for a cup. They had enjoyed a cup every night since.

Terce ended. Unlike Maria Magdalena, Sister Barbara and the others emerged from the church in an almost festive mood. No doubt when they returned to Montjoix tonight, they would pray for forgiveness from the sin of vanity, or gluttony, or lust, or however they defined enjoying themselves. For now, they laughed and smiled as they started again on this holiday from the never-changing routine of their daily lives.

The march resumed. The levity of Julian's party contrasted with the heavy sameness that hung over the men and women they passed in the fields, the burden of poverty that was their earthly lot and the earthly lot of all the serfs in Europe. Poverty in their cottages, poverty in their clothing. The women wore long-sleeve ankle-length tunics, course wool, mostly brown, or if the owner could not afford dyed cloth, gray. The men wore woolen stockings tied up with garters above their knees. Over the hose, knee-length tunics, again of wool. Even the nobility wore the universal costume of tunic and hose, except that their tunics were made from finer cloth and did not smell of sweat and manure and the animals that lived in the humble cottages during the winter months.

"Master Julian, all these days, today our last day, and you've never asked me why I'm in the convent." Those hazel eyes beamed up at him from the lovely face within her cowl, mischievous and playful, lights of their own that the darkness could not overcome.

"No, Sister Barbara, nor have we asked any of the others. The call you received from our Savior is a personal one, and need not be explained."

Barbara had chosen her time well, while Maria Magdalena was busy reciting personal devotions as she walked along. "Nor have you ever asked where I lived, or what I did before I joined the convent."

"No, I have not." The lights blazed at him. He took the hint. "Where are you from, Sister Barbara, and what did you do before you joined the convent"?

"You are more than a blacksmith, aren't you, Julian? You know the magic that makes the iron come forth from the rock. You can forge the dull lumps of metal into unbreakable shining steel."

"Yes."

"Are you married, Master Julian"?

"No." The breeze rustled the trees at the edge of a woodlot, shaking down the dying leaves.

"I'm from that village, Master Julian, Ronzières. My uncle is the smith. When I was a girl, I enjoyed visiting him at his forge, watching him turn the iron into tools and nails and horseshoes. Sometimes I helped, building the fire, pumping the bellows, holding a second set of tongs on the piece to keep it steady, even some of the finishing work." Barbara's hands moved as she demonstrated her holding skills in her bubbly voice. The nun's cheerfulness belonged in some happy family cottage, not in the somber surroundings of Montjoix's convent.

"How did our Savior call you to the religious life, Sister Barbara"?

"It was more my father than our Savior who called me to Montjoix, Master Julian."

"Your father"?

"I was sixteen. My uncle's assistant was twenty. He was handsome and I was weak. Or strong. He was intended for a girl in the village, but I wanted him. All the other boys my age, they were taken. Or they were stupid. I didn't care about the woman he was to marry, that simpering baby. I wanted him."

"Sister Barbara, I…"

"Not only did I want him, he wanted me. One day I drew myself to him at the forge and kissed him. At first he admitted his love, but then he shoved me to the ground and called me a witch. 'No, no,' I said, 'I love you I am a woman in love not a witch.'"

"And that's why you entered the convent? To atone for the sin of lust"?

"I entered the convent to remove temptation from my uncle's assistant. That was my choice: embrace Christ as his Bride or be denounced for fornication, for lust, for seduction, sins that only a woman in the thrall of Satan would do. Serve Christ at Montjoix or be burned as a witch. It was an easy choice."

They walked several paces along the road before Julian spoke. "We all suspected that you had not truly welcomed the religious life, as Maria Magdalena has done. We guessed that you had a child, Sister, perhaps by a married man."

CLERMONT

At the request of Bishop Durand of the Auvergne, Pope Urban did not hold his Council in the Clermont Cathedral. Instead, he used a parish church in the Portus market district. Clermont, at a crossroads on the Allier River, was not Rome, but it was growing, and the Portus district was growing with it. Two and three story shops and residences lined the narrow streets radiating away from the church square, with cross streets linking the spokes from time to time. Many of the timber buildings stepped out as they went up, creating an arch of square shapes closing in the sky overhead. As in all towns, animal waste and human waste and discarded food collected in the roadways, creating an aroma different from the country but pungent nonetheless.

Julian and his party arrived to find the square in front of Notre Dame du Port nearly full. The church seemed a larger version of Ronzières, with a square stone tower on one corner and a door in the center. The smith quickly picked out the boisterous voice of Baron Jaufres of Lapeyrouse and followed the sound towards its well-fed owner. The Montjoix monks and nuns stayed close behind him as he maneuvered through the crowd. They realized that Julian's course was bringing them ever closer to the place where the Holy Father would speak.

"My lord," Julian said as Jaufres turned towards his arrival. The Baron surveyed Julian's small army as the monks and nuns and men-at-arms all bowed towards the nobleman. "The Abbott of Montjoix allowed these religious to accompany us." Jaufres waved his assent and turned back to his conversation. Julian felt a tug on his sleeve.

"Is the Count inside, Master Julian"?

"Yes, Sister Barbara. Raymond is a devoted servant of God and a loyal supporter of His Holiness, so he is inside for the Council."

"You have favor with the Count, Julian. All the others look to you for guidance, to tell them what to do. Yet you are not a member of his family or a nobleman yourself."

"It's the skill I have, Sister, the same one you learned as a girl. He values that skill, and so he values me and he favors me."

Maria Magdalena stepped between Barbara and Julian. "Sister Barbara, we have not come here for idle talk. These men are leaving today. The time for foolish speaking is over. Stand in silence, bow your head and turn your thoughts to sacred things. Prepare yourself for the Holy Father's words."

"It's all right, Sister Maria Magdalena. Sister Barbara is simply being polite. Those of us not in the religious life often converse as a way to pass the time."

"Sister Barbara is in the religious life, Master Julian! She has devoted herself to God. She is Christ's Bride.

She has no need of polite conversation. You place your own soul in danger of eternal damnation if you tempt her to break those vows. Barbara is here to see the Holy Father, to pray and to contemplate our Savior's sacrifice, not to talk with men from Toulouse."

Julian smiled at the rebuke and smiled at them. "Baron Jaufres thinks that the Pope will call for a military pilgrimage to take Holy Jerusalem back from the Saracens. Have you heard that, Sisters"?

Sister Barbara opened her mouth to speak, but no mere mortal could tempt the Old One. She glared Sister Barbara into silence. Both women bowed their heads, leaving Julian standing alone.

A commotion in front of the church broke the awkward silence. The doors opened and several nobles exited, among them tall and blond Count Raymond, fourth of that name to rule Toulouse, their liege. He walked towards them with all the authority of his office, the most important nobleman in Languedoc. Julian bowed to his Count as Raymond joined them, as did all of his men, and the monks and nuns.

"My lords," Count Raymond said, "His Holiness will speak to us. He will set for us a most remarkable challenge." He looked around his court and found his armorer. "Julian, we will have need of your skills, my friend."

Julian gave a deep bow of acknowledgment and straightened up. A moment later, he felt a body bump up against his. He looked into the hazel eyes of Sister

Barbara. Maria Magdalena was trying to join them, but the Count's men had crowded around Julian, cutting her off.

"Will you honor us, my lord, with what the Holy Father has decided"? asked the Baron of Lapeyrouse.

"He has repeated Pope Gregory's decrees against simony. Against the lay investiture of the clergy. And against the marriage of priests."

"That is bad luck for the priests, my lord," Jaufres said. A smattering of laughter began, but under the glare of their pious liege, it faded away immediately. The baron quickly moved on. "What of the King, my lord"?

"The Holy Father has excommunicated King Phillip. France cannot repudiate his lawful wife, Queen Bertha, and marry Bertrada, the Countess of Anjou, simply because he wishes to do so."

Sister Barbara pulled on Julian's sleeve. "Were you ever married, Master Julian"?

He looked down, annoyed at the interruption, even though only he had heard her whisper. How had she managed to get such an innocent look in those lovely eyes?

"I was, but my Willelma died giving birth to our first child. The babe, my daughter, could not come out, and they both perished in agony. I have prayed for understanding ever since that day, Sister Barbara. The will of God, the purpose of God, can be difficult to understand."

Barbara took his hand and held it for a moment. Julian felt an uncomfortable stirring in his loins as she rested her other hand momentarily on his forearm.

"What else, if I may beg more information from you, my lord"? Jaufres asked.

"Baron Jaufres, the Holy Father will be out presently. Turn your thoughts to God and wait for his arrival. Julian, come here, we must speak."

The crowd separated to allow Julian to make his way into the Count's presence. He bowed again once he stood before his liege, even though the Count was smiling at him as he approached. "Have you hired a personal confessor, Julian? Who is this sister who joins you"? Julian turned to find that Barbara was still with him. Looking back, he saw the Old One trying to follow, but five rows of Raymond's supporters cut her off from her charge.

The nun curtseyed deeply. Then she put her hazel eyes to work. "I am Sister Barbara from the convent at Montjoix, my lord. Before I joined the convent, I was the daughter of a serf, a bondsman in the village of Ronzières. My given name, before I took the name of the saint, was Monica."

"Monica. Monica. Also the name of a saint, Sister Barbara." The Count considered her, standing before him, smiling again. "You are quite saucy for a nun, Sister. Why are you here with my armorer, Master Julian"?

"If you need help with the explanation, Julian," Jaufres said, "just ask me."

Sister Barbara smiled, and Jaufres received the gift of those eyes. There was something magic about them, the way they made all of them melt. Was she a witch, not a nun? She certainly had bewitching ways.

A shout went up from the front of the crowd. Bishops poured from the entrance to the church, crossing the terrace and standing on the steps. People surged forward, carrying Barbara and Julian and Jaufres and the rest of the Count's court along in the flood. With the jostling and the pushing, it was possible that anyone, even a nun, could stumble and be trampled underfoot. Julian moved Sister Barbara in front of him, facing her forward with his arms around her body.

Lord Christ, I am protecting Your bride. Forgive me from the sin of holding her so. He could not keep the two of them from being pushed with the crowd, but it flowed like a stream around them, Julian a rock protecting Sister Barbara from the current.

The movement stopped. Julian realized that they were all still together, Jaufres and his men, Count Raymond and the others. The crowd had brought the Montjoix monks and Sister Maria Magdalena close to them again. He released Sister Barbara and she took one step away, a step closer to Maria Magdalena. Julian wondered if Hazel Eyes had enough time left in her life for all the prayers of penance that the Old One would fix upon her for the sin of touching a man.

The end of the Papal procession moved onto the terrace in front of the church. Despite his age and the gray in his beard, the Pope made a most resplendent figure, with the sunlight glinting off the gold threads in his clerical robes. Bishop Durand processed just behind him, and all the priests of the Vatican bustled around, jockeying for the position due their station in the Papal entourage.

The Pope himself appeared oblivious to all the maneuvering. Without a pause, he came to the head of the steps, stopped and waited for the crowd to quiet. He looked out at the throng, hundreds of knights and commoners, clergy and laity. Hose and tunics, their cloth fine and rude, colorful and gray. Knightly standards blew in the breeze, and soon their snapping was the only sound to be heard. The Pope bowed his head in silent prayer, looked up, and began.

"My Lords, My Bishops, Friends of our Lord Jesus Christ. I, Urban, by the grace of God elected Chief Bishop and Prelate over the whole world, have come into these lands to bring you a divine admonition." A deep, firm, inspired voice issued from the Holy Father. From the mouth of Urban, Julian heard the majestic, the powerful, the omnipotent Voice of God.

"From the Emperor Alexios in Constantinople we have learned of horrible things. A race from the kingdom of the Persians has invaded the Christian lands of the Eastern Empire. They have put Christians to death by sword, by pillage and by fire. They have destroyed the churches. They torture the men and rape the women. The Eastern Empire has lost territory in Asia Minor so vast in extent that it cannot be traversed in a march of two months."

Singly, in groups, in ever-increasing numbers, the religious in the crowd, monks, priests, nuns, fell to their knees. Urban's words transfixed the knights. Their hands went to the hilts of their swords as their minds filled with visions of fitting revenge.

"Of holy Jerusalem, I dare not to speak, for it is a sin and a source of shame for all Christians. Jerusalem, where our Lord Christ Himself suffered for us, died for us and rose again in triumph from the dead, has been overcome by the enemy and withdrawn from the service of God. The Lord's Holy Sepulcher has become a place of shame. We can no longer speak of the suffering of Jerusalem. Instead we weep, we weep like the Psalmist, and in us the prophecy is fulfilled:

> 'God, the nations have overcome your inheritance. They have defiled your holy temple. They have laid Jerusalem to waste. The dead bodies of your servants have been given as food for the birds of the heavens, the flesh of your saints to the beasts of the earth.'"

The Holy Father stopped. He looked towards the heavens, and then fixed his look around the crowd, starting at the left and moving to the right. To the right, the side of The Majesty on High on which Our Lord sat down after His Resurrection.

"But there is more. You knights, you are arrogant and full of pride. God has given you dominion over the peoples in your lands. They are yours, to defend and to protect. Yet you rage against your Christian brothers and cut each other in pieces. You are the oppressors of children, the plunderers of widows. As vultures smell fetid corpses, so do you sense battles from afar and rush to them eagerly. This is the worst way, for it is utterly removed from the way of God"!

His arm lunged into the air.

"If you wish to spare your eternal souls from the pains of Hell, you have two choices. Either cease this robbing and this pillaging, or advance boldly, as knights of Christ, to the defense of the Eastern Church, to the redemption of the Holy Land. Under Jesus Christ our Leader, may you struggle for Jerusalem in Christian battle line. Struggle, that you may drive out the Turks, more awful than the Jebusites whom Joshua drove from Jerusalem of old"!

The hand came down now, pointing out, sweeping along the Papal audience.

"My lords, undertake this journey with the assurance of the imperishable glory of the Kingdom of Heaven. Enter upon the road to the Holy Sepulcher; wrest the sacred land from the wicked race, and restore Jerusalem again to the service of our Lord"!

Count Raymond's sword leaped from its scabbard and shot above his head. His voice boomed across the square.

"*Deus Lo Volt!* It is the Will of God!"

Jaufres' sword was out next, and fifty others in the crowd.

"It is the Will of God! It is the Will of God!"

Now Julian, and the monks, and Maria Magdalena, and Barbara, joined in,

"It is the Will of God! It is the Will of God"!

Now the whole throng, swept up, inspired, the vision of the Earthly Jerusalem and the Heavenly Jerusalem united into one, the place where Christ lived on earth and the place where He reigned in Heaven brought together, open to true believers, the foe that held them now defeated for all time.

"It is the Will of God! It is the Will of God! It is the Will of God!"

The Holy Father stood in the midst of the storm, his head bowed before the waves of sound. Minutes passed as Urban prayed before them. Finally he turned to Durand. The Bishop's hands went up, stilling the crowd, allowing Urban's voice to soar over the multitudes.

"My fellow Christians, today our Lord has manifested what He said in the Gospel: 'Where two or three are gathered together in my name, I am there in the midst of them.'

"For as you all uttered the same cry, the same prayer, so are we certain that it was the Lord our God who was the source of your prayer. Although your cry issued from many mouths, the origin of the cry was the One. Let this then be your cry in battle, because it was given to you by God! When you stand before Holy Jerusalem, ready to take it from the Saracens, let this cry be raised by all the soldiers of the Lord: It is the Will of God! It is the Will of God"!

"It is the Will of God! It is the Will of God! It is the Will of God"!

Through the uproar that followed, the chanting, the cheering, the pounding of swords against shields, Julian heard the voice of Sister Barbara whispering in his ear. "You will be going to the Holy Land, Julian. That's why your Count came here, to embark on this pilgrimage, this quest."

"So it appears, Sister Barbara," he whispered back. He looked towards Maria Magdalena, expecting to be interrupted. Instead the Old One knelt on the ground, arms upraised to heaven, tears of joy at the redemption of Jerusalem streaming down her face. She did not notice their polite conversation.

The crowd quieted, the Pope resumed, but Julian's attention remained with the nun.

"Monica is my name, Julian. I'm not a witch. I was a sixteen-year-old girl in love with the wrong man. I've paid the price of that kiss for eleven long years. Do you know what I learned in all those years? What my prayers taught me"?

"No."

"If you ever have the chance again, be smarter and find a better man." She glanced towards the Pope, and back again. "I look at the stars at night, so many stars. Which is the one star that shines through eternity only for me? I know the answer now. If I were not a nun, would you love me"?

Willelma, darling Willelma, I've thought about that so many times these past weeks. I'm lonely, my love, and this Sister is lonely. She is intended to be Monica, a mother, not Barbara, a Sister. Together, O Lord Our God, her star joined with mine, together we would never be lonely.

"Yes, I would…..I do. But you are a nun, Sister Barbara."

She let him go and turned back to the Holy Father.

"Remember again what Our Savior has said: He that does not take up his cross and follow after me, is not worthy of me! Be worthy of the sacrifice of our Lord, our Redeemer, you men of France! Take up His Cross, and follow Him! Follow Him, and redeem Holy Jerusalem"!

"It is the Will of God! It is the Will of God! It is the Will of God"!

Urban turned to Durand and retrieved his crook. With a small final bow towards the crowd, he re-entered the church, all the bishops and priests following in order after him. The door finally closed behind the last man, but by then, no one was watching.

Sister Barbara turned to Julian and put her hands on his arms. Her decision, and his, was taken. "Master Julian. I have the skill. I know how to work the steel. Marry me and take me with you. We must join this campaign together. It is the Will of God."

Maria Magdalena was alongside in a moment, but it was too late. Julian reached out and pulled the hood and the cowl off Barbara's head, handing them to the stunned Old One. Monica's auburn hair, cut short and dirty, saw the light of the sun for the first time in eleven years. Maria crossed herself furiously but could think of nothing else to do in the face of so great a sin.

"My lord Count," Monica cried as she fell prostrate into the offal. Her large wooden cross came up, her arms extended in front of her, a look of intense excitement on her face. The Count and Jaufres turned and sought the sound, found Julian and then looked down at the space beneath them. The Count was surprised, and then smiled.

"Is this your saucy confessor again, Master Julian? Whatever is the matter with her? What does she want"?

"I know what she wants, my lord," Baron Jaufres said. "And what Master Julian wants. Stand up, woman, stand up and speak your piece."

Julian reached down and helped Monica to her feet, put his arms around her waist and drew her close again.

"My lord. I know the magic of the iron. I am the assistant that Julian needs. Command the Abbess of Montjoix to release me from my vows. Let me be Julian's apprentice, and his wife. Let us take up the Cross together and follow Christ. Let us stand together at the Holy Sepulcher. It is, my lord, it is the Will of God."

PART ONE

Jabil al-Hadid, County of Tripoli
April 1222

1

Hugh, sixth Baron of Jabil al-Hadid, stepped from his Keep into his castle yard. For a moment the bright sunlight blinded the Baron, causing him to squint his blue eyes against the pain. Before him, the horses of his mounted escort, led by Sir Frederic, his Marshal, snapped and shuffled against each other, snorting their impatience. The full suits of chain mail armor on Jabil al-Hadid's military commander and its men-at-arms displayed the wealth of Hugh's fief. The Christian nobility in the Holy Land always wore armor, but many nobles could afford only heavy leather vests to protect their men in battle.

Baron Hugh strode across the yard towards his own mount. Tall and slender at twenty-one, his light brown hair glowed in the sunlight. He kept his hair long in the noble fashion, but thought his youthful beard too scraggly and preferred to endure the razor.

He wore the well-made clothing of a wealthy noble, gray woolen hose and knee-length fitted tunic.

"Good morning, my lord." Jabil al-Hadid's Seneschal, its master of the household, bowed before his master as he held the reins to his horse.

"Good morning, William." Hugh looked up and addressed the rider on the pillion behind his war saddle. "Lady Agnes, are you ready?"

Agnes of Jabil al-Hadid sat sidesaddle, with her embroidered slippers peeking beneath the hem of her long silk tunic. A blue silk cap tied under her chin with white silk ribbons shielded the fair skin of her face from the sun.

"Yes, my lord."

Hugh took the reins from his Seneschal and swung into the saddle. Lady Agnes wrapped her arms around his waist, wiggled herself comfortable and leaned forward to whisper. "Thank you for not wearing your mail, brother. It's uncomfortable on my arms when I hold onto you."

"The wish of such a lovely member of the fair sex is always to be honored, sister, always." The baron looked down on his waiting servant. "William."

"Yes, my lord."

"Find Lady Anne. Tell her that I require her attendance upon me in the Great Hall when I return."

The skinny man fretted. "It is still early, my lord." Hugh looked at the sun, already high in the sky. He glared at his servant. "As you command, my lord."

"Go tell her now, William, now, so that she can prepare. I will receive her as soon as I return." Without waiting for a reply, he spurred his horse for the short trot to the column.

"Good day, Sir Frederic."

"Good day, my lord."

Born fifteen years before his Baron, Hugh's leading knight carried the dark hair and dark eyes of his Lebanese Christian mother and grandmother. He carried a body and spirit hard from fighting the Saracens, experienced in the constant challenges and occasional skirmishes that defined life in Outremer, the "land across the sea." The skill of such men and the careful leadership of its Barons had allowed Jabil al-Hadid to prosper at the edge of the County of Tripoli for over a century.

"Open the gates for the Baron of Jabil al-Hadid"! Frederic called. The double column set off at a walk through the castle entrance.

Sir Julian of Blagnac built Jabil al-Hadid in 1099 following the holy pilgrimage that freed Jerusalem from the Saracens. Hugh's grandmother Athèné strengthened the castle's wall while she was regent for her son Joscelin, after her husband Olivier died in the disaster at Hattin. She raised its height and built a gate tower over the single entrance, secured at each end by a heavy wooden door and iron-plated portcullis. Any attackers who penetrated the outer entrance would be trapped in the space under the tower, shot at with arrows through slits in the side walls and burned by boiling oil and molten metal poured through the murder holes in the ceiling above.

"Mind the guerdon"! Its bearer lowered the banner for the passage through the gates.

"Shield bordered in white and divided in half horizontally," the heralds called when Hugh's men approached a noble assembly with his guerdon held high, "Base color top half red, with an Occitan cross in gold." An Occitan cross, one with triangular points at the end of each arm, the cross of the Counts of Toulouse in Languedoc, founders of the County of Tripoli in the Holy Land. "Base color bottom half silver, with a brown bear on its hind legs over the words, *'Plegar le Ferre.'*" *Plegar le Ferre*, "Bend the iron" in the Occitan language of Toulouse, the motto of Jabil al-Hadid.

Horseshoes reverberated in the narrow space under the tower as the men rode through the gates. Brief coolness gave way to bright light that flooded the land and sparkled on the green of Hugh's Syrian villages, stretched along the Orontes River that lay east of the castle. Further north the Orontes entered the ancient reservoir near Homs. Legend said that the Romans built its dam while they ruled *Palestina*. Others claimed that some Pharaoh was responsible. Either way, its irrigation canals still watered a large area, but that area was in the lands of the Emir of Syria, beyond the County of Tripoli.

The Baron led his men downhill, north, to the road between Tripoli on the Mediterranean and Homs in Syria. To the west, the Lebanon Mountains formed a rugged wall between the Orontes and the Mediterranean plain. Snow melted on the higher peaks, filling the river for its northward journey to the sea, near Antioch, where Prince Bohemond ruled.

The rocky knoll where Julian placed his castle dominated the eastern end of the Homs Gap Pass as the Tripoli Road entered the Lebanon Mountains. Controlling the road created a valuable source of income, yet that wealth paled in comparison to the peak that rose some distance away, at the southern edge of their fief. *Al-Jabil al-Hadidiu*, the Saracens called it, the "Iron Mountain."

The family chronicles recounted Julian's urgency in seizing the Iron Mountain. Even as their men-at-arms and serfs and hired men from Tripoli dug the foundations and cut the stones and fortified the knoll for Christ, Julian and his Baroness, the Lady Monica of Ronzières, diverted their most skilled laborers to the nearby bank of the Orontes. The noble couple completed their smelter and their forge even before their castle was enclosed, before their fief was safe against Saracen attacks. The first sword came from its foundry on Christmas Day 1099, a gift for Count Raymond IV of Toulouse, also Count Raymond I of Tripoli, their liege.

Plegar le Ferre, "Bend the Iron." Steel had flowed from the banks of the Orontes ever since.

A dust plume trailed the baron's passage as the column turned West towards the Pass. Its narrowing walls heightened the tension as they entered. Without orders, two men from the rear broke away and galloped ahead, seeking any sign of an ambush. When the outriders returned, Frederic waved his hand. Everyone pulled up to a stop. Gritty powder settled gently back to earth as the same two men rode into a narrow valley just south of the Pass Road. In a minute, they were back.

"All clear, my lord."

"Continue on your way to Krak, Sir Frederic. We do not want to keep the Hospitallers and their caravan waiting. Lady Agnes and I will be fine."

"You two wait here," Frederic ordered. "The rest, follow me." The column set off at a walk.

Hugh's men-at-arms saluted their Baron as he rode past them, up the stream that flowed down the gorge. Despite the green closer to the river, this higher land remained rocky, barren and dry, at least until they reached the canyon's far end.

Coming around the last bend revealed a small pool, as deep as a man was tall. To one side, water poured steadily from a small crevice in the rock. At this time, in the early Spring, snowmelt joined it, running down the walls of the gorge, overflowing the pool and filling the stream. In the dry season, that stream always dried to a trickle, but the flow from the crevice kept the pool filled all year. Grass and even some trees grew here, creating a cool, shaded and quiet spot.

The Baron dismounted and tied his animal to a tree, out of the sun and with room to reach the spring. His sister waited on the pillion, holding onto the pommel.

"I'm right next to you, Agnes," Hugh said. "Let me reach up and help you down."

Agnes turned her blonde head with her lovely but sightless blue eyes towards the sound of his voice. *Al-Zarqa'*, the Syrians called her, Blue Eyes. "Don't let me fall, brother," she answered in a soft, low voice.

"I'll catch you if you promise to help me with my problems. You're the clever one, not me."

Agnes smiled, a warm smile on a pretty face. She always loved that exchange, that compliment.

Hugh put his hands around her narrow waist as *al-Zarqa'* let herself slide into his arms. His walked clumsily, holding his sister upright while her arms clung around his neck. He tripped just as they reached her favorite shaded rock, but he managed to seat her without dropping her. Agnes felt around with her hands while Hugh straightened her dress and her legs.

"Could you move me a little, Hugh? I can't move my legs, but I can feel them, and the left one is resting on a bump in the rock." He slid his hands under her tunic, feeling how shriveled, how bony her thighs had become.

"Is that better"?

"Thank you, yes." She turned her vacant gaze towards his voice. "This is such a happy place and yet such a sad place, brother."

Hugh looked around the pleasant spot. "We did have good times here, Agnes. The four of us splashing around in that pool naked while Mother and Father watched."

"And the servants waiting around the corner." Her lip quivered. "And then that wretched disease. It took Madeleine and Roger so quickly, unable to breathe. But those demons only played with me, Hugh, they played with me and left me alive. Alive, blind and paralyzed from my waist down."

That catastrophe struck just over two years ago, at Christmas in 1219. The crippling sickness, that came from time to time, killing some and paralyzing others. "You know what the Arab doctor from Homs thought, Aggie. The wasting of your legs, that was the disease that killed Maddie and Roger. The blinding, no."

"The demented sickness, he said."

"Yes, the headache before you lost your sight reminded him of the headaches old people get before they become crippled and demented. They think the same disease blinded you. No doubt there is other damage, but it is hidden by the crippling disease. " He lifted her soft hand to his lips and kissed it. "The good news, sister, is that you are hardly demented. Far from it."

"Maybe not, but I'm helpless and useless, Hugh, a lump who can only drag herself through the straw and the offal, bumping into things. I depend on your kindness to be sure I'm even carried to the table and fed."

Hugh turned away so that she could not see his pain, pain that she could not see. Before the disease took her, this broken body and her sister rode bareback with their brothers, straddling the horses like men. Up and down the canyon in their long tunics with their bare legs showing, shrieking and giggling and waving their make-believe swords. It was most unladylike, but their mother could never get her husband to make them stop until the disease brought it all to a tragic end.

"I'd rather have you as you are, Agnes, than lose you altogether. You're a very brave woman."

"That is kind, Hugh, although I am more a burden than brave." She took in a deep breath, and smiled. "Did I ever tell you that Mother thought that I was conceived here by the side of the pool on a warm summer night? She was explaining where babies come from and told me a little more than she should."

Hugh imagined the embarrassment on Mother's very proper face, realizing what she had said. Her marriage was arranged, like all the nobility, yet when Joscelin and Marguerite finally met, they fell in love. It was not something that the fourth baron, Olivier, and his wife, Athèné of Jerusalem, expected when they agreed with Count Angibert II of Alberensa that Joscelin would marry Angibert's infant granddaughter.

"Mother told me a lot of things before she died, Agnes, but conceiving any of us wasn't part of it."

Madeleine and Roger two years ago, and now their parents this year. Baron Joscelin took ill with a terrible fever two months ago, in February. Having lost so much, two children dead and one maimed and helpless, Marguerite could not leave her beloved husband to the care of the servants, so she tended him herself. Her husband died first. Within days, Marguerite had taken ill with the same sickness, and with the same result. Hugh remembered her bedside, her final moments, looked at his sister, and fought back his tears.

"Hugh? Are you here"?

"I'm here." He kissed her hand again. "It's the sixth of April, 1222, Agnes. Happy nineteenth birthday, sister."

"Thank you."

He kissed her hand again. "Will you be reminding me yet again that Easter Sunday fell on your birthday in 1203"?

Agnes cocked her head. "You just reminded yourself, brother. And again in 1208, but not again until 1287, when I'll be 84. Somehow I don't think that I shall have another Easter birthday." She smiled into the unseen distance. "You had me dressed up for the occasion in something new. What am I wearing"?

"Mother ordered this tunic for you last fall, and two others. She wanted you to look nice, even in your chair with wheels. They arrived from Tripoli two days ago. It's silk from beyond the eastern mountains, deep blue, the color of Alberensa. As you can feel, it's more fitted around your upper body than a tunic. The sleeves are tighter to the elbow, too, before they open out. Your belt is leather with a silver buckle, loose with the long end dropping in front of the tunic." He fingered her long surcoat, a loose garment with no sleeves, worn over the dress with the front open. "Your coat is white, and you have a blue square silk hat with silk ribbons under your chin. You really do look lovely, Aggie."

"Thank you." Hugh's sister put her hand to her mouth as she always did when she was thinking, then took it away. "You didn't need to dress me in silk for a dusty ride in the country. You have news for me. Family news, which is why we are alone."

"I need your advice, Aggie. You're the clever one, not me."

2

The noonday sun brightened the top *pied* of the gorge, six *toises* above the little pool. The *toise*, the height of a tall man, with six of them keeping the solar heat from reaching into the cool glen. Agnes poised on her rock in her silk gown as Hugh began.

"The Toulouse line of Tripoli counts ended after Hattin, Agnes. Now the Prince of Antioch rules both counties. Our parents thought that a closer union with our new liege would strengthen our position, given our place at the frontier with the constant wars. In rank we are a minor house in Tripoli, but the wealth of the smelter enabled the promise of a huge dowry, something to help pay for those constant wars. Bohemond IV, Prince of Antioch and Count of Tripoli and his wife Plaisance of Gibelet agreed that you would wed their son and heir, the future Bohemond V."

"An agreement made when I was five and he was nine. 'Princess Agnes of Antioch,' it did have a nice ring, once I was old enough to understand what it meant."

"And what was expected of you."

Agnes reached down and touched her womb. "Perpetual gravidity. Many heirs."

"Your marriage makes Jabil al-Hadid a major house in the County. Because my children are closely related to the Prince of Antioch, vacant fiefs and higher titles fall to us. Surely the pangs of childbirth are worth enduring for such a boon."

Agnes snorted and frowned. "I trust you smiled as you said that, brother. Men afflict those pangs upon us with abandon, perhaps because no man has ever died in childbirth."

"Yes, I was smiling." He reached out and caressed his sister's cheek. "Your engagement still stands. As soon as Mother and Father died, Prince Bohemond started demanding payment of the dowry. Pay or be guilty of felony, that's the message. It sounds like they'll throw you over the saddle along with the money, to make it legal."

"Felony. A disloyal act by a vassal against his liege. Resulting in his death and the forfeiture of all his property to his lord."

"That would be the effect, yes.

"A century of service to the cause of Christ and they insist on this"?

"Knowing that you cannot burden your liege with an impossible marriage, you'll be expected to beg to be sent to the Maronite Convent of Saint Elizabeth in Tripoli, there to spend your days in prayer, repenting of the sins that struck you lame and blind."

"My sins? A convent? I'll cut off his…."!

"To decline is felony, Lady Agnes of Jabil al-Hadid."

"Ah."

"Although it won't be the Maronites. Bohemond and his new Princess, Melisende of Jerusalem, promised the Temple Knights a portion of the dowry in return for their support. The Templars will place you with the Carmelites."

Agnes shook her head. "Delightful." Her hand went to her mouth as water trickled down the stream. A breeze briefly swirled down into the glade, ruffling the surface. "Alberensa"?

"Yes, Alberensa, a large and fertile county nestled against the Pyrenees. To the west, the Duchy of Aquitaine, a jewel of the English Angevin Empire. To the south, the Kingdom of Aragon, constantly seeking to push north. And to the north and east, the County of Toulouse, pressed by the English and the French and the Spaniards."

"Mother's plan," Agnes said, "strengthen her brother Count Jacme's ties with Toulouse, the weakest of the three. Mutually fortify each other's position against England, France and Aragon. That means you marry Maura of Colomiers, a niece of Raymond VI of Toulouse. Her dowry coming in replaces my dowry going out. Toulouse promises to send fighting men to

Jabil al-Hadid each year, where they support Antioch and its young princess."

"It had a ring I could understand, once I was old enough to understand."

"And to understand that the quite gorgeous and very eager Alzalaïs of Sidon was not in your future after all, despite your mutual eagerness for that mutual future."

For a moment the siblings sat quietly, listening to the water gurgle from the spring.

"The Preacher in Ecclesiastes was right, Aggie. 'The race is not to the swift, nor battle to the strong, but time and chance happen to them all.'"

His sister nodded her head. "You're all that's left of Jabil al-Hadid now, Hugh. You must send for Maura and marry her, quickly. Under the Salic Law, if you have no male heirs, your fief will go to your nearest male relative descended through an entirely male line from Baron Julian. That would be a great-grandson of Baron Guilhabert's brother Robert. He married a noblewoman of Constantinople. Third cousin Phillipicus is Greek, not Latin. He won't care if this place falls to the Saracens."

The silence resumed, but only briefly until Hugh broke it.

"Once Mother learned last year that her brother died childless and she was the Countess of Alberensa, she named Gauthier of Moustalon as her Viscount. She remembered him growing up and trusted him. I see mischief once Alberensa's barons learn that Mother has died. English, French, Spanish and Toulousian mischief, to say nothing of my barons, perhaps even my Viscount."

Aggie's blind eyes glinted. "At least there's no Salic Law in Alberensa, Hugh, although Mother was the first woman in generations to inherit the title."

"In fact, perhaps only the second ever. The chronicles relate that once our ancestor Roland enlarged on Lothar's small holdings, he found himself with only daughters. He decreed that the eldest, Harildis, would be Countess after his death and that her son Oddo would inherit from her."

"One wonders, my lord baron, how much of the wealth of his county went to Our Holy Mother the Church to ensure that the *loi Salique* never applied in Alberesna."

"Perhaps none. After all, Alberensa is not the only place where it does not apply. Eleanor of Aquitaine brought her Duchy to King Henry. Maybe Roland told his knights that Oddo would inherit. Then Countess Harildis had her husband kill all those who disagreed."

Another moment of silence, contemplating that distant, almost legendary past, until Agnes smirked. "Even more, my lord, one wonders what the men of Alberensa thought when the Countess Harildis first summoned them into her presence."

"I suspect, my lady, that Alberensa's Service of Acknowledgement stems from that moment." Hugh smiled into her smile. "We are here, Aggie, so she must have been a woman of strength and purpose, one who could bend capable men to her will."

"Indeed." Silence again as Hugh let the Clever One think clever thoughts. "If the *loi Salique* did apply, Hugh, do we know who inherits Alberensa"?

"No, but whoever it is, he does."

"Exactly, brother. This war, these battles over the Cathar heresy, that man might approach the Holy See, claiming our uncle Count Jacme was a Cathar heretic. Under the Third Canon of the Fourth Lateran Council, our lands are then forfeit to our cousin, all with the blessing of the Holy Father."

"Delightful." Hugh took Aggie's gloved hands in his own. "You're right, Agnes. It's time for me to marry Maura of Colomiers." He straightened his sister's cap. "I won't send for her, though. I'll go to Languedoc and marry Maura there."

Agnes sat up straight, almost falling over. "That's not why you're going! You're taking me to France! You plan to leave me at a convent in Alberensa, someplace in the Pyrenees instead of Tripoli"!

She panicked and ran away, except that her legs just folded under her as though they weren't there. A silky fish flopped on the beach, except that even a flopping, dying fish didn't look so sad. Hugh reached down to help, but she batted at him from her darkness.

"No! No! Don't touch me! Leave me alone!" She flailed wildly, slapping and punching, sometimes hitting him, sometimes the air. "Go away! Leave me here to die!" And then she began to cry.

Hugh knelt down, picked up his sister and set her on his lap on her stone. She struggled at first, then put her arms around him and hugged, sobbing and shaking. He had never held her so tightly. He found her small breasts soft against his body.

"I must not spend all day feeling sorry for myself, Hugh, but it's so hard. I'm alone in the dark all the time, and I never liked the dark. I must be carried everywhere by someone, or pushed around in a chair with wheels. Mother took care of me so much that the servants never did, and they still don't, not really. Now you want to send me away like some worn doll cast off by a little child. Please Hugh, please don't do that to me. Please."

Hugh put her face against his chest and stroked her back. It felt strange. She was his sister. She was still the five-year-old girl who sat formally on her stone, talking to the baby in Mommy's belly like a proper noblewoman, except that she was quite naked.

"A convent, Aggie? A convent? You know that Jabil al-Hadid never dedicates anyone to a convent unless she asks to go. That's why I'm not letting you be taken to Tripoli so that you can be jailed by the Carmelites. I don't know why, but according to Mother we just don't do that. Otherwise Lady Anne would be there now, praying the Hours every day for forgiveness."

Agnes laughed, sobbing and laughing at the same time at the mention of their aunt. Hugh set her down on her rock again and sat on his own.

"What of the felony if you take me away"?

"A problem to solve, yes. Money will solve it and we have money."

"But still you want to take me away from here, Hugh. It's the only place we've ever known and you want to take me away."

"Baron Julian was clever to ask for the iron mine when Raymond of Toulouse established his holdings in the County of Tripoli. We have a small fief but a rich one. The iron ore with its traces of gold and silver, the things we make in our smelter and foundry have made us wealthy for generations, and there's still plenty left."

"Yes, so…"

"While I'm away, you'll be blind, alone, in a wheelchair and the only thing standing between that wealth and the greedy ones who want it for themselves. Antioch. The Hospitallers. The Saracens, including our good customer Hassan ibn Ishaq al-Haddad. Even our own nobility."

Agnes shook her head gently. "I do worry about Outremer, Hugh. The Franks crusade against the Greek Christians in the Eastern Empire, looting the cities, setting up their Latin Empire in Constantinople. The nobility of Tripoli and Antioch plot against each other, inviting the Saracens to help them. Year by year, the Saracens take back the Holy Land that our ancestors won for our Lord and Savior Jesus Christ."

Hugh picked his sister's cap from the ground and tied it back on her head. She reached up to adjust it, and he fixed it again afterwards. "Our family took up the Cross long ago, Hugh. We took a holy vow to defend the cause of Christ and His church in the Holy Land. I should not run away."

Hugh laughed. "You can't run away, Agnes, as you just proved. Yet you can't stay if I'm gone."

"It will be hard for me to travel, Hugh."

He put his hands on her shoulders, man to man. "Well, you won't ride sidesaddle the whole way." He kissed her gloved hand. "We'll go to Alberensa. I'll marry Maura. At some point I'll bring her back to Jabil al-Hadid, at least for a while, until I decide what's really happening in Outremer. When I leave Languedoc, I'll appoint you as my Vice Countess, my deputy to rule in my place while I'm away."

"Like this"?

"Of course. You are the daughter of the Countess Marguerite, a lineal descendant of Lothar the Founder. Like the Countess Harildis, you are a woman of strength and purpose. You will bend the necessary men to your will. You will see what's happening without seeing and move around my lands without walking. You, my beloved sister, you are the only person worthy to guard our family's estates in Languedoc."

He knelt down in front of her and put his hands on her silk, over her knees.

"Now if there is nothing further about my plans for Alberensa, my lady, shall we move on to the immediate threats to our fief here? We cannot leave until they are resolved."

Agnes held her head high as they rode back down the gorge. She would not go on being a helpless and hopeless cripple, ignored, waiting in the dark to die. Viscountess Agnes, descendant of Harildis of Alberensa, descendant of Monica of Ronzières would not fail her brother.

3

Hugh rounded the last bend in the canyon. The Homs-Tripoli Road appeared.

Something is wrong.

He stopped and backed the horse away, out of sight of the road.

"Our men are gone, Aggie," he whispered.

"What? Have they…" With that, her mouth closed, understanding perfectly.

"I'll lift you off, then explore." He reached up and took her by the waist again, bringing her down. She spoke softly into his ear.

"Don't leave me, Hugh, please. Being alone in the dark, it terrifies me."

The Baron considered the terrain. The gorge grew narrower and deeper as the stream neared the pool. From here, closer to the entrance, he could scale the wall and reach the ridge above.

"You are indeed the clever one, Agnes," Hugh whispered back. "We'll climb the wall here. That way

I can search for the threat from above instead of just walking into an ambush at the mouth."

He tapped the horse's rump, sending it back into the gorge to water at the pool. He slung his sister over his shoulder with her chest on his back. Other than the slightest "oof" she made not a sound.

"Grab my waist. I'll take your legs with one arm and use the other to steady us on the trail."

"Did you…? Do you…"?

"A dagger, that's all. And I left my armor off to meet the wishes of a certain member of the fair sex. Yes, we are very exposed."

Hugh started up the wall, stepping from protruding rock to ledge back to protruding rock. Six *toises* with his sister on his back, hard work.

Be careful. Kick no stones loose. Do nothing to alert any ambushers that you're here.

His head and shoulders reached the top of the wall. He sat Agnes on the ridge and laid her back, then pulled himself over the ledge without standing.

"We're up. I stayed low so we made no silhouette against the sky." He pushed her so that she rested securely in a bowl on the ridge. "Are you comfortable"?

"Yes."

"You're safe here. I'll crawl towards the road and see what I can see." Terror crossed her face, but she gritted her teeth and nodded.

Hugh looked west. Rough and rising terrain made it nearly impossible to proceed alongside the gorge past this point. Julian or Peytre or Guilhabert had scouted the terrain well, all those decades ago. No one could threaten the family from above while they enjoyed the pool.

The Baron looked east. I can see my castle. My banner is flying, the gate open, no sign of any fighting. Further east, the smoke from the smelter chimney on the Orontes is drifting away across the Syrian fields.

No Saracen raiding party waits for you. It's your own kind, Christians.

Christian traitors.

The Baron of Jabil al-Hadid slithered along the bare rock on his belly like the serpent God punished for deceiving Eve. Sounds. Animal sounds, horses shuffling. Men murmuring, nervous, anxious, talking when they should stay silent.

Take a look.

Hugh craned forward just enough to see the mouth of the canyon. His guards, tied and gagged and sitting out of sight of the road behind a pile of rockfall from the wall. Three other men-at-arms in Jabil al-Hadid armor, all looking down the gorge, waiting for Hugh to appear.

He slithered back, gently. The leader, that is… is…. Josse, that's right, Josse.

Josse, squire to Sir Guy.

Josse, a second son of… of… Godfrey yes Godfrey of Sarlant, one of Mother's barons in Alberensa. Josse of Sarlant.

Not Mother's, yours. One of your barons in Alberensa. His son is waiting to kill you.

Hugh turned and crawled back to Agnes. "It appears that the threats to our own fief have arisen sooner than we expected, Aggie. Guy's squire Josse of Sarlant is waiting to kill us."

"Aunt Anne's latest lover? He's my age, maybe nineteen. She's thirty-five."

"She likes them young and eager."

"Yes," Agnes answered.

"Stupid, waiting to ambush us. Just ride in and kill us."

"Are you complaining, my lord"?

"No."

"Do you suppose Lady Anne learned of your plans"?

"No. As always, she has plans of her own."

"And yours"?

"For her? Unchanged."

"I mean right now," Agnes hissed. "I'm not quite ready to meet our Lord"!

Hugh reached out and moved Aggie's cap to shield her face from the sun. "Time is on our side. They're waiting in the road. Someone will come along soon enough, forcing them to leave. If they get bored and come down searching, they'll find the horse but not us."

"And if they do find us"?

"I'll stab them to death with my dagger." Hugh's sister shook her head. "Stay quiet. I'll go back and watch the road." Again the terror, but she nodded, letting him go.

Hugh regained his spot. This time he did not look out, merely listened. The threesome kept whispering among themselves. Soldier talk, mostly, of different women in the Tripoli brothels. They wore full armor, the knee-length coat of mail over leather called the hauberk, the mailed stockings and boots, the chausses, and the mailed hood over head and shoulders, the coif.

Movement brought the Baron's eyes east. He watched as a single horseman started from Jabil al-Hadid. The rider reached the road and turned for the Pass at a trot. "Josse," said one of the ambushers. "I hear someone coming."

Hugh's vassal looked towards the sound. "Only one horse." He pointed to one of the men. "Audric, you watch the prisoners. Godelot, you come with me. We'll kill the faggot and the witch, then come back and kill this rider if he stops."

Josse and Godelot drew their broadswords and started down the gorge on foot. Their mail rustled softly as they passed beneath Hugh's position.

The Baron studied the wall of the Pass. There, then there, then a leap of about two *toises* to the ground. Or rather, to Audric.

Hugh paused. You are wearing only a tunic. He is wearing a full suit of armor. Yes, but the mail protects best from a swinging blow, a slashing blow in close combat. It does not always protect its owner from a sword thrust or an arrow. The force of the blow from a skilled fighter can snap the links between the rings and let the weapon penetrate.

A skilled fighter. Your skills in the martial arts are limited. Everyone knows that. They are all testing you, testing your resolve since your father died.

The rider will be alone. Without you, it will be three on one. You must even the odds.

You are the Baron. Skilled or not, you must defend your own fief.

"No one knows what he will do in battle," Hugh's father said, as his father had said before him. "All that is asked is that you fight as well as you can until you no longer can, and then, that you trust in Our Savior's merciful grace."

Hugh drew his dagger from his belt.

Not my will but Thine will be done, O Lord my strength and my Redeemer.

Go!

Audric heard the movement and looked up, seeing the Baron half-leaping, half sliding down the rock. "What the…" His hand reached for his broadsword as Hugh jumped from the rock. The stunned assassin waited to take the blow rather than moving aside, "OOOOFFFFF"! Hugh's body slammed into him, knocking him on his back, stunning him.

Quickly, Hugh, quickly, before he recovers, sits up and runs you through.

The Baron raised his knife high over his head and brought it down hard on the mail covering Audric's chest. The sharp blow from Jabil al-Hadid steel parted the links, pushed aside the rings of mail, penetrated the leather underneath, drove through the padded gambeson and entered the man's chest, sliding sideways off a rib as it plunged in.

"AAAAIIIIYYYY"!

A fountain of blood spurted into Hugh's face as he twisted the knife in the wound. With a huge shove, Audric pushed him aside.

"SHIT"!

Another spurt, another, spraying warm blood all over the Baron while his opponent sat up and reached for his sword.

"I'll kill you, you bastard"!

The fountain stopped after the third spurt. The man-at-arms blinked. "Shiiii….." His head crashed back on the road while his soul departed, leaving behind the metallic smell of his blood and, after a moment, the scent of his offal and urine. The Baron reached down and took the heavy broadsword from the dead man's hand.

Eternal rest grant unto thy servant Audric, O Lord. May light perpetual shine upon him.

Thanks be to God, who gives us the victory through Our Lord Jesus Christ!

"Am I too late to be of assistance, my lord"? Hugh looked up as the rider approached with his sword drawn. Giles, one of Sir Guy's sergeants. A handsome man, around thirty, with the dark eyes and dark hair that said he had some Maronite ancestry. A hard man like Frederic, steeled by the battles in the Holy Land. "That knife looks rather well placed." A loyal and trusted man, assigned by Baron Joscelin to guard his elder daughter, the affianced Princess of Antioch. Giles pointed towards his liege's chest, at the tunic soaked with Audric's blood. "Delivered from up close, it appears. His blood is dripping off your nose."

"Yes." Hugh put a foot on Audric's chest and pulled his blade from the dead man's body. Gore dripped from the steel as he walked behind the rockfall.

"When you did not come back on time, my lord, I decided to explore."

The Baron freed one guard's wrists with the knife, dropped it beside him and stepped into the road. The pool of Audric's blood and urine diminished as they soaked into the dirt.

"Thank you, Giles. I can still use your help."

Hugh's two men-at-arms appeared from the behind the rocks. "My lord," said one, "They surprised us, saying that we…."

Hugh put up his hand to stop them. "Your names"?

"Edgard," said the taller one.

"Michel," said the shorter.

"Can I trust you"? Edgard offered back the dagger, still wet and red with Audric's blood.

"Yes, my lord," they chorused, dropping to their knees as Giles dismounted.

"We will deal with what happened later. Right now I need your help." The Baron pointed up the canyon. "Josse of Sarlant and a man named Godelot went up there on a mission of murder, Giles. On foot."

"Where is my lady of the Blue Eyes"? Giles looked at the sun-washed rock, the castle outside the pass, the fields beyond, not finding her. "Is she safe"?

"I put her up on the ridge, out of sight. Those traitors will not find her before we find them."

"How is she, my lord"?

"Blind, crippled, alone and fighting her fear bravely, Giles. A most special woman, waiting for us to rescue her from those killers."

"Wait here, my lord. The three of us will go up the gorge and bring down those other two."

"I'll join you, Giles. They went to kill my sister, and on her birthday."

4

Sir Frederic and his ten-man column reached a junction in the Tripoli Road and turned north along a ridge into the mountains. The lush fields of the Homs Gap surrounded them as they made for Krak. Krak, *Krak des Chevaliers*, the Castle of the Knights, the headquarters, since the disaster of Hattin thirty-five years before, of the Sovereign Military Order of the Knights of the Hospital of St John in Jerusalem. The occasional walker stepped out of the road as the column trotted by, then closed his eyes and held his breath as the cloud of dust swept over him.

The serfs looked up from their farming as Frederic's column rode by. No smiles, no scowls, no emotions at all crossed their faces. The Knights of the Hospital were their liege, but their lives would not change if their liege became Sultan Al-Mu'azzam 'Isa Sharaf ad-Din, Emir of Damascus and nephew of the great Saladin. Frederic had no doubt that the farmers would prefer the Sultan.

The garrison at Jabil al-Hadid alone could not protect a holding so near to the Saracen lands. Hugh's fief remained Christian only because it was so close to Krak. If the Syrians attacked, the Baron would yield up the ironworks without a fight, make a stand in his castle and wait for the Hospitallers to ride down from their fortress.

Krak appeared in the distance after the column had billowed clouds on walking men for about half an hour. The castle dominated a spur of a high hill, Gebel Alawi, surrounding it, Christianizing it, turning God's creation to the defense of His Holy Land. The outer wall reached up ten *toises*, as tall as ten men standing on top of one another. Farther uphill, a higher, thicker inner wall surrounded the castle buildings, the stables, barracks, kitchen, refectory and chapel. The builders created the platform on which those structures stood by covering the top of Gebel Alawi with earth and leveling it with stone. When they finished, they had shaped the largest and most impressive Frankish fortress in Outremer.

"Krak always amazes, Sir Frederic," said Petrus, the guerdon-bearer to the knight's side.

"Have you ever seen the Temple Mount in Jerusalem, Petrus"?

"No, my lord. It is in Saracen hands now."

"Neither have I, but those who have marvel at how Krak's platform resembles King Herod's wondrous structure, constructed during the Roman era before the birth of Christ."

The column rode a few steps further before Petrus, encouraged by his lord's friendly tone, risked another question. "Do you think the wagons will be ready for us, my lord? We should get as close to Tripoli as we can before nightfall."

Frederic laughed. "I don't think any wagons will be waiting, Petrus. We should be home in Jabil al-Hadid before nightfall."

Petrus pondered that reply. He decided not to follow up, but instead to take advantage of the knight's candor to resolve a debate in the barracks. "Do you know what Baron Julian did during the battle of Hisn al-Akrad, my lord? What he did to earn Jabil al-Hadid"?

All in Outremer knew the history, how the Castle of the Kurds once dominated Gebel Alawi as Krak did now. Count Raymond IV of Toulouse and his knights seized Hisn al-Akrad in battle with the Seljuks early in 1099.

"Jabil al-Hadid's chronicles relate that the forces of Toulouse gained the wall of the castle during the final assault. Two cowardly Saracens attacked Count Raymond from behind. Sir Julian saw them, ran one through the heart, wounded a second and pushed him over the battlement. The enraged Saracens turned on Julian, but Baron Jaufres of Lapeyrouse, the Count's Marshal, sent men to Sir Julian's rescue before he was overwhelmed."

The column suddenly seemed silent, even though the hooves still pounded against the earth. Frederic could read their minds as he remembered what the man who trained him as a soldier always said.

"No man truly knows what he will do in combat until he is there, Frederic. All that is asked is that you fight as well you can until you no longer can, and then that you trust in Our Savior's merciful grace."

Baron Julian had done that and survived, and received the Iron Mountain as his reward.

■ ■ ■

Hugh let Giles lead them up the canyon. "By now they know you are not there, my lord," the sergeant whispered. "What weapons do they have"?

"Only swords," Hugh whispered back. He pointed up the wall, "Lady Blue Eyes." The sergeant nodded. They continued quietly, staying to either side of the flowing water. Edgard and Michel carried crossbows retrieved from their mounts as well as their swords.

Giles raised his hand. They stopped.

Yes. Footsteps splashing in the stream. Giles motioned one man to each side. He took one side himself, Hugh the other.

Josse's voice. "They must be up on the ridge, Godelot. We'll kill the guards, take Audric and climb up from the Pass road where the wall isn't so steep. Then we'll look around until we find them."

"What of the rider, Josse"?

The two men rounded the corner.

"Indeed, what of him"? Giles replied.

Josse and Godelot froze, swords in their hands. "Yield"!

Godelot turned and ran back into the canyon, making for the pool. Before Josse could do the same, Hugh got in front of him, turning Josse his way. "Take him alive, Giles, alive"!

"Yes my lord."

The sergeant moved in from other side. The assassin backed against the wall. Edgard stepped into the middle between Giles and Hugh, pointing his weapon at the face of Sarlant.

"Give it up, traitor"! Giles ordered. "Beg for mercy from your liege or meet Satan right now"!

A moment, then two, with only the sound of Godelot's splashing footsteps to break the quiet.

"I yield." Josse lowered his arms and dropped his sword to the rocks. In an instant, Giles grabbed his arm, twisted it and drove the man to the ground.

"Give me your crossbow," Hugh said to Michel. "Then help Giles tie him up."

Giles looked up from his work. "My lord, you should not…."

"I've always been good with this weapon, Giles. If I need help, I'll call for it." He smiled. "I must say, it is unfortunate that *al-Zarqa'* can no longer see. She was even better." He pointed at Josse. "Tie him up and then retrieve her. Bring everyone down to the pool."

"Yes my lord."

Hugh started up the canyon, staying out of the stream, listening. Next turn, wait, listen.

My horse. My horse is still up there. Godelot isn't running into a trap. He's running back for the horse, planning to ride through the men on foot and make his escape into Syria.

The Baron looked around the corner into the glade. The animal was enjoying its freedom, backing away as Godelot reached for its reins, giving Hugh enough time to position himself in the entrance.

"Yield, Godelot! You cannot escape"!

In reply, the man leaped at the horse, panicking it, starting it running for the canyon mouth. The assassin ran behind, lifting his sword for the attack, using the animal to shield his rush. Hugh contemplated briefly if honor required a swordfight even though he had no sword.

What honor? He came to stab you in the back!

The horse ran faster than Godelot, leaving him ten paces behind as it swept past the Baron.

Make this count. Don't waste your only bolt trying to wound him.

TWANG!

The steel of the bow launched the arrow, punching through the mail into Godelot's stomach, tumbling him over with a shriek of pain. He and sat up and looked down, scrabbling at the bolt as it protruded from his belly. Blood began to ooze along the shaft, a sign more bleeding beneath.

"You've killed me"!

Hugh reached down, dragged the man clear of the stream by his hauberk and leaned him against the wall of the glade.

"I have, but not just yet. If you do not bleed to death first, you will get very sick, then die in two or three days." Blood began trickling from the bottom of Godelot's hauberk. He did not have two or three days. "Before that, we have to talk."

Until this morning, you had never killed anyone. Now you have killed two men.

Killed men defending yourself. Saving your sister's life. It is not murder.

5

Stephen of Orcival, Castellan of the great fortress at Krak, stood on its ramparts with his friend and lieutenant Simon of Apamea. They could be brothers, although they were not. Each man's black tunic displayed an embroidered white Crusader cross. The eight-pointed white star of the Order, each point a reminder of one of the Beatitudes, adorned the lapels of their black cloaks.

Others in the Holy Land might indulge their own desires. For more than twenty years, Sir Stephen and Sir Simon had indulged only their duty. Piety. Loyalty. Honor and glory. Courage. Contempt for death. Their eyes remained bright with dedication even as they grew too old to sally forth against the enemies of the Lord. With their gray hair and gray beards, they governed now while the younger men fought.

"It's the guerdon of the whelp of Jabil al-Hadid, Simon."

"Yes, my lord."

Stephen snorted. "Generation after generation, they are nothing but merchants with a title. They stay on their little fief and run their dirty smelter and sell their products to those of us actually fighting to defend the Holy Land. In times of peace, they even sell to the Saracens."

The Castellan and his lieutenant watched as the dust cloud approached.

"Right now, I am told, they are trying to get the ore hot enough so that the iron metal flows from it like water. That will make it much easier to work."

"Has that ever been done, my lord"?

"Not that I have heard," Stephen answered. "The Saracens told the whelp that it has been done somewhere far to the east. They are trying to do the same."

Another moment of silence settled on the ramparts as they watched the column trotting up.

"In fact, Simon, they are so valuable to the heathens that the Emir's raiding parties never damage their smelter. They pass by Jabil al-Hadid, not besieging it, because they know its barons will not come out and fight."

Simon spoke softly, reverently, "Hugh's grandfather Olivier fell at Hattin, my lord."

Stephen snorted, "So it is written." His face showed displeasure at this reminder that Jabil al-Hadid had indeed been committed to the work of God in the Holy Land, at least once. "Since then, Olivier's son and now his grandson have been content to work their metals, in trade, like commoners."

"They keep us well-armed and equipped, my lord." Simon drew his sword and let it glint in the sunlight. "They can even obtain the Damascus steel."

Stephen looked upon Simon's blade with its distinctive fine banding, reminiscent, some said, of flowing water. "A gorgeous weapon indeed. I am afraid that its source, my friend, proves that the barons of Jabil al-Hadid are not committed to the work of God. They are committed to money."

The column drew close to the lower gate.

"His Marshal, Sir Frederic," Simon said, pointing at the leader. "A true warrior for Christ."

"Yes," Stephen replied. "The *Custos* of our Order, Pierre Guérin de Montaigu, keeps urging me to recruit new men into our ranks. We must replace our losses from the battles in Egypt. A man like Frederic is exactly who we need."

"You came out from the Auvergne together with Sir Pierre, did you not, my lord"?

"I did. He appointed me as Castellan here as we returned together from Damietta." Stephen turned his thoughts to the men lost to the heathens in Egypt while this baron's father sold iron in Tripoli. Lost without reward, without recompense. The Ayyubids still rule Egypt and Syria and the Holy City Jerusalem.

Not my will but Thine be done, O Lord my strength and my Redeemer.

"A man like Frederic, a true warrior for Christ should hold Jabil al-Hadid, Simon, not the merchant. Sometimes it can be difficult to ponder the ways of our Lord."

Simon replied firmly as the column reached the lower gate. "The Iron Mountain's loss should be our gain, my lord."

"Yes, Simon, it should," Stephen agreed. "Let us make it so, today."

■ ■ ■

Giles appeared, carrying Agnes in his arms. Edgard and Michel escorted Josse, now with his hands tied behind him and a short rope between his ankles hobbling him. His coif was gone, exposing his head and neck and a crop of dark hair.

"Put Agnes on that stone, Giles," Hugh said, pointing. "How are you, sister"?

"Much happier now, my lord. I am glad to find you still alive." Hugh watched as the sergeant set her in place.

"And I am glad to find you in the same condition, my lady."

Hugh turned to Edgard. "Seat Josse next to Godelot."

Edgard and Michel slammed the assassin down beside his accomplice, causing the wounded man to wince in pain. Pain filled Godelot's face, pain and panic and fear at the sense of his imminent death.

"Godelot," Hugh said, standing over him. "You're dying. Tell the truth now. Save your soul."

"My mother, my sister…"

"Tell the truth and they will not be punished."

Silence.

"I make that a holy oath before Almighty God, Godelot. Tell the truth. Save your family. Save your soul. Did Lady Anne send you"?

"She sent Josse. He recruited Audric and me." The man spoke through grunts of pain. "Where is Audric"?

"Dead. She offered gold"?

"Yes."

"What else"?

"Last night, we… her bed…. all of us."

"What else"?

"She promised to knight us once she became the Baroness."

"What about her husband"?

"What husband"?

"Hassan al-Haddad. Is he part of this? Are Anne and Hassan plotting to take the fief for the Emir"?

"I know nothing about the Emir. Anne thinks the fief is hers by right."

"Did she promise to marry Josse"?

"Yes." Blood flooded from under the hauberk now. Godelot looked down, tears in his eyes. "I'm thirsty. Can I have some water"? Thirsty from the loss of blood. His end has come.

"Fetch him some water," Giles said to Edgard as Godelot's head slumped forward.

"Not necessary," Hugh said. "He's gone." Whether to Heaven or to Hell, that is in the hands of the Lord.

"No one has ever died in this happy place, Hugh," Agnes said. "It is a sad moment, even if he came to murder us."

"He died in a place like the Saracen vision of Paradise, my lady, in gardens with rivers flowing beneath."

Giles turned on Josse, putting his sword against the man's bare throat. "Lady Anne. Why does she think she deserves this fief"?

Silence.

"Speak or I'll have you thrown in the pool to drown"! He motioned to Edgard and Michel to pick up the miscreant. Fresh panic crossed the face of Sarlant.

"Stay, Giles," Hugh said. "This fool is the victim of a harlot. She has already caused two good men to lose their lives. I want information about her, not the death of this idiot. Josse."

Silence despite the panic.

"Josse, you are a son of Sarlant in Albernesa. I do not yet know your father. I do not wish to make an enemy before I even arrive. That is your good fortune, Josse. It means that you will not suffer the fate of Audric and Godelot as long as you cooperate. Answer or be thrown in the pool to drown"!

Josse looked up as Edgard and Michel reached down to lift him. He gave in.

"You are a faggot, Anne said. You like men. That's why you go to the smelter. You like to fornicate with sweaty men in leather aprons. She read Leviticus to us: 'If a man lies with a man as with a woman, both of them have committed an abomination; they shall be put to death.'"

"So it says. Did she mention the first chapter of Romans"?

"Yes."

"What of my sister? Why must she die"?

"Lady Anne says that you two fornicate in this glade. You screw a blind, hopeless and useless cripple, a witch struck down by God for her sins."

Giles, Hugh could tell, was ready to slaughter both Josse and dear Auntie Anne. The Baron could only marvel at her cruelty.

"And for those sins we forfeit our claim to this fief? And she is next in line, the sister of Joscelin, the only survivor of Olivier and Athèné"?

"Yes."

"Agnes"?

Joscelin's daughter looked towards the sound of Josse's voice. "She tricked you, Josse," she said in her soft, low voice. "In Alberensa where you grew up, a woman may inherit a title in default of male heirs. In Tripoli, we have the Frankish law, the Salic Law."

"You mean…"

"Exactly. I cannot inherit Jabil al-Hadid. Neither can Anne. If Hugh dies before he has a son, the fief passes to Phillipicus, a descendant of Baron Peytre, the second baron. He lives in the County of Nicaea."

6

Frederic's column passed through an inner gate and reached the upper yard. No wagons awaited, no drivers, no cargo.

It is as you expected. Prepare yourself.

"By God's bones, Sir Frederic! They are not ready at all"!

Frederic smiled as he looked to his guerdon bearer. "Mind your language, Petrus. We are among holy men."

"Sorry, my lord, but…"

Frederic called to the column, "Dismount"!

The knight swung down from his own horse in a squeak of leather and rustle of mail. He wiggled his hauberk, smoothing and adjusting the padded gambeson underneath that protected from the weight and movement of the mail.

"Sir Stephen sends his compliments, Sir Frederic, and asks if you would join him." A young man without armor bowed before the knight, wearing a black tunic embroidered with the Order's cross. Light hair, blue eyes, he appeared to be a Frank from the north.

"Petrus. Take two men and find food and drink. We'll probably be leaving within the hour."

"Yes my lord."

Frederic turned to his guide. "Lead on, …"

"Lucas, my lord. I am a novice in the Order."

"Lead on, Lucas." Frederic followed the man from the bright of the yard into the cool of the first passageway, dimly lit by only a few candles. "Where are you from, Lucas"?

"Amiens north of Paris, my lord. I felt a strong call, an overwhelming call from Our Savior to serve him here. When I inherited my fief last summer, I donated it to the Order and set sail for the Holy Land."

"A large fief, Sir Lucas"?

"No, my lord, it was rather modest, but like the widow with her two mites, it was all that I had."

They walked up the dim corridor, passing and acknowledging other Hospitallers. "And you took the monastic vows when you arrived"?

"Like all of the men here, I took the vows of chastity, poverty and obedience. I pledged my life to the protection of the pilgrims on their journeys to the holy places. I swore to defeat the Saracens wherever they might be found."

Indeed, Frederic knew, the survival of Outremer depends on the faith of men like this Hospitaller, on the faith of the knights from The Poor Fellow Soldiers of Christ and of the Temple of Solomon, the Templars, on the faith of the men of the German Order, the Teutonic Knights.

"Sir Lucas, the warrior monks of the Military Orders serve as Christ's soldiers with a devotion as complete as that of any man copying scrolls in a European monastery. I commend you on your devotion to Our Lord's cause."

"Thank you, my lord."

Frederic smiled. "Thank you for coming to Outremer. We can certainly use your help. The Saracens never give up."

Lucas put his fist to his heart. "I am honored to hear that, Sir Frederic. I shall do my duty to our God, that I have sworn."

The novice led Frederic past chamber after chamber filled with tapestries, gold, silver, fine carved wood furniture. For a century, Christians making the pilgrimage and Christians remaining in Europe sought a path to the Kingdom of Heaven by supporting the Hospital, the Temple, the Teutonic Knights. Their generosity made the Military Orders wealthy here and wealthy in Europe. Jabil al-Hadid was a serf's hovel compared to the Castle of the Knights.

The two men stopped at the entrance to the Knight's Hall.

"Sir Frederic of Jabil al-Hadid"! Lucas called.

"Enter"! echoed from within.

Frederic found the Castellan sitting on a heavy wooden chair with the cross of the Order carved on its back. Behind him, above his raised dais, the Order's banner. Stone arches created a series of domes that marched overhead to the far end of the long room. Flags of the Order and arms of its members hung from the supporting pillars. The whole space glowed with candlelight from chandeliers and wall sconces.

"Welcome, Sir Frederic," Stephen said as the knight approached. "You honor us with your visit. Do you remember my friend Sir Simon"?

The Castellan motioned to his right, where Simon sat in the first of many chairs set in the niches between the pillars. The senior members of the Order took those spots, on seats upholstered in silk. Their green damask pattern would be at home in Homs, or Damascus, or Cairo, or Baghdad. The junior members stood in the open rectangle before the Castellan's seat.

"I do indeed, Sir Stephen." He bowed towards Sir Simon. "The honor, I assure you, is all mine."

"Thank you, my lord," Stephen answered. "I would offer refreshment but we fast until Nones." He turned to the guiding squire. "That will be all."

"Yes, my lord."

"God bless you in your work, Sir Lucas," Frederic called as the man turned to depart.

"I pray continually that he does, my lord." Lucas slipped quietly away.

"Is that new"? Frederic asked, pointing to a small shrine in the wall beside the dais.

"I have had the altar refreshed," Stephen answered. "It is to the memory of Roger de Moulins, the *Custos*, the Guardian, the head of our Order who led the Hospitallers at Hattin. After the battle, Saladin beheaded every member of a military order that he captured, save Gerard de Ridefort, the Templar Grand Master. Roger and his Hospitaller knights knelt bravely, knowing that the blow from Saladin's steel served only to lift them into the Heavenly Jerusalem."

Frederic fixed his gaze on the Castellan. "My father Fulk and his half-brothers the Baron Olivier and Jourdain also fought bravely that day, my lord. All three died during Count Raymond's advance, trying to battle through to the water."

Yes, Stephen thought, the knights of Jabil al-Hadid died on their feet while the Grand Master surrendered to his fate. Yet Raymond de Moulins might have dined with his knights in victory that evening had not the foolish Count Raymond III of Tripoli charged through the Saracen host, taking his entire force out of the main battle.

Stephen bowed. "I did not mean to suggest…."

"Your father's brothers, is that what your said, Sir Frederic"?

"Yes, Sir Simon."

"Same father, different mothers or the other way around"?

"Same father, my lord. Olivier and Jourdain were the sons of Baron Guilhabert by his first wife, Madeleine of Montpelier. My grandmother was his second wife, Mariam, a Maronite Christian, a young maid at Jabil al-Hadid who earned Guilhabert's favor. My father Fulk was about fifteen years younger than Olivier and Jourdain."

Simon and Stephen exchanged a glance as they worked through the relationships. Frederic and the Baron Joscelin were half-first cousins. Anne the Whore, Joscelin's sister, a half-first cousin too. Frederic and Hugh are half-first cousins once removed, yes, that's it.

"Baron Hugh has told us, Sir Frederic," Stephen went on, "That in default of his issue, the fief passes to a distant cousin, one Phillipicus who lives in the County of Nicea. He is a descendant of Guilhabert's brother Robert. How can that be? Your claim is stronger, through the Third Baron, not the Second."

"It may seem so, my lord, but it is not."

The two warrior monks exchanged another glance.

"How so"? Stephen asked.

"While Guilhabert was courting Mariam, he was also trying to arrange a marriage between Olivier and Princess Athèné of Jerusalem, a cousin of Amalric, Jerusalem's King. The King balked at the possibility that the offspring of a maid might inherit a fief once possessed by a royal daughter's husband. To permit the marriage to proceed, Guilhabert agreed that none of Mariam's offspring could ever inherit Jabil al-Hadid."

Again the Hospitallers exchanged a glance.

"And this agreement still stands"? the Castellan asked.

"It is perpetual, my lord, and blessed by Our Holy Mother the Church in the person of Amalric of Nesle, the Latin Patriarch of Jerusalem."

Simon stood up and stepped down from his niche. "Then nothing has changed," he began. "You have no ties to Jabil al-Hadid. We renew our offer that you join our Order."

Frederic bowed gently towards both Hospitallers. "Once again I am honored, my lords, but I have promised my cousin that I will act as his Viscount while he visits his County in Languedoc. He expects to remain there about three years. We can discuss this matter again when he returns."

Or not. Somehow I don't see my beautiful Sophia, may she rest in peace, thinking that it would be a good idea to bring Jean and Luc into the Order with me.

"Will he return"? the Castellan asked. "If he does, who will act for him in Languedoc"?

"His sister Agnes will be his Vice-Countess."

"A woman"?

Frederic nodded. "Yolande of Brienne is the reigning Queen of Jerusalem, Sir Stephen, even if she must rule from Acre. Hugh's mother was the Countess of Alberensa in her own right."

Stephen shook his head at the strange idea. "Will Hugh still marry Maura of Colomiers, the niece of

Raymond VI of Toulouse? She is older than he is, I'm told, plain and fat. It will simply be a dynastic marriage, nothing more."

"All marriages among the nobility are dynastic, my lord. In my case, not being eligible to inherit, I married for love. My wife Sophia came from Chadra, the same village as Mariam and my mother. It will be a comfortable place to retire, among friends, among family, once I am no longer able to serve Jabil al-Hadid."

Stephen nodded, but with a vacant look that showed that his mind was not in Chadra. "I would counsel your Baron against that marriage. The Albigensian heresy threatens Languedoc. Ever since the Papal Legate Pierre de Castelnau was murdered in 1208, the Holy Father has encouraged a campaign to exterminate those heretics. Maura's uncle Count Raymond has been excommunicated more than once by the Holy Father for his Cathar sentiments."

Frederic's face hardened. "All of us in Jabil al-Hadid are aware of the battle against the Albigensians, the Cathars, Sir Stephen. Guilhabert's daughter, Olivier's sister Claire perished at Beziers in 1209. She and her family were devout Catholics, but that made no difference when the final assault came. The new Papal Legate, the Abbot of Citeaux, gave the order to kill everyone in the city. 'Kill them all,' he said. 'The Lord will know his own.'"

Simon dismissed the Abbot with a wave. "It was a harsh order, yes, but a necessary one. This heresy threatens the cause of Christ just as the Saracens do. The martyred Catholics of Beziers are certainly with Our Savior in Paradise, where your aunt waits for you, even now."

Frederic waved that away. "Princess Athènè, Claire's mother, never understood how the Pope could wage war on his own faithful. She sought refuge in a church not ruled by the Holy Father. She spent over a year in Homs, in retreat at the Syriac Orthodox Cathedral of Saint Mary of the Holy Girdle."

"A heretic church, my lord," Simon replied, "Not unlike the Cathars."

Frederic concentrated. "You test my knowledge, Sir Simon, but I believe the Syriacs are quite unlike the Cathars. The Cathars deny the humanity of Christ altogether, believing Him only divine. The Syriacs merely err in the nature of His earthly and divine persons." Fredric smiled. "I suggest that we leave such matters to the priests and turn to the caravan for Tripoli. My men are waiting in the upper yard to begin the journey."

"My lord," Simon said, "Sir Guy is more than capable of acting for Hugh while he is away. A man of your skill and experience…"

Frederic raised his hand, palm forward. "Please, my lords, let us speak no more of this. Baron Hugh must go to Alberensa. He must bring his sister to the safety of Europe. He must wed his betrothed. He has honored me by naming me his viscount. I have accepted. I must honor my oath, my lords. It is the Will of God."

Stephen stood up from his chair, surprising Simon. "I admire your devotion to your oath, to your family, to the Lord, Sir Frederic. We will not speak again of this topic until your cousin has returned from Languedoc."

"Thank you, Sir Stephen." He waved in the general direction of the yard. "I take it that we are not needed to escort the caravan to Tripoli"?

"That is correct," Stephen said. "We sent a messenger to inform you, but he did not arrive in time."

"He did not, my lords," Frederic replied, ignoring the obvious lie. "Then with your leave I shall return to Jabil al-Hadid. If we leave immediately, we should make it back by nightfall."

"Lucas"! The novice appeared immediately. "Escort Sir Frederic to his men"!

"Yes my lord."

"May God the Father, God the Son and God the Holy Spirit be with you this day and forevermore, Sir Frederic."

"And with you, my lords."

■ ■ ■

The sound of Jabil al-Hadid's chausses against the stone receded into the distance. Simon turned to his lord. "You let him go quite quickly, Sir Stephen. I thought we were turning him to our work today."

Stephen waited to reply until the sound of Frederic's departure died completely away.

"We have been fools, Simon. What is our purpose here"?

"To honor the request of our *Custos* to build up the Order. Service with us offers Frederic something far greater than life with a weakling lord on a small marcher fief. The *Custos* will certainly call him to Acre. As he grows older, perhaps he will be Castellan of a European fortress of the Hospital."

"To what end, Simon? Why do we exist at all"?

"To protect and serve the cause of Christ in the...."

"Exactly! With the Whelp gone, Frederic is in charge of Jabil al-Hadid. He will fight where Hugh will not. He is already in the Order without being in it! And so shall I report to Guérin de Montaigu."

"When the Baron returns"?

An excited Stephen stepped off the dais and turned back. "We misunderstood Frederic's place, Simon. Now we know that he stands number two to inherit"!

"Except that he cannot inherit, given this agreement."

Stephen shook his fist in the air. "Think, man! Frederic's title is obstructed only by an agreement made with King Amalric over fifty years ago on behalf of a woman who became a Saracen"!

Simon froze, stunned by the Castellan's vehemence. "A Saracen"?

"A Princess of Jerusalem traveling safely to Homs, that is impossible without help from the heathens. Perhaps she spent time with the Syriacs, but more likely she passed that year in the harem of their trading partner, this Hassan of the Iron. Perhaps she even became a Saracen herself."

Simon shook his head. "That does not seem likely, my lord. Her husband was murdered by the heathens at Hattin."

"Her marriage was arranged. Her daughter was her own, and she died at Christian hands."

Simon paced towards the rear, and back, thinking. "I do not think Sir Frederic would ever betray his oath to Hugh, my lord."

"We would not expect that he would," Stephen said as he put his hand on Simon's shoulder. "If the whelp dies without heirs, on the voyage, in Languedoc, we will counsel Frederic to petition Queen Yolande to annul the agreement. I'm sure he will make the petition rather than become the vassal of this Phillipicus."

"Queen Yolande needs the aid of our Order. Prince Bohemond, too. You are right, my lord. If the choice is some spoiled Greek or a true warrior of Christ, the agreement will be dissolved."

"At that time, the Order will approach him again. Join us. Donate your property to our work. Serve as our Castellan at Jabil al-Hadid, you and your sons after you."

The Castellan watched as Simon paced away again and returned.

"Jabil al-Hadid has always honored requests from our Order to give our new men field experience, patrolling in the mountains. Frederic did get on quite well with Lucas."

Stephen took his lieutenant by the shoulders, gripping him warrior-to-warrior. A grin, a positive moment of joy crossed his face. "Brilliant, Sir Simon, brilliant! The devotion, the financial sacrifice of Sir Lucas will inspire Frederic! Our novice will stand as a personal reminder that our Order seeks to welcome him"!

From without the Knights Hall came the sound of men on their way to the chapel.

"It is the hour of Nones, Simon."

The Ninth Hour in the mid-afternoon, the moment on Good Friday when the Lord and Savior uttered the words, "Father, into thy hands I commit my spirit." Uttered those words and died on the Cross.

Stephen and Simon stepped from the Hall into the corridor to join their comrades.

Died on the Cross and rose again in glory on the third day, the first Easter.

"If the whelp marries and has heirs"?

"Then there will be no need to petition about the agreement. The Order will approach Hugh in Languedoc. Surely there is something we can offer him to remain in Alberensa and to donate Jabil al-Hadid to our work, with his cousin as our Castellan."

7

Hugh cradled Agnes in his arms as he carried her into the Great Hall of Jabil al-Hadid. "You are the Baron, Hugh. One of the servants should carry me, not you."

"Father liked to do this, Aggie. So do I." No need to tell her that even William was not waiting when they rode in. No one here either, on the ground floor of their family residence, the Keep tower. The servants had lit only half the sconces in the room. Instead of a steady glow to illuminate the space, the candlelight made a shadowy dance on the stones.

"Audric's blood has dried in my tunic. It's not ruining your new dress."

The baron strode through the straw and food scraps and animal waste on the stone floor. His sister's silk fanned the embers on the open hearth as they passed by, adding a tinge of smoke to the other aromas. And adding fresh soot to the stone arches in the ceiling that supported the weight of the floor above.

Still no one.

Like the chapel, like the stables, the Keep served as a fort inside a fort, a place of last refuge in case the enemy penetrated the outer walls and took the courtyard. A single door and narrow slits for loosing arrows created the only openings, making the candles necessary, even in the middle of the day.

Hugh mounted the raised wooden dais set along the back wall where the Great Hall abutted the ramparts. He put his sister on her chair at the family's dining table. William appeared through the kitchen door, turned and attempted to retreat. Too late.

"William! Come here!" The Seneschal approached his master and bowed. "Where's Maud? Catarina? Joanna? The other servants"?

William bowed even lower. "I don't know, my lord." He looked up. "My lord. Your tunic. It's…"

"You're my Seneschal, William! Go upstairs, find my aunt and send her down! Find the servants and get these candles lit"!

"Yes my lord."

William passed through the narrow door into the tower staircase. The steep circular steps could be a challenge, but the major domo seemed to fly above them in his eagerness to escape.

"I've found you a companion for our journey, Aggie. A woman who will be a reliable lady-in-waiting. She'll read to you and bathe you and attend to your needs."

"Certainly no one here then. Who"?

"Sister Ekaterina from the Convent of Saint Mary the Virgin at Chadra in the mountains. A young woman, a Maronite Christian, Aramaic-speaking. You can teach her French. The Mother Superior agrees that she can come to Languedoc for five years. That should be enough time to find someone in Alberensa to take her place."

Agnes smiled. "I don't want to ask exactly how this happened, my liege. Something tells me that the work of St. Mary's has recently been enlarged by a substantial donation."

"You need a companion you can trust."

Servants emerged from the stair tower and scuttled into the room, bowing.

"Light the candles, Joanna."

"Yes, my lord."

"William. Have the tables set up for dinner."

"Yes, my lord. Your tunic, my lord, it…"

"Now, William"!

"Yes my lord."

Hugh took his own seat at the family's wooden dining table. Joanna bustled about, getting the candles alight. William directed four men as they took the trestle tables from against the side walls and began to set them up for the common meal.

Lady Anne appeared from the staircase wearing a dark red woolen tunic. Her gown fitted tightly around her upper body before it fell over her hips to the floor.

Her girdle belt hung loosely around her waist. She wore a black surcoat and a silk cap of red, like her dress. On her feet, closed shoes with toes that came to a point. A well-dressed noblewoman, the sister of the late Baron Joscelin of Jabil al-Hadid, called to the servants.

"Joanna, bring me some fresh water." Joanna turned to comply.

"Stop, Joanna," Hugh replied. "Finish the candles first." The servant froze. The candles remained unlit and the water unfetched. The men setting up the tables ceased their work. "Come sit with Lady Agnes and me, Lady Anne. Everyone, back to work."

Anne carried herself towards the table as the beautiful woman that she was, her hair still dark and her form still shapely even at the age of thirty-five. Wrinkles had begun to show around her eyes, but the allure of Joscelin's baby sister remained the envy of all the women her age.

So calm, yet she must be surprised to see us alive. She knows that Josse made his attempt today She must notice the blood on my tunic. Be careful for treachery, even now.

"What do you want, Hugh"? Anne sat down directly in her chair, not bothering to bow or curtsey. Her surcoat flopped back to the floor while she challenged her nephew with her bright brown eyes. "The flowing iron of the Men of the East can't be all that important. My brother Joscelin thought it was a myth."

Over Anne's shoulder, the servants froze again, locked in place by the tension between their masters.

"Joanna. The candles"!

Motion resumed, again. Hugh did not look away from Anne as he gave his order, and neither did she look away from him.

"Our father thought it was a myth," he said, "But your husband has seen the iron flow beyond the eastern mountains."

Anne flared. "That Syrian deceiver was never my husband, Hugh! I was only fifteen, seduced by a man of thirty-five! It was a heathen Saracen ceremony, not a wedding like the one blessed by Our Lord in his first miracle at Cana in Galilee. Father Sebastian agrees that I'm still a maiden." She smirked while brother and sister considered the formal truth but absolute absurdity of that statement. "I've told you two all I know about the flowing iron. Don't bother me about it again." She stood up and walked away.

"Sit down, Aunt."

"What?" Anne looked back, bemused.

"Sit down." Anne stopped walking. "Now"! Sudden menace flowed from her nephew's voice, and in that menace, danger. "You would be wise to remember the charity of my father, your brother. Princess Athèné, your mother, our grandmother, wanted you tossed to the dogs."

Anne returned to her seat at the table. She waved towards Homs in Syria. "Was I supposed to languish in the harem, day after day, night after night, never to…."?

"Athèné was a princess of Jerusalem, Anne, the granddaughter of one King, the cousin of another. You fornicated with a Saracen, ran off with a Saracen, abandoned the One True Faith and married a Saracen. To so betray the cause of Christ, a cause for which your father died at Hattin, your mother was sure that Satan had you in his grasp."

"That doddering fool and her tales of life at court before Hattin 'when Christ still ruled the Holy City,' she never…"

"Fortunately for you, aunt, Joscelin was more practical than Athèné. He accepted the Will of God, especially since his new brother-in-law was Hassan al-Haddad. They had, after all, a very profitable relationship, trading our smelter's iron to both sides. That is, until the calls from the harem stopped coming to you."

Anne flared again. "Every night for three years Hassan took me to his bed. He couldn't get enough of me, but I'm barren. A Syrian peasant took my place in his affections. I rebelled against the mockery of the heathens"!

"Even more, you rebelled against a lifetime of chastity."

All in Jabil-al Hadid knew what happened next. Anne filched the clothing of a eunuch and went over the harem wall. She stole a horse and rode hard for the castle. Athèné told the guard to leave her outside for the Saracens, but Joscelin ordered the gate opened and sent her to the family quarters in the Keep, the Solar.

"Agnes and I were still infants, but everyone over thirty remembers the morning after you rode in from Homs. Hassan and a hundred of the Emir's armed men crossed Guilhabert's stone bridge. You came out on the ramparts in your eunuch's clothes, screaming in Arabic. You promised Hassan that he would be in Hell by nightfall because your brother was going to kill him."

"He will be in Hell, that filthy old man, once the True God…"

"Instead, Joscelin walked downstairs and exited the castle, leading the stolen Arabian and one our horses. He went alone, without armor, unarmed. He sympathized with his old friend. He understood why Hassan would want to throw such a disrespectful wife out of the harem. He offered the bag of gold draped over our horse's back as an apology. They laughed, embraced and went back to business."

Anne glared at her nephew. "I am a daughter of Jerusalem, Hugh! Did that Saracen dog really think he could treat me like that"? She crossed herself. "I was wrong to claim that Jesus was just a prophet, not the Son of God, God from God, Light from Light. I repented that night and returned to the way of our Lord. He welcomed His lost sheep, His prodigal daughter back into the fold."

Agnes turned towards the sound of Anne's voice. "Returned to the way of the Lord? Hardly." She leaned across the table. "You are a harlot, Anne, not a maiden. You succumb to the willing and seduce the unwilling. There is hardly a man in this place who hasn't had you."

Anne snorted. "I'm a harlot"? The Daughter of Jerusalem turned on her niece. "You're a blind, hopeless and useless cripple punished by Our Lord for your sins! You should be spending your days in prayer, repenting for the evil that caused Him to strike you down! Instead you dare to mock me"!

The servants knelt on the floor, trying to bury themselves in the straw.

Control yourself, Hugh.

"That 'blind, hopeless and useless cripple' is your niece, Anne, a beautiful woman who should be married to Bohemond of Antioch but instead sits in the dark. No one understands why a loving Creator permits such things, but He does. Do you remember the Prophet Samuel's visit to the family of Jesse, when he was searching for a successor to King Saul"?

Anne blinked. "What"? Blinked again. "Oh. Yes, yes. The Lord directed him not to choose the strongest son, but the youngest, David."

"'Do not look on his appearance or on the height of his stature, for the Lord sees not as a man sees. Man looks on the outward appearance, but the Lord looks on the heart.' Agnes is blind and crippled, but the Lord knows that she has a beautiful heart. You are still beautiful, aunt, but I wonder what Father Sebastian would say about your heart."

"He would say…"

"He would say that I'm treated quite poorly by the servants since our mother died," Agnes said. "They dress me in mismatched clothes. They are never around to help me to the chamber pot. They leave me in a wet tunic if I cannot drag myself there in time. You have ordered this behavior, Anne, telling them that I am a witch, being punished by God for my sins, and that I will soon be gone."

Anne glared. "I would never do that."

The blue eyes turned vaguely towards the Great Hall. "Joanna"?

Joanna looked up from her place in the straw. "Please, my lady, please. I'm sorry, my lady, very sorry. I'll do better, really, I promise"!

"Not only that," Agnes went on, "These lovers of yours, you seek one bold enough to help you seize this fief from Hugh. That is felony, my lady."

Anne froze at the sound of that word in her niece's quiet voice. She stared at her, at Hugh, at the servants buried in the straw.

"You've been trying to find a man, any man, to get rid of us," Hugh said. You tell them that I like men and Aggie is a pawn of Satan and God has destined you to rule this fief. You promise to marry our murderer and rule Jabil al-Hadid together."

"That is complete foolishness." Be careful. She's reaching behind her surcoat.

"Josse tried this morning, and failed. Audric and Godelot are dead at my hand. This is Audric's blood on my tunic."

"Who"?

Hugh pointed at his aunt. "You are reaching for a knife behind your back, Anne. Take it out and lay it on the table. Don't make me kill you right here. It's over."

The bright brown eyes darted around the room, seeking escape, seeking a champion, finding none. They returned to her nephew, defiance giving way to fear. "No, Hugh, I could not…"

"The knife, on the table."

Slowly, cautiously, Anne placed the blade on top of the wood. "What now"?

"You sent those three men to assassinate us, Aunt. As Aggie says, that is felony. There is a punishment for felony."

"No"! Anne dropped from the chair to her knees. She started to cry, to shake. "No, no, no my lord, no that is not true." She put her face down in the straw, the bones, the animal leavings. "Never"!

Hugh looked at her trembling, hunched-over body. "Don't you care what happened to Josse"?

"Yes. No. Please, my lord Baron, please stop. You are confusing me. You are frightening me." Hugh waited. "What happened to him"?

"I don't want to anger Sarlant even before I get there, but his son tried to kill me. Josse will work in the mines on the Iron Mountain. Three years at that hard labor, then he will be banished from both Alberensa and Jabil al-Hadid."

"The mines"?

"That's not your punishment, Anne. The miners think that a woman underground is bad luck."

"Please, Hugh, please! Don't kill me"!

Hugh nudged her hunched-over form with his toe. "Get up out of the dog shit and take your seat, Lady Anne." She obeyed with fear streaking across her face. Hugh turned to the servants. "Leave us." The room emptied even before he finished his words.

"Hugh, please…"

"What are we to do with you, Aunt"? Agnes said. "Can we really trust you not to try again"?

"Please, yes, I'll never…"

Hugh frowned, stopping the felon. "You are still a Christian noblewoman, Anne. Sophisticated and attractive and most of all lusty. But only Father Sebastian considers you a maiden. No one would marry a woman who fornicated with a Saracen, until now."

Her eyes started up. Her mouth opened, and closed. She sat, back erect now, the perfect vision of a Christian lady, except for the straw and dog turds sticking to her face. "Until now?"

"I must travel to Languedoc, to Alberensa, to claim my mother's County. To arrange for my marriage. I cannot leave you here alone to scheme, to plot, to try again, but I know that my father would not want me to behead his sister."

"Athèné might welcome that," Agnes added, "But our father would not."

"Then… then…"?

"It cost me much treasure, Lady Anne," Hugh continued, "But you will finally have a Christian husband."

"What? You can't…." Of course he can, Anne realized, surrendering to the inevitable. At least she was spared the sword. "Who "?

"Baudoin of Saissouq."

Anne leaned over the table, stunned. "Baudoin of Saissouq? He is old, over fifty. He is a fat belching pig. He has a poor fief and no vassals. No one will have him. Men say he… he… he…"

"Leviticus, Anne? Romans"?

"Yes."

"You could offer our aunt another way, Hugh," Agnes suggested. "Let her return to al-Haddad's harem. Of course, she will sit alone, night after night for the rest of her life, served by the most insolent woman in his palace, but at least she will not be forced to live with Baudoin."

The felon glared. "Not that, you witch! You know I won't just sit there! That Syrian deceiver will treat me as an apostate! He'll cut off my head with a Damascus blade forged on our own anvils"!

Hugh shrugged his shoulders. "Then you have chosen Baudoin, Lady Anne," he declared. "He is the only man who will have you." He swept the straw off her cheeks. "Your days as a harlot and a traitor are over. Giles will take you to Saissouq tomorrow."

"Tomorrow"?

"Obey your new husband. Repent of your sins. Turn your thoughts to God. Seek His forgiveness. Prepare yourself for the Heavenly Jerusalem."

8

Agnes sat on her rock in the glen. Hugh sat facing her on another. Mother's gift, a silk tunic with a red bodice and alternating red and black panels in the skirt glowed softly in the skylight against the water. In the round of endless farewells, it was time to say farewell to the little pool.

"You look quite lovely today, Agnes." She beamed, happy for the compliment. She cramped and flowed in her monthly time, so her womb must still be working. Not that it mattered, except in her dreams. The miserable disease had taken away her legs, and her eyes, and any chance for children, for love.

"Giles has been a great help to me, Hugh, very loyal." Even after nineteen years, her voice occasionally surprised Hugh with how deep, how soft it could sound. Seductive, perhaps. Like now. "And, I am told, a skilled fighter like Frederic, not an amateur like Father and you."

"Thank you for the compliment, sister. Still, I will do my part if the time comes."

"You proved that on my birthday. It frightens me. You may not be as skilled as many, but you are as courageous as any. In my nightmares you die bravely, like our grandfather." She crossed herself. "A Viscountess should not be protected by a mere sergeant, Hugh. You should knight Giles."

"Even if that sergeant is a skilled fighter, one of our best, not an amateur"?

Those sightless eyes, afire again. "I trust you are smiling, brother"!

"Let me discuss it with Frederic. I think you should let him serve you for at least a year before I do that. Then we'll decide."

"Yes, my lord." Her voice remained deep but no longer seductive. Her head bowed in submission, but only barely. The sulk on her face meant that the topic would come up again in less than a year. Next week, perhaps. Like all the nobles, Agnes of the Blue Eyes did not enjoy taking directions from her liege lord.

■ ■ ■

Hugh and Frederic sat on benches at the wooden table in the Solar's common room on the second floor of the Keep. They wore no armor. Their weapons leaned against the nearest stone wall. Above their steel, a tapestry portrayed a hunt in a European forest, a forest filled with green trees and flowing streams and the mythical one-horned beast, the unicorn. A forest lush beyond anything in Outremer, even high in the Lebanese Mountains. A forest like those near Toulouse, the source of the richly woven cloth.

"Lady Agnes," Maud announced, pushing her charge into the room on a chair mounted on a platform with four small wheels at the bottom.

"End of the table, Maud," Hugh ordered, "Then leave us." The maid adjusted Aggie's tunic and departed down the stairs.

"Thank you for rejecting the Hospitallers and staying with Jabil al-Hadid, Frederic," Hugh said, pouring some water from a flagon into an earthenware cup. "We need to get Agnes to a safer place."

"It's a wise decision, Hugh. Alberensa is worth far more than Jabil al-Hadid. Once Antioch took control of the County of Tripoli after Hattin, our family was eclipsed. Our new liege did not trust a family so close to Toulouse. The disease thwarted Joscelin's plans to remedy that with Agnes. If we didn't make iron, we'd have been gone a long time ago. I must hold this place for you, for me, for my sons. I don't think Sophia would see them as Hospitallers."

Hugh nodded at the memory of Frederic's gentle wife. A quirk of history facilitated the marriage of Mariam, of Frederic's mother Elizabeth, of Sophia, of all the native Maronite Christians into Jabil al-Hadid's Frankish descendants. The flood of Islam into the lowlands drove the flock of John Maron into the mountains while still speaking the ancient Aramaic tongue of Jesus himself. And while adhering to the Roman view of the nature of Christ, not the heresy of the Syriacs and Copts. They were the only Christians in the Holy Land in full communion with Rome.

"Jean and Luc remind me of their father, Frederic," Agnes said. "At least they did two years ago when I could still see."

"Dark complexion, dark hair, dark eyes on all of us, Aggie. My father's mother, my mother, my wife, all Lebanese. The Frankish blood grows thin in Jean and Luc."

"Yet it is still there," Agnes replied. "They are, what, seven and five now"?

"Yes."

"I believe that your Sophia is with Roger and Madeleine, Frederic, the three of them killed by the same disease that crippled me, the three of them together with our Savior in Paradise, waiting for us to join them."

"Amen, Agnes, amen."

Hugh let the silence hang in the ancient room, a moment of memory for the victims of the crippling disease. "A happier thought. Do you know the story of Juviler, my lady"?

"Of course, Hugh. In the Year of Our Lord 950, the fourth Count of Alberensa, Angibert the First, called "The Builder," married Ermessenda, the eldest daughter of the Baron of Juviler. The Baron had no living sons. Angibert quickly convinced the Juviler cadet lines that the *loi Salique* did not apply in Juviler. That made Angibert and Ermessenda's son Pau the heir to the fief."

"One assumes, my lady," Frederic said, "That this agreement was obtained while the lawful heir lay on his back with Angibert's sword at his throat."

"Quite possibly." Agnes smiled. "Taking Juviler nearly doubled Angibert's domains. When Pau became Count, he never separated his claim to Juviler from his claim to Alberensa. All counts since that day have been both Counts of Alberensa and Barons of Juviler, with the Count as their liege."

"Until today, my lady," Hugh said.

"Today"?

"A woman as my viscount will be helped if she has a title of her own. I have prepared the deeds that name you as the Baroness of Juviler." He rapped the tabletop, twice. "If you accept, I will expect the full amount of my feudal dues given in a timely fashion, my lady."

Agnes could never move much, but now she could not move at all. Her mouth opened and closed, opened and closed. "I… The income you will lose…"

"I have a plan for that. Do you accept me as your liege, my lady"?

She shook her head. "It is too great an honor for one in my condition, my lord."

"Our mother would approve, heartily. 'Your sister, so clever, Hugh.'"

Agnes grinned. "In that case I accept."

Hugh stood. "Sir Frederic. Please take Lady Agnes from her chair and help her kneel."

For a man of Frederic's strength, it proved a simple matter to lift Agnes around the waist, move her chair aside with his other arm and use his foot to push back her calves as he lowered her to her knees. Hugh retrieved his sword and scabbard as he watched.

"Lady Agnes. I hold the sword brought from Toulouse by Sir Julian of Blagnac, the first Baron, when he accompanied Count Raymond on Pope Urban's pilgrimage." The baron removed the broadsword from its scabbard and held it aloft, twisting it in the candlelight. Its two-edged blade fitted into a hilt set at the end with a single ruby. "It has been carried by each Baron of Jabil al-Hadid since."

Deep silence filtered into the room, a sense of something ancient, something holy. The Barons who ruled before Hugh were gone, but their sword rose into the air even now. They lived on in the glowing light of its steel.

"Lady Agnes of Jabil al-Hadid, I, Hugh, Count of Alberensa, name you as my vassal, granting you the fief of Juviler." He tapped her right shoulder, her left with the sword. "Rise, Lady Agnes, Baroness of Juviler."

Frederic quickly hauled Agnes up from the straw, moved her chair into place and set her down. He lifted her hand to his lips, "I am at your service, my lady the Baroness of Juviler."

Hugh held the sword aloft again.

"Aram has taken Julian's blade, worked off the scale and sharpened the edge. He wrapped the hilt and the guards in new leather."

"It looks almost new, Hugh," Frederic replied.

Hugh turned the hilt towards his cousin. "Julian's sword should not accompany me to Languedoc. He pledged it to the defense of the Holy Land. It must remain here, in Outremer. You should carry it, Sir Frederic, grandson of Guilhabert, son of Fulk its rescuer, and use it to defend Jabil al-Hadid, to the greater glory of Almighty God." The Baron took his sister's soft hand and placed it on the blade, over his. Together, they extended the hilt to Frederic. He took it and held it aloft.

"May I always use this sword of the Barons of Jabil al-Hadid in your service, my lord Baron, and to the greater glory of our Lord and Savior Jesus Christ."

"Amen."

Frederic put the sword back in its scabbard and leaned it against the wall.

"Might I ask you something, Sir Frederic"? The deep, seductive voice was back, a hint of the question to come.

"Of course, Baroness."

"I'd like to bring Guy's sergeant Giles into my service as a knight. My brother wondered what you thought of that idea."

Indeed. It had only taken two hours for the topic to come up again.

"You did well to choose Giles, Hugh. He's a trustworthy man and quite loyal. May I offer you some advice, my lord"?

"Please, Sir Frederic."

"You fought cleverly on Aggie's birthday, but that is not the same as fighting a battle. You will never be a great warrior, Hugh, but you should improve your skill. Alberensa has known no Count for two years. You will be challenged. Take advantage of the skills that Giles has. Train with him."

"That's good advice, Frederic."

"A Count should not be trained by a commoner, my liege." The demons had taken her legs and her sight, but her spirit remained untamed. "You should knight Giles. Without his help we might be dead."

"Your wish is noted once again, Baroness."

Frederic laughed. "Now I know what this is about, Hugh. She remembers what Giles looks like. He was her guardian for years, after all."

Hugh put his hand under his sister's chin. "Was there some affection between you, my lady? Was he the source of Mother's admonitions that 'A Princess of Antioch must always remember her station, Lady Agnes'? Lady Anne did find him rather handsome."

A deep red of embarrassment swelled across the face of the new Baroness, beginning at her neck.

"I'm sure I have no idea of what you two are talking about"! She waved away any romantic notions even as her face and hands turned bright red. "If this foolish topic has ended, perhaps it is time to visit our forge, Hugh"!

9

William lifted Agnes onto the bench of a small wagon. Other servants lifted her chair into the bed. Things ran more smartly now, as though a wheel with three flat spots had suddenly become smooth and even again. All at Jabil al-Hadid had learned the lesson of Audric and Godelot, of Josse, of Lady Anne.

Hugh climbed up beside his sister and took the reins from a groom.

"Lady Agnes, are you ready?"

"Yes, my lord."

Hugh shook the leather and guided the mule towards the tower gate. Hoofbeats and wagon wheels clattered in the opening as Hugh drove downhill and turned right.

Julian and Monica put their ironworks on the west side of the Orontes River, just north of the Tripoli-Homs road. Workmen fed ore from the Iron Mountain and cedars from Lebanon into its furnaces, melting the rock and freeing the iron from its bond. Their work left a brown blot to darken the green fields of the valley, a place of hard-packed dirt where nothing grew.

"The smelter chimney is belching smoke, Baroness. They must be trying again."

At first, Julian drained the molten waste into the river. He soon realized that he was slowly blocking the flow and damaging his fields. After that, for over a hundred years, wagons had taken the hardened slag across the Orontes to the Syrian side and dumped it in a large dry gulley outside the area irrigated by the ancient reservoir.

"I can smell it, Hugh. And hear it too."

Fortune smiled on Julian and Monica while they built their smelter. Conflict in Syria between two Seljuk brothers weakened the initial Saracen resistance. The victor, Abu Nasr Shams al-Muluk Duqaq, seized and fortified Homs, preventing further Crusader advances from Tripoli and leaving Jabil al-Hadid as the County's border fief. Soon after, Duqaq's *atabeg* overthrew Duqaq's son and founded the Burid Dynasty.

"I'm driving directly to the smelter."

The quality of the work from Jabil al-Hadid quickly became known among the warring Saracens. In a decision that provoked hostility among the other barons, Julian sold first to the Seljuks and then the Burids, helping them make war on each other. To encourage the trade, he built a wooden bridge to carry the Tripoli road across the river into the Emirate of Damascus.

"We can hope that they've been successful."

The Burids fell to the Kurdish Ayyubid Dynasty while Julian's grandson Guilhabert ruled Jabil al-Hadid. The demand for quality did not slacken. The third baron grew tired of the constant Spring washouts which interfered with the Saracen commerce and made it harder to get rid of the slag. He replaced Julian's bridge with stone, a copy of one built when the Roman legions ruled *Palestina*.

"We're there, Aggie."

A dozen men stood in the open as they approached, at platforms of brick that held open-hearth charcoal fires. A bellows blew under each hearth, heating the coals and making the iron glow red. Hammers rang on anvils as the workers beat the hot metal into endless rings of chain mail, swords, horseshoes, nails and tools.

Hugh drove not to the forges in the middle of the hard-packed dirt but to the smelter furnace by the riverbank, a tall brick cylinder lined inside with clay. Laborers pumped its bellows as the passing wind took the acrid smoke off towards Syria. Other men worked nearby, crushing iron ore and limestone. Sawing cedars from the Lebanese mountains into logs that would be burned into charcoal. Hard work and sweaty work and for six generations at Jabil al-Hadid, very profitable work.

Hugh's foreman stepped away from the smelter as the Baron's party drew up. The Syrian covered his hose and tunic with a long leather apron against the heat. Slightly bent and with rough hands, the short, thin and bearded man showed the wear from a lifetime of heavy labor.

"Peace be unto you, Aram," said Hugh, "In the name of God the All-Merciful, the All-Compassionate."

"And peace be unto you, my lord. Would that you truly accepted the witness of the Prophet, may the blessings and peace of God be always upon Him."

"In the name of the All-Compassionate the All-Merciful, Aram, I accept that God sent down iron with its great military might and benefits for the people. It has certainly benefitted this family for generations. May it always be so, *inshallah*."

"*Inshallah*, my lord."

Hugh had no doubt where his man's true loyalty lay, but they did share a common bond. Both of them knew, as their ancestors had known, that the magic of the smelter worked the same for every man. It made no difference whether a Christian or a Muslim put the ore and the limestone and the charcoal into the furnace. No one understood how it happened, but if the ore held *al-Hadid*, the iron, it always appeared.

"You look quite lovely today, my lady," Aram proclaimed.

"Thank you, Aram," answered Agnes, speaking in Arabic as she turned towards the sound of his voice. Like all descendants of Julian and Monica, Hugh and Agnes spoke not only French and the Occitan language of their Languedoc ancestors but also Arabic. Pleas for mercy in the local tongue would not help them if the Saracens retook the land, but speaking Arabic made it much easier to deal with their serfs.

Hugh looked towards the smoke-belching smelter chimney. "Have you ever seen this work, Aram? We've been making iron here for years but I've never seen it flow."

"Hassan ibn Ishaq al-Haddad has seen it, my lord. He has traveled to the east of Persia. On the other side of the great mountains there, men make the iron flow like water."

Hugh nodded at the mention of Anne's former husband and their best customer in Homs. "We can make copper flow like water from the ore, and zinc, and tin, but never iron. Once we tap away the slag, all we have is a bloom, a lump of hot iron, full of holes. We can't get it hot enough to flow. So the smiths must forge the bloom into shape, heating and hammering it to close up the gaps and pound out the impurities. Whatever the Men of the East do, Aram, it is a prize of great value."

A second Syrian walked up, a younger man, Aram's assistant, Mahmud. "*Salaam aleikum*, my lord, my lady."

"*Aleikum salaam,* Mahmud," in a chorus.

"Some of it might have flowed, my lord," Mahmud said, "But there is still a bloom. I let the liquid drain onto the dirt. It hardened into a flat platc. We're taking it to a forge now."

"Aram," Hugh said. "Have the men lift Lady Agnes into her chair. We'll go watch the forging."

"You'll watch, Hugh," Agnes said as they lifted her down. "I'll hear."

Hugh pushed his sister across the hard-packed dirt, worn by a century of feet into a surface as smooth as a well-paved road. Mahmud and Aram and a half-dozen men gathered around a hearth and forge. The flat plate and the roughly-shaped bloom rested on the coals. Two men pumped the bellows, keeping the iron hot.

"Would you like to try, my lord"?

"No, Aram. You made this. You try."

Mahmud took a pair of tongs, lifted the round billet from the fire and rested it on an anvil. He held it while Aram reached for a hammer. The metal's reddish color began darkening as the foreman gave it a gentle tap, getting the range.

"In the name of God, the All-Compassionate, the All-Merciful."

"Verumtamen non mea voluntas, sed tua fiat," Agnes added, "Not my will but Thine be done."

Aram raised the hammer over his head and brought it down hard on the metal. With a dull thud, the piece shattered into six pieces and dropped onto the dirt. Disappointment and defeat filled every watching face.

"Mashallah," Aram said after a moment of silence.

"Mashallah," the workers echoed.

"As God wills," Hugh agreed.

"What happened"? Agnes asked.

"It shattered into pieces, Aggie."

Mahmud took the tongs, pulled the bloom from the coals and set it on the anvil. Aram took another ranging tap, then delivered a blow. The hot metal deformed where he struck it, closing a hole. The foreman nodded and Mahmud dropped the bloom back into the fire.

"The solid bloom can be worked, Agnes." The foundrymen drifted back to their workplaces.

"But what flowed, was it iron"?

Aram picked up a chunk of hot metal from the ground with the tongs. "Yes my lady. It is metal, not cooled slag."

"Then some iron flowed. Hassan did not lie about the Men of the East."

Hugh took the tongs and looked at the piece. "We put in more charcoal, trying to get it hotter. Perhaps more got into the iron, causing some to melt at a lower temperature. Probably it can be cast into things that do not need to be worked like pots and pans. We cannot work it, temper it, make it into something that must stand up to blows. Like a weapon."

Agnes turned her head towards the foreman. "Cool the smallest piece for me, please."

Aram dropped a hot chunk of the iron into the quenching trough. The water boiled around it, releasing a hiss of steam to drift off towards the Orontes.

"If what flows is brittle," Agnes continued, "We cannot pound out the added charcoal. We need to find another way."

"We must find a better fuel," Hugh said, "Something that gives off more heat could cause the iron to melt at a higher temperature."

The Baroness put her hand over her mouth. "We suspect that the charcoal does something to the iron. It doesn't just melt the ore, it changes it, too. The iron looks rusty in the rock, but the charcoal gets rid of the rust. And only in the furnace. It doesn't work in the open."

"Yes my lady," Aram said.

"If we find something hotter than charcoal, will it still bring the iron from the rock"?

In the silence that followed, Mahmud pulled the iron from the trough and tested it. "This piece is cool enough, my lady."

He placed it in her hands. Hugh watched as she worked her fingers around the warm metal, gauging its shape.

"I shall take this piece with me to Alberensa and treasure it as a memory of the progress we made today, my friends. For the first time, we matched the fabled Men of the East. We made the iron flow."

10

With the chair and Agnes loaded on the wagon, Hugh steered the mule towards the castle. As they approached, a flurry of activity broke out on the gate tower. One man bellowed towards them, "Hurry, my lord! Saracens approach from the Syrian side"!

Hugh stopped the mule, stood and looked across Guilhabert's stone bridge. Nothing. He shouted back, "How many"?

"Two, riding hard"!

Hugh looked down at his sister. "That sounds more a visit than an attack, Baroness. Shall we wait here to see who it is? That way we do not need to invite them inside where they can see our dispositions."

"An excellent idea, my lord."

Guy appeared on the wall, then Frederic, then a dozen men spreading along the rampart battlements on the side towards Syria. Hugh shouted towards the tower, "We'll meet them here"!

Guy and Frederic looked at one another, then Frederic called something to the gate tower. The portcullis slammed down. The heavy door closed behind it.

"They've locked us out, Agnes."

"A wise move."

Hugh looked towards where the men on the ramparts were looking. Two riders appeared, a man and a boy. They slowed their white Arabian horses as they approached the bridge. No, not a boy, a woman, because she was entirely covered in black. Hugh shaded his eyes against the sun, trying to make out the man.

"I think it's al-Haddad, Agnes. The other rider, it's a woman."

"Then she must be *mahram*, Hugh, a relative. Otherwise he could not be out alone with her."

Hugh looked beyond the castle, towards the road to the Pass, the road beyond Guilhabert's bridge, the entrance to the canyon with the glade. No other threats, just two riders on white Arabians riding past the smelter.

Hugh waited as his father had done, twenty years earlier. He sat with his sister, without armor and unarmed in front of his castle as the Saracen riders approached.

Hassan ibn Ishaq al-Haddad pulled up in front of the mule, dismounted and held the reins of his horse. He wore the flowing trousers and shirt of the Saracens, a cape and a turban. Almost sixty now, very old, only God knew how many children. Wrinkles marked his face. White hair peeked from under his turban. His eyes, though, they were still shrewd and alert, like the skilled and wealthy merchant he had been all his life. A little heavy from too much food, but not fat, despite his age.

"*Salaam Aleikum*, Abu Khalid," Hugh said. "Blessings upon you and upon your house." He climbed down from the wagon and walked forward, taking the mule by the bit to keep it in place.

"*Aleikum Salaam,* my lord *Sheyk*."

The second rider sat astride her mount like a man, but she dressed in the full-length black gown, the *abaya*, of a Saracen woman. She wore the *niqab*, almost a hood, fitted to cover from the forehead and to surround the neck, with only a slit for the eyes. Over the *niqab*, her *hijab*, a large scarf wrapping her shoulders and her head, concealing her hair.

Hugh turned and called towards the walls, "Rest at ease"! The archers removed the arrows from their bows and stepped back.

"You took a great risk riding out here alone, Abu Khalid. Alone, that is, except for this relative. How may Jabil al-Hadid be of service to you, my good friend"?

Hassan helped the woman to dismount, lifting her down so that her legs never showed as she reached the ground. He handed her the reins of both horses. "I have a desperate problem." He pointed towards his companion. "My daughter's life is in danger. I need your help." The Syrian woman was full-grown, but slender. Fright showed in her dark brown eyes, yet they challenged at the same time. Perhaps Anne had given birth after all.

"What's her difficulty, Hassan, father of Khalid"?

"Jamilla bint Hassan is the only child of Safiya, my fourth wife. She is my youngest child, my baby, the delight of my old age. She has been disgraced by a man."

"Disgraced? She bedded with a man before she was married?"

Hassan scowled and shook his head violently. "She is sixteen, My Lord Baron, sixteen! She is the light of my ancient eyes, a lovely girl, gracious and refined yet full of spirit and fire. She is a beautiful woman, my lord"!

"Was the man married, Abu Khalid?"

Hassan was so upset that he forgot himself. Hugh did not object.

"Hugh, you speak our language and you know our ways. A man tried to rape her, Hugh, rape her! He did not succeed, but yes he was married. He accused her of seducing him. He claims he has witnesses. Adultery is a Hadd offense."

"What happened to him, Hassan"?

"First I must protect Jamilla. I will wait my time and deal with him and with his false witnesses." Hassan's hand on the hilt of his Saracen sword hinted at the pleasure of a father's revenge. "For them, the Fire awaits."

"Jamilla is not married, Hassan. Does the Hadd punishment still apply"?

Hassan waved off the legal question. "Even though she was attacked, her brothers insist that she has disgraced the family and must be tried under the law. I cannot let them do it, Hugh."

Hugh did know their ways. "It" meant that Jamilla bint Hassan al-Haddad would be buried up to her neck in the ground and killed by stoning. While still wearing her hijab and niqab.

The eyes looked at Hugh from behind their niqab, waiting, watching. "I hid Jamilla in my rooms. When her brothers came to me, I told them that she had run away. They are out now, searching the brothels. Her mother is mourning her as though she was dead."

Hugh was stunned by what happened next. Hassan dropped to his knees, reached out and took the Baron's hands into his.

"Please, My Lord Baron, please, give my baby sanctuary. Take her into Jabil al-Hadid. Ask Sir Frederic to keep her safe until her brothers find the reason that eludes them now. Until they find the mercy that God the All-Merciful wants them to find. It should take me but one or two months to convince them to direct their anger to the rapist. Please, Hugh, please, I beg of you. Save Jamilla's life. Save my soul."

11

Hugh drove the wagon south along the Orontes, making for the Chadra road beyond the Iron Mountain. The sun sparkled on the river and brightened the green of the fields on both sides. It deepened the black and brightened the red on Agnes's gown.

The Baron turned to the rear of the wagon as he drove. Jamilla al-Haddad sat with her back against the side wall, watching the river.

"Your father is our friend, Jamilla, but many in Jabil al-Hadid have suffered losses at Saracen hands. It isn't safe to leave you there. We are driving to Chadra to fetch a companion for Agnes, Sister Ekaterina from the Convent of St. Mary the Virgin. We will ask the sisters to give you sanctuary. I'll get word to your father secretly."

"Will the polytheists make me pray to their three gods"?

"No. They will ask you to help with the chores, though. Have you ever helped with the chores"?

"No."

Of course not. Jamilla is the light of Hassan's ancient eyes, a lovely girl, gracious and refined yet full of spirit and fire. Servants waited on her, hand and foot, satisfying her every petulant teenage desire until her brothers decided it was time to stone her to death.

"Poverty, chastity and obedience is the way of the sisters, Jamilla. They will expect you to humble yourself, to do menial labor, to become a part of their community." He paused. "It is either that, or Jabil al-Hadid, or Homs."

The bolt of black shifted on the wagon bed. "I will help."

"They speak Aramaic, not Arabic. The languages are close but different."

"I will learn the words I need."

"You will not need many, Jamilla. The sisters do not talk much. Silence, stilling the evil fire of the tongue, that is part of humility."

Silence followed as Jamilla contemplated silence.

"It will not be for long. Once your brothers calm down, you can return to your home."

Hugh turned the wagon up the narrow dirt track towards the mountain village.

"Do you speak French, Jamilla"? Agnes asked.

"No, my lady."

"French is easier for Hugh and me. Do you mind if we speak French"?

What?

"No, my lady."

"The flowing iron and the bloom together, Hugh, that is interesting." Ah. French so that Jamilla could not discuss their trade secrets when she returned home. "I wonder if that is part of the secret of the Hinduwani steel."

"How so, clever one"?

"Bronze and brass are alloys that can easily be made. When heated, the copper flows like water. The same is true for zinc and tin. To make bronze, we add molten tin to molten copper in the right proportions. The tin flows into the copper like wine poured into water."

"You think that the Hinduwani, the Damascus steel might be an alloy"?

"Not of two different metals, Hugh, but of the brittle iron and the bloomery."

Hugh pondered that concept as the mule plodded diligently up the track. "Not so much a true alloy, but rather a mechanical mixing like two kinds of grain stirred in a bowl. Each type of iron remains separate, yielding the banding, the flowing water effect."

Agnes nodded. "Once we get to Alberensa, we must experiment with the smelting, Hugh. Letting the bloom cook in the molten iron. Maybe that will change both, making the brittle soft enough to beat into the bloom."

The animal snorted at the exertion as it dragged the wagon uphill. They rounded a turn, bringing the convent into view, silhouetted against the sky on the top of the nearest peak. Byzantium, the Eastern Roman Empire still ruled Tripoli when the builders put the first of those ancient stones into place.

"Making the Damascus steel in Languedoc, that will be a prize of great value for Alberensa, Agnes."

"And if we can make the bloomery iron flow, perhaps a prize of even greater value." She put her hands together, clasping them as though in prayer. "I only regret that I must leave Jabil al-Hadid before that happens here."

Hugh put his hand over his sister's. "All of the women of our family leave Jabil al-Hadid, Aggie, beginning with seventeen-year-old Bonassias, the daughter of Julian and Monica, when she married Hugues de Barlais in Tripoli. Were it not for the cruel disease, you would be in Antioch now, a Princess. Instead, you will be in Alberensa, a Baroness."

"That is true."

"This Sunday, Father Sebastian will say the Mass, our last before we depart. At the end, I will pray the prayer that Julian prayed when Bonassias left, the prayer offered ever since by every Baron when his daughter departed to bc wed."

Hugh stopped the animal on a flat spot, letting it rest while he spoke.

"In the name of God, Father, Son, and Holy Spirit."

"Amen."

"Agnes, we bid you farewell from among our midst, but not from our hearts. Our parting is sorrow, like unto death, but we trust in God's mercy that our parting, like our death, shall be but a brief moment in eternity. The trumpet shall sound in the latter days. Death shall be swallowed up in victory. In this flesh shall we all see God."

PART TWO

County of Alberensa
September 1222

1

A small boy stood in the village street, watching the approaching riders. Mud-daubed wooden cottages lined both sides of Brassat's muddy road. Within each dirt-floored dwelling lived a family, and if they had no barn, their animals.

Behind the horsemen, in the distance to the south, the peaks of the Pyrenees Mountains waited for their first coating of snow. In front, downhill to the north past the edge of the village, the lane joined a small stream, the Barièja. Stream and lane proceeded down-hill to Fonta, where the Barièja flowed into the Arget and the lane met the road to Foix. On the far side of the Arget Valley, the Bear's Tooth, a sharply pointed mount of stone, erupted from the ridge. To the east, Foix Castle, home of its Counts, shimmered in the distance beyond the hills.

The column kept to the center of the damp lane as they rode through Brassat. The child squatted and stood, squatted and stood, making up-and-down motions like the men on their horses. A door opened behind him, "Tibaut"! The bright sun glinted off his mother's blonde hair as she snatched up her child and dashed into the blacksmith shop. "Tibaut," she said, setting the dark-haired boy down on the small bench inside. "You must always avoid the men in the metal clothes, always. They are very dangerous, Tibaut, very dangerous." She sat down next to him to catch her breath as the sound of the hooves passed by outside.

The men in metal clothes feared no threats from Brassat's serfs, now cowering in their thatch-roofed cottages. They rode with their helmets and their coifs hung from their saddles, allowing the wind to blow through long and stringy hair. Each man's white tunic bore a large red cross, a Crusader's cross. Hooves pounded a few paces past the shop before one of the lead riders pulled to a stop, halting the column.

"Did you see that young peasant with the glowing blonde hair? A nice one."

"Yes," answered one of the men behind him. "Her breasts jiggled nicely in that loose brown tunic as she bent over to pick up her little boy."

"I got a look down her cotte," announced a third man. "Nice and round, like two perfect moons."

"Gorgeous blue eyes, too," said a fourth, "Especially when they glint with fear"!

Laughter followed that sally. Their animals pawed and snorted, surprised at the sudden stop, eager to move on. The first man turned to their leader, "My lord, that woman could be a Cathar witch. We must find out." Without waiting for an answer, he turned his horse towards the village. After a moment, the others turned to follow, leaving their leader to bring up the rear.

The blacksmith heard the order to turn back, although he could not make out the words. "They've been visiting Sir Arnald, Aenor. They must have caught sight of your golden hair. Take Tibaut and hide in the corner behind the forge, my love."

Aenor needed no encouragement. She clutched her three-year-old son to her bosom and carried him into the gloom behind the heat of the fire. Until her new baby came, this precious little boy was all she had. Her first child, a girl, had died soon after she was born, four years ago when Aenor was still seventeen.

"Be careful, Guilhelms, please be careful. There are at least eight of them. Don't forget your place. You've worked hard to give us a good life."

He nodded, not convincingly, "I will, love."

Guilhelms looked around his home, thinking. His success as a tradesman earned him a shop and cottage larger than any of the other buildings that lined Brassat's rutted track. He paid others in the village in coin to keep the roofing thatch fresh and the mud on his walls properly daubed. Aenor kept a large green garden to supplement their simple diet on a plot outside.

The thunder stopped as the men drew up in front of the shop. Their animals snorted and their harness crunched as they trampled Aenor's late-season vegetables. Guilhelms picked up a piece of hot iron with his tongs. And a hammer. A crash and the door flew open, kicked in by a young knight in chain mail armor.

"Stand back, peasant. Kneel for your liege, Henri, Baron of Épernay." Arrogance oozed from his youthful face as he waited for the serf to comply.

Guilhelms remained on his feet as Henri stepped in. Gray hair ringed a balding head on a man nearing fifty. Both men had the same long nose, but the older was the taller of the two. Surprise registered in his blue eyes when he saw Guilhelms still standing. "What is this, Charles"? Full beards covered the cheeks and mouth of both men, although gray speckled Henri's beard and Charles still had his dirty blond hair. Father and son, Guilhelms guessed. "This dog should be kneeling before his lord"!

Guilhelms squared up with the young one, Charles. "It's easier to lift the latch and open the door, my lord."

Charles had given his order in French, but Guilhelms answered in the language of Languedoc, Occitan. Henri scowled, annoyed at the arrogance of the peasant before him. Usually they knelt with their faces to the floor and begged not be hurt. He glared at his son.

"Kneel, dog" the Kicker said in horrible Occitan, horribly pronounced. "Name."

The blacksmith let the iron move so that the Arrogant Kicker could sense the heat. "I am Guilhelms

Faure," he said, in French this time, "The blacksmith in this village, as was my father before me." He took a step towards the young knight, forcing him back. "As for your dog, it's outside, holding the reins to your horse."

Charles and Henri exchanged glances. By rushing in, the two Frenchmen had given Guilhelms the advantage. The low ceiling made it difficult to draw and swing their swords. Although they wore armor, leaving their helmets hanging from their saddles exposed their heads to blows. The man before them held a hot piece of iron in one hand and a hammer in the other. With his large shoulders and very strong arms, the brown-haired Guilhelms impressed even without the hot metal. The Épernays backed away from the anger that flashed from his dark eyes.

"As for my liege," turning to Henri, "I hold this shop in free tenancy, without duties to any lord." He gave a gentle bow in acknowledgment of the nobleman's station. "Although I'm surprised to see you, my lord baron. We hear that the northern knights are retreating to the east, to the County of Trencavel, below Carcassonne, near Limoux."

Henri recoiled at the insult, but the glowing iron remained in the smith's hand. "Perhaps you have not heard of the Third Canon of the Fourth Lateran Council, blacksmith. The Holy Father decreed that all lands belonging to heretics are forfeit to the man who rids them of the heresy. Alass, Baron of Fonta, was a heretic. I now hold his fief, including these villages of the lord Arnald, including the castle at Fonta, for my liege, His Majesty King Philip of France. The heretic of Toulouse no longer rules here."

It was as the villagers feared. These Épernays were not leaving Fonta until they were driven out.

Sir Arrogant the Younger put his hand to his sword. "My father and I have stopped here on God's business, peasant. We have taken up the Cross to drive the Cathar heretics out of France. Where is the woman we saw outside? Bring her here."

Guilhelms shook his head. "Brassat is in the County of Alberensa, not Toulouse, my lord. Marguerite, our Countess, is a good Catholic. There are no heretics here."

"When last we heard, your Countess was in Outremer, smith," Henri said, "with her husband Baron Joscelin of Jabil al-Hadid, making iron in the mountains of Tripoli. She has no interest in Languedoc." His hand went to the hilt of his sword. "No heretics? Sir Alass was a heretic. We have consigned him to the flames, and all his family. We hold Fonta for the King of France, under the Council's decree. Her lady the Countess of Outremer has no sway here. Obey my son Sir Charles, now. Where is the woman?"

"We are good Catholics, my lord. There are no heretics here."

"Where is the woman"!

The two knights separated. Guilhelms could no longer threaten both of them at the same time. Henri, farther away, drew his sword. Time to get them out of here.

"Aenor, put the boy down and come out."

Her face appeared very slowly. She took a hot poker from the fire as she passed. In a moment, she was standing next to her husband. Unlike Guilhelms, she curtseyed deeply and kept her eyes on the floor.

"We are good Catholics, my lord baron," she said in Occitan. "You can ask Father Ricartz if you are in doubt. We are in church every Sunday."

Her eyes still were on the floor, speaking to the dirt in humble submission. Charles eyed her carefully, vaguely grasping her words while dwelling on every part of her anatomy, leering, challenging Guilhelms. The smith ignored him, turning his back to put the iron in the fire. He kept the hammer.

"My lords, please, there are no heretics here." He came back from his forge. "One of our neighbors needs that piece for his plow so that he can sow the winter wheat. I can only offer you some cool water. You are welcome to it but please let us get back to work."

Charles took a step towards Aenor. She stepped back, keeping the same distance. "Stop, woman. We must see if there are any marks of Satan on you."

Aenor struggled with the French, but she understood the meaning. "Please, lord, no." Her voice trembled now, real fear. She sank to her knees as Guilhelms turned towards Charles with his hammer. She patted her womb. "Baby, baby, please. No hurt." She turned towards Baron Henri, a pleading look through her tears. "Catholics, lord, no hurt baby no no." She was crying, but she still held the hot poker.

"My lord baron, my wife has done nothing to harm you, nothing to insult you. You do not need to search her body. Please leave so that I can get back to work. We pray for our Lord and Savior to bless your holy crusade."

Henri looked at the hammer and the poker. Once again he had given in to his heir's foolish lust. Charles didn't care if this woman was a Catholic or a Cathar, pregnant or not. He wanted her, now. For Henri, it made a difference. He could not let his son rape a pregnant Catholic woman. That would be an offense to the Holy Crusade.

"Charles, leave her alone." The sharp tone brought the younger man up short. "We shall visit with the priest, Guilhelms Faure. We are rooting out Cathars in our fief. If you are one, we will be back."

Henri turned and went out the open door. Charles waited for only a moment before following him. Aenor dropped the poker and bent over, trembling. A moment later, some loudly spoken orders and the horses rode out of town, towards Fonta.

Guilhelms pushed the door closed and studied the broken latch. He reached down and took the poker from the floor. His hand went briefly through Aenor's hair before he turned and jammed the iron back into the fire. Sparks flew from the speed of his thrust.

"Tibaut. Come out now, son. Go to Mama, Tibaut." The boy came around the forge, trembling. The strange men had frightened him and he had stayed out of sight, but now he ran to his mother. She caught him as he ran into her arms. She hugged him tightly. They were both crying.

"I'm sorry you had to go through that, Aenor. I'm afraid that's not the end of Baron Henri and Sir Charles. We were lucky today. They came unprepared and we had more of an advantage than we should. They will not repeat that mistake. They must never see us again."

2

Father Ricartz hurried from his tiny rectory into the nave of the Brassat parish church, urged along by Henri of Épernay and his son Charles. Even with their swords still in their scabbards, the Épernay scowls provided more than enough menace for the simple priest. The Father's parishioners fed him well from the produce of their fertile land, making the short man bulky, even rotund. Priest and baron might be the same age, but unlike Henri who looked quite fit in his mail, the Father's cassock grew steadily smaller each day, forcing his belly to bulge against it above his waist. Father Ricartz had not moved so quickly for some time.

Sir Arnald's ancestors tore down an older wooden church to build this sanctuary, over a century before. It joined the many parish churches built across Languedoc in the same period. A simple rectangle of cut stone blocks rose from the fields, with a rounded apse behind the altar in the style of an ancient Roman basilica. Natural light entered through two small windows high up on each side, while at the front, the builders raised a square bell tower towards Heaven. The round arches holding up the gable roof matched the round arch over the single entrance doorway. Only a pair of gold candlesticks and a golden cross, a gift of the brother of the noble builder, struck out against the poverty and the simplicity of the Lord's dwelling place in Brassat.

The knights did not bare their heads as they marched the priest to a row of wooden chairs. Ricartz waited patiently while the baron asked meaningless questions, answering carefully but knowing that they didn't really care what he said. After only a few minutes together, Henri stood, surprising the young one. "Father Ricartz, you have been most helpful." A pause, and then the Baron sat back down. "I almost forgot. We have but one question more. The blacksmith, Guilhelms Faure. Do you know him"?

Now they would be interested in his answers. "Of course, my lord. In his business he earns money, coins. He is very generous with them here. With his gifts we are able to buy things in Foix, in Alberensa, even in Toulouse when someone is traveling so far away." In truth, Ricartz feared that the Faures were among Brassat's Cathars, using their donations to his church to encourage his silence.

The young one, Charles, barely paid attention to the answer. "What of Aenor, his wife, Father"? The man's interests lay elsewhere, definitely. The father's grimace told the priest all he needed to know. No doubt the baron had made a good noble match for his son up north in Champagne or Picardy, but the younger man had an unfortunate penchant for pressing his affections upon the best-looking daughters of their serfs. All the nobles took advantage in this way, especially if the woman flirted with them, hoping for a liaison that could benefit her family. Too much of it always angered the peasants and led to trouble. No doubt Charles often caused that trouble.

Be careful, Ricartz. These Franks are dangerous men. The Cathar heresy threatens the Faures, threatens the souls of all its believers, threatens Christ's One Holy Catholic and Apostolic Church, but you doubt that these knights even know what all the fuss is about. Charles wants the young girls. Henri wants the land.

"I asked you a question, priest! What of her"!

"Yes, my lord." Ricartz bowed his head in humble submission. "They attend Mass as good Catholics do. They are popular in the village, helpful to everyone."

"Is that so, priest"? Charles growled. "They insulted my father when we stopped to visit. Threatened him, even. We prayed to our Lord for patience and held our tempers. Without His divine help, we would not have been able to contain ourselves against such arrogance." He rested his hand briefly on the hilt of his sword. Ricartz might be struggling to keep up with the French, but that movement took no translation at all.

"He said he was a free tenant with no feudal obligations. Is that true"?

"Yes, my lord. He pays a fixed rent to Sir Arnald, but has no duties."

"How is that? All the other peasants in this village are serfs, working Sir Arnald's lands. How is this blacksmith free"?

"Aenor was a serf, the daughter of a local farmer, until she married Guilhelms."

Henri stood and glared down at the priest. "We did not ask you about the woman. We asked you about the smith. Answer us, Ricartz. His Majesty King Phillip is waiting for our reply."

This is most peculiar, the priest thought. Yes, Guilhelms challenged them and they did not like the challenge. Still, they did not need to talk to the village priest if they wanted to ride down the street and kill him.

"His father was a free man, too. He was the village smith until he died about five years ago. I think that his wife may have died giving birth to Guilhelms, and his father never re-married."

"You test my patience! Why is he a free man? Why was his father a free man"?

You need to get these men out of the village, Ricartz, before one of the eight outside grows bored and does something threatening. Sir Arnald is dangerous, too, but at least he has to live among his people. The Holy Father has set these northern interlopers upon the Languedoc faithful like a plague. The Pope cannot convince the Holy Roman Emperor to embark on his promised Crusade to free Jerusalem, but he's had no trouble keeping the Albigensian Crusade, the Cathar Crusade, alive in Languedoc. Saracens hold the Holy Sepulcher while the Holy Father unleashes these northerners on my flock.

Charles put his hand on the priest's shoulder.

"My father asked you a question. Why are they free men"?

"They are related to the Counts of Foix. Guilhelms's cousin owns an iron smelter in Farga de sant Matèu. It is not far from here if you climb over the hills east of Ganat, but the easy route is to ride down to Foix and then go up the Ariège Valley to Farga. The smelter is very successful and the family is quite well off."

Charles leaned in, threatening. "Related to the Count? How so, Father"?

"Guilhelms has an ancestor, a woman who returned from Outremer to marry Count Roger III not long after Pope Urban's Crusade freed Jerusalem. Roger and his Countess built the smelter at Farga almost as soon as she arrived in Languedoc. Many of their descendants have been metalworkers, like Guilhelms. The smithy was purchased for his father in some sort of family settlement many years ago, even though it is in Alberensa, not Foix."

"If he is descended from Foix, why is he not noble"?

"Roger's Countess returned from the Holy Land a century ago, my lord baron. Roger and his countess made a settlement among their children. The heir continued to rule Foix, but one of his siblings took over the ironworks. That man's descendants have been commoners but free ever since. Guilhelms Faure is one of them, and his marriage to Aenor freed her, and their children as well."

"Who was this woman of Outremer, Father"?

"I have told you all I know, Sir Charles. Guilhelms Faure's ancestors are noble, but other than Roger III, I do not know their names. You must ask the Count to search his family records if you wish to know more."

Now the good Father understood. Guilhelms was related to the ironworkers of Farga. And they were related to the Counts of Foix. If Foix was a heretic, his family's properties were forfeit. If the smelter's owners were heretics and Foix was not, the result was the same. The freehold ironworks would be forfeit to Épernay. And they sat not far over the hill from their new holdings at Fonta.

"Good day, Father."

The two knights walked into the center aisle and turned towards the door. They did not bow to the altar, or genuflect, or cross themselves. They walked as though they were leaving a dining hall or a tavern. Ricartz watched them, but did not rise to follow. He waited in his seat while they marched away, armor rustling, swords knocking against it as they walked. They left the door standing open as they reached the street.

Ricartz wondered why God allowed these things to happen. A mother rescues her small boy from a threatening group of knights. They see her beauty and think to rape her. They are disgraced in the ensuing confrontation, requiring them to seek revenge on the man who disgraced them. Which leads them to find the Farga smelter and its relationship to the Count of Foix.

The priest of Brassat believed in God the Father Almighty, Creator of Heaven and Earth, of all that is, visible and invisible. Still he faced the daily challenge to the Holy Church, explaining to its people that sickness, death, and the plague of these northern knights could exist in the Creation of their loving God.

Guilhelms and Aenor Faure gave the Cathar answer. Their books spoke of a universe divided between the divine, the light, and the dark, the profane. God ruled only in the heavens, in the divine place of light. Satan created the earth and ruled it as his domain. Nothing in the long history of the Christian faith, back to the time of the Apostles and before, supported the Cathar belief, nothing. You must admit though, Ricartz, that the Cathar theology explains why Henri and Charles can sit in God's holy church and threaten you, threaten Guilhelms, threaten the lovely Aenor Faure even as she is with child.

Satan sent these knights as his creatures to rule his evil world of earth.

■ ■ ■

Henri's men lounged in the small square in front of Saint Gregorio's Church, waiting for their lord. Mud and debris from last night's rain littered the stone paving, but the serfs who swept it every day stayed away, waiting for the soldiers to leave.

While they waited, one rode a short way down a second lane that led from the square to Ganat, a thirty-minute walk away. Although seldom used, Sir Arnald ordered the serfs of Ganat and Brassat to keep the path open. Late Spring and late Fall, they worked their way between Arnald's two villages, cutting away the fresh brush. For the rest of the year, they farmed their strips and Arnald's strips and grazed their stock on the rich bottomland along the Barièja.

The sound of boots against stone echoed through the church door, under the arch with the small carved statues of the four Evangelists. At least the waiting men thought they were the four Evangelists, the authors of the four gospels. The people in church statues always held the traditional symbol of the person being depicted in their hands. The eagle, that's one gospel author's symbol, yes. The lion, another. Which statue was supposed to represent Matthew, Mark, Luke, John, in that they had no real interest.

Henri and Charles appeared. One of their men led up their horses, but neither Épernay reached out at first to take the reins. The soldier stood waiting while father and son looked at each other.

"Your wish, Father"?

"What do you think, Charles"? You will be lord of Épernay before too long. What would you do"?

Charles moved closer to his father, allowing him to speak quietly without their guard overhearing. "Yes, a difficult question and yet an easy one. We must learn how close the family is to the Count. How long ago did they gain the smelter and lose their nobility? This woman from the Holy Land, was she related to the Counts of Toulouse, of Foix, or was she just a daughter of one of the nobles"?

"All true. What else"?

"Most importantly, Father, are any of them heretics? The priest spoke very carefully in describing those Faures. He suspects they are Cathars."

Charles looked around at the others, a leer coming over his face. They smiled knowingly in response. He wore the same look when he took one or two of them to the cottage after he claimed that the serf's daughter loved him.

"I think we should go ask them some more questions, my lord. With some prodding, they may admit something useful."

3

Guilhelms guided his family uphill through the trees, using the spot where the sun brightened the clouds to keep them headed east. He carried a sleepy Tibaut on his back while Aenor's sack contained only a few items of clothing. It also contained, wrapped tightly in a large piece of leather, the gold and silver coins they had saved from their work.

The leaden sky began to appear between the tree trunks. The downhill side opened in front of them a few minutes later. "We're at the top of the ridge, love."

"Yes. We've crossed into the County of Foix." She slung her sack to the ground. "It must be midday. Shall we stop to eat"?

Guilhelms gladly let Tibaut slip to the ground behind him. "Watch him, Acnor, please." He made his way along the ridge until he found a small outcrop with a view of Farga in the valley below. He got on his belly and slithered out so that he did not make a silhouette against the sky.

Good visibility beneath the low clouds allowed Guilhelms to see far to the east, beyond the Ariège valley, towards the Lavalenet road to Limoux. The leaves, already changing into the colors of autumn, rustled in the damp breeze as the smith looked carefully over the valley. After a few minutes, he slid back, waited for his wife to look his way, and motioned his family to come.

"Aenor. Lie on your stomach and slide out. Don't let your body show against the sky. The village of Farga de sant Matèu is just to the left below us."

Guilhelms enjoyed the shape of Aenor's rear as she slithered out. Like her husband, she took her time, looking carefully over the whole valley, then backed off without turning around. Her tunic rode up as she did.

"I've always enjoyed the look of your legs, my love."

"Stop that in front of the boy, Guilhelms. You should know better." Aenor stood up in the woods and straightened her clothes. Her belly was beginning to swell under the cloth, but only someone who looked closely would see it now. "The town looks quiet, and I saw no one on the road. We've escaped Fonta and the Épernays, Guilhelms."

"Yes. Lunch is a good idea. Let's eat the bread and drink some wine and get down into the valley."

Aenor pulled a little picnic from her sack. A loaf of her bread. A piece of cheese that they had purchased from a neighbor, and some water mixed in with wine. The family sat on the hard ground, amid the brush and pine needles and fallen leaves. Husband and wife folded their hands and asked Tibaut to join them in a simple grace. Aenor divided the food and they began to eat.

"Mommy, have the men in metal made us run away? Daddy made them leave. Why do we have to go away"?

"Daddy made them leave, but there are lots more of them and they will come back. The men in metal, the knights, they do not like it when people make them look bad." She looked at his portion. "Do you have enough, Tibaut? Do you want some more cheese"? She held out a piece of her portion for him to take. In the way of hungry children everywhere, he took and ate without noticing that his mother's share was now very small. She noticed, but in the way of mothers everywhere, she did not care.

"Careful, Aenor, you need to eat too, for the little one." Guilhelms handed her half of his cheese.

"Why was Aunt Eva crying, Mommy"?

"She was sad that we were leaving, Tibaut."

"You took everything from our house and gave it to her." The Faures feared that even one night in Brassat could be dangerous, but the smith took the time to hide his tools and their household goods with Aenor's sister.

"She will take care of everything while we are away."

"We left early, Daddy, and you left the shop door open."

"I did. That way the neighbors can go in and find their things." The Épernays would certainly return, and when they did, they must find the smithy empty. "You saw some new places, Tibaut."

The overcast sky had barely begun to lighten when they started from Brassat. Their path took them up into the still-dark square before the church and then east along the rain-soaked lane to Ganat. They left the road before the village and started through the dew and the stubble of the fields. The rising mist on the forest floor enclosed their phantom shapes well before the farmers woke at sunrise. Within minutes, they began the climb up the ridge.

"Yes, Daddy, but will we go home again? Will we go home tomorrow? It's cold out here."

The couple looked at their three-year-old, and Guilhelms spoke. "You remember how we told you about my cousin in Farga, Tibaut? Gervais Deslegador? He owns our grandfather's smelter."

The boy's face said I don't understand. He was only three. "Yes, but are we going home? The metal men have left."

"No, little one. We're visiting my cousin for a few days. Then we'll decide if we can go home." Tibaut looked decidedly unhappy. It was too early for the truth. "It won't be long before you're back in your house, Tibaut, and your friends will still be there. First we must stay with Gervais." The little boy understood that they were not going home, but his father confused him with the rest.

The family started downhill, passing under the rock outcropping and disappearing into the forest. Downhill was easier, and their pace was faster now. A rivulet became a brook and they followed it down. Their goal was not the village of Farga de sant Matèu itself, but a foundry, *la farga*, that lay about five hundred paces south of the town, where their brook joined the Ariège.

The Faures slowed up along with the rushing water as the land flattened out, moving carefully through the woods to the low brush bordering the farmland. The fields of Farga spread out to their left, brown in the early Fall, into the broadening valley of the Ariège.

"Let's stop here, Aenor."

To their left, Farga's single village street matched the street in Brassat, in Ganat, in every village of Languedoc. Thatch roofs, mud-daubed woven-stick houses and a small stone church provided homes for almost a hundred people. Beyond the village, down-river towards Foix, some of those hundred were at work in the yard of the manor house of Sir Josèp, near a small copse of woods on a little rise.

"It looks quiet, Guilhelms."

"Yes." Husband and wife looked to their right, where the valley narrowed as the land rose towards the Pyrenees, just as it did in Brassat. "Nothing up the valley, either."

Smoke poured from a smelter's chimney across the field in front of them. Two others stood idle, but the hammers in the forges added their ring to the tumbling Ariège. The three furnaces stood in the open, but a high wooden roof protected the hearths and workbenches of the forge. The smiths were cold in the winter and hot in the summer, but at least they stayed dry.

"We are free, Aenor, but I'd rather not argue the point with Sir Josèp. We'll watch from here to make sure everything stays quiet. Once it's safe, we'll cross over to my cousin's house."

Time passed slowly for Tibaut. A few moments' play, and then it was time to ask Aenor again, could they go home. Finally the dozen workers put away their tools and began their walk to Farga de sant Matèu. "Soon now, Tibaut," Aenor said as they watched the parade. Not for the first time, Guilhelms wondered why his Outremer ancestors named their forge after Saint Matthew.

"There's your cousin, Guilhelms."

The couple watched Gervais Deslegador hang up his leather apron on a peg and start for his house. In a moment, he was out of the muddy foundry yard and crossing the vegetable garden to his dwelling. He opened his door and went inside. Quiet settled over the yard as the workers neared their village.

"Okay, Aenor, Tibaut has been patient long enough. Let's go knock on my cousin's door."

The Faures stepped from the woods into the brown furrows of a field left fallow for the year. They walked steadily through the soft dirt, Aenor carrying their sack and Guilhelms carrying Tibaut.

"What's that sound, husband"?

Yes. "Hoofbeats, very faint." They froze as the faint sound of many men riding hard echoed faintly across the fields. "Turn back for the woods! We've been betrayed"!

Aenor needed no encouragement. The sound grew louder as they regained the trees. Guilhelms let Tibaut down. "Take him back into the woods, deeper. I'll see what's happening." Within seconds, Aenor was lost in the changing leaves, down on the forest floor, hiding behind a log. Guilhelms lay down at the edge of the brush.

The smith thanked God he had waited as the riders finally pounded into view on the far side of Farga de sant Matèu. They did not slacken their pace as one man turned off for Sir Josèp's house. Mud flew from the hooves of nine chargers as the Crusaders galloped through the town, making straight for the Deslegador forge. They rode through the workers as though they were not even there, forcing them to jump into the wet grass on both sides of the road. Someone, Guilhelms thought, someone told these Épernays about his cousin's foundry. It would not be a safe place to hide after all.

Shouting floated over the field and into the brush, but the smith could not make out the words. The workers quickly climbed out of the grass and ran hard for the town. No one turned back to chase them. The nine paused in front of the empty foundry.

"The house"! Charles shouted. The column trotted through Petrona's empty vegetable garden and pulled up in front of a substantial dwelling. Gervais Deslegador was as wealthy as Sir Josèp, his home said, perhaps more wealthy. His ancestors built a home a full two stories tall, quarried stone covered with stucco. Clay tiles fired in a smelter covered the roof instead of thatch. The smoke of the kitchen fire wisped from a chimney on one end. Two windows on each floor let in the light and a solid door gave a feeling of importance.

Henri shouted orders. Two men rode behind the house. The baron, his son and the six others dismounted, crushing more of the stubble left from this summer's growth. Charles pounded on the door with his mailed fist.

"You, in the house! Come out! Kneel in the presence of Henri, Baron of Épernay."

Gervais and Petrona spoke little French, so nothing happened. Charles motioned and two men kicked in the solid door. It was but a moment before Gervais stumbled out, shoved by the man behind him. The drift of the generations made him ten years older than Guilhelms, already in his mid-thirties. With the brown cloth they all wore and the bald spot on the back of his head, Gervais always reminded his cousin of a tonsured monk.

"Kneel before Baron Henri, dog"!

Again, no understanding. His guard shoved Gervais down in the vegetable garden and held his sword to his back. Gervais ate as well as any monk, as the bulge in his tunic showed. His family did not suffer like their neighbors when the local crop failed, because they could always purchase more in Foix.

Some shouting, some crying from inside. Petrona ran out, holding the hand of a young girl. "Kneel, woman." Petrona hesitated, so her guard pushed down into her garden. Her frightened face with its dark hair turned towards her husband and back to their daughter, brown eyes darting from side to side in panic. Blonde-haired Lisbetta thought that this must be some kind of game. The ten-year-old child giggled and knelt down like the grownups.

Intense curiosity overcame Aenor's caution and she slid forward. Tibaut came with her, but he recognized the metal men and stayed quiet. They settled into the brush just as another man emerged from the house. He bowed quickly to Henri and made his report. Guilhelms could not hear, but he knew what the report must be. No crosses in the house, my lord, nothing Christian. They do not believe in the Resurrection of Our Lord and Savior. And that was true. Like Guilhelms and Aenor, the Deslegadors were Good Christians, what the Catholics called Cathars, Albigensians.

"Thank God Andreva is away, Guilhelms." Aenor looked protectively at Tibaut. "We have to do something."

"I have a knife. There are nine of them in armor, with swords. And one more over with Sir Josèp." Aenor's face grimaced. "It is too late to give ourselves up to them. They now know that my cousin's family are Good Christians. They are seizing their property under the Third Canon."

"How did they…"?

"Some traitor in Brassat told them, to make them go away."

There was a whoop, a shout from inside the house. Yet another man appeared, dragging a woman who was slapping at him, beating at him, to no avail. Sixteen-year-old Andreva was tall for a girl, thin with small breasts, and with dark hair brushing against her pretty face. The order came quickly from Charles. "Take off your tunic, girl. Strip off your cotte. We must check you for the Marks of Satan."

Forgive me, Gervais. I sowed the wind with Satan's messengers. You will reap the whirlwind.

4

Andreva did not understand the French. A hand movement from Charles and one of the men ripped tunic and cotte over her head, both at the same time. The young woman didn't know what to do, what to cover, so she just stood, trembling and naked in the cool air.

"Aplanta!" Stop, she called as Gervais rose to his feet to protect her. The man guarding him ran him through from behind, sending blood spurting from his chest and back. Petrona shrieked, Andreva shrieked, Charles laughed. Lisbetta threw herself on her father, begging the dying man to get up.

"He murdered him, Guilhelms, just like that."

"According to the Holy Father, it's not murder, Aenor. The Church says that the lands and the lives of Cathars are forfeit. I protected you from rape and now my cousin's family will die for it."

Charles pulled up Andreva and shoved her, face forward, against the wall to her own house. He put his arms around her waist and spread his legs around hers. She struggled at first, but the nobleman from Épernay slapped her face hard with his open hand. She gave up and let her upper body bend towards the ground. Charles lifted his armor over her back and then drew her onto him. The young woman cried out only once when he entered, his face twisted in ecstasy. Soon her body betrayed her, her breath coming hard, long hair brushing the dirt as she writhed over him, moaning in spite of herself. Gervais stopped moving as Andreva's moans grew louder.

Petrona turned from her dead husband and shrieked at Charles. *"Aplanta"!*

"Shut……her……up," Charles replied, in rhythm with his thrusting, "shut….her….up." Another man yanked Petrona to her feet and ripped off her tunic and then her cotte. His move revealed a plump woman with rolls of fat around her belly, the nun to her husband's monk. Her tormentor said something to the others, pointing at her large breasts as she tried to cover everything.

"Aplanta"!

The man drove his sword straight through her throat.

Lisbetta shrieked, jumped up from her father's body and began dashing along the little brook, directly towards Guilhelms and Aenor. Blood stained her cheeks and her hands and soaked the bodice of her brown woolen tunic. A stumble. She reached down to pull the hem above her waist and run as hard as she could.

Perhaps because he felt himself too dignified for a stand-up rape, the Baron of Épernay left the others to take their turns on the skinny young heretic. He remounted and trotted after the running child. He was in no rush, so he did not mind that she reached the woods before he caught her. He rode in, pushing the brush aside, ducking his head under the lower branches. The girl had stopped screaming, but Henri knew which way she had gone. He rode forward towards where she must be, still pushing aside the branches.

The girl appeared where he expected, standing in a clearing, but she surprised him by holding the hand of a small boy. A quite attractive blonde-haired woman stood beside them, her tunic and cotte pulled high on her thighs while she adjusted her boots. Her legs were quite shapely, quite shapely indeed.

It took Henri of Épernay about one second too long to realize that the lovely legs belonged to Aenor, the wife of the smith Faure of Brassat. Guilhelms reached up, pulled down on his right arm, his sword arm, and plunged a knife along the muscles between his shoulder and his elbow. The shape of the blade and the force of the blow forced apart the chain mail. Blood fountained from the deep wound.

Aenor straightened up in an instant, grabbing the horse's bridle, jerking the reins from Henri's hands. The smith levered down on his knife and dragged the baron from his saddle. With a cry of pain and anger and fear, the Lord of Épernay crashed to the ground alongside his mount. The fall stunned him for a moment, just the moment Guilhelms needed to sit on his chest and hold him down. He pulled the knight's own dagger from its sheath, lifted the coif away from his neck and held the blade to his throat.

"Yield or I'll gouge out your eyes before I cut your throat, my lord Baron. Aenor, get his sword."

"A knight cannot yield to a peasant, you imbecile. Get off me while there is still a chance that I might let you live." He glared at Guilhelms while Aenor leaned over his legs, unbuckling his sword belt and pulling it free.

"Let me live, my lord? You're the one losing blood. Your murdering son is a useless piece of shit. I should kill you, but I need you."

"They are Cathar heretics, Faure. Their lives and their goods are forfeit to me."

Guilhelms laughed. "Yield now, my noble turd, or in five minutes you'll bleed to death and be reborn again as a serf into this world of pain."

"You're a heretic, too, Faure? I should have let Charles have that wench"!

"We are Good Christians, yes, my lord. And that wench is my wife." Guilhelms wiggled his own knife in the wound, renewing the fountain of spraying blood.

"AIY! AIY! STOP! I yield! I yield"!

"Better." The blacksmith pulled the coif from the knight's head and threw it on the ground. "Stand up."

■ ■ ■

A strange parade left the woods. Henri led the way, walking without his armor and with his right arm tightly wrapped in blood-soaked strips of cloth cut from his Crusader tunic. Other strips tied his hands behind his back. Guilhelms walked behind, with the Baron's sword pushed lightly into his spine. Aenor held the reins to the knight's charger in one hand and his dagger in the other. Lisbetta held Tibaut's hand. The Baron's hauberk lay on the forest floor, along with his coif and helmet.

Andreva was still against the wall as a third man took his turn with her, riding her, thrusting into her like a bull into a cow. Shrieks of pain echoed against the stone wall as their victim begged them to stop, *"aplanta, aplanta."* The others only laughed.

"She says she likes it, Pierre," said one as he urged on the bull.

A shout from the left, "My lord Baron"! Guilhelms turned towards the sound. The knight who stopped at Sir Josèp's manor trotted towards them through the fields behind the village. He had seen his liege go into the woods and not come out. He decided to investigate.

"Call to them, Baron," Guilhelms ordered. "Tell them all to stop."

"Charles"! A loud voice, a voice accustomed to command. "Sir Martin! Stop! Stop now"!

The group around Andreva looked towards the call, all except the man who was in her. The others drew their weapons and spread out in a line. The knight trotting towards them drew his sword and prepared to charge.

"Stop him." Guilhelms kept his voice calm, low, threatening.

Henri turned towards the rider. "Sir Martin! No! Stop! I am grievously wounded, my friend! My arm is nearly cut off! Do what he says or I'll bleed to death"!

Martin did not stop, but he slowed his mount to a walk and approached carefully. Concern filled his wrinkled face, but his body, like that of the Baron, remained hard despite his age. Guilhelms felt his warrior energy, with his sword making little movements, looking for the opening that would let him kill them all and rescue his liege.

Energy, yes, but Guilhelms could also sense the friendship, the respect between the two older men. The smith knew that Sir Martin must be everything that Charles was not. A man could trust his life to Sir Martin in a battle. He could trust his daughter's virtue to Sir Martin on a journey, even if the two of them traveled alone.

"Dismount," Guilhelms ordered, but instead Martin only kept his horse alongside as the little party walked towards the house.

"Please, Martin, do as he says. I'm bleeding badly. Put up your weapon and help me." A brief moment as Martin regarded the broadsword in Henri's back. His own sword went into its scabbard, and he dismounted.

Guilhelms stopped twenty paces from the house, just as the third man finished with Andreva. He let her go and she fell into the dirt. Her legs went into her chest to be hugged by her arms, trying to conceal her breasts and her sex. Her mother's open eyes stared at her in death from where she fell. Andreva closed her own, as if she could sleep this nightmare away and wake up safe in her bed.

"Charles," Guilhelms called. "Give her back her tunic and send her over here."

Charles leered and stabbed her through her breast instead. Andreva's eyes shot open with a look of fear, of anguish, of disbelief as the blood spurted from her chest. Ten minutes ago, she was a virgin helping her mother with supper. Now she was sitting naked in her empty vegetable garden, raped three times and dying. She held her wound, trying to stop the flow, choking.

"Lis! Lis"! Blood sprayed from her mouth as she called her sister's name.

"Andi, no, Andi"! Lisbetta shrieked.

Andreva knelt up to stand, fainted into a heap and died. Charles kicked her head to make sure, picked up her tunic and dangled it on the corpse. "I'm giving her the tunic, smith, but she doesn't seem to want it."

"Guilhelms," said Aenor, in the flattest, calmest voice Guilhelms had ever heard from her. "Let me kill the father. I want to kill him, now." She laid Henri's dagger against his cheek.

"Charles!" Henri called. "No more! Do what the blacksmith says! Do it or I'll disown you! I need help"! The knights spread out to rush the smith's family. "No! Stop! This woman will kill me! Charles, I mean it! Stop"! His eyes turned towards his friend, pleading. "Martin, come here. My arm is nearly cut off."

"Stay there, Martin," Guilhelms ordered. "The rest of you. Mount up and ride out. Come back to the house tomorrow. The baron and Sir Martin will be there, alive. Ride out now."

"It's a trick, Father. The Cathar pigs will kill you as soon as we leave"!

"Ride out! Do as he says! Martin, help me. The pain is most grievous." Henri slumped to his knees and fell over. Guilhelms held the sword to his unconscious throat.

"Sir Charles," Sir Martin called over. "I must tend to your father. Ride out"!

Charles hesitated. "I want the smith's wife first! Send her over"!

"What are you thinking, Charles"! Martin called. "A man who lets his father die to gain the title, His Majesty will never accept you"! Martin called to the column. "All of you! Mount up! Ride out"!

Charles joined the others in following the command. A moment of confusion as the column formed and the horses thundered away. Mud splattered over Gervais as he lay face down in his garden, and over the naked bodies of Petrona and Andreva sprawled nearby. Andreva's dress piled up on her body as blood trickled from her mouth.

Sir Martin dropped the reins to his horse and walked to his lord. He limped slightly as he did. "I have served my lord the Baron Henri for many years, smith," the knight said as he knelt down. "We have fought many battles together." He unwrapped the bandage, looking with expert gray eyes at the welling blood. He bound it again, more tightly. Henri awoke, screamed from the pain and slumped back down. "That's a deep wound. Make me another strip so that I can fashion a tourniquet." Aenor dropped the reins to Henri's horse and leaned in to cut the cloth. "His arm will never be the same. He may lose it."

"The woman they raped lost more than her arm," Aenor snarled, tossed the cloth and stormed away.

"I was present when Sir Charles was baptized." Martin's scarred hands twisted the tourniquet. "He is….." The knight stopped, looking towards Andreva. Guilhelms said nothing. Instead he watched as Aenor and Lisbetta laid the bodies out side-by-side and covered them with a cloth from inside the house. Tibaut stayed with his father. He did not ask when they were going home.

Aenor and Lisbetta returned. "Turn around," Guilhelms ordered. "Aenor, tie his hands behind his back, and his legs. Tie the two of them together, back to back." She cut strips from Martin's tunic and began her work.

The grazing horses, Martin's and Henri's, lifted their heads. One whinnied. "Hurry." The horses trotted towards the village, towards the faint sounds of hoofbeats. "It appears that tomorrow has come early, Sir Martin. I will not stoop to murder today, but you can tell your fucking Baron of Épernay and his dog shit son that if I ever get the chance, I'll kill them both."

Charles and his men charged through Farga de sant Matèu as the two riderless horses fell into the column. Sir Henri and Martin sat tied together back-to-back in the field across the road. The column rode past them towards the woods, but the smith and his family were nowhere to be found.

5

The smith, his family and the newly orphaned Lisbetta reached the overlook before dark. "The sun is setting earlier all the time, Guilhelms. The days and nights are almost the same." Darkness finally ended the commotion in Farga de sant Matèu, all the checking for the Marks of Satan, leaving behind a rising full moon to light the mercifully cloudless sky.

Slowly, carefully, the Faures led Lisbetta off the hillside, around Ganat and onto the road to Brassat. They moved along carefully, a hundred paces at a time, watching and waiting. A smell of burnt wood grew stronger as they drew closer, carried towards them on the wind.

Just before they reached Brassat, the blacksmith left the road and took his family down to the Barièja, near a place where he played as a boy. The water slowed and meandered as it crossed the fields behind the village, making it easy to walk along its banks. Wind blowing through the trees and water flowing in the stream covered any sounds from their passing feet, but that wind carried a strong scent of charred timber.

"It's our shop that we smell, Guilhelms," Aenor said. "Those pigs must have burned it before they started for Farga this afternoon."

The huts of the serfs darkened the darkness above them as they passed behind the village. The last fields fell away, the lane through the village ended and they began their climb into the hills, into the narrowing Barièja valley. The riverbank grew steeper as they entered the forest. Even the light of a full moon could not fully illuminate their path now, slowing their progress.

The Faures struggled uphill for half an hour before they came to the edge of a clearing. Moonlight sparkled on the waterfall at the far end. Grass still with the green of summer filled the pleasant spot, softening the ground, gentling the landscape. The Trysting Glade, everyone in Brassat called this place. More than one baby had been created here through the centuries as the parents lay side by side near the flowing stream, gazing on the starry blaze of heaven.

"Wait here." Guilhelms disappeared into the woods. The sound of the waterfall masked his steps as he made his way around the edge of the meadow, staying just inside the trees. Aenor watched carefully, because the sound of the waterfall could mask other footsteps too.

Guilhelms returned after ten minutes. "I found the hidden trail. Let's go up a little way, share what food we have and wait for sunrise."

■ ■ ■

Charles of Épernay and seven men rode into Ganat early the following morning. They drove everyone from their huts and stripped the young girls to check for the Mark of Satan. Finding that they all bore the stain of the Prince of Darkness, Charles pleasured himself with one while his men took the others. Afterwards, they whipped three serfs and rode off.

Guilhelms, his family and the newly orphaned Lisbetta watched it all from their place in the woods overlooking the Barièja Valley. "Henri did not bleed to death, love," the smith said. "Martin must be tending him, in Fonta."

In response, Aenor threw up in the way women often did in the morning when they were early with child. Lisbetta held Tibaut's hand, still trying to grasp how the game with the knights had left her an orphan.

■ ■ ■

The blacksmith's party started up the hidden path from the Trysting Glade. "We're looking for a clearing in the woods on our right." Two or three came and went, but not the one they sought. Finally, in one little break in the tree line, they saw the tower of St. Gregorio's in Brassat lined up with the Bear's Tooth on the far side of the Arget. "This is it." Guilhelms turned to look behind them.

No one in Brassat remembered how long ago the first villager discovered this hidden spot. A grove of thick brush marked out by the line of the Bear's Tooth and the church tower concealed a small defile in the hillside. Only a diligent search would give even a hint of what lay behind the cluster of bushes. A casual walker would pass by without seeing anything.

Guilhelms pushed aside the bushes and held them back for the others to pass. Brambles clutched at wool while Aenor shielded Tibaut's face from any whipping branches. The smith checked the brush after they passed, being sure no tuft of cloth, no broken branches stayed behind to betray their passage.

A cold rain began as they climbed through the defile, onto a higher ledge and into a hardwood forest where the leaves were just beginning to change. Ten minutes brought them to a small clearing with two small cave mouths in the hillside.

"Lisbetta, take Tibaut and hide in the woods. Aenor, wait here, in the open so that they can see you. I'll go back down the path and be sure we weren't followed."

Guilhelms walked down the trail and hid in the forest. Once he was thoroughly soaked, with rain dripping from his nose and no sounds down the trail behind him, he returned to the clearing. Aenor was gone.

"Husband." A whisper from the cave to the left. "Husband, in here, quickly." Guilhelms slithered through the entrance on his belly, and disappeared.

■ ■ ■

Behind the entrance, the cave opened out into a large room, large enough for three serf's cottages to fit at the same time. This cavern had once been a mine, but whatever ore the ancient miners sought had been found and extracted. At the rear of the space, a natural crack in the rocks, or perhaps an airshaft carved by the miners, let the smoke from a cooking fire escape into the trees above. All the twists and turns in the crack thinned the smoke before it emerged, as long as the fire was not allowed to grow too large.

Guilhelms joined his family and their neighbors the Formatgièrs, the village bakers, husband, wife and three children. "We came up here as soon as those Épernays left your house, Guilhelms," Diegos, the father, said. "We told Father Ricartz that we wished to go into the mountains on retreat, to meditate on our sins."

"He suspects we are all Good Christian *Credentes*, Believers, Diegos."

"He is from Lengadòc, a native speaker of our language. As long as we attend Mass, he will protect us."

Guilhelms pointed to an older couple, Brassat farmers tending the small fire. Both had changed into the simple black robes of a *Parfait*, a Perfect of the Good Christians. "Rothan and Francesca came up with you"?

"Not right away. They came up after those northern killers burned your blacksmith shop. 'We have received the Sacrament of the *Consolamentum*, the Consolation,' Rothan said. 'Our community is threatened. We must join them.'"

Even as Diegos spoke, Rothan and Francesca broke away from the fire to join the little group. "The Faures," Rothan said. "You escaped the knights after all."

Guilhelms gave a gentle bow, an acknowledgement of Rothan's position in the community. "We did, barely." All among them believed that, just as the Holy Spirit descended upon the Apostles on the Day of Pentecost, so also had the Holy Spirit descended upon this couple, through the laying on of hands by other Parfaits, back to the time of the Disciples themselves.

"Who is this little girl"?

"Lisbetta Deslegador from Farga de sant Matèu, my cousin's daughter, Tibaut's second cousin. They murdered Gervais and Petrona and Andreva yesterday while we watched from the woods. I nearly cut off the arm of the old Baron when he followed Lisbetta into the forest. They will harass and threaten everyone in Brassat, Ganat, Cazac until they find us to take their revenge."

Rothan nodded. As a *Parfait*, he ate abstemiously, only fish and vegetables, no meat or eggs. Those things came from fornication, from the world of Satan. They must be avoided if the believer expected to escape rebirth into Satan's world and be accepted instead by God into the heavenly paradise.

"Where will you go"? Francesca asked. Since becoming *Parfaits* ten years before, Rothan and Francesca had lived together as husband and wife, yet without once engaging in the act of carnal love. Which was more than the Formatgièrs or the Faures could claim, especially Aenor in her present condition. It was so difficult to live as a *Parfait* that many *Credentes* did not take the *Consolamentum* until they were near death.

"Father Ricartz tolerates you, Rothan, and he has always been grateful for our gifts. I'll give you more for him now. If you can give us some provisions in return, the four of us will leave immediately. We'll go into the mountains and cross over to Aragon before the snows begin."

"If we don't remain here too long," Francesca said, looking at Rothan, "We can spare them a few days of food. Enough to sustain them until they reach the first Aragonese village."

"You should not stay up here too long, Francesca," Guilhelms answered. "Give us a one day head start. Return to the village tomorrow, before Sir Arnald asks the Épernays to start looking for you. Tell Ricartz that we have run away to Aragon and will not be coming back."

"Where will you go after that"?

Guilhelms and Aenor exchanged glances, and blue-eyed Lisbetta, so fair for this part of the country, waited to hear the answer, too. "We'll go to Al-Andalus, to the Saracens in Iberia, Rothan. They will welcome a skilled smith and ironworker, and they will tolerate us as People of the Book. It will be safer for us with the Muslims than with the Catholics."

6

Lady Elizabeth waited alone in the common room of the Solar for her son Sir Frederic. On her wedding day, the Maronite woman stunned Jabil al-Hadid with her sensual beauty, but now gray filled her curly black hair and the thick of age filled her waist. Her youth lived on in her dark eyes, eyes that still sparkled with passion. Passion to fulfil her mother-in-law Mariam's dying wish. To protect Sir Frederic's rights, despite King Amalric's decree. To end that demeaning insult and free their line to inherit Jabil al-Hadid.

"Good day, Mother." Elizabeth presented her cheek for a kiss. Frederic placed one there, smelling the perfume in her simple blue wool tunic. The knight unbuckled his weapons belt and laid it on the table. "William," he said to the waiting Seneschal, "We can begin."

Frederic enjoyed the roasted meat and figs and chicken that they shared from the common plate, but he knew that Elizabeth felt her appetite fading. Her age, of course, but she held on, true to her pledge to Frederic's grandmother.

"Will you ride as far as Saissouq today, my son?"

A chicken bone, picked clean, found its way to the straw on the floor. "To Saissouq, yes, but not the castle. Sir Stephen has asked our assistance with a caravan coming up to Krak."

Lady Elizabeth remained silent for a moment while she watched her son eat. "You should move into Hugh's room, Frederic. I've found the Cripple's to be very pleasant."

Sir Frederic held his knife, waving it vaguely in her direction, more of a pointer than a weapon. "I wish you had not ordered that, Mother. I'm Hugh's Viscount, not the Baron. It's only been a few months. He probably just got to Alberensa. It's not appropriate."

"Rooms are for the living, Frederic."

"What does that mean, Mother"?

"Baron Guilhabert's wife died when your grandmother was still a maid. Madeleine of Montpellier left him with three children, his heir Olivier, his daughter Maria and his son Jourdain. Plenty of space, but changes were soon afoot."

"The two marriages."

"In 1164, Guilhabert married Mariam and Oliver married Athèné. Guilhabert kept his bedroom on the second floor, and gave Olivier the other, and together they started filling up the Keep. Maria created some space when she married Guy of Sidon in 1168, but Jourdain remained home, unmarried. Your father Fulk joined him a year after Guilhabert and Mariam married. The Keep at Jabil al-Hadid grew steadily more crowded, and I had not yet arrived from Chadra."

"Mariam had only Fulk. Athèné birthed five children."

"A toddler daughter and a teenage son died before I got here, leaving only her son Joscelin and daughter Claire. Claire married John of Beziers during his pilgrimage in 1186 while I was pregnant with you. The following Spring, Anne arrived. Her Royal Highness did not believe it was possible for her to have another baby, but it happened."

"Your point being, no one really has a room here." Elizabeth nodded, but her eyes said that she was suddenly far away. "Mother"?

"Hattin." Her hand reached out to rest upon the scabbard of Julian's sword.

"Hattin"?

"After the battle, Athèné became twelve-year-old Baron Joscelin's regent. She tried to send Mariam and you and me back to Chadra."

"Yes."

"Instead, Mariam insisted on her rights as the Dowager. Athèné's own mother advised her to accept the demand. We stayed, Mariam in the Keep, you and I in a farmhouse in the village outside, at least until Joscelin knighted you and you moved into the barracks."

Yes, we stayed, Frederic thought. For the next twenty-five years, the cobra circled the asp and the asp stalked the cobra. Dowager Baroness Mariam blessed my marriage to Sophia without ever telling Dowager Baroness Athènè. Then the cobra died, and the asp, and then the catastrophe of the crippling disease.

"I still remember the day Joscelin rode down to the village after his mother died. 'You have been treated poorly by Princess Athènè, Lady Elizabeth. You are welcome to join us in the Keep. Or if you wish, I will build a home for you in Chadra and send servants to care for you.'"

"You chose the Keep."

"That kept me close to you, my son, and to my grandchildren. And to the nobility of Tripoli, able to plead our case against the insult of Amalric's decree."

"I don't see how…"

Elizabeth frowned. Her hand took the scabbard and drew out the sword of Baron Julian. She surprised Frederic and William as she twisted the weapon in the candlelight, hefting it, pointing it. "If it wasn't for my husband, your father Fulk, this sword would be decorating a *souk* in Baghdad right now."

"Leave us, William. I'll call if we need you." The viper was about to spit poison, and perhaps it was not best for the servants to hear. William scurried away, scuffling quickly down the circular stone staircase. Frederic stood at the top and shouted after him. "Don't snoop from downstairs, William! Go to the kitchen. There is work to do there." He turned back. His mother's smile for her son could be quite warm, if one could ignore the viper's fangs.

"Always remember the Horns of Hattin, Frederic. The Fourth of July, 1187."

As if anyone in Outremer could forget Hattin.

"Every Christian remembers Hattin, Mother. It was a disaster for the cause of Christ. After it, Jerusalem surrendered to Saladin. If Richard of England and Philip of France had not arrived, the Saracens might have expelled the Franks from all of Outremer. Her Majesty Yolande may still be called the Queen of Jerusalem, but she now reigns from Acre by the sea."

"She reigns. Frederic? She is a ten-year-old girl. Her father John of Brienne rules for her while the Holy Father and the Holy Roman Emperor scheme about her future."

"Hattin, Mother"?

"Baron Olivier and his brother Jourdain were already in their thirties at the time. My husband Fulk was only twenty-one. Olivier and Jourdain, they were like all the Barons, ironsmiths, merchants with a title. They preferred to work with the serfs and the Syrians in the forge, making gold and silver trinkets. Making iron and steel for better men to use."

And making the family very rich, Frederic thought. Someone had to make the swords or there would be none. That's why Olivier's wife had been a princess of Jerusalem.

"Raynald de Chatillon, Lord of Oultrejordain, provoked the Saracens, but Saladin was looking for an excuse," Elizabeth said. "And that idiot Guy de Lusignan" – she spat out the name – "he took the bait."

The story of Guy, that, too, Frederic knew. Guy's wife was Athèné's cousin, the Queen of Jerusalem, Sybilla. Sybilla's son died. Her leprous brother died. The Kingdom fell to her in her own right, but she adored Guy. She crowned him King with her own hands, elevating the Lusignan family, disappointing many others, and dooming her Kingdom.

"When Saladin invaded Galilee and besieged Tiberias, the whole Christian army in Outremer marched out to meet him. Jabil al-Hadid was with Raymond III of Tripoli at the Sephora Spring when King Guy ordered the army to march to the relief of Tiberias."

Yes, Frederic thought. The Franks started on the morning of the Third, reaching the springs at Turan, six miles from Tiberias, late in the day. It was time to stop and fortify for the night, but King Guy pressed on. When he finally realized that his army would not reach Tiberias and the Sea of Galilee that day, the King ordered it to make for another spring, at Hattin, below a mountain with two peaks, the Horns.

Guy did not realize that the spring was seasonal. The army found it dry. The prey had taken the bait, and the predator snapped closed the trap.

During the night from the Third to the Fourth of July, Saladin's army surrounded the Christian host as it camped below the Horns. They fired the grass, adding smoke to the misery of their thirst. Volleys of arrows fell into the Christian ranks all night. The Saracens massacred any Franks trying to reach the water at Galilee or Turan. Evenly matched when the Christians started from Sephora, by morning the Saracen host had gained the advantage in numbers.

On the Fourth, the Crusaders fought as though their lives depended upon it, as indeed they did. They charged Saladin's line three times, and were repulsed each time. The Saracens counter-attacked, and the Christians drove them back. It was brave but it could not last.

Saladin captured King Guy, and Prince Raynald, and the Grand Masters Roger de Moulins of the Hospital and Gerard de Ridefort of the Temple. Saracen custom held that if the victor gave a drink to a defeated man, that man's life was not forfeit. Saladin himself offered Guy water with snow from the Lebanese Mountains. The King drank and turned, unbidden, to pass the cup to Raynald. Saladin's Damascus steel flashed, taking the Prince's outstretched arm off his body before he could drink. A Saracen soldier beheaded Raynald from behind even as his severed limb bounced on the ground.

"The story I tell you now happened early in the day, Frederic, as the Saracen numbers steadily wore down the forces of our Lord. I learned it from the Hospitaller who was with Fulk when he died."

Elizabeth set the point of the sword in the straw, on the stone floor. Her hands rested on the leather-wrapped guards. The ruby on the handle sat chest-high. Two crosses of Christ, the one around her neck and the one made by the weapon, blessed the story to come.

"On the morning of the Fourth, Raymond of Tripoli attacked towards Tiberias, trying to force an opening to the water. Saladin let Raymond through his host, then attacked."

"Cutting him off from the main army. Separating the Christian host."

Elizabeth's nostrils flared, her eyes blazed. "When the Saracens counterattacked, they overwhelmed those two lame idiots, Olivier and his brother. Fat and clumsy Jourdain was the first to go. An Arab stabbed him in the leg. Your father saw him fall. He saw the heathen reach down, take Jourdain's own sword and use it to kill him. He turned to Olivier to do the same."

Again those eyes, those wistful eyes. They must have been quite in love, Frederic, your mother and your father. Years in the village, yet no other man ever caught her eye.

"Your father Fulk was a true warrior for Christ, my son, a fighting man. He dispatched two or three atheists as he fought his way to the Baron's side. The loathsome murdering Arab put his dagger in Olivier's chest just before Fulk reached them. The heathen reached down and took Julian's sword from his hand.

Fulk leaped to the attack, landing a single blow against Julian's upraised steel that drove the filthy Arab to his knees. The jaws of Hell opened before him. Fear crossed his face as he saw Satan waiting for his soul"!

Frederic had fought in many fights, but never in a battle like Hattin, where whole armies fought to the death. Where the losers dropped their weapons and ran from the field in a rout while the victors chased them and cut them down and sold any survivors into slavery.

"Another Saracen attacked Fulk before he could deliver the killing blow, forcing him to turn away. That man quickly tasted steel in his mouth, but Julian's sword made its way into Fulk from behind. Your father turned without pausing and sent the backstabbing coward's head flying into the Saracens. He reached down while blood still fountained from the quivering corpse and pulled the Baron's sword from its dead hand"!

Julian's steel flickered in the candlelight, remembering. A red-blue hazy nick glowed near the hilt where the Arab had fended off Fulk's attack.

"But my father's wound was mortal."

"Yes. Fulk was not bleeding badly, but he knew that he would get the fever and die. He knelt next to Olivier. He pulled the Arab's dagger from the Baron's chest and threw it on the ground. The two of them began to stagger from the field. Olivier had not gone twenty steps when he knelt, fainting from the loss of blood. He put his head down, rolled on his side and died."

All that is asked, Frederic thought, is that you fight as well you can until you no longer can, and then that you trust in Our Savior's merciful grace.

The chaos. The shouting. The arrows singing through the air. The cries of encouragement, of pain, of surprise at the moment of death. The banging and ringing of steel on steel. The injured horses, baying and thrashing. The dead and the dying ignored while those still able to fight battled on.

And in the rear of the Christian line, one badly wounded man limping away, leaving his dead half-brothers behind. Losing blood, growing fainter each moment, clinging to consciousness as he clung to the sword he had rescued. Until someone dumped him into a wagon with other wounded men and drove him to Tripoli. Where he held onto life for three days, his pain relieved only by wine, until he died.

"The Hospitaller knight brought the sword home to Jabil al-Hadid, Frederic, and told the tale. Mariam was overcome with grief. Still, that haughty bitch Athèné of Jerusalem, she did not care. She took the sword from the Hospitaller and said that she would hold it for her son Joscelin until he reached maturity. There was not one kind word to Mariam, Frederic, not one, nor one kind word to me, not one, even though Fulk rescued the sword for the family."

Elizabeth's face flushed as though she had drunk too much wine. "That's why I'm glad you finally have the sword. Fulk would be proud. You're a chivalrous knight, a man worthy to carry the weapon of the hero of Hisn al-Akrad, Julian of Blagnac. A man worthy to carry the weapon rescued by your father, Fulk of Jabil al-Hadid, the flower of Tripoli's chivalry."

She lifted the Sword of Julian, offered it to her son, put his hand on the hilt to take it. She closed her hand over her son's.

"The Lord intends for you to be the Baron, my son. That is why your father rescued the sword, for you. That is why the Lord kept you here while filthy Athèné's cowardly grandson ran from the fight in Outremer, hiding behind his crippled concubine witch."

Frederic started. "Mother, be careful. Agnes is Hugh's sister, not his concubine. Close your eyes and pretend you cannot walk. That is Agnes, completely helpless, and there are too many enemies here. Our lord the Baron of Jabil al-Hadid has done the right thing to take her away. And the right thing to go with her, to protect her. Whom would you send, Mother, Lady Anne"?

Elizabeth snorted. "At least the sailors would enjoy the voyage then, every one of them."

Frederic put the sword back in the scabbard and stood to buckle it on. "You say that I'm a chivalrous knight, Mother? A chivalrous knight honors his oaths. I have sworn to use this sword to protect Jabil al-Hadid as the Viscount of its Baron, Hugh. And we are friends, Mother, you know that."

"Friends with your liege"? Elizabeth waved that away with a flourish. "Are you worried about Amalric's agreement, my son? His descendants no longer rule Jerusalem. That slip of a girl barely rules the outhouse behind her palace in Acre."

Frederic recognized the look in his mother's eyes. She always had that look when she was plotting with Mariam against Athèné. "It is a matter of honor, of justice, of righteousness, Mother. Of course none of them are alive any longer, but Guilhabert gave a binding oath. The Patriarch of Jerusalem blessed it. Hugh, Baron of Jabil al-Hadid, is a most worthy liege. It is our Christian duty to honor him."

"The decree does not apply to Lady Saissouq, Frederic."

"Of course not, mother. Anne is Athèné's daughter, but it does not matter. She cannot inherit."

"Her new husband is fat and old. He likes boys. She must be lonely for a real man. I know you had her. Everyone here had her. Was it good?"

Frederic pointed his finger at his mother. "You must stop this behavior. I don't want to hear this kind of talk again."

"Your son Jean needs a fief, Frederic. You can rescue Anne from Saissouq's clutches and marry her yourself. Marry her on the condition that she joins your petition to the Count of Tripoli to allow your marriage to Athèné's child to annul the effect of the King's decree. She will do it, I'm sure. You will be the Baron, and Jean after you."

"You're forgetting Hugh, Mother."

"He will never be back, my son." She dismissed the Runaway and the Cripple with another wave. "Ride to Saissouq today. Renew your carnal association with Athèné's harlot daughter. Surely she will be able to think of something to provoke a war with Fat Baudoin."

PART THREE

County of Alberensa
March – June 1224

1

Guilhelms stood at their cottage door, ready to leave for the ironworks. Aenor sat at the table, nursing their infant daughter Isabèl.

"It's still cool, Guilhelms, but I think that winter is past. The days are longer, the ground is warmer. I'll start preparing for our garden today."

"I'll help, Mommy," Tibaut said.

"I'll help with Isabèl," Lisbetta added. After eighteen months together, Tibaut remained a little boy, just slightly bigger. At nearly twelve, Cousin Lisbetta was becoming a woman.

Guilhelms smiled as he left their home and started up the Petrousset village street for the Count's foundry. A cool day, yes, but a hint of Spring hung in the air.

Lent always began in the short dark days of winter, but as the celebration of Easter approached, even the heavens brightened with joy at the coming celebration of the Savior's Resurrection. Or so the Catholics claimed. The smith could not understand why anyone believed that God would actually appear in His own flesh on Satan's evil earth. Incarnation, Crucifixion, Resurrection, it was superstition, not faith, all of it.

■ ■ ■

"Water never boils while you watch it," Aenor always said as she shooed Guilhelms away from her cooking. That had been the smith's experience at the Petrousset smelter too. He stood on the brown packed dirt, watching two laborers pump the bellows while smoke rose from the brick chimney. Inside the furnace, the ore and the limestone grew hotter under the heat of the charcoal, working the mystery that brought forth the metal.

Wait, watch, and wait some more.

Not yet.

A lucky moment for the family, Guilhelms, arriving in Alberensa just as the Count began building this smelter. "His lordship wants a way to make money besides fleecing the pilgrims," Walter said while he watched Guilhelms shape a horseshoe. "That's good work, excellent work in fact. Do you know how to run a smelter"?

"Yes."

"You're hired. A couple of the men will help you build a cottage in the village." Walter frowned as he considered his mystery expert. "You're not a runaway serf, are you"?

"No."

"Good."

Guilhelms doubted that Walter cared. He needed someone to run the smelter. Until the Brassat smith appeared, all that he had was farmers.

The Count's ironworks stood in a forest beside the Alberensa River, an hour's ride north from the city of Alberensa. The Pyrenees Mountains dominated the view to the south, just as they did at Brassat. Here the highest and most prominent peak flattened into a table at the top, earning it the name of *"Lo Grandautar,"* the "High Altar." The route through the Sárdalo Pass into Aragon traversed the notch on its eastern slope.

Aenor was heavy with Isabèl when the Faures came down the Pass last Spring, as the Catholics said that Mary was heavy with God on her way to the first Christmas. Much as the people of Bethlehem looked briefly at the Holy Family, the serfs of Alberensa's villages spared a moment to be curious about the Faures. Then they returned to tending the winter wheat and plowing under last year's fallow strip to prepare for the spring planting. The weather and the manor lord ruled their days, not passing families.

"What do you think, Guilhelms? Is it ready?" The smith's assistant brought him back from his reverie.

"A moment more, Bernart." He looked towards the larger smelter, where workmen tended a charge that should become molten iron. The Count had learned to do that in Outremer, but the iron he made was hard and brittle. It could be cast into molds, but not shaped by forging and tempering. For that, they still worked a bloom.

"Now"?

"A little longer." The breeze rustled the trees, making the smoke columns curl to the ground under its force. "You know, Bernart, I think this forest grew back over ancient farms."

"No one remembers a time without these woods, Guilhelms."

"Yes, but when they started cutting those trees," pointing towards the edge of the clearing, "They found a couple of old hearths, like in a village. Dragging the logs to the big smelter furrowed the dirt and revealed some flat stones, as though a road once went up this side of the stream."

Bernart crossed himself. "Don't talk like that among the men, Guilhelms. They'll think the forest is haunted."

Not haunted, just once occupied by people now long forgotten. As we too will someday be long forgotten, just as the Bible says.

Not today, though. Today we are here. Today we are here, making iron, turning nature to our will.

"Bern. It's time."

A shout of warning. The men at the bellows stopped. Bernart knocked open the tap, letting the liquid rock pour forth into the slag pit. Both men felt the intense heat against their faces, heat like a hot sun on the hottest day. Bernart pissed into the flowing slag, watching his urine boil instantly and steam into the sky. It was the old farmer's idea of a joke. The others backed away to avoid the pungent scent.

"When you're done with that, Bernart, open the door."

Guilhelms reached in with the tongs and dragged the glowing bloom from the furnace. He carried it twenty paces to a hearth that stood under a high wooden roof, just as at Farga de san Matèu. He tossed it on the coals as the smelter laborers started working the bellows on the forge, pumping air into the fuel from underneath.

"Pump harder, men." Guilhelms called as he turned the lump and pushed it to the heart of the fire. "Get the glow back."

A single horse entered the smelter yard. The bellows stopped as everyone turned towards the newcomer. A young man, almost a boy sat astride the animal, dressed in the Count's livery. His tunic bore a white cross quartering a blue field, the color of Alberensa. He dismounted as Walter approached.

"I seek Guilhelms Faure"! the herald bellowed into the ironworks, ignoring Walter. The foreman simply pointed.

"Come here, Guilhelms Faure"!

Guilhelms looked around. Everyone else seemed just as confused. "He looks useless, Guilhelms," Bernart offered, "But he did come from the Count. Maybe you'd better go."

The smith nodded and walked over. The boy looked down his nose as he announced, "Your skill is well known in the castle, Guilhelms Faure."

The smith considered slugging the pimple-faced weakling in the face. Instead, he regarded the Alberensa blue livery, remembered his family and answered.

"I am honored to hear that, Herald."

"Our liege Hugh, Count of Alberensa, requires a special sword for Raymond VII, Count of Toulouse."

Of course. In Outremer, Jabil al-Hadid once served the descendants of Toulouse. In Languedoc, that union lives on in the marriage of the Count to Maura of Colomiers, Raymond's cousin.

"This sword will be a baptismal gift for the son of one of Raymond's vassals. It must be of the finest quality, smith, the finest."

Guilhelms leaned in gently, forcing the boy to lean back. "My work is always of the finest quality, Herald. Otherwise we would not be speaking."

Pimple-faced arrogance responded in a voice dripping with disdain. "What shall I tell my lord the Count, Guilhelms Faure"?

Guilhelms bowed, "I will begin work immediately. It will take perhaps a week."

Without a word, the boy walked off, mounted his horse and rode away. Guilhelms turned towards Walter. He shrugged his shoulders.

A gift for Raymond to give a vassal, of course. With Pope Honorius continuing Innocent's attacks on the House of Toulouse, Raymond needed the support of all his vassals. Especially now, since the Count was in Trencavel, besieging the French crusaders in Carcassonne. In times of strife and battle, a liege worked hard to keep his vassals friendly.

Guilhelms rejoined his men. Bernart and the others stood around, smirking. "Well, my lord"?

"I have to make a sword for the Count." He turned to the bellows men. "Pump it up. Let's see what we have here."

A minute, maybe two brought back the cherry-red glow of hot iron. Guilhelms lifted the mass from the hearth and set it on his anvil. Cavities pocked the shapeless bloom where the rock had melted out, oozing heat in all directions. The men at the bellows stopped pumping and walked over to watch. "Let's see," Guilhelms said. The smith took a large hammer and struck, looking, listening.

"What do you think"? Bernart asked. He picked at his tunic, pulling the scratchy wool from his skin for a moment. The bellows men waited for the answer, too. Guilhelms struck a few more blows.

"Close, I think, very close. We may need to cook it with some charcoal, but I think we got lucky this time. It's almost steel already, and it's enough to make a sword. Mark the rest of that wagon load of ore and set it aside." He put the iron back in the forge and turned to the laborers. "Make those coals glow! I only have a week"!

2

Father Esteve, the Catholic priest in Petrousset, accompanied Guihelms on a walk after Mass on Sunday. Unlike the aging Ricartz in Brassat, the aging Esteve remained thin, almost a stick. He reminded Guilhelms of Rothan and Francesca, the abstemious *Parfaits* of Brassat, partaking of only of water and wood.

The smith led the priest south from the village, past the idled smelter and forges to the edge of the forest. "This place, Father." Guilhelms pointed to a stone hearth set in the ground. "When we cut the trees here last week, we found the remnants of what must be a village. Was there one here, back before there was a County of Alberensa"?

Esteve looked down at the rocks, still darkened by the flames that once burned on them.. "It is hard to tell the difference between history and legend, Guilhelms. All the charters in the Cathedral refer to

'Alberencidum,' but that could simply be a monk giving a Latin name to Alberensa as the County arose."

"What do you think, Father"?

"Walk with me." The priest turned from the ancient hearth and started deeper into the forest, away from the river. His cassock swept over the fallen leaves as he passed. "The chapel at the Benedictine convent on the Tolosa Road is more ancient than the convent's other buildings. The figures in its mosaics wear the ancient Roman clothing, the toga."

"So Alberensa goes back to ancient times." Spring might be coming, but the air remained chilly as they walked among the trees. The branches overhead had barely begun to bud.

"Yes, but in those days, I suspect that it was just the final village at the edge of the rich farmland under the Pyrenees. The village boys drove their goats into the mountain valleys every summer while their fathers farmed the bottomland. The families passed the winters in their cottages, living on the summer's produce while snow clogged the passes to Iberia above them."

"When did that change"? Esteve was guiding them along a path, faint but present.

"In the Year of Our Lord 814, the year that the Holy Roman Emperor Charlemagne died, the hermit Pelagious made an amazing discovery at Compostela near the Atlantic Ocean, on the Iberian side of the mountains. He found the ancient tomb holding the remains of Saint James, brother of John, son of Zebedee, one of the first disciples to follow Jesus. Although James preached in Iberia after our Lord's death, he died in Palestine, beheaded by Herod Agrippa in 44 AD."

The priest stopped and turned towards the smith.

"Only a miracle could explain how the remains of a man beheaded in the Holy Land found their way into an Iberian tomb among his converts. The Way of St James, *El Camino de Santiago de Compostela*, soon became the third great Christian pilgrimage, after Rome and Holy Jerusalem itself."

Guilhelms could not decide from Esteve's expression if the priest believed the story he recounted or if he was merely recounting a story.

"And so Alberensa no longer found itself at the edge of the world."

"Pilgrims returning home described a gorge in the Alberensa River that started just south of a small village. It offered a wonderfully gentle climb into the mountains under the High Altar, over the Sárdalo Pass and down into Aragon."

"The Count's family became wealthy because they controlled that route"?

"Not at first. In 851, Charles the Bald, Charlemagne's grandson and King of the Western Franks, appointed Lothar, a local landowner, to administer Alberensa. Lothar promptly installed his second son Bedolf as the priest of the parish church. The power of the family grows from those two appointments made nearly four hundred years ago."

The trees separated, revealing a circle of large rough stones in a small clearing. A bowl filled with the rain-caked ashes of a huge fire lay in the center of the rugged chunks of rock. An smoke-stained altar made from two stone posts and a stone lintel straddled the bowl.

"Are you a Cathar heretic, Guilhelms, a Good Christian"?

"Is this a place where they meet, Father"?

The priest tapped the smith's chest. "Are you a Cathar"?

"No."

"I will ignore that obvious lie, smith, as I ignore that lie when others in my flock give it. I am not interested in burning anyone at the stake."

"Truly, Father Esteve, I'm sure there are no heretics in Petrousset."

The priest smiled, "We all have our secrets, Guilhelms."

"Are you a Good Christian, Father? You are certainly as thin as their *Parfaits*."

"No." He pointed towards the circle. "How long until you reach this place with your woodcutting"?

The smith turned around, looking back the way they came. They had walked for thirty minutes at least. "One year, maybe two."

Father Esteve frowned, seeking a better answer, reminding the smith that we all have our secrets.

"Actually, Father Esteve, this is so far back from the river that we will probably never get here. We'll keep cutting upstream along the riverbank, floating the logs down to the ironworks." He swept his hand over the clearing. "The Good Christians did not build this place."

"No. My ancestors did, in the ancient days before the Goths destroyed that village." The priest pointed south, where the flat-topped mountain could be seen in the distance, rising above the forest. "Each winter on the darkest night of the year, we light a bonfire here. We celebrate the moment when the Bright Shining God Belenus descends from the heavens to kindle a great conflagration on *Lo Grandautar.*"

3

A shout went up from the edge of the smelter clearing. More shouting, and then the sounds of hooves and harness as a mounted column came into view on the village road. Ten men in mail rode in front of a wagon with ten more behind. The lead rider carried the guerdon of the Count, a white cross quartering a blue field, with yellow castles at the lower left and upper right, for Alberensa in the south of the County and Juviler in the north. An Occitan cross filled the other two quadrants. "CML" embroidered the center of the cross.

CML, Guilehlms thought. This year is MCCXXIV. This family has ruled this place for a long time.

A visit by a mounted column carrying the banners of Alberensa and Jabil al-Hadid happened often enough at Petrousset. Women making the difficult journey in an open wagon added something different to today's visit. Centuries of neglect had left the paved roads of the ancient Romans in poor repair. Only a horse could easily negotiate the rutted dirt tracks cut in later times. A wagon lurched into every hole and climbed over every rock while the passengers struggled to keep from falling off.

Work stopped as the caravan drove in. The bright blue war blankets protecting the flanks of the animals contrasted sharply with the dirt and mud and slag and black charcoal ash underneath. Walter ran forward and held the bridle of the his liege's horse while he dismounted.

With a nod to his foreman, the Count walked back to the cart. It was a simple affair, with a driver's bench in front and a flat bed in the rear for freight. Four solid wheels turned on axles fastened to the bottom. Two mules waited patiently in the harness.

"Let me help you, my lady," the Count said to the woman sitting next to the driver. For the first time, Guilhelms saw Maura of Colomiers, Countess of Alberensa. She looked older than the Count, and all hips as she turned her back and felt down with her foot, seeking the little step under the bed. The Count reached up and helped her down with his hands around her ample waist. When she turned, Guilhelms saw her brown hair and eyes, a face not quite plain but not quite pretty either. She wore an expensive tunic made of light gray wool and a black cloak of heavier wool. As she stood, looking imperiously over the works, Guilhelms decided that she weighed as much as the Count himself.

A nun stood up from the cart's bed and removed a blanket from around a seated woman. A Christian from Outremer, Guilhelms guessed from the sister's darker skin and brown eyes. Certainly her habit, the cowl covering her head, was unlike any he had seen in Languedoc.

The blanket's removal revealed a chair on small wheels tied securely to the bed of the wagon, with its occupant tied securely to the chair. Two soldiers loosened the ropes keeping the conveyance in the bed. A quiet word and they lifted it to the ground. The nun climbed down and removed the silken ribbons holding her lady's arms to the arms of the chair. She left in place the ties around her waist, under her shoulders, around her legs. The whole process moved smoothly, quickly, with each actor performing a familiar role.

"I fix, lady," the nun said in French. Or at least it sounded like she said that through her thick accent. The Baroness of Juviler gazed quietly into the distance while the sister arranged her pale blue tunic, wool with vertical silk panels in the skirt and a girdle of tooled leather. Fixed her surcoat, her cloak, her cap. "Almost done, lady."

A knight still wearing his helmet stepped up beside the chair while the work went on, his dark eyes searching for threats. Guilhelms recognized the lean, firm body of a skilled warrior, like Henri of Épernay, like Sir Martin. This must be Sir Giles, the champion of the Baroness of Juviler, a handsome man, several years older than his Count. Even now, he stayed coiled, ready to strike anyone who threatened the woman he had sworn before God to defend with his own life.

The men at Petrousset had not lied when they said that the Count's sister was a quite attractive blonde. The troubadours had not lied when they said that she was blind and paralyzed. The songs of her injured beauty, so chastely tended by the handsome and chivalrous Giles, had spread from Alberensa through Lengadòc and across the Pyrenees into Iberia.

As the Count approached, Guilhelms realized that all work had stopped. Everyone was on their knees by their workstations. Guilhelms knelt down himself just as the Count reached him.

"Guilhelms. The Baroness of Juviler wished to go for a ride. She favors Petrousset. '*Plegar le Ferre*,' that is our family's motto."

"Yes my lord Count, " Guilhelms acknowledged to the packed dirt.

"It's my birthday, Guilhelms," said the Baroness in a very sweet voice, soft and low. "I'm twenty-one today. Father Aribert and Bishop Stephen both agree that when my birthday falls in Lent, I may relax the rigors of my Lenten vows for the day."

"Yes, my lady Baroness." He bowed from his knees towards her unseeing smile.

"Have you begun the work for the Count of Toulouse, Guilhelms"? the Count asked.

"A few days ago, we smelted a bloom that is very close to steel. I am now forging it."

"Show me." The Count in his fine blue hose and linen tunic and woolen cloak followed Guilhelms in his sweat-stained brown wool towards his hearth. Everyone else stayed down on their knees. After a moment, Maura decided to look, too, and followed. The workers bent over to touch their faces to the ground as she walked past. The soldiers followed her in, arranging themselves to protect Count and Countess.

"Get it hot, lads." Guilhelms pulled the roughly shaped broadsword from the glowing coals and took a couple of strokes. The metal rang slightly under the dull thump of the hammer.

"Do you hear that, Countess?" the Count asked. "Usually if the iron is right for steel, it will ring when struck, like that. This should make a nice blade for Lord Villebrumer's son." Sudden surprise crossed the Count's face. "Are you unwell, my lady"?

"The ride has left me ill, my lord. I trust you are right about the sword. I find this making of metal from rocks to be almost witchcraft." She frowned as she looked at the red-hot metal resting on Guilhelms's anvil.

"Not witchcraft, my lady," said the Count, "although we know little of why things happen as they do. Our Lord used things of smelted and beaten metal in His own life."

"Brother," Agnes called. "It's very quiet here. Why don't you acknowledge the men and let them get back to work?" Hugh and Maura started up and looked around. Even Guilhelms was bowing again, waiting for their conversation to end. A wave and the hammering sounds began.

The Baroness spoke and the nun began pushing the wheelchair towards the nobles around the forge, rocking from side to side over the rough ground. Guilhelms understood the silken ties now. Being blind, the Count's sister could not anticipate the movements and could easily be thrown from the chair.

"Sister Ekaterina," the Count said as they arrived. "Please help the Countess. Take her to the wagon. She feels sick."

The Sister bowed her head submissively. "Yes, my lord," again with a very thick accent on her French.

The nun let the heavy woman lean on her as they made their way to the cart. There was something gentle in the sway of the Sister's hips under her habit, Guilhelms thought, born down by the weight of the other. He caught himself. Like a *Parfait*, the Sister had dedicated herself to a life of chastity, of poverty, of virginity in the service of God. He was wrong to think of her as an object of lust.

"Guilhelms," the blind noblewoman said, "Walter says that you have an idea for an animal-driven drop hammer to forge the iron."

"Yes, my lady. The early work, drawing the bloom into a rough shape, a mechanical hammer of some kind will speed that up."

"And not require the skill of an experienced smith"?

"Correct, my lady, once some simple instruction is given."

"Walter," the Count said, "Guilhelms and you should try to make such a device."

"Yes my lord."

"You speak French well, Guilhelms," the Baroness said. "Where are you from?"

If Sir Arnald or Sir Alass or the Count had asked him such a thing, Guilhelms would make something up. They would be offended by the truth, that he left Brassat to save his family from noble threats and rapes and murders. Something about the wholesome face and complete vulnerability and gentle sound of the Baroness caused him to let down his guard. He already knew that the Count did not have the typical arrogance of the nobility, but his sister seemed positively tender.

"I'm from a village called Brassat. I'm a free man, but that village is in the fief of Sir Arnald, and his liege is the Baron of Fonta. Fonta's liege was Alberensa until the fief was declared forfeit for heresy while you were in Outremer. It was seized by a French knight from Épernay, two years ago."

Hugh studied Guilhelms for a long time before speaking. "A river flows from the mountains through Fonta, is that right?"

"Yes, my lord. We call it the Barièja. It leaves a gorge just above my village and starts across a plain."

"I'm told that deposits of iron ore lie high up in the Barièja Valley, still in Alberensa."

"They do, my lord Count."

Sister Ekaterina rejoined them, taking up her station behind the Baroness. "Is there a place to dam the stream and put a smelter alongside"?

Guilhelms found the questions strange, but even a free man answered any question posed by a nobleman. Think about the terrain. The Trysting Glade. "Yes, my lord, there's a good place above Brassat where that could be done."

The Count turned to his sister and spoke, yet Guilhelms understood nothing. It was not French, or Occitan, or Poitivin, or Catalan, or any other language the smith had ever heard. The Baroness answered straight away in the same confusing tongue. They went back and forth several times. Finally the Baroness spoke again in French.

"Guilhelms. Are you still there"?

"Yes, my lady," causing her head to turn to the sound of his voice.

"Walk beside me as Sister Ekaterina pushes me to the wagon."

"I will push you myself, my lady." He stepped up to take the handles from the nun.

"Mercés," in her thick accent. Guilhelms began the walk over the rutted ground.

"Bishop Stephen put a condition on breaking my Lenten vows of fasting and penitence, Guilhelms. I must invite someone from Petrousset to Easter at the castle. Your family will join us there a week from today, next Saturday morning. You will take part in the Great Vigil of Easter that night and the High Mass on Easter morning. You will be among our guests of honor for the Easter dinner."

"Yes my lady."

Guilhelms stepped back as the soldiers lifted the chair onto the wagon. Sister Ekaterina bent over, helping the men tie it down.

The Count stepped up alongside the smith. "At dinner, we will discuss the place above Brassat, Guilhelms."

"Yes my lord Count."

The Count strode off while Guilhelms quickly bowed, while everyone bowed. The nun draped the blanket over the Baroness and sat down on the floor. Maura gripped the driver's bench. The Count mounted, Sir Giles mounted, the column mounted. The hostler snapped his whip over the mules and the wagon began to lurch down the road.

Bernart and Walter looked at Guilhelms. The smith shook his head, bemused. He thought about the sweet-voiced Baroness of Juviler and the polite Count of Alberensa. He thought about the aloof Sir Henri and the brutal Sir Charles. Were these Alberensas all that different from the Épernays? Whatever brother and sister had been saying to each other, they had set his family's plans without bothering to ask him.

Forgive me, Gervais, forgive me, Petrona, please forgive me. I must take your daughter to celebrate the heathen Feast of the Resurrection.

4

Holy Saturday dawned somber and gray after a night of storms. Last night the thunder made the ground shake, just as it shook on the first Good Friday, at the moment of the Savior's death. Today, on the day between His death and His Resurrection, all of God's Creation mourned the sacrifice of the Son of Man. Tears of rain dripped from the trees whenever the wind blew in the cloudy sky. A morning fog entombed the land as the Lord's body had been entombed by Joseph of Arimathea. The whole earth awaited the glorious moment when He would rise from the dead, to be commemorated that night in the Mass of the Great Vigil of Easter.

The Faures awaited the Count's column.

"Should we start walking, Guilhelms?" asked Aenor. She sat at the wooden table at the side of their cottage, cradling Isabèl in her arms, wearing her second tunic, the brown wool she saved for church.

Guilhelms tried to decide if she was older than the blind Baroness. Her smile was every bit as beautiful. No. Even more so.

"Walter told me they were sending men to get us, Aenor. That pimple-faced herald came back Wednesday to tell him." He wondered which of the Count's servants had dared to mention to their noble lord that it was a long walk to Alberensa.

Here in Petrousset, five people lived in a space five paces wide and five deep. Aenor cooked at the small hearth in center. The smoke from her fire escaped through the hole in the thatch above. They ate together at the table. They slept on the dirt floor, on beds of straw. They had left behind a much larger shop at Brassat, with its separate kitchen below and two-roomed loft above. They had also left behind the fief of Fonta where the Épernays came calling, seeking out the Marks of Satan. They traded size for safety. Aenor was content.

"Will they be metal men, Papa?" Tibaut asked from the floor where he was playing with Lisbetta. The five-year-old boy looked more like his father every day. His cousin played with her living doll as a child might, even as she looked more like a woman every day.

"Probably, Tibaut." He looked at his wife. "You're right. We should start down the road. If they do come, we'll meet them going the other way."

The sound of hoofbeats echoed into the house as they had at Brassat that terrible morning eighteen months ago. Aenor looked at the sword lying among their things on the table. "Her well-fed ladyship Maura of Colomiers, Countess of Alberensa, wants her cousin's sword, Sir Blacksmith of Brassat. Today, we ride."

■ ■ ■

The wagon crested a small hill in the village of Dactalanne, bringing the walls of Alberensa into view before the Pyrenees. Guilhelms sat on the bench with the driver while Aenor held Isabèl in her lap on the rain-damp floor. Beside her sat Tibaut and Lisbetta, all three with their backs to the bench, watching where they had been, not where they were going. Everyone tried to balance themselves as the cart lurched over the narrow muddy track. The driver leaned back.

"Easier in a minute, lady."

They bumped from the mud onto a smooth causeway, freshly paved and leveled with square stones, like the roads the Romans left behind. The teamster snapped the whip over the mules and the column picked up the pace.

"Why has the road become so smooth"? Guilhelms asked.

"Look down to your left, that small pool in the river."

Guilhelms found a spot where a sandy bar quieted the rush of the Alberensa. Trees beginning to show green hung over a rocky ledge above the flow. "I see it."

"Our liege and his sister found this place soon after they arrived," said the driver. "He ordered that the road be improved to make the ride easier for the Baroness. The men of Dactalanne worked all last summer until they satisfied the Count."

Guilhelms and Aenor exchanged a glance. Every day, those serfs had farmed their own fields. They had done their share farming the fields of the lord of Dactalanne. Then they came here and cut stone and laid it in the mud under the supervision of the Count's overseer until the twilight gave way to night. A hundred men worked extra time all summer so that one woman would not need to be tied up when she fancied a ride in the country.

If any of the serfs had a daughter like Agnes, she would lay all day on a straw bed and wait to be fed. No one would have time for anything more.

The solid wheels rolling over the smooth stones set the wagon to vibrating, massaging its occupants. "If we went the other way from Petrousset, driver, what would we find"?

"This is the main road from Tolosa south to the Pyrenees and through the Sardálo Pass to Aragon." Tolosa, *Toulouse* in the French. "It follows the Garona River, the *Garonne*, south from Tolosa to the mouth of the Salat. It strikes up the Salat until that river meets the Alberensa. That's where it leaves the County of Tolosa and comes into our liege's lands. Four days by wagon from Tolosa to Arguenos on the Alberensa frontier, two more days to the city of Alberensa itself."

Guilhelms looked out upon the rich and rolling land that lined the river from Arguenos to the city.

"And then"?

"One more day to the top of the Pass and into Aragon."

"The Counts maintain that road"?

"They do, keeping it brushed, bridges over the streams, rocks and gravel in the low spots every Spring."

That Sunday at the stone circle, Father Esteve shared the legends of the Compostela Road. "From the beginning, Guilhelms, pilgrims paused in the village of Alberensa, resting before the climb. Every summer night, they filled a tiny sixth century Visigoth church that stood to the east of the path leading into the gorge. Those who could not fit inside camped in the fields behind, next to the river. The travelers left gifts to support the work of the church and to pay for the damage they had done to the land."

"And then Charles the Bald appointed Lothar."

"Yes. With his son Bedolf as the parish priest, they took the alms left by the pilgrims, tore down the worn and ancient wooden sanctuary and replaced it with brick. Alongside their new church they built a large dormitory, a place for the pilgrims to stop and rest."

Guilhelms considered the stone altar while Esteve spoke. No ancient priest, no druid could pray at that altar while the fire raged. In their worship of Belenus, the ancients rendered burnt offerings of animals, perhaps even humans on that post and lintel.

"Papa, the road is smooth now." Tibaut brought Guilhelms back from his remembering. "Why don't we have these stones in Petrousset?"

Papa looked at Mama. "Our life here is hard, Tibaut," she said, "but we will not need this pavement when we go to our reward in Heaven. That is what Jesus promised to us when He rose from the dead to rejoin His Father on the first Easter." She was being careful in the presence of strangers.

Father Esteve recounted how the descendants of Charles the Bald fought each other over his kingdom. "So much fighting, so much chaos at the top, Guilhelms," said the priest of Jesus and Belenus, "It gave the local lords space to increase their power and independence. Their rights became hereditary. That is what happened here in Alberensa."

Through force and guile, Lothar's grandson Roland compelled all the other landholders between the Sárdalo Pass and the Salat to swear fealty to his house. He donated the alms of the pilgrims to the Holy Father in Rome. Pope Formosus responded by consecrating Roland's grandson Berenguer as Alberensa's first Bishop. Alberensa became a formidable estate, although not as large as Tolosa, with Roland recognized as its first Count and his grandson Oddo recognized as his heir.

Lisbetta slid her tunic up on her legs, rubbing her calves. Aenor shoved it down without a word. Her glare turned to the soldiers riding behind, and they averted their gaze. "Never do that, child, never. They will think you want what Andreva fought. That is only for your husband, only."

"What is only for my husband, Aunt Aenor? What you and Guilhelms do late at night? Is that the thing that makes babies grow in women?"

"Our Lord God makes babies, Lisbetta, but yes that is part of it. A proper woman does not show herself like that, does not tempt men to sin."

"Did Andreva tempt those men to sin, Aunt? Or was that evil the work of Satan"?

The driver looked around at the young woman and back at Guilhelms. He seemed to agree, but Guilhelms thought it too dangerous to assume he was a *Credente*. He said nothing.

"With Roland," Esteve had continued, "the House of Alberensa truly begins. After him many names, but Angibert, the grandson of Count Oddo, the man who married Ermessenda of Juviler in the year 950, he stands out. 'The Builder,' they call him."

The Builder took the gold of Juviler and the alms of the pilgrims and built a high stone bridge to connect the two halves of his city. He tore down Lothar's pilgrimage church and replaced it with the Cathedral Church of Our Lady of the Pyrenees. He removed Roland's cramped castle and put up a new one five times as large, demolishing an entire district of the town to make room for the works. He constructed a new city wall, enclosing city, castle and the suburbs on both sides of the river.

"It's larger than I remember, Aenor," Guilhelms said as the column approached The Builder's wall. Church spires speared the sky behind the ramparts, their stone standing out against the stone of the Pyrenees.

"I'm surprised you remember at all, Guilhelms, since we passed around it at night, on the other side of the river."

The pimply herald raised his hand, stopping the column. He called up to the gate tower. "Open, on the command of the Count"!

The handsome soldier Ferrandos rode up and cuffed him on the head with his armored gauntlet. "Be still, you fool. The gate is already open. It is a day for quiet thought, not for noise and boasting."

The young soldier's height and his craggy features, his blond hair and blue eyes made him quite attractive to the women. At least Lisbetta must think so, Guilhelms believed, based on her flirting this morning. Both the Catholics and the Good Christians blamed women for tempting men, but today a man was tempting women simply by being alive.

The column entered the city through a double gate tower. Their horseshoes echoed from two-story wood and stone buildings as they passed along the narrow street. Merchants came out from their shops to bow towards the Count's flag, just as the serfs had done in the countryside.

Their route soon took them through a square with five tiny streets entering at different angles. "This quarter is Saint Luke's," said their driver.

Aenor pointed to the church that stood at the end of the square. "Is that the Cathedral?"

"No, lady, that is St. Luke's. The cathedral is coming up on the left. You'll see the tower again in a moment."

Our Lady of the Pyrenees lacked the ornate touches of cathedrals built a century later, and certainly it lacked the elaborate statuary, the flying buttresses, the peaked windows of the French Style now being built in the north. Angibert constructed a large but simple Roman basilica, a rectangle with an apse behind the altar and a gable roof. He used red brick, as did many of the churches in Lengadòc, including St. Sernin's in Raymond's Tolosa.

Only one alteration had been made to Our Lady since the tenth century. Count Hugh's great-grandfather Angibert II, known as the "Glassmaker," rebuilt his namesake's straight nave into a cruciform, creating a transept on each side below the high altar. There he arranged for the bishop to install two astonishingly beautiful and inspired stained glass windows on each side, works created by a craftsman known as the Master of Alberensa, works that rivaled the luminescence in the new cathedral in Paris.

"If you have the chance, Guilhelms," Esteve said, "Visit Our Lady and see the Master's work. I'm sure nothing quite so magnificent has ever been done anywhere else, even in Rome."

As recounted by the Father, the lower panel of the north transept depicted the beheading of St James by Herod Agrippa, with Satan guiding Herod's hand as he wielded the executioner's sword. The upper panel recalled the miraculous transportation of the Saint's remains to Iberia. Angels laid him gently in his grave while sheep and lambs looked on.

In the lower panel of the south transept, Saint James welcomed his brother Saint John into Paradise after the Evangelist's long life drew to a close. In the panel above the Sons of Zebedee, the Risen Christ and His mother Mary the Virgin, the Queen of Heaven, looked with warmth upon the happy reunion. Behind them, the cherubim and seraphim and prophets and martyrs bowed down on the glassy sea before the splendid golden throne of God.

"Who was the Master of Alberensa, Father Esteve"?

"A man called Garnier of Normandy. The Count brought him down from the north, from Paris. He returned there when the work was done."

The leading soldiers reached the front of the cathedral. They turned west, from the Highway of Santiago de Compostela onto the Avenue of Our Lady. The Count's castle came into view, five hundred paces along the market street. Sitting backwards, Aenor and the children had an excellent view of the cathedral's tall square tower of patterned brick alongside the entrance doorway. The description of this prominent landmark at the entrance to the Sárdalo Pass had spread throughout Christendom.

The castle guard opened the gate once the herald answered the challenge properly. Their party rode through another double gate into the large forecourt. They found the Lebanese nun Sister Ekaterina waiting for them along with many servants. She held a green cap and with white silk ties in her hand and a green silk tunic and white surcoat draped over her arm.

Ferrandos waved his hand and a man in the Count's blue livery took the family's belongings from the bed of the wagon. A governess stepped forward and pried Isabèl from Aenor's arms. Another liveried servant took Tibaut's hand. Ferrandos offered his arm to Lisbetta. She did not decline.

Ekaterina motioned another woman forward and pointed at Aenor. "Give bath. Hair. Perfume." That thick accent on her French again, almost impenetrable even with the single words, but the maid understood. Sister Ekaterina turned to Aenor and held out the dress with a smile. "Baroness send. You wear. Look nice."

5

The Count presided over his Easter dinner in the Great Hall, the most festive event of the year. He sat on the dais at the center of the head table, wearing a linen tunic in the deep blue color of Alberensa. Before him, his guests took food from the common bowls on the trestle tables and put it on trenchers of bread. They dined on eel from the Alberensa fish ponds, and pork, and even some beef. Cooked vegetables from the store that survived the winter filled other bowls. White bread, fine and expensive, piled in mounds on every table. At the end of the feast the cooks would send out a marvel, something sweet and surprising and filled with honey.

"Yes, my lord, the ore comes from the valley of the Barièja above Brassat," Guilhelms said from his place at the far end of the head table. "Gervais brought it across the ridge to the Ariège, the river that flows down to Farga. Except for a few places, a cart can pass down that way. My cousin cut the bank to make room for the wagon."

The name "Great Hall" fit well for the large space in which they ate, yet it was only one of two large rooms on the ground floor of the Alberensa Keep. In the middle of the last century, Angibert the Glassmaker enlarged upon the work done by Angibert the Builder two centuries before. He extended the Keep into the castle yard and made room for both this Great Hall and a formal reception chamber. Tapestries woven for many Counts hung from its walls while candles added to the faint sunlight coming through the slit windows. Straw covered the stone floors as in Outremer, steadily filling with scraps as the meal progressed.

"And this place in Fonta, Guilhelms, this 'Trysting Glade,' how about that"?

"Even easier, my lord. They are in the same valley and so it is merely a matter of bringing it downstream."

Bishop Stephen leaned forward from his place among those to the right of the Count. Hugh liked Stephen, a reasonable cleric who served his people well. He had a certain softness under his cassock, like many clergymen, but his dark eyes still sparkled under his gray hair.

"Is there a road down the Barièja, Guilhelms"? the Bishop asked.

Stephen did indeed understand the problem of Alberensa, a summer rush of pilgrims followed by a penurious winter. Petrousset produced another source of income for the County, payment for iron in golden coin instead of goods. Gold that could be traded for things Alberensa needed from far away, from Tolosa, from Aragon, even from the Saracens in Iberia.

The smith frowned, then smiled. "No, but that is no impediment. The quarry is not that far up the river from the Trysting Glade, two thousand paces, three at most. Put winches in place, load the ore on boats, let them down and winch them back."

The Count blinked. A clever idea.

"With your leave, Guilhelms Faure," the Countess said, cutting Hugh off before he could pose another question.

"Of course, my lady." Guilhelms dropped his eyes to his trencher and resumed eating. Maura leaned over to her husband.

"This witchcraft should wait, my lord Count," she whispered from her place of honor to Hugh's left. "It is long past the moment when you should greet and recognize your Consuls." She wore a tunic of blue silk, the color of purity, of the Holy Mother of God, of Alberensa. "In Tolosa my cousin does that immediately after the cleric blesses the meal."

"Yes my lady, you are right." He lifted and kissed her hand. "I trust that you will always help me do things properly."

"It is my honor, my lord." Yesterday morning, when her monthly flow appeared after nearly three months, Maura had cried and sobbed. The pain of that disappointment still lingered, but she remained the gracious Countess of Alberensa, presiding over her Easter dinner, assuring that all went as it should.

Hugh rose to his feet. Conversations stopped. Eyes turned his way.

"My lord the Bishop of Alberensa, Father Aribert, my lords and ladies, distinguished guests. When my ancestor Count Angibert II ruled this city, he recognized that a place so prosperous would prove easier to govern if he sought guidance from among the people. Like the Count of Tolosa, Angibert enlisted five townsmen to form a council of advisors. Like Tolosa, he called them 'Consuls,' using the ancient Roman word. Together they made up his *Capitolum*."

The Count turned to the man on his right, placing his hand on his shoulder. "Beside me sits my First Consul, Garcias Lana, a leading merchant in the St. Matthew's Quarter wool district. Unlike me, First Consul Lana did not inherit his position." The Count lifted his pewter cup. "He holds that position because, despite long service, he remains quite vigorous and active, a man with a reputation as a shrewd trader and negotiator. Garcias Lana, I thank you for your service."

A cheer rose in the room. The old man stood and bowed to his liege.

"You are most gracious, my lord Count. It is an honor to serve you as it was an honor to serve your grandfather Count Roland III and your uncle Count Jacme."

Hugh knew from his mother that Lana's advice helped Jacme guide Alberensa away from Pope Innocent's campaign against the Good Christians. Hugh saw no reason to replace him. Many of the wool merchants of Lengadòc were rumored to be Cathars, but Hugh found no value in attempting to discover if Lana was among them.

The Count turned to his other side, to the man to the far side of the Countess. "My *Capitolum* has no formal Second Consul, but I think all agree that if Consul Lana were not here, we would all turn to Consul Anton Legros, a most prosperous baker in our St. Luke's Quarter." A lifetime of eating his fill of his own products had left the balding Legros quite heavy for a man his age. Hugh had quickly learned that Anton was clever with numbers, the kind of person who seemed to know instinctively if things were costing what they should. "We also thank you for your service, Consul Legros."

The Count motioned further down the table, to the place where the Baroness of Juvilier sat. Agnes, you are the brightest thing in this dark room today, wearing our mother's gift of the tunic with a red bodice and alternating black and red panels in the skirt. You do like looking nice in nice clothing, even if you can't see any of it.

"I also greet my sister Agnes and her companion, Sister Ekaterina from the Holy Land." The nun sat behind her lady in her plain dark habit and large wooden cross, cutting her charge's food and helping her eat. "Did you all know that the Baroness was born on Easter Sunday"?

"So we have all learned," replied Consul Anfos Lodet, owner of the largest souvenir shop on the Highway of Santiago de Compostela. "It was Easter again on her birthday in 1208, but not again until 1287, when she will be 84."

Agnes could be quite the flirt, laying her deep and seductive voice on the men, flattering them, gaining favors from them. The merchant widower was not yet forty, still of handsome mien, and quite willing to be flattered by anyone, even a blind and crippled woman who had no idea how handsome he was. Since Aggie needed someone to help her do everything, Hugh never complained how she found her helpers, even if it was by blatant coquetry.

"Does she think she shall have another Easter birthday, Consul Lodet"?

"No my lord, but we all pray that she does."

Cheers and applause rose in the room.

"Let me also introduce a newcomer among us, Father Felipe Vilalba." The intense young man to the right of Agnes wore the white cassock and black cape of the *Ordo Praedicatorum*, the Preaching Order founded a decade before by the Castilian Dominic de Guzmán. Felipe's skin matched de Guzmán's Iberian olive, but his blue eyes came from the Basque people just across the Pyrenees. "Father Felipe arrived during Holy Week."

Felipe rose to his feet, surprising the Count. "I am here," he began, unbidden, "To preach among you against the heresy of the Cathars." He turned to look down on Agnes. "You were born on Easter, my lady, the Feast of the Lord's Resurrection"?

"Yes. I always think of that as my real birthday even though last week...."

"A most marvelous coincidence, my lady. Do you believe in our Lord's Resurrection"?

Hugh remained upright, wondering if he should challenge this impudent friar with his impudent questions to your sister, a noblewoman, the Baroness of Juviler.

No. We are merchants with a title. Don't let honor get in the way of knowledge. Find out first what this Papal emissary is doing here.

"Of course I believe in the Lord's Resurrection, Father Felipe," Agnes continued. "The men and women who knew him witnessed it themselves. At the tomb, an angel told them that He was risen."

Felipe frowned. "Do you believe that the Lord who rose from the tomb died on the Cross"?

Agnes nodded, firmly. "God came among us, Father, through the womb of the Virgin Mary. He lived among us, truly human and truly God. This, too, is testified by those who knew Him."

Felipe frowned again. "You certainly know the answers, my lady, but do you truly embrace them? Blind and crippled, perhaps our Lord struck you down for the sin of being one of those awful Cathar heretics. Many of them seem to prosper in this County."

No one moved, no one spoke in the Great Hall. Clever Agnes seemed at a loss for words, her mouth opening and closing while she tried to process once again the insult that God hated her enough to take away her legs and her sight. Hugh motioned at Giles, resume your seat, take your hand from your sword.

"That is a terrible thing to say, Father Felipe," Hugh said. "Everyone here knows the Baroness of Juviler to be a most devout Christian. A sense of our Lord's own presence fills our chapel whenever she worships there."

Felipe dismissed the Lord's Own Presence with a wave. "It was my great good fortune to be welcomed into the Order of Preachers by Father Dominic himself, my lord Count. He was an inspiration to us all in our quest to rid Christendom of this awful Cathar heresy. There is too much tolerance of these Albigensians in Fois, in Tolosa, even here. That is why the Holy Father sent me, to rid Alberensa of this pestilence."

Maura's brown eyes flared. She rarely spoke in public, but Hugh knew from the look on her face, and Aggie's, that the priest had annoyed them both.

"Parainça, tolerance for the ways of others, has illuminated our culture for a long time, Father," the Countess said. "It is part of Lengadòc, like our troubadours, like our language. I am a faithful Catholic, but I do not feel threatened by the Good Christians."

Maura's words brought a certain shuffling to the trestle tables. Not all among them were faithful Catholics. The words of the Countess might reassure, but the Preaching Friar's scowl did not.

"Such sentiments worried Father Dominic, my lady. They worry the Holy Father. All heresy threatens Christ's One Holy Catholic and Apostolic Church. It is treason against God. This *parainça* is the work of Satan. It is abhorrent to the Lord."

A soft, low voice appeared on Felipe's left, firm, not seductive. "My mother the Countess Marguerite spoke favorably of *parainça* as well, Father Felipe. We are open to learning here, to knowledge and education among our women. We do not want that light taken from any of us."

Father Felipe turned his back on the unseeing Agnes, looked past Maura and spoke directly to Hugh as though the Countess was not even there.

"I have learned, my lord Count, that the Baroness of Juviler meets with a group of women in the nave of St. John's Church, where this supposed knowledge and education take place. They are commoners, all of them, wives of merchants, except the Baroness. They discuss the Lord's Word, the Holy Bible, which some of them can actually read. They discuss it untutored, unguided by any clergy, in fact unguided by any man at all."

Hugh motioned to Ekaterina. She placed a gentle hand on Agnes's shoulder, warning her not to reply.

"That is true, Father Felipe," Hugh said. "Sir Giles carries her there and Sister Ekaterina remains with her. The women insist that Sir Giles wait outside, even if it's raining." That image brought forth laughter, breaking the tension. "My sister has little to amuse her, Father Felipe, so the companionship of her friends at St. John's is most important to her."

The priest shook his head. "I am afraid it is not as easy as that, my lord. Some of those women are Cathars, heretics. Do you know of Etienne de Metz"?

"No."

"He is also a follower of Father Dominic. He advised Esclaramonde, the sister of the Count of Foix, that she keep to her spinning, the place of a woman."

"Keep to her..."! Ekaterina gripped the shoulder of the Baroness, silencing her.

"Yes, my lady," Felipe said. "Keep to your place as a woman. Or dedicate your life to Christ and enter a convent. There is little of value you can do here in your condition."

The eyes of *al-Zarqa'* blazed. Her nostrils flared. She almost forgot again that she couldn't stand up. "What of the value of the women who followed Jesus, Father Felipe? They were the first to find the empty tomb"!

"Stay, Baroness"! Hugh ordered. "You too, Sir Giles! Sit down"! Hugh turned to the Friar. "My sister does keep to her spinning, Father Felipe, the spinning of a noblewoman. She sits with our subjects and hears their needs. I find her to be most astute in conveying the concerns of Alberensa's women to my *Capitolum* and to me."

Hugh motioned towards Giles again, sit down. Finally the knight obeyed.

"As for a convent, I will never send Agnes to a convent if she does not wish to go, and she does not wish to go. Instead she remains among us with her afflictions, an inspiration to us all, as our troubadours so rightly sing."

Father Felipe looked towards Stephen for support, but found the Bishop busy cutting some meat from the common plate. Felipe's blue eyes, Hugh realized, could burn as brightly as his sister's.

"I must be allowed to preach to those women, my lord Count, to guide their study of God's Holy Word, to keep them from the path of this loathsome heresy."

Murmurs arose. Yes, now you know why he is here, my lord Count. The Holy Father has sent Felipe as a spy even as the war goes badly for his northern allies.

"As for your plans for the iron of Fonta. That fief was forfeit under the Third Canon. You have no claims there."

Hugh drew himself up. "I rule in Alberensa, Father Felipe, not His Holiness. The northern knights from Épernay falsely accused my vassal Sir Alass of heresy. Falsely, for Alass was a good Catholic. Fonta remains part of this County. I will restore it, and its iron ore, to my service. I will work with the Count of Foix for the return of the foundry at Farga de sant Matèu to Lisbetta Deslegador." The Count bowed gently towards the Preaching Friar. "I ask for the Holy Father's blessing on my quest."

Now Felipe stood dumbfounded, trying to comprehend why he should convey such a request. Bishop Stephen spoke into the silence.

"How could Lisbetta lose a forge? She is but a child."

Tibaut had been squirming for an hour alongside his mother. His stiff linen tunic rubbed and chaffed. He wanted to take it off, but he could not. Stupid Lisbetta kept talking to that boy, flouncing around in her yellow dress instead of playing with him. The tunic gleamed as she twisted and turned, the first time he had ever seen fabric do that. Now, at last, a question that he understood.

"The metal men killed everyone," he announced with assurance in his little boy's voice. "They stabbed them." The boy made stabbing motions with his hand.

"Metal men," said Father Felipe. "You mean soldiers, boy, knights"? Tibaut had not expected the Black Cape to speak. He buried his face in his mother's lap.

"Yes, Father," Guilhelms answered for him. "The same men who scized the fief of Fonta. The same men who threatened us in our shop in Brassat. The Épernays, Baron Henri and his son Charles."

The priest looked at Tibaut, his face still buried in Aneor's lap. "Why did the knights kill them, boy?"

His voice was firm, not threatening, but not the tone to comfort a child, either.

"Because we are Good Christians, priest"! Lisbetta stood up from her place beside Tibaut. "They murdered my mother and my father and my sister because we are Good Christians"! She stood trembling, her blue eyes kindled into fury by the memory of the murders. The beauty to come was apparent now, if she lived past this night so that it could blossom.

The black-robed priest looked at Hugh, the Bishop, and finally at Guilhelms. "There was no murder there. Their lives were forfeit if they were offered salvation and did not repent."

"My sister was offered something other than salvation, priest! By Sir Charles and two other men! Then Charles murdered her"!

Father Felipe looked at Hugh, at Stephen, waiting for them to do something about the heretic in their midst. They looked back, waiting themselves. Waiting with Agnes and Maura. Finally the Father spoke.

"This saucy wench with her harlot ways is a heretic, my lord Count. Her eternal soul is threatened by Hell. I must guide her away from this heresy and into the true faith." Lisbetta glared at Felipe and he glared at her. "Father Dominic established the convent of Saint Mary Magdalene at Prouille, near Fanjeaux. Once this heretic is reconciled to our Holy Mother the Church, you will send her there. She will dedicate her life to God in thanksgiving for the saving of her soul."

Lisbetta laughed. Aenor reached up and slapped her across the face. The stunned girl looked towards her new boyfriend but he averted his eyes. The tunic that was too big for a child not fully a woman disappeared out the door. Tibaut, frightened, ran after her. Silence followed, a stillness like that before a summer thunderstorm unleashes its fury on the earth.

"My cousin's daughter is spirited, Father Felipe," Guilhelms said. "For that I apologize to you. I beg forgiveness in her name. She watched the Épernays kill her parents when she was but a young girl."

"We have discussed that. What of repentance and the convent?"

"Not in our family, Father Felipe. It is a very ancient rule. No one can be forced into a convent against their will. No one."

6

Hugh honored Father Felipe's request to meet in the castle's tenth-century chapel. The Count entered a place like all chapels from that long-distant time, so simple that it might have served as a fourth-century church in Alberencidum. For nearly three centuries, every baptism, every wedding, every funeral of Alberensa's ruling family had taken place in this space.

The Count found Father Felipe praying devoutly before the golden cross on the stone altar. The Black Friars, the people called the Preachers, after the black cape that marked their Order. Its priests traveled from place to place, living as mendicants on alms, preaching God's Word, combating heresy. The Order's rapid growth continued even after Dominic de Guzmán's death in 1221, with new foundations all across Europe.

Felipe finished his prayers before he stood up and turned to face Hugh. "Good morning, my lord Count." The priest did not bother to bow as he stood before the altar. "Duty compels me to thank you for your generosity. I have not passed a week in such pleasant surroundings since I joined the *Ordo Praedicatorum* ten years ago."

"It is an honor to have an emissary of the Holy Father among us, Father Felipe."

The priest nodded, accepting the tribute that was is due. He pointed towards a window. "This glass, it is unique in the old family chapels I have visited, my lord. Most have the typical slits high up on the walls. How did this happen"?

"True windows, those our family chronicles credit to Ermessenda of Juviler, the bride of my ancestor Angibert who built this castle. "Let there be one place in this giant pile of rock," she said, "where light can stream in."

"But she did not install the glass."

"No, Father. That began when Pope Urban issued his call for a sacred pilgrimage at Clermont in 1095. The count at the time, Roland II, installed the first of the six windows in Ermessenda's large openings." Hugh pointed to their left, to the window nearest the door. "That one, the Return of the Prodigal Son from the Gospel of Luke." An older man stood beside a younger, both dressed in fine tunic and hose. A second young man knelt before them, dressed in a peasant's short garb.

Felipe read the inscription at the bottom of the glass. *"Perierat, et inventus est.'"* The priest crossed himself. "He was lost, and is found."

"Yes." Hugh pointed towards the altar. "Roland also replaced Angibert's silver altar cross with that cross of gold on a golden reliquary." The ornate box held the crown of thorns from an early Christian martyr, persecuted by the Romans while Lengadòc was still *Gallia Narbonensis.* "He purchased it from Raymond IV of Toulouse in 1096 as a donation to Raymond's quest to take up the cross, answering Pope Urban's call at Clermont the year before."

"Roland himself did not answer the Holy Father's call"?

"No."

"Do your chronicles relate why he failed the cause of Christ"?

This priest does grow tiresome. No apologies for ruining Easter dinner. Now this insult towards a man long dead. "The Count's second son Lucratz joined Raymond on Urban's pilgrimage to Jerusalem, Father."

Felipe moved to the chapel's most beautiful window, one so perfectly crafted in shape and color that it stood out against the others in the way that fine silk stands out against coarse wool. "And this one? The woman looks Hebrew." He leaned forward and read the inscription.

"*Et consolatus est David Bethsabee uxorem suam.*" Felipe frowned. "'Then David comforted his wife, Bathsheba.' From Second Samuel. David and Bathsheba displeased the Lord, so He took their firstborn."

The King of Israel knelt at the foot of an exquisitely beautiful Hebrew woman, with the dark eyes and dark hair and high cheekbones of the Semitic people of Outremer. David's head lay in her lap, kissing her hands, while a look of great sorrow crossed her lovely features.

"Theirs was a great love birthed in sin, Father Felipe, with the death of Uriah the Hittite, yet the Lord rewarded David and Bathsheba with a second son."

"King Solomon." Felipe pointed to a small black symbol, the letter L turned upside down and backwards, with a small vertical stroke at the bottom of the left side. "What is this"?

"The mark of the Norman craftsman Garnier, the man we call the 'Master of Alberensa.' My great-grandfather the second Angibert hired him away from the work on Notre Dame de Paris to create this glass."

"The Count they call the 'Glassmaker.' The one who executed the windows in the Cathedral of Our Lady."

"Exactly."

Felipe turned and moved across the chapel to the far side. "This one, my lord Count, *sed ut manifestentur opera Dei in illo*, 'that the works of God might be made manifest in him,' it is Jesus healing the blind man at the pool of Siloam."

"Yes. I filled the last available space with that glass."

"You have put your sister's face on the man, my lord, her pale skin, blonde hair, and vacant blue eyes."

"Yes." The Count swept around the chapel. "I suspect, Father Felipe, that all my ancestors have done the same. The Return of the Prodigal, that could be Roland with his sons Drogos and Lucratz."

"Do your chronicles recount the return of… of"?

"They say nothing of any return, but the *Gesta Francorum* recounts that, 'Then Lucratz of Alberensa and Jaufres of Lapeyrouse charged the Saracens. They fell side-by-side on the walls of Jerusalem.'"

"He embarked on the holy pilgrimage in penance, my lord Count, is that your meaning"?

"Yes. He died as a martyr for our Lord, lifted in a moment, in the twinkling of an eye from the walls of the Earthly Jerusalem into the Heavenly."

Felipe pointed to Agnes. "Are you not concerned, my lord, that you have defiled your family chapel with the face of a woman struck down for her sins"?

These insults to our family do indeed grow wearisome. "I beg of you, Father, as I begged of you after dinner yesterday. Cease these insulting remarks towards my sister. As the Evangelist said of the Pool of Siloam, God makes His redeeming Grace manifest in her life, a woman chaste and pure, suffering under her afflictions without complaint. Our Lord sent her to inspire us all."

Felipe turned his back on Alberensa's Inspiration. He swirled his cape, adjusting it around him as he sat down in a chair on the aisle. "That girl yesterday afternoon in the yellow silk. I must speak with her. She is a rude peasant, but she is a child of God. Her soul is in grave danger of eternal damnation."

Hugh sat down beside the Friar. "She has run away, Father. I don't know where she is."

Felipe glared at the Count. There was no respect for Hugh's station, for his rule over this part of Lengadòc. *The eternal battle between the Holy Father and the nobility, you are part of it now, Hugh.*

"You do know, my lord, but you refuse to say." The Preaching Friar stood again, taking on a preaching pose, body square, finger out to make his point. "You tolerate this heresy in Alberensa. The Sárdalo Pass Road to Compostela passes through here, a holy route, filled with pilgrims, but you allow it to be defiled by these heathens. The Holy Father has called upon all faithful Christians to take up the Cross against them, but you do not join in."

You did not lie about Lisbetta, Hugh. Agnes knows where she is, and Ekaterina, but you have not asked them.

"Father Felipe, Lucratz died on the walls of Jerusalem. Sir Julian of Blagnac took up the Cross for the same great pilgrimage. Raymond of Toulouse, first Count of Tripoli, granted Julian the fief of Jabil al-Hadid, a fief which my cousin and Marshal Frederic now guards for me. My grandfather Oliver died with his brothers at Hattin. This family has been most diligent in the pursuit of God's work."

Felipe dismissed six generations of crusading with a snort. "I'm sure your cousin in Outremer carries forth the battle against the Saracens, my lord. The Holy Father needs your help here, in Languedoc, to defeat these Cathars."

"The Saracens threaten God's work in the Holy Land, Father, far more than these Good Christians threaten His work here. What brings these men down from the north to fight in Lengadòc instead of battling for Jerusalem, where the Saracens still possess the Holy Sepulcher of our Lord"?

Another preaching finger, making a point. "I answered that question at dinner, my lord Count. Heresy here threatens Christ's Holy Church as much as the Saracens in Outremer. That is why the Lateran Canon 'On Heresy' grants the same indulgences to those who campaign against the Cathars as he does to those who go to the aid of the Holy Land."

"I acknowledge that, Father, but I do not understand it."

More rounding, posturing, pointing. "The Pope is Christ's Vicar on earth, my lord, before whom all earthly kings must bow! It is through the Holy Father that Christ's true purpose for us is revealed. Pope Honorius has declared that these Cathars are a threat to Christ's kingdom on earth, to the Holy Catholic Church, to the immortal souls of us all. You are required to obey."

The earthly kings bowing and obeying, yes, the battle does continue. This priest truly believes that the Holy Father rules Alberensa, not me, and that he is the Holy Father's legate in that rule.

"This heresy places their souls in mortal danger, my lord. While they live on earth, they can enjoy the beauty of God's own Creation. After they die, they will be cast into the pit of Hell, to suffer in agony forever and forever. You must help me find this woman and save her. Find where she has gone so I can preach to them all. I will bring them the True Light of Christ while there is still time for them to repent and achieve salvation. It is my calling. It is why God placed me on this earth."

Look upon Felipe, Hugh, and marvel. He is no ordinary priest like Aribert, dutifully serving his flock. The fervor of the Apostles themselves, of Andrew and Peter and James and John and Paul, fills his soul. He is a passionate Christian, a man without doubts, a man dedicated to spreading Christ's Saving Word. In him you see the kind of man upon whom God built His Holy Church.

You can only hope that Saint James of Compostela had more compassion than this Preaching Friar. That instead of insults, James would put his arm around Agnes and comfort her with the assurance of her Savior's eternal love.

"I'm not sure how I would find Lisbetta, Father. Our Good Christians do not harm us, so we do not harm them. I will get little co-operation in finding the girl, even from among the Catholics."

"This tolerance, this *parainça* of yours, it threatens the souls of all in Alberensa." Felipe drew a parchment out from under his cloak and handed it across. In Latin, with a red wax seal at the bottom that certainly looked like it had been impressed by the Papal ring.

Hugh read the document. "Bishop Stephen is retiring to the Benedictine monastery in St. Girons, immediately. Jerome, a Bishop from the Roman Curia is being sent to take his place."

"Yes, and Father Aribert is moving to the north, to Orléans."

"Aribert speaks little French, Father Felipe."

"Perhaps that is why he was unable to urge you to be more vigorous in your pursuit of these heretics." Felipe stepped up to the altar and turned as though he was celebrating the Mass. "The Holy Father asks that you indulge me with your generosity for a year. I need a place from which to preach, and to supervise the new Bishop and your new priest. I hope that His Holiness can count upon your support."

"A year seems rather more than is needed, Father."

The Friar glowered. "Never forget, my lord Count! The Third Canon not only declares that the holdings of heretics are forfeit. It decrees that a nobleman who does not rid his lands of heresy may be excommunicated. Excommunicated, and after a year, deprived of his lands so that they may be made available for faithful Catholics. Help me so that you are not excommunicated! Join our Crusade and protect your lands from the King of France"!

7

Hugh stood with Giles on the road between Brassat and Fonta. Hugh's barons and their men surrounded Fonta Castle, besieging it. Its defenders remained inside, not sallying forth to break the encirclement, but rather waiting for help from their liege Henri of Épernay, encamped to the east beyond Foix, in the Trencavel lands near Limoux.

"This village of Fonta without its castle, Sir Giles, it is how Alberensa appeared before the commerce of the Sárdalo Pass Road grew it into a great city." The two men looked down on the cottages of the serfs lining the junction where the road to Brassat joined the Foix Road to Alberensa, where the Barièja joined the Arget. From the top of a small knob near the river junction, the dark gray stone of Fonta Castle loomed over the fields while the Bear's Tooth across the Arget loomed over the castle.

"In 895, my ancestor Roland convinced the lords of three fiefs in the Barièja Valley that he was their liege. He sent a favored vassal to build that castle and secure Alberensa's border against Foix." Hugh pointed towards the castle's round tower. "The Keep fills half the space inside. A man can walk around the walls outside in ten minutes, even though the ground is rough."

Giles surveyed the terrain. You found yourself a true knight, Aggie, dedicated, determined, committed to the cause of his lady and her liege. Just as men like Felipe built God's Holy Church on earth, men like Giles built the County of Alberensa. You inherited something you might never create yourself, Hugh. Like your ancestors before you, you must give thanks to the Living God for men like Sir Giles.

"Your sister, so clever, Hugh." Yes, Mother, you are right. I saw a sergeant. Aggie saw a warrior. She knighted him while Gautier of Moustalon and I held her up, letting Giles guide the sword to his shoulders himself.

"A week now, Sir Giles. The northern Crusaders remain where Raymond VII of Toulouse has driven them, into the region south of Carcassonne. Will you carry an offer to Fonta Castle under flag of truce"?

"Of course, my lord."

■ ■ ■

Guilhelms approached the Count and Sir Giles as they stood in the road by his old shop. We've been here a week, the smith thought. Henri of Épernay's banner flutters above the Fonta tower. The banner of Alberensa flutters over Hugh's tent. Sometimes I see movement on the battlements, but the Count's men are staying beyond arrow range. I wonder how long this goes on?

"Ah," Giles said. "Here's Guilhelms, my lord. I'll take him as my flagbearer."

"He is not a soldier, Sir Giles."

"We won't be fighting, my lord. If we get close enough, he may be able to see if there have been any changes to the works." Guilhelms felt the power of the imposing soldier before him. Broad shoulders from years of training. Brown eyes that calmly surveyed every scene, no matter the threat. For Giles, no battle was ever beyond hope. As long as he was alive, there was always something to do.

"Can you ride, Guilhelms"?

"No."

"Time to learn."

■ ■ ■

Guilhelms soon found that riding wasn't so difficult if your horse was old. A waiting soldier handed up the white flag. The smith let his animal follow Giles up to the castle. They rode close to the wall, within range of the archers on the gate tower. "I see nothing different, Sir Giles." He did not add that the serfs tried to stay as far from the place as they could, even when Baron Alass was Sir Arnald's liege.

"We'll dismount. You hold the reins of both horses."

Guilhelms looked up at a four crossbows aimed directly at him from the tower. He felt naked, armored only in his brown woolen tunic. At this range, even the mail on Giles would not afford much protection from a well-placed bolt.

"Steady, Guilhelms. You're doing fine. Hold the flag. Survey the works. Count the people looking out. Remember everything."

The small sally port opened in the main gate. A man carrying a white flag stepped out, followed by Sir Martin, Henri of Épernay's close friend, the man who helped him with his wound at Farga. Both defenders wore armor. Martin worked hard to conceal his limp as they approached.

A moment of quiet followed as the two knights faced each other. Both men, young Giles and older Martin, carried an aura of dignity, of pride in their station. Menace, too, the very present threat of the coming battle, and death. Martin's eyes recognized Guilhelms and grew angry, but he did stoop to acknowledge a peasant.

"I am Sir Giles, sent by my liege, Hugh, Count of Alberensa. My lord the Count has an offer for you."

"I am Sir Martin, enfeoffed in this place by my liege, Henri, Baron of Épernay. Wrongly besieged by your stripling from Outremer. Disperse and go home." He waited, arms crossed.

Giles kept a calm, cold look. "Sir Alass was not a heretic. Henri's claim was false, made to seize these lands wrongly."

"Alass confessed before being burned at the stake. I was there, and I heard his confession. He died with his family, all of them reconciled with our Savior."

Giles motioned to the host behind him. "Your position is hopeless, Sir Martin. You have no well, no water. The Count offers this: Surrender and abandon Fonta, and you are free to ride out. He demands no ransom, no compensation."

Martin turned his own cold look to Guilhelms.

"My lord of Épernay lost his arm from your cowardly attack, peasant." Hold steady, Guilhelms. Do not flinch. Do not step back. Meet his noble fury with your own. "He granted me this fief. I will not yield it up to a blacksmith."

The knight turned his attention back to Giles.

"Your so-called Count? I take no instructions from a boy who knows only how to smelt iron and fuck fat women. The Holy Father has blessed our campaign against the heretics. The Lord will provide water for my cisterns."

Guilhelms felt the effort Giles was making to remain calm in the face of the insult. "There is no dishonor in our offer, my lord. You cannot hold this place against us without help from Foix. The stripling from Outremer has received Roger-Bernard's pledge that Sir Henri will not be allowed across his county. Raymond of Toulouse has promised help as well. You have too few men to hold your castle. We will let you ride out, without ransom and with your honor."

Martin scowled. "You, Giles, I do not yield to you, either. You are a peasant from Syria. Dubbed a knight by your Count's concubine, who is also his sister. Agnes the Harlot of Outremer, a witch struck blind and crippled for incest with her brother, for her many other sins. You are a pawn in the thrall of Satan."

Guilhelms could taste the violence. The Baroness depended upon Sir Giles, his strength, his loyalty, his devotion to her needs. The troubadours sang of his chivalry across the whole of Lengadòc. Martin wanted Giles to lose his temper, to break the truce so the archers on the gate tower could strike him down. Anger flowed both ways now. Even Martin's soldier showed surprise at the sudden hate.

"Guilhelms told me that you were a reasonable man, Sir Martin. He was wrong. Agnes of Jabil al-Hadid, the Baroness of Juviler, is a beautiful and gentle lady who suffers her trials with great nobility. I tolerate no insults to her honor. If we meet on the battlefield, I shall yield you no quarter."

Guilhelms grabbed his saddle pommel and held on tight as they rode quickly down the road. Sir Giles reached back, yanked the flag of truce from his hand and threw it in the mud.

8

The Baroness of Juviler and Sister Ekaterina sat on the roof of the Keep in the cool of a mid-May morning. From five floors above the ground, the streets of Alberensa and the pilgrims emerging from the Cathedral spread out as though being seen from a hilltop. "See like birds up here, my lady," Ekaterina said, and Agnes nodded. The Sárdalo Pass beside the snowtopped *Grandautar* notched the wall of the Pyrenees.

"Lisbetta is in our family, Sister Ekaterina. That is why we must try. My brother is busy regaining our fief. I will regain our cousin."

"Yes, my lady," Ekaterina said, wrapping Agnes in a blanket. "But how you know she is cousin"? The sister's French was improving, but it remained poor. Agnes spoke slowly.

"The Count and I are descended from Sir Julian of Blagnac through his son Peytre. Peytre's sister Esquiva, Julian's elder daughter, returned from Outremer and married the Count of Foix around 1120. Gervais

Deslegador and Guilhelms Faure are descended from the union of Esquiva and Roger of Foix."

"But, my lady, that was…one…hundred years…. ago. How you sure"?

The Baroness smiled. "That is not so hard, Ekaterina, really. Try."

The nun held her cross between her hands as her brow furrowed. "They work the metals."

"Good. Guilhelms's father told him the legend. A woman from Outremer convinced the Count of Foix to build Farga de sant Matèu. She brought the knowledge with her."

Ekaterina nodded, she understood. "They are free men, not serfs."

"Free because of a settlement made by the Count of Foix upon their grandfather, at a time when the business of the Farga foundry was separated from a noble title. Guilhelms's own father remembered that event, although he was only a young apprentice. One more thing."

Sister Ekaterina smiled, although of course her lady could not see. "Guilhelms tell Black-Cape Priest that Lisbetta not forced into convent. No member of his family can be forced into convent."

"That is our tradition, too, Ekaterina. Otherwise my Aunt Anne would be there now."

"Yes. Did you know tradition so old? Back to Julian and Monica of Blagnac"?

"No. Monica was noble, too, the daughter of the Lord of Ronzières." Her hand went to her mouth, thinking. "There is a convent nearby, in Montjoix."

"Maybe Monica not noble, just a sister who does not like convent."

Agnes grinned. "The story of Julian on the battlements of Hisn al-Akrad is not consistent with our family's military skills."

"Maybe they know the iron, my lady. Maybe that is why Raymond give them Jabil al-Hadid, name them *sheyks,* because they make the iron for everyone."

"*Plegar le Ferre,* Sister Ekaterina, *Plegar le Ferre,* that is certainly our family business."

"The Sword of Blagnac, maybe Julian does not get from his father. Maybe they *plegar* themselves, on the Orontes."

"Perhaps." Agnes sat up, her musing over, her bearing regal. "Perhaps my ancestors did improve upon the legends of our family, Sister Ekaterina. They served us well, those improvements, for we are certainly noble now."

"Yes my lady."

Agnes put her hand to her mouth, took it down. "We will find Lisbetta Deslegador and bring her here. She will remain under my personal protection. Once times are better, my brother will ensure that the Count of Foix restores the ironworks at Farga to her." She pounded her fist into her hand, softly. "He will ensure that her husband does not marry her for her money. My parents were very much in love. I want that for Lisbetta, too."

9

Two weeks passed. The Épernay Marshal still occupied Fonta. Three days of late Spring rain restored both the castle's cisterns and Martin's faith that God blessed his enterprise. Emboldened by the Lord's favor, he sent out a foraging party one dark night to restore his pantry.

Ferrandos spotted the men letting themselves down the wall at the rear of the castle, not far from the Arget. He let them form and move uphill towards the village of Cazac. Once they were out of range of the castle's defenses, he ordered his archers to unleash. Their ranks broken, the foragers scattered, only to be run down and slaughtered. Father Ricartz buried them all in the Brassat churchyard. Food in Fonta grew short, but the Épernay banner still flew over the battlements.

■ ■ ■

Hugh followed Guilhelms as he led his liege uphill past the fresh graves, up the gorge of the Barièjja into the Trysting Glade. Farther up the valley, Hugh's soldiers guarded the iron mine seized from Martin's men on the day the Count arrived. That same day, he sent word to Count Roger-Bernard of Foix that the works at Farga de sant Matèu belonged to Lisbetta Deslegador, not Henri of Épernay. Alberensa would make no deliveries of ore until the works were restored to their rightful owner.

"My idea is this, Guilhelms," said Hugh, standing in the Glade. "We can make the iron flow if there is too much carbon in it, but it's brittle when it hardens, unable to be worked. If we try to raise the temperature by pumping harder, the charcoal is burned up completely and the iron does not appear."

"Yes, my lord."

The Count placed his hand on the smith's shoulder. "Relax, Guilhelms, I'm appointing you to head my works at Brassat. There's no need to be afraid of me."

"It is not you, my lord. So many of your soldiers are here. Aren't you worried about traitors back in Alberensa? Her lady the Baroness of Juviler is alone."

"Were you in Petrousset when Sir Giles rode in with Godfrey of Sarlant, Guilhelms"?

"I was, my lord."

The Petrousset men had seen the soldiers heading north in February, just before the Catholic Ash Wednesday. The following afternoon, Sir Giles and four others rode into the Petrousset yard with Sir Godfrey tied over the saddle of his horse. The scent of his arrival reminded Guilhelms of a roast that had been left on the fire too long. The soldiers had seared his body with flaming torches and broken his arms and legs. Godfrey was passing in and out from the pain, but he woke up in a rush when one of the soldiers untied him and shoved him to the ground.

"Question him here," Giles said to his man. "He must know more, and he may not live to reach Alberensa."

"My family." Godfrey was almost beyond agony, yet he could still speak. "Have mercy on my family."

"Your holdings are forfeit for your felony, traitor. Still, in his kindness, our lord the Count has granted your wife's plea. She will take holy orders, with your daughters, in the convent at Fanjeaux. Two men are escorting them now. They will not take advantage." He nudged the broken lump of flesh with his boot. "Talk quickly now, Godfrey. Tell us what you know. Spare yourself further pain."

Guilhelms wondered how the troubadours would sing of Giles that afternoon.

"Guilhelms"?

"I remember the day, my lord."

"I've had no problems with traitors since then. I will have no problems here, either, once I have installed a loyal vassal in Fonta."

"Yes my lord."

The Count motioned towards the flowing Barièja. "I need your help with the iron, Guilhelms. We need a way to raise the temperature. My idea is a furnace piled high with wood. A powerful bellows blows through the fire, making it hot. That bellows blows the hot smoke from the fire into the smelter, adding to the heat of the charcoal mixed with the ore."

"You get the smelter air very hot before it reaches the smelter."

"Yes. Now the mass grows so hot that the bloom melts. If it melts, it can be cast as workable iron, iron that can be forged and tempered into steel."

"Iron that is easier to work than trying to create the Damascus steel, the Hinduwani."

"Exactly. Properly done, our flowing bloomery iron will be superior to the Hinduwani."

Guilhelms considered the concept. "Men and animals cannot pump the bellows hard enough. You'll use falling water to power a wheel and the wheel will turn a crank and crank the bellows. That will produce a powerful blast, my lord."

Hugh's face lit up. "An excellent name, Guilhelms, a blast furnace. We'll experiment here. If it works, we'll put a wheel in the Alberensa near Petrousset and build a larger blast furnace there." The Count's eyes glowed with enthusiasm.

"We can use a wheel to power the hammer forges too, my lord. It will never tire as an animal does."

"Exactly, Guilhelms, exactly"!

Sir Martin was right, Guilhelms. Hugh does care more about iron than fighting.

I hope that the part about the Count and his sister is a lie. For nobles, they are reasonable in their arrogance. And for some reason, the Count and his sister think we are all related. That's why Lady Juviler sent Sister Ekaterina dashing from the Easter dinner into the castle yard, spiriting Lisbetta away from the clutches of the Preaching Friar.

■ ■ ■

With a great struggle, Sister Ekaterina explained her problem to the stable hand. Finally he understood what she wanted. He agreed to help.

"The Baroness is not, uh, large above, Sister."

"Large"? He motioned. "Yes."

"Dress her as a boy. Veil her face like a leper. Put her on a mule."

"How stay"?

"Tie her on, Sister. Lead her up the Sárdalo Pass Road. If anyone speaks, do not answer. They will understand, a vow of silence."

The nun nodded, "Yes."

"Wait behind the shrine to Saint Mary of Egypt. Be patient."

It took a few times, but finally Ekaterina was certain that she understood.

10

Another week passed before Fonta. A week with no rain. A week with a second slaughtered foraging party. Without relief, this castle would soon fall without a battle. Someone from Limoux must try to break the siege, to fight through the lands so recently regained by the Counts of Toulouse and of Foix. If that happened, the battle would finally begin.

Guilhelms stood in in the Count's tent, looking at the blast furnace sketches, discussing the construction. A guard called in.

"Ferrandos is here, my lord."

"Send him in."

Guilhelms recognized the soldier who had guided them from Petrousset. His blue tunic with the arms of Alberensa covered his mail. His heavy leather belt held both a sword and a knife. In the siege he had proven himself a formidable warrior, engaging and destroying two armed parties sent out to seek food and water.

When the battle came, much would depend on how Ferrandos handled the yeomen, and himself.

"The lookouts on Guilhelms's outcrop above Farga have seen dust on the road from Lavelanet, my lord. Whoever is coming from Limoux will be here by tomorrow."

"They must have Count Roger's leave, so they will ride through Foix, not come over the hill. Send five men down from the outcrop into the woods along the Farga-Foix road. Get a count. Do not attack them. Observe and come back. Leave the lookouts on the outcrop to warn if a larger party approaches later."

"Yes my lord.

"Find Sir Giles and send him here."

■ ■ ■

Agnes summoned Hugh's seneschal. "Peter. Sister Ekaterina and I will be in retreat at the convent of the Sisters of Charity, in the St. Matthew quarter across the river. We must turn our thoughts to the words of Father Felipe, understand them, pray on them, embrace them."

"Yes my lady."

"We leave in the morning. I do not know how long we will remain cloistered. We are not to be disturbed in our devotions for any reason."

"Yes my lady." He paused. "If my lord the Count should…"

Agnes waved him silent. "I said, 'For any reason,' Peter! Is that clear? We are not to be disturbed for any reason"!

The man bowed deeply towards his unseeing liege, struck by the steel in her usually soft and gentle voice. "Very clear, my lady." This was not a request to be lifted onto the chamber pot. It was an order.

■ ■ ■

Ferrandos joined Giles and Guilhelms in the Count's tent. "The men are in place along the Foix-Fonta Road, my lord Count. So far, only the one column approaches from the distance."

"Thank you, Ferrandos."

Ferrandos bowed and made to leave.

"Wait," The Count turned to Giles. "Have we found Sir Arnald, the Brassat manor lord, Sir Giles?"

"No, my lord. The serfs believe he is in Foix."

Hugh pointed at Guilhelms. "The smith's sister-in-law Eva says that you have become fond of a woman of this village, Ferrandos. And she of you. What's her name again, Guilhelms?"

"Prisca Formatgièr, my lord." Guilhelms smiled at Ferrandos while the soldier blushed.

"Yes, Prisca. It appears that Sir Arnald is not available to discuss the disposition of the serf Prisca. Therefore, I have emancipated her. If you feel that she needs protection in the battle to come, you may send her to Alberensa to await you."

Ferrandos bolted out, without bowing, without stopping. Guilhelms watched as he took an unsaddled horse and rode up the road towards Brassat. Prisca stood, stunned but excited, as her handsome soldier rode the animal through the ripening winter wheat. He dismounted and spoke to her. Immediately she clung to him and kissed him. She did not mind that the horse was nibbling the crop, although her mother was moving quickly to pull the animal's head out of the grain.

11

Sister Ekaterina led the donkey, walking beside in her habit. The nun's beads hung around her waist and her large cross hung from her neck. Agnes sat in the animal's saddle, held in place by a hidden rope passing through loops that Ekaterina sewed on the inseam of her man's hose. The leper's veil across her face concealed her blindness and the gloves her soft white hands. Binding her chest left a man's tunic easily able to conceal her womanhood.

Agnes felt embarrassed by the Sister's success. It made her less than a woman, just as her blindness and paralysis left her less than a woman. She tried to remember what a boy looked like while he rode and to relax into the saddle like he would.

"Where are you from, lad," a pilgrim asked as they left the city gate, heading south on the Sárdalo Pass Road. Ekaterina put her finger to her mouth. Those with them on the way understood immediately. The sister and her young charge had taken an oath of silence in hopes of a miracle at Compostela. They were not bothered again.

The shrine to Saint Mary of Egypt, the patron saint of penitents, lay only six hours up the road to the Pass. Agnes spent the time getting into the rhythm of the *ase*, steadying herself with the pommel but trying to keep her balance without leaning against the restraints. Occasionally the hooves of the animal clomped across a wooden bridge or echoed against a low spot filled with gravel. The river murmured and the pilgrims murmured, never far away. When Ekaterina paused to rest, Agnes heard their fellow travelers give her food and water. The nun waited for a quiet moment and shared them. Refreshed, they forged on.

"Valley still wide, my lady, trail not steep. Think we are close." The donkey clunked across a long wooden bridge. "Yes. We are here. Shrine *Maria Aegyptiaca*."

Ekaterina led the animal towards a small square tower of red brick, open on one side. It shielded an Occitan cross of stone raised on a granite boulder. Pilgrims were leaving the road to pray before the shrine. Ekaterina knelt down to join them, holding the donkey's lead. Her voice in prayer joined the voices of many in the darkness surrounding the Baroness. Agnes folded her hands and bowed her head and prayed with them.

"Please, brothers," someone said, "what does the inscription say"? After a pause, a pilgrim monk answered.

"Entreat me not to leave you or to return from following you. Where you die I will die, and there will I be buried."

"What does that mean"? asked another voice.

"It is from the Hebrew Book of Ruth, the words of Ruth to her mother-in-law Naomi." After a silence, another traveler spoke.

"Look at the date on the shrine. The first of April in 1176. St. Mary of Egypt died on April first in a year when it fell on Holy Thursday."

"That means Easter was the fourth of April in the year she died," added another traveler. The date of Easter each year depended on the lunar calendar, Agnes knew, on the date of the first full moon after the first day of Spring.

"It is a good guess, brothers," said yet another voice, "That April first was also Holy Thursday in 1176. That is why the pilgrims erected a shrine to Mary of Egypt."

The first monk spoke again. "Certainly the passage from Ruth commemorates something that happened here on that Holy Thursday, the death of a mother or a daughter on the road to Compostela. It is a most peculiar inscription, but the emotion is sincere."

Agnes heard clothing shuffle as the monastic party moved on. New pilgrims took their places, and again more pilgrims. And then, while the sun was still warm on her face, the place went silent.

"We alone, my lady. I lead us behind shrine, into woods."

Ekaterina led the *ase* behind the shrine, away from the road, into the woods. Agnes could sense the humidity, even though she could not see. Hugh, Giles, Ekaterina, all of them had told her that the land was covered in green everywhere. Green in the fields where the serfs worked, green on the mountains from thousands and thousands of trees. Green from the European rain that fell all the time. She could feel the grass, hear the trees, and yet she was sure that her vision of the place still held too much bare ground.

One hundred paces, two hundred and Ekaterina stopped the donkey. "I'll untie you now and help you down, my lady. We're in a little glade, very fresh and green. The mountains are rugged and the trail is narrow, with many trees bearing in on us."

The sister had spoken in her own language, and Agnes answered in the same. "Help me change, please. They are expecting a Baroness, the sister of their Count."

"You are very brave, Agnes *al-Zarqa'*, very courageous. Your troubadours will sing of this night. May God the All-Compassionate, the All-Merciful, bless you in your work."

"*Inshallah*, Jamilla bint Hassan al-Haddad, *inshallah*."

■ ■ ■

The Cathar Credente who appeared soon after dark helped Ekaterina lift Agnes onto the donkey, side-saddle now that she was in a blue woolen tunic and surcoat. He blindfolded the Maronite nun and, as a precaution, Agnes.

"Put Sister Ekaterina on the donkey so she doesn't stumble around on the trail," Agnes said. "The animal can carry us both."

Leaves brushed the face of the Baroness from time to time. Her forehead cleared all the spider webs on the trail. The walk uphill became much steeper than the Sárdalo Pass Road, moving up the west side of the valley towards the ridge above.

Agnes had been hanging on for at least an hour when they stopped. Someone removed her blindfold, making no difference at all. Strong arms lifted her and placed her in a chair. She tried to wiggle around to make herself more comfortable.

"Please smooth the fabric under my legs, Sister. Where are we"?

"Small village, my lady. Maybe fifteen cottages. Hidden by trees. We sit in the center of street."

Agnes heard a man's voice, deep, firm. "Is this the Baroness of Juviler"?

"Yes," Lisbetta answered. "That's her, and her lady-in-waiting, Sister Ekaterina, the Maronite nun from the Lebanese Mountains."

"I am Bishop Thomas, my lady. Do you understand the reference"? The Cathars had a false gospel, Agnes knew, supposedly written by the Apostle Thomas. Doubting Thomas, who had not believed in Christ's Resurrection until he saw him in the flesh, marked with the nails from the Cross.

"Yes."

"Why are you here? You are a Crusader, and there is a crusade abroad. The Black Friar Felipe has established himself in your castle. Times have never been more dangerous for the Good Christians of Alberensa."

Agnes straightened her back and sat up, the Baroness of Juviler, sister of the Count of Alberensa. "Or more dangerous for the nobility of Lengadòc, Bishop Thomas. For Tolosa, for Fois, for my brother, the Count. The Papal threat is real and the threat of the King of France is real. We could simply burn you all and end those threats. We do not do that, Bishop, we do not do that because like our *parainça*, like the Occitan language, like the troubadours, you are part of the fabric of this land. When we protect you, we are protecting our way of life. We protect you even though you place your mortal souls in jeopardy with this heresy."

The Bishop took up a preacher's pose. "This has been our way to Christ in Lengadòc for a long time, my lady. In the past, we could live in our villages, unmolested. Now it is wise to hide from our neighbors. That is not fair, my lady. This dispute does not give the Holy Father the right to exterminate us. He cannot prove, no one on earth can prove, which of us is right. Remember what St Paul said, when he discussed fasting on the Sabbath. Some men did so, he said, and others did not. Both were acceptable to the Lord because, 'He who eats, eats in honor of the Lord, since he gives thanks to God; while he who abstains, abstains in honor of the Lord and gives thanks to God.'"

"In that same passage," Agnes replied, "St. Paul said, 'None of us lives to himself, and none of us dies to himself. If we live, we live to the Lord, and if we die, we die to the Lord; so whether we live or whether we die, we are the Lord's.'"

"When we die, Lady Juviler, we will know the Lord's judgment. It is not for a mere mortal, even the so-called 'Holy Father,' to take the God's place in making that judgment."

Rustling began in the woods around Agnes, a little noise in the distance, the sound of the community about its evening work.

"Bishop Thomas. I have come for Lisbetta, the daughter of Gervais and Petrona Deslegador. I wish to bring her to Alberensa under my protection."

The Bishop did not speak. For a moment no one spoke, until Lisbetta.

"I don't want to come, my lady. Maybe you will hold against the King, the Pope, maybe not. One thing is sure. If you bring me back, that Father Felipe will chase me night and day to confess and repent. His terrible crusade murdered my parents, my sister. I won't do it."

This Lisbetta is brash in the face of the nobility, Agnes thought, as she was brash in the face of the priest's threats.

"You should think about your answer, Lisbetta. Things are going well for the Count of Tolosa, the Count of Fois. The northerners are being driven back. My brother will speak to the Count of Fois about the Farga ironworks. They are yours."

The Baroness heard a snort. "Until the next northern knight shows up, rapes me and kills me as a heretic. I will wait up here, my lady, to see if your brother can drive the Baron of Épernay away from Fonta. And if he can stand up to the Pope's threats delivered through this loathsome Father Felipe."

The commotion in the camp grew louder. Shouting began downhill on the trail. Without warning, Agnes found herself lifted into someone's arms, carried off at a run. Noise surrounded her, footsteps surrounded her, shouting surrounded her as her heart raced and a cold chill ran down her spine. Her bearer laid her on her back on the ground and shoved.

"Wait here. Lie still. Don't move. It may be a long while." Branches whipped nearby, and she was alone. Completely alone, while the noise roared on around her.

"Stop them! Catch them"! Father Felipe? "Bring the heretics back"! Yes, Loathsome Felipe. Lie still.

Footsteps thundered through the underbrush. Men fell in the darkness, yelling and cursing. Several people ran right past the Baroness, but no one stopped.

The running faded into the distance. It grew quiet in the nighttime forest. Very quiet. Agnes felt around. She was on her back under a ledge, her face almost in the rock above, like a coffin. Some kind of bush shielded the opening. She was getting cold. She had to go.

Someone betrayed us. At the convent, perhaps, where the Preaching Friar might have learned of the strange behavior of the Baroness, dressing myself as a boy and being lifted to ride a donkey like a man. Or maybe he just ordered the guard to follow me from the castle and waited for us to set off.

Thank you, Lord, Agnes thought, thank you for Your gift of the *Credente* who shoved me into this cave. I will not be found among the heretics, accused of heresy myself. Forfeiting Juviler, which has belonged to my family almost 400 years. Forfeiting my own life to the flames.

The night sounds of the forest returned. Jamilla was right after all. This was a foolish idea. It's one thing to be blind and paralyzed when you're sitting in your bedroom, a noblewoman surrounded by trusted servants to do your bidding. It's another to be alone, outdoors in the open, at night.

The wild beasts always attack the cripples first. They are easy prey. I want to cry, but I'm too afraid. It will attract an animal. It will attract Father Felipe.

Agnes couldn't wait any longer. She pulled up her cotte and tunic and surcoat, feeling around to be sure they were above her waist. She wiggled with her shoulders toward one end of the hole, crumpling up her legs, and relieved herself. Then she pulled forward, dragging herself straight, away from the warm, damp earth.

Cold, still cold. She pulled her arms inside the surcoat and wrapped it around her. Better.

Time to pray. Pray, among other things, that the sound near her, rustling in the leaves, was not a soldier searching for heretics. Or a wolf.

■ ■ ■

Agnes woke with a start.

"Baroness Juviler. My lady, where are you? They've all run off and left you. Call out and we'll bring you back to Alberensa."

Felipe again. Yes, let's go back to Alberensa. Away from this wretched hole that smells of my piss. And of animal piss, from the family of something that lives deeper in the cave. Something that sniffed around my body, between my legs. Something that ran over my face to get out.

No. Mark his sound. He must be calling from the camp. If no one comes after you have peed twice more, drag yourself in that direction and find the trail.

"Baroness! We have your heretic bishop! You must repent and think of your soul, my lady"!

No. They don't have anyone. That's what all the soldiers were cursing about as they crashed around in the underbrush. "What're we gonna tell that fuckin' Friar if we don't come up with the blind witch, don't come up with no one."

12

They will not be enough, Hugh thought. The men on the outcrop see no one moving up the Ariège, trying to cross over and come down the Barièja behind us. The scouts rode in, no one is advancing on the other side of the Arget from Foix. The messenger arrived from Alberensa this morning, everything calm in the County.

This is not a feint while they attack somewhere else. The hundred men approaching are all that the Épernays brought. Roger-Bernard accommodated the Papal Legate by letting Henri's force through Fois, but he did not join the northern knight.

Hugh disappointed Sir Rodrigo when he ordered his men to watch Fonta Castle instead of joining the fight against Henri. "You know your position is important, my lord," Hugh said. "We cannot have Sir Martin coming out to take us from behind during the battle. He will try, and you will have your share of the fighting."

Hugh worked hard to sound bold and assured for the benefit of his men, but he had not really slept last night. Good planning, good dispositions, but he was not a warrior. He was a merchant with a title who had gotten lucky one day in the Tripoli gorge. He was scared to death.

"Everyone is scared to death while they are waiting, my lord," Sir Giles told him. "Whoever is coming from Épernay is just as scared as you are. Go into the woods, shit your diarrhea, throw up your breakfast, and get ready." Then Giles took the edge from his encouragement. "Try to avoid a one-on-one fight, my lord. I have trained you but your skills are mediocre at best. A man with real talent will defeat you. He may play with you while he kills you, wound after wound, until finally he tires of the sport."

A pleasant thought. Yes, Father, yes. All I can do is fight as well as I can until I no longer can. Then I must trust in our Savior's merciful grace.

Hugh moved his battle into position, facing east on the Foix-Fonta Road with Foix Castle before them in the distance. A hundred mounted men and two hundred archers watched the cloud of Épernay dust draw near. Hugh looked back towards Fonta Castle. Only three men on the ramparts, watching. Martin has the rest formed up inside, ready to join the battle. Rodrigo's men are waiting just out of range of the walls, ready to charge.

The Épernay column appeared. It drew to a halt. Accompanied by shouted orders, Henri lined up his own battle. A hundred men sat astride their mounts in their armor, lances up and waiting. Plumes in the green of Épernay adorned each helmet. The Épernay coat of arms fluttered on the guerdons. Blankets of Épernay green covered the heads and sides of the horses.

Henri has only mounted men. You have at least as many mounted, and two hundred foot. If he charges, your archers will cut down half his force before they even got close. Still, these northerners make a gallant sight as they wait to be slaughtered. The beginning of their charge will be beautiful, thrilling, until you order the arrows to fall among them.

Hugh looked up. Clouds scudded across the sky, the kind that always yielded showers. Birds fed on the killing ground between the armies. The Épernay left flank stretched into the fields towards Brassat. Fortunately for the serfs, those strips were fallow this year, sparing their crops from destruction in the coming charge.

The Count turned to Giles. "Sir Giles, my compliments to Sir Bertrand. I pray that he take his knights to that knoll to our right. Sir Henri has not properly covered his flank." Hugh adjusted his helmet again, a clumsy movement with his hands in his gauntlets.

"That will be a good placement, my lord Count," Giles replied. "If they are not needed for Henri, they can turn to support Rodrigo when Martin tries to break the siege from within." He motioned to a messenger, leaned over with the order and watched the man dart away. In a moment, ten knights rode off to Hugh's right.

"Sir Giles. Ride to the other side of the archers. Remain away from me in the battle. If I fall, leave the field. One of us must return to my sister."

Giles shook his head. "I shall not obey your command, my lord. You will not hide behind Agnes, and I will not hide behind her either."

"Sir Giles, you are to….."

"My liege, this is a foolish conversation. I have a better idea. Let's stay together now and greet her together when we return." The man with the guerdon smiled.

"Then join me now." The Count rode down the front of his line to where Ferrandos stood among the crossbowmen, all of them wearing the blue Alberensa livery over their armor. Giles followed, and the man carrying Hugh's guerdon. He faced his host. They looked up at him, expectantly.

"Men of Alberensa! Our enemy murdered Sir Alass and his whole family. He burned them at the stake and stole their lands. He slaughtered the family of Gervais Deslegador, the peaceful owner of the forge on the Arriège, without cause, without provocation. They raped his daughter and, having satisfied their lust, ran her through."

"Murder"! shouted Ferrandos.

"Murder"! shouted the entire army.

Hugh motioned towards Henri's men. "The Épernays claim they are Crusaders, but they are not. I am a Crusader, the Sixth Baron of Jabil al-Hadid in Outremer. My family has held that fief against the Saracen host for generations. That is what a Crusader does, men of Alberensa! He takes up the Cross against the enemies of Christ in the Holy Land"!

Hugh swiveled in his saddle and took a moment to regard Sir Henri's dispositions. Nothing had changed.

"Those men are not Crusaders, they are pirates! They are thieves from the north! They ride south to steal Lengadòc, to loot our lands and pillage our homes and rape our women, as they did to the family of Gervais Deslegador"!

Ferrandos raised his fist. "No, my lord, never, it shall never be"!

The shout went up. "No! No! No! No"!

Hugh lifted up in his stirrups. "They ride south to steal our way of life, our freedom, our independence. To take our Lengadòc for the King of France."

"No! No! No"!

"If the King of France wants to take up the Cross, let him go where he will do some good! Let him go to Outremer, if he has the courage!"

"Ou-tre-mer! Ou-tre-mer! Ou-tre-mer"!

Hugh waved his arm over his battle. "Stand fast, my loyal men of Alberensa! Stand fast, and today we shall have the victory! It is the Will of God!"

"It is the Will of God! It is the Will of God! It is the Will of God!"

The Count felt lifted by his own words. We have the advantage in numbers and position. Wait to see what Épernay intends.

One minute. Two. Scudding clouds, Feeding birds. Nervous and snorting animals.

Motion appeared on the Épernay side, the first motion since they had ridden up.

"Bowmen, ready"! ordered Ferrandos.

"Here they come, my lord"! Giles drew his sword and held it over his head. The knights lowered their lances, preparing for the countercharge that must meet a charge.

"Hold, Sir Giles, hold! They are opening a gap in their line, that's all." In proof, two horsemen rode out from the center, carrying the Épernay flag and a white flag. "A white flag, Sir Giles. They want to parlay." Hugh turned and motioned to the young knight behind him, come. The man rode smartly forward, pulled up and saluted with his arm across his mailed chest.

"At your service, my lord Count"!

"Your name and your liege, sir"?

"I am Laurent of Burgalays, in the service of Gautier of Moustalon."

"My compliments to you, Sir Laurent. Pray take my guerdon and see what they want."

■ ■ ■

Men from both sides quickly placed a table in the Fois Road and erected a canopy against the coming rain. They found a white cloth for the table and six chairs. Ferrandos stood on one side with five soldiers in the blue of Alberensa. An officer of Baron Henri stood on the other with his five in the green of Épernay. The two armies remained in place, separated by three hundred paces.

It began to drizzle. Both groups of guards moved under the canopy, then realized that they were too close to draw arms and fight. Both groups stepped back from under cover. The drizzle turned into a heavy shower. The soldiers stood in the rain, enduring.

The parties made their formal introductions quickly. For Alberensa, the Count and Sir Giles. For the Épernays, Henri and Charles and Martin, granted safe passage from Fonta so that he could join his liege. Henri's right arm was missing from below the shoulder, but his hauberk concealed the loss.

"My lord Count," Henri said, "May I present Bishop Jerome, the new diocesan for the See of Alberensa."

A quite young man stepped forward. A bishop's purple fringed his new cassock. He lacked the occupational softness and rotund belly of the long-serving cleric. His dark eyes and hair signaled both a heritage from Languedoc and a fervor to rise up within the Church. Not just Christ would evaluate his work today, but also the Holy Father who had granted this young priest a See.

"Greetings, my lord Count." Jerome extended his hand so that Hugh could kiss his ring. "I come from Quillan." The east of Lengadòc then, south of Limoux. "I look forward to this opportunity to return to Lengadòc, the land of my birth." Hugh kissed the ring. "I am eager to get to take up my new position. There is much work to do, combating this heresy."

"You are most welcome to Alberensa, my lord Bishop," Hugh replied. "Indeed, you have already arrived, in my fief of Fonta. We shall discuss this question of heresy later, in my castle." He looked towards Henri. "Thank you for your courtesy in escorting Bishop Jerome, my lord Baron. With your leave, I shall bring five men forward to escort the Bishop on his way."

Jerome raised his hand, no, no. "Thank you, my lord Count, but the Holy Father has asked me to act as his Legate in this dispute. Shall we all be seated so that we might begin"?

Six men sat down as the heart of the storm broke overhead. Rain sluiced from the tent to the soft ground, drenching the guards, soaking the waiting armies.

From up close, Hugh, Henri looks old and tired. A wound so severe, an amputation, takes years from a man, assuming he survives. The son next to him, Charles, he is the warrior Giles warned against. Arrogant and vain and a killer. Eager for his father to die so that Épernay can be his.

"My lord Count," Jerome began, "the Holy Father affirms that Fonta is forfeit for heresy under the Third

Canon of the Fourth Lateran Council. However, His Holiness recognizes that the family of Jabil al-Hadid has protected the Christians in Outremer since the time of His Holiness Pope Urban the Second. The same was not true of Count Jacme."

"It was true of the Countess Marguerite, my lord Bishop. She was in the Holy Land when the Épernays wrongly seized this fief."

"So the Holy Father has learned, my lord Count. Because of that service, he does not wish the Third Canon enforced against Alberensa, as long as you cooperate with me and with the Preaching Friar Felipe Vilalba as we work to root out this heresy." The Bishop turned to his side. "Sir Henri, please."

The old knight rested his only hand on the table. "Sir Martin, I must ask a difficult thing of you, my loyal friend."

Martin already knew what it was. "You have but to command, my liege."

"Sir Martin, you have my thanks again, as always." Henri turned towards Hugh. "My lord Count, it is the Holy Father's wish, as expressed through his Legate, that I surrender Fonta back to you, on the condition that you seek no ransom to allow my men to leave."

Hugh nodded towards the others. "Sir Giles, at my instructions, carried the same offer to Sir Martin three weeks ago. The offer still stands."

"Excellent," said Jerome. "Then we may…"

Hugh raised his hand, cutting off the Papal flow. "However, I do not accept that you are surrendering something that is rightfully yours. It has always been mine, wrongfully taken."

Jerome reeled back. Henri scowled. Charles coiled, a snake hoping for battle. The negotiator, the merchant with a title continued. "There may be no need to dispute the point further. We can simply agree that, after this meeting, Fonta is a fief of Alberensa, without further description."

Henri looked towards Charles. His evident disappointment convinced his father. "Yes, I can accept that, my lord Count."

"Excellent," said Bishop Jerome. "Sir Martin and his men shall evacuate Fonta immediately. No ransom shall be paid. Fonta is acknowledged as a fief of Alberensa. Let us be on our way to Alberensa, my lord Count."

"Sir Giles," Sir Martin said, surprising them all. He rose, stiff from his old war injury. "By your leave, my lord."

Giles nodded. "Of course, Sir Martin."

"I insulted the Baroness of Juviler during our parlay. I deeply regret what I said. It was unchivalrous and cruel. I have never before spoken of a woman in such a way. And I said it under flag of truce, to provoke. That was an even more cowardly deed. You will certainly have the advantage over me, my lord, but I am prepared to give you satisfaction, with the weapons of your choice."

The rain beat on the canopy. A trial by combat would not help the truce.

"My lord Count," Giles said. "What is your wish"?

"Sir Giles, it is not my place to wish. The offense given was double, to you and to the Baroness. She has accepted you as her champion."

The rain beat even harder, or perhaps the silence between the two knights made it so.

"Sir Martin, the Baroness would consider that you have given a deep and sincere and proper apology for words spoken under threat of battle. She would find your apology most chivalrous, and she would accept." Giles put his hand against his chest. "I, too, gave offense in our parlay, my lord, threatening you with murder. I ask that you accept my own apology. The Baroness and I only hope that after this day we might be friends."

He held out his hand, and Martin took it. "That is my hope as well, Sir Giles."

Certainly the ten soldiers, relieved of the upcoming battle, needed no further satisfaction. Or the Bishop. In fact, of all those under the canopy, only Charles appeared to regret that there would be no violence today.

13

Agnes felt the urge again, the second time. How could she be so thirsty and still have to go? How long could she go without water?

Dew lay on her face now, her clothing. Insects crawled on her, and those animals, sniffing all over her body. She swatted at them, but only succeeded in hurting herself on the rocks. She was already in her grave, just waiting to be dead.

My God, my God, why have you forsaken me, and are so far from helping me, from the words of my groaning?

"My lady." A whisper. In Arabic, thanks be to God, the All-Compassionate, the All-Merciful! "Shake the bush, Agnes, so I can find you."

Out of the depths I cried to you, O Lord, and you heard my voice!

In a moment, Agnes felt Jamilla's hands under her shoulders, dragging her clear. "You did very well, my lady." She touched her face and Agnes grabbed her hand. "Your troubadours will sing of you, Agnes *al-Zarqa'*. They will sing of Agnes of the Blue Eyes, *Sheyka al-Hadid*, the Baroness of Iron." Jamilla sat up Blue Eyes, brushed off her face, straightened her tunic and coat. Straightened and re-tied her cap on her head. "I was hiding not far away, but I couldn't move until that Black Friar finally left. A day, a whole day he spent searching for you until he finally took his soldiers and departed."

"Did they find anyone, Jamilla"?

"The others are in Aragon by now, my lady. Felipe and his soldiers burned their camp."

Both women froze as they heard rustling in the brush. Jamilla leaned Agnes against the mouth of her cave. "I have a dagger, my lady. If that is one of Felipe's awful men skulking around hoping to rape us, I will slaughter the Infidel."

The scent and the breath of Jamilla disappeared without a sound. The rustling continued, drawing closer, step by step as the Infidel felt his way through the dark. Suddenly a rush arose in the bushes nearby, a footstep, another, followed by the crash of one body into another. Sticks cracked as the two thudded together to the ground.

"Tarnut ya kalab kefiran"!

"No! Stop! Don't kill me"!

Lisbetta? Call out, Agnes, call out!

"Al-Jamiliat! La! 'Anaha Lisbetta! Tawqafi"!

The sounds of struggle subsided. "Sorry," Ekaterina said. "Is mistake."

"Are you harmed, Lisbetta"?

"No my lady." Agnes listened as the two women untangled themselves. After a moment, she felt their bodies next to hers. She reached out, finding Ekaterina's robe, Lisbetta's tunic. "It's night again," Lisbetta said. "I'm going back with you. I have a plan to deal with this Black Friar so that he does not threaten any of us."

"I am glad to hear that, Lisbetta. I will protect you, just as I promised."

"What was that language, my lady"?

"Ekaterina is a Maronite, Lisbetta. They speak Aramaic, the language of our Lord Christ himself. We have many Maronites among us at Jabil al-Hadid, so I am familiar with the tongue."

Lisbetta rustled beside her. "This notion that God would actually appear as a man on Satan's earth, it is most peculiar."

"Yes," said Ekaterina, then caught herself. For Jamilla, Agnes knew, this notion that God even had a son was the highest blasphemy. So it was revealed in the Noble Qu'ran, in the *Surah* that the Saracens called *al-Iklas*.

Suddenly her terror overwhelmed Agnes. She had been so helpless, so alone. She did not feel like *Sheyka al-Hadid*, no, not at all. She pulled Ekaterina to her and hugged her tightly, bringing her to the ground in her embrace, crying and shaking. She felt the sister's body against hers, melding, flowing, as though they were lovers.

"Sister Ekaterina, is there something you want to share with me"?

Ekaterina kissed her cheek. "No, lady. Tell if time comes."

14

The crops on every fief needed tending and serfs to tend them. Sir Rodrigo, Sir Bertrand and Sir Gautier took their men from Fonta and returned directly to their estates. The Count's own force rode west in a column of twos, with heaven shining on their victory under a soft early summer sky.

Late in the day, they left the open land and smells of the country and entered the narrow streets and smells of the capital. Hugh's subjects bowed as his column passed through the St. Matthew's Gate, but they smiled, too. The upright bearing of the soldiers, the perfect angle on the guerdons, the neat order of the supplies tied to the wagons, all told them that their Count had been victorious over the northern invaders.

A celebration began as the column proceeded through the Quarter. The workers repairing Count Angibert's bridge cheered as the hooves clattered over the span into the Cathedral Village. Hugh ordered a halt at the side of Our Lady and, together with Sir Giles, escorted Bishop Jerome into his new See. They knelt with him, in their armor, beneath the south transept window.

"Holy Mother of God," Hugh prayed, "we give thanks to you for your gracious protection over us." As he spoke, the sun came out from behind a cloud and brightened the golden sea around the throne of God. "May our lives always be dedicated to the service of our Lord and Savior Jesus Christ." The gathered Compostela pilgrims began the *Magnificat*, the Song of Mary, "My soul proclaims the greatness of the Lord, and my spirit rejoices in God my Savior."

Word of the victory spread quickly. The town's enthusiasm grew with it. The merchants on the Avenue of Our Lady stood in front of their shops, chanting their Count's name. Upstairs windows on the houses flew open as they approached, and dresses, robes, coats, anything of blue, Alberensa blue, streamed out into the breeze. A crowd surged around the column and followed it along, reaching out to touch the legs of Giles, Hugh, the men behind them.

"God bless you, my lord Count," the people chanted, "God bless you."

The Count's triumphant progress ended in the castle yard where the entire household waited for their liege. On a signal from Peter, they bowed as one. Grooms ran forward and held the horses while the column dismounted. Guilhelms hurried quickly to his family, hugging his son and kissing his wife and his toddler. Hugh walked steadily to Countess Maura. She curtsied as he took her hand and kissed it. "I am pleased to see you safe and unharmed, my lord."

"Thank you, my lady. And we possess Fonta and its ore again. And we have a truce with the Holy Father. A most successful endeavor." He looked around the yard. "Where is the Baroness of Juviler"? Everyone looked at the dirt of the yard, all except Maura and Father Felipe. "Peter. The Baroness and Sister Ekaterina."

"My lord, they...."

"Have run off with the heretics in the Sárdalo Pass, my lord Count," Felipe answered harshly. "They are Cathars, too, like that wench in yellow."

Hugh turned to the Father, but Giles spoke first.

"Be careful how you speak of the Baroness, Father Felipe. I have sworn to protect her against all harm, including such slander."

Felipe glared at the knight. "I am well aware of your oath, Sir Giles. The traveling minstrels in this place, indeed everywhere in this heresy-infested Languedoc, remind me of it constantly." He made the sign of the cross. "You cannot be bound by an oath to a Cathar witch, my lord. You are bound by your duty as a Christian knight to help me root out this heresy."

The Black Friar spoke with the certainty that his words defended the One True Faith. Giles wanted to kill him anyway. Hugh doubted that the knight would reject Felipe's offer for satisfaction, if one could only be coaxed from the priest. "Father Felipe," Giles began. "If you were not a priest…."

"But he is, Sir Giles," Hugh said, cutting off the threat. He tuned to his Seneschal. "Peter. Where are my sister and her lady-in-waiting? They are not in the mountains with the Cathars. That is frankly preposterous."

"We followed them up the Sárdalo Pass Road, my lord. The Baroness was dressed as a leper boy, riding on a donkey. They….."

The Count allowed his hand to touch the hilt of his own sword, momentarily. "Father Felipe. Please, Father. Do not interfere while I question my servants. If I have a question for you, I will ask it." The Friar's mouth opened, but he regarded the fury in Sir Giles and remained silent. "Peter. My sister."

The entire household starred carefully at the ground in front of them while the major domo answered. "She took Sister Ekaterina to the convent of the Sisters of Charity, my lord Count, several days ago. She said they wished to think about the words of Father Felipe, pray on them, embrace them. She gave strict instructions, my lord, that she was not to be disturbed in her devotions for any reason."

"That sounds more reasonable. Fetch her now. We will put an end to these ridiculous claims."

"My lord, she gave strict instructions….."

"Enough. Sir Giles. Put pillions on two horses. Take ten men and bring those two back here. Carry them if they resist. They have been devoted long enough. It is time for them to tell Father Felipe what they have learned. We will all wait here to learn ourselves." He looked around the gathered crowd. 'Magdalena. My lady the Countess may withdraw. Assist her to do so. Peter. Release the kitchen staff. Everyone else will wait here."

■ ■ ■

Hugh ordered an armchair brought for Agnes. He spent time with Guilhelms and Aenor, talking about the blast furnace. He listened attentively and respectfully to the priest's tale, told softly, of following the nun and the leper boy towards the Pass.

"My lord Count," the guard called from above the tower. "The Baroness of Juviler approaches."

Sir Giles rode in, with Agnes on the pillion behind, her arms around his waist. Ekaterina rode on the pillion on the next horse, and Lisbetta sat across the front of the saddle of the third. She wore the yellow tunic last seen on Easter Sunday, two months ago. Sir Giles drew up to a halt before the waiting crowd.

"My lord, I have fetched the Baroness of Juviler. She has obeyed the command of her liege, but she is most displeased. You have interrupted her devotions, her meditations upon the words of Father Felipe."

A scowl, amazed and stunned, darkened Felipe's face. "Her meditations? Her… her…This is a ruse, my lord Count, a…."

"Please, Father. Peter. Two men to help my sister into her chair."

The Baroness appeared most elegant in a deep red tunic of fine wool. Ekaterina bustled about, arranging her white surcoat and straightening the silver cross around her neck. Save perhaps Father Felipe, everyone in the yard recognized the ancient jewelry in her blonde hair. It was the Tiara of Juviler, worn by the Baroness Ermessenda at her wedding to Count Angibert I in 950.

Giles dismounted, walked back and lifted Lisbetta to the ground. She ran to Guilhelms, hugged Aenor and stood holding the hand of Tibaut. Triumph shone out from her eyes, not suppressed quite quickly enough. Felipe turned to approach, but Giles was moving, too.

"Sir Giles. My compliments, Sir Giles. Pray stand with me, my lord. Father Felipe. There will be time for Lisbetta later, Father. Agnes does not appear to have been with the Cathars, but with the Sisters of Charity. We'll hear her story first."

Hugh stood in front of his sister, with Giles alongside. She posed in the chair, regal, commanding, as though she could actually see and then get up to look more closely. "My lady. Father Felipe says he saw you in the Sárdalo Pass, my lady, but Sir Giles found you at the Sisters of Charity."

Ekaterina curtsied deeply. "My lord. Baroness, oath of silence." It was the first time that most in the castle had heard her voice. They found her French strange, filled with guttural sounds from deep in her throat. "Angry you disturb. Control temper. One hour."

Hugh motioned silently for the Maronite sister to rise. Another silent motion to Peter, and a few more servants slipped away quietly. Aenor disappeared with Tibaut and Isabèl while Guilhelms waited with Lisbetta. Hugh surveyed the servants, the yard, his knight and the priest glowering across the ground at each other.

"The sand has run out on the hour, my lady. I am sorry that you were disturbed, but Father Felipe claims that you were in the mountains with the Cathars. We are pleased that it is not so, but I must beg you to explain."

Her head turned towards the sound of Hugh's voice. Her nose went up in the air. "The sand has not run out, brother, but your patience has, and that of Father Felipe. You two are the disciples whom our Lord chastised in the Garden of Gethsemane on the night before His crucifixion. 'Could you not watch with me one hour'? Jesus asked." Agnes swept away their impatience with the back of her hand. "Apparently not."

"My lady," Felipe began, only to be interrupted by that lady.

"Our Lord made a mistake that night," she said with an edge of annoyance in her soft low voice. "He took men. He should have taken Mary and Martha and the Magdalene."

Felipe's mouth opened in shock at the blasphemy. He crossed himself. "That is…"!

"A woman in the St. Matthew's Quarter found Lisbetta hiding in the shed behind her shop," Agnes continued. "She brought her to the convent for sanctuary. Sister Ekaterina and I found her there when we went for our devotions."

"You… you…"?

"Yes, Father Felipe. We have prayed with her daily. She has repented and accepted the True Faith. She will serve us now, here, as one of my ladies, assisting Ekaterina."

A frustrated Felipe finally exploded in outrage. "That is a lie! They brought the harlot wench back after we found their village! They were all up there, taking the *Consolamentum*, helping the heretics! Juvilier is forfeit to the Holy Father under the Third Canon of the…."!

Hugh watched Giles's hand move to his sword.

"Stay, Sir Giles! He is a priest of God! Do not put your immortal soul in jeopardy"!

"As you command, my lord." And only because you command, Hugh.

"Father Felipe. There is no way that my sister could be in the mountains. She can barely get around her room. Can you not accept that through some holy mystery she has rescued this poor child from Satan"? He turned to her. "I'm going to lift you, Agnes." And he did, holding her gently under back and knees while she put her arms around his neck.

"Lisbetta is accepted as lady-in-waiting to the Baroness. She is to go with Father Felipe now to receive the Holy Sacrament in our chapel. After that, she will come to you, Peter, to be given her livery. You will bring her to Lady Juviler's room."

"Yes, my lord."

"You may dismiss the servants. Sir Giles, dismiss the guard. Father Felipe. Lisbetta is in your charge."

Hugh swept away with his sister's skirt fanning the dirt as they passed. Ekaterina hurried quickly behind.

■ ■ ■

Hugh set Agnes in her wheelchair and waited while the servants hurried in with her luggage. "Ekaterina. Chapel. Watch. Be sure, Lisbetta to Peter."

"Yes."

Hugh barred the door after the sister left and lowered his voice to a whisper. "Aggie, what have you been doing? No woman from any quarter brought Lisbetta to the convent. You got her out of the city and she disappeared. The Mother Superior will not lie if the Black Friar or Bishop Jerome asks her what happened."

This time the a smile and a sparkle in her eyes joined Aggie's dismissive sweep. "We did bring Lisbetta to the Sisters of Charity and ask the Mother Superior for sanctuary. Of course, that was after we rode down from the shrine of Saint Mary of Egypt, not when we arrived the first time so I could change."

"Then how…"?

"That time, we bribed the sexton and used the barn." She smirked. "The Leper Boy of the Sárdalo Pass was born in a stable, like our Lord. And he rode a donkey, as our Lord did when He rode into Jerusalem on Palm Sunday."

"Agnes, what were you thinking? You put….."

Now anger accompanied the sweep. "As you well know, Lisbetta Deslegador is a descendant of the Countess Esquiva of Foix," she hissed, "and therefore of Julian of Blagnac and Monica of Ronzières, the founders of Jabil al-Hadid. A member of our family cannot spend her life hiding in the mountains. What I did was completely foolish, but it worked. She is here again, safe under our protection."

"I do rejoice in that, my lady."

His lady wiggled in her chair, pulling at the tunic to get comfortable. "Did you do as well, my lord? Did we regain Fonta or does that terrible Charles still remain to threaten Aenor, our cousin's wife"?

"Yes, my lady, we did. The sacrifice of Baron Olivier at the Horns of Hattin still counts for something in the Church. The Holy Father has ordered that the Third Canon be suspended here for as long as Father Felipe and Bishop Jerome consider we are not assisting the heretics. We hold the entire County again, and we have a truce."

"So there was no battle"?

"We held the siege and killed any who sallied forth for food or aid. When the relief came, we were too strong for the force that Fois allowed to cross his lands. Had the Baron of Épernay chosen to engage, we would have destroyed him." He leaned forward and kissed his sister's cheek. "The northern knights have been driven back all across Lengadòc. This business about Outremer merely allowed Sir Martin and Épernay to retire with honor."

Agnes smiled. "Then we have both done well, my lord. You have protected our family before Fonta, and I have protected it in the Sárdalo Pass."

"As long as Father Felipe cannot prove that you were up in the mountains with the Cathars, taking the *Consolamentum* and becoming a *Parfait.*"

She shook her head. "I am a faithful Catholic, Hugh. I was born on Easter. I will never become a Good Christian." Her lip began to quiver and her hands to shake. "He almost caught us, Hugh. That Black Friar almost caught us. They hid me in a small cave. I was in my coffin and I was cold and I lay in my own piss while animals and bugs crawled on me and….and….and…."

Suddenly the memory of her grave was fresh again, the urine in her nostrils, the bugs on her face. She collapsed into tears, shaking. "I was so frightened, Hugh, so helpless and so frightened. I laid there in the damp and the filth and the cold and the animals….the animals…" She lunged her brokenness at him and he caught her as she fell. He carried her and sat her on her bed and held her as she cried. "Why did God leave me alive, Hugh, alive like this? He took our handsome Roger and our beautiful little Maddie to Himself and He left me….He left me…half dead….I went to help and I was….was…in my tomb and….."

Hugh put his hand against her cheek. "Stop, Agnes, stop." He rubbed her back, softly, gently, the way their mother used to do. "He left you alive because we all need you, Baroness." He kissed her forehead, the way their father used to do. "It is your strength that gives us all our inspiration." Her tears subsided to sniffling as he carried her back to her chair. "That was very brave, what you did, Agnes. You were clever in the yard, too, but then we know you're the clever one, not me."

"I'm sorry, Hugh, sometimes I just…."

"Let me tell you about Fonta and the truce while we wait for Lisbetta."

15

Two years passed without Sir Frederic heeding Lady Elizabeth's constant admonitions to visit Athèné's Harlot Daughter.

"It is not as simple as it seems, Mother," he told her more than once. "Perhaps Baudoin of Saissouq has no real interest in Anne, but his honor is at stake. I see no reason to get into a dispute with a knight I respect, even if the rumors are true."

Frederic grew suspicious when the topic disappeared after Easter. He returned to Jabil al-Hadid after escorting a merchant caravan through the Homs Gap, only to find that it had not disappeared, not at all. Six armored men wearing the colors of Saissouq waited in the castle yard. He had no reason to expect a visit from Sir Baudoin.

The knight found the two conspirators at the table in the common room of the Solar. Twins in gray tunic and surcoat, one with gray in her hair as well.

Lady Elizabeth explained how she had invited "your cousin" to pass some days at Jabil al-Hadid. "Lady Anne is languishing in Saissouq, Frederic. She misses the companionship of her family, who never visit even though they are often so close by."

Frederic waited for the meaningless prattle to stop. He gave the expected response. "Jabil al-Hadid is honored by your visit, Lady Saissouq."

Elizabeth smiled, "William, some wine for Sir Frederic." The knight sat down with his cousin the asp's daughter and his mother the viper, daughter-in-law of the cobra. Or was it the other way round, the cobra and the asp?

He should find some reason to busy himself at the smelter. No, that ruse would fail, since he never went there. He had been tricked and trapped by a woman, but that woman was his mother. Sit, be gracious and enjoy the pleasant company, because Anne of Saissouq is indeed pleasant to look upon. Sit, and wait for the inevitable.

It was not long in coming. "My lady," William said upon his return with Frederic's drink, "Catarina is having difficulties in the kitchen. She would like you to come."

Her son thought that Elizabeth did a quite commendable job of appearing irritated. "What would those difficulties be"?

"I do not know, my lady." William was a far poorer actor, which gave Frederic comfort. He did not want a Seneschal who could dissemble and not be caught.

"Sir Frederic, Lady Saissouq, if you will excuse me." Elizabeth followed her servant, shaking her head as though she was offended by the interruption.

Alone now, just the two of them. Anne sat waiting with that formal, sophisticated pose she had adopted soon after returning in her eunuch's clothes. Frederic turned back to her, smiled, and received her smile in return.

"I think we have dealt with the weather and the crops and the Saracens, my lady. How are you"? That unleashed a torrent, as he knew he would. It was the reason he had resisted so long.

"Sir Frederic, my nephew treated me very badly, marrying me to this Baudoin. The fat oaf likes his sex the Greek way, with men and boys. It is offensive to the Lord. Leviticus tells us that 'If a man lies with a man as with a woman, both of them have committed an abomination; they shall be put to death.' In Romans, St. Paul says, 'They know God's decree that they who do such things deserve to die.' I beg of you, speak to Father Sebastian, my lord. Have my marriage annulled so that I may leave that den of degenerate lust and iniquity. Let me return to Jabil al-Hadid."

Frederic looked upon his cousin and her still-evident charms. "Does he never treat you as his wife, my lady"?

She snorted in disgust and waved her hand. "When he does bed me, it is a duty. He wallows over me like a pig in the sty. Please, Sir Frederic, show some pity."

Frederic lowered his voice, even though they were alone. "Don't you do what you did in Jabil al-Hadid, cousin? Just satisfy your needs with others"?

Anne dismissed such foolishness with a wave. "I can't imagine what you're speaking about, my lord." She took some wine and lifted into her up-straight pose. "Soon after our marriage, Baudoin accused a squire of adultery. It was of course a false charge, but my husband forced the lad to join the Hospitallers. It is just another example of Baudoin's disgraceful behavior. Please, Frederic, please help me escape this torture."

Anne had seduced the squire, of that there was no doubt. Saint Paul disliked adultery and fornication, too, but Frederic thought not to mention that now. "Was he one of Baudoin's own lovers, Anne? That would not have been wise."

Her dark eyes flashed and her dark tresses bounced as she shook her head. Her perfume wafted into the space. "So I was informed, later." A scowl. "Not that it mattered to me, because of course the charge against me was false."

"Of course. But afterwards, no one else was interested in being the subject of false rumors."

""My lord, I...."

"I cannot denounce Baudoin as perverted on the testimony of a woman, Anne"!

Despair overpowered anger on Anne's face, the fear of earthly damnation to a life devoid of her earthly pleasure. "Please, Frederic, you must..."

"It cannot be helped, Anne. Your husband likes to fight, and he is good. Such charges must be followed by a trial by combat, and one of us will die. Leviticus or not, Anne, both of us are too valuable to Tripoli and the Hospitallers to sacrifice because of his strange desires." He leaned back and crossed his mail-clad arms across his chest. "You are alive, despite your felony here. You are cared for. You are safe. You are the wife of an important knight of Tripoli. You should learn to be content, my lady of Saissouq."

Anne rose up, leaned over the table and pointed her finger directly Frederic. Her perfume, her full chest, they flowed to the center of the knight's attentions. "Content, my lord? Content? You sound like simpering Hugh! 'Turn your thoughts to God,' that idiot told me! I am not content to be treated so poorly, my lord! I need someone loyal to champion my cause"!

Anne sat down again, leaned back and ran her fingers through her hair, outlining her shapely body in the tunic. "Do you remember King Amalric's agreement with Baron Guilhabert, Sir Frederic"?

"Of course. Lady Elizabeth reminds me that it insults her, constantly."

"Except for that agreement, you are next in line for Jabil al-Hadid after Hugh. You, not some distant cousin roaming around the County of Nicaea looking for a fief."

"Yet the agreement does exist."

"It does. Made at a time when Toulouse not Antioch ruled Tripoli. Made for the benefit of my mother, the Princess Athèné to cut off the rights of your grandmother. If you rid me of Baudoin, I will marry you. And I will petition the Count of Tripoli to lift Amalric's decree and allow Jabil al-Hadid to pass down to you."

Frederic smiled, a broad smile. "What a surprising proposal, Lady Anne. Strangely enough, my mother had the same idea." His face grew more somber, and he touched the hilt of Julian's sword. "The agreement does seem unfair, so long after the event. Should Hugh die without heirs, it is better that the fief pass to those who have worked to preserve it. Certainly Sophia prayed that Jean and Luc not be deprived of their rights."

A thin shaft of light from an opening door, an exit from her earthly Hell, brightened Anne's face. "That is exactly…"

"It won't work." Her face darkened as the door went closed. "Even if you were free of Sir Baudoin, which you are not, we are first cousins, very close. We cannot wed."

"Half first cousins."

"It makes no difference to the Church."

Another wave of dismissal. "Yes, so we need a dispensation. I'm barren. We won't be having any idiot children." Her dark eyes glowed with mischief as she ran her hand along the side of his face. "I think some donations to God's work in Tripoli, to the Bishop, will solve that problem. It's common enough."

Frederic nodded and kissed her hand before she took it away. He certainly had more than enough money to satisfy the bishop. "Yes it is." She crossed her legs, letting her ankles show. "From all that I have heard, my value to you would lay in bed, my lady. Your value to me would be your petition to the Count of Tripoli. Would you still make the petition after we are wed"?

Anne beamed with mischief now. She leaned forward and kissed him. "Don't be so crude, my love," she whispered. "We both know that we are very good in bed together. We have proven it many times. You are better, far better than my deceiving first husband, the very nimble Hassan ibn Ishaq al-Haddad. Once we're married, we'll never need anyone else."

"You will never need anyone else"?

"My lord! What are you implying"! Anne smiled. "Of course I will make the petition. Just rid me of this clown and let me marry someone I can truly love"!

PART FOUR

County of Alberensa
September 1224 – March 1225

1

Supper ended, with the Great Hall emptying and the servants beginning to take down the tables. A man-servant carried Agnes up the circular staircase to her room, followed by Sister Ekaterina and Lisbetta and the Countess.

Hugh remained behind as the women left, taking the chance to speak to Sir Laurent of Burgalays and Sir Bertrand, his guests of honor for the evening. Laurent had done well as Hugh's envoy before Fonta. Bertrand's second daughter was of marriageable age, but her betrothed had died of a fever during the winter. Once he raised the topic, the Count bid his vassals good night. He bowed to Bertrand's three women, waiting patiently, and disappeared up the staircase.

Angibert's extension to the Keep created separate bedchambers for Count and Countess on the third floor, with a smaller room in between for their servants. Angibert built several more bedchambers on the floor above. Agnes slept in one room and Ekaterina another and Lisbetta in yet another.

Hugh found the privacy between Count and Countess quite unusual. He wondered if that had been the whole purpose of his great-grandfather's work on the castle, to create a secluded space for himself to entertain his lovers.

Maura's servant Magdalena waited outside her door. That was the signal, the sign that the Countess was undressed and waiting in their marriage bed. Magdalena's head bowed down in silent prayer, as it always did when Hugh entered, silent prayer for an heir.

The candlelight flickered as he opened the door, making the silver and golden threads in the tapestries glisten. On the finest cloth, a view of pilgrims making their way through the Sárdalo Pass, the threads of snow shimmered in the candlelight as real snow shimmered when a thin cloud passed across the sun.

Hugh made for Maura's bed, then realized it was empty. He had looked right past her, sitting in one of her chairs. "My lord Count," she said, motioning towards another chair. "Pray have a private conversation with me this evening, my lord. Away from the servants. Away from the others." A look most intense, most earnest filled her plain face. "It is a matter most urgent to my family."

Never before in their eighteen months together had the Countess been so bold, so direct. They lived in a dynastic marriage, filled with formal respect but completely lacking in emotion. Their ancestors had linked the fortunes of Toulouse and Blagnac in Outremer a century ago. Now they linked those fortunes to those of Alberensa in Languedoc. No importance attached to Hugh and Maura themselves, only to their ability to join their bloodlines and increase the wealth and power of their descendants.

"May I have leave to sit, my lady"? Maura had worn her finest gown this evening, her blue silk tunic, her golden cross and her finest slippers. Sir Laurent of Burgulays, handsome though he was, did not merit such elegance. Now Hugh understood. Maura had dressed for this meeting, not for Sir Laurent.

"Please, my lord, and have some wine." Hugh poured himself a cup from the side table while the Countess took a sip of hers. As he approached, she reached out her hand, stopped him and plucked something off his tunic. The show of personal affection, personal attention, made her blush. She gathered herself as he sat. "My lord. This truce at Fonta, my lord. I have been working up my courage to speak of it for months."

Hugh calculated. The truce, early June. Now it's harvest time, late September. "Please do so now, my lady."

"The arrangement distresses me. It is not a woman's place to question, but I must know if you understand what happened that day."

Hugh smiled. "Agnes thinks it's a woman's place to question whenever she wants. You should have the same privilege, Countess." He leaned forward, took her hand and kissed it. "Are you worried that I have been tricked into giving up the battle against the Pope's Crusade? Threatened by this Felipe and Jerome so that I'm isolated from your cousin, Raymond VII"?

"Yes, my lord." Her arms went on her thighs and she leaned forward, urgently. "You were still a boy in Outremer when this so-called Albigensian Crusade started. The death of Pierre de Castelnau. The Abbot of Citeaux at Beziers, 'the Lord will know his own.' The surrender at Carcassonne soon after. That awful Simon de Montfort and his son Amaury. When my father's cousin Raymond VI escaped to England in 1214, our family fled to Aquitaine. De Montfort gave our holdings in Colomiers to one of his men in the same way that Henri of Épernay gave Fonta to Sir Martin."

"Since we were betrothed, my mother received news of all this, my lady."

Maura nodded. "Montfort's man pressed our Cathar serfs to recant. Those who did were forced to wear the yellow cross of shame. Those who did not were tied together and burned in a single fire."

"Mother heard of those mass burnings as well."

Maura began trembling, the emotion shaking her bulk. "For two years, our family lived on the generosity of others. We survived on what we carried away with us, and on the small amounts of money that

Raymond sent from England. My father had promised me to you before the Crusade began. The time was drawing near, and we had no money for my dowry. No lands. Nothing. We thought Lengadòc, our way of life, our power, our wealth was lost forever."

Hugh reached out, put his hand on her cheek and gently wiped off the tears. "Yes, but Montfort and the northerners ruled so badly that they provoked a revolt. Raymond returned, Simon de Montfort was killed in 1218 and his son Amaury has been driven into a corner of Trencavel. Even the Count of Trencavel has returned to Carcassonne. It's a great victory for your family."

Maura took his hand away. The tears stopped as her face grew hard. "A victory in which Alberensa played no part, my lord! Played no part but earned a great boon, the defeat of these northerners"! The Countess stopped to control her emotions. "I am sorry, my lord, but I must speak frankly. It is what Count Raymond would expect of me."

Hugh nodded, "Please, my lady. Go ahead."

"We have a dynastic marriage, my lord. Its purpose is the mutual support of the positions of our families. Yet your uncle Count Jacme did nothing throughout this whole terrible business. Nothing except collect his tolls from the Compostela pilgrims and use them to bribe Montfort's knights to stay away. Since your arrival, you have done nothing except to bribe the northerners to leave the one piece of Alberensa that they did bother to seize"!

"Bribe, my lady"?

"Bribe, my lord! By promising the Holy Father that you would let his Bishop, his Preaching Friar into our lives, spying on us, threatening us"!

"By the time that Agnes and I arrived, my lady, the battle was nearly finished. And it was important for us first to be sure that the vassals of Alberensa remained loyal to my family. I could not ride off to Fanjeaux or Castelnaudery or Carcassonne."

Maura actually snorted. "Yes, that would have interfered with building your dirty smelter at Petrousset." A scowl crossed her face. "Why do you think God consecrated you as Count of Alberensa, Hugh? So that you could make your family richer by finding a better way to make steel? No. That is the job of Guilhelms Faure, your fourth or fifth cousin once or twice removed."

"It is something of which I know quite a bit myself, Countess. More than Guilhelms, in fact. As does the Baroness of Juviler."

"Indeed." Maura actually wagged her finger at him. "You inherited a county that your ancestors built through generations of fighting and struggle. That means that God has given you a job, my lord. You hold this fief to protect your people. To preserve their way of life, the life of Lengadòc. To keep them from being harmed in the wars of King Louis, the wars of Pope Honorius. From being forced to believe in a resurrected Jesus if they don't want to." Maura appeared quite regal now, as Agnes had been regal in the castle yard. She was of the family of Toulouse, her demeanor said, he only of Blagnac, of Alberensa.

"The steel is important, my lady. It gives our County something besides farming and overcharging the pilgrims. We are on the verge of a great breakthrough."

"So I have heard your sister say. She seems most excited." A sip of wine calmed any excitement that Maura might feel. "Did you know that Simon de Montfort gave Toulouse to the King of France, to Philip II, in 1216? That Amaury de Montfort gave all his claims in Languedoc to Louis VIII, his son and successor, this year"?

"So I have heard you say."

"Once this new King, this Louis VIII, feels secure, we can expect him to assert those claims. His wife Blanche of Castile is said to be most religious, most devout and most ambitious for her husband. And clever, very clever herself. She will urge the Crusade again. This victory is a lull, Hugh, a lull. They will be back. This time, you need to stand with Tolosa, with Fois, with Trencavel against these northern invaders. To protect *parainça*, the Good Christians, the troubadours, our whole way of life, our independence. I am not interested in living on English alms in Aquitaine, or having our children carry chamber pots for the King of France."

"What is it that you wish me to do, my lady"?

"There is no threat now. But there will be. Prepare yourself. Lengadòc will need your help." She finished her wine. "You have been most gracious to listen to me, my lord Count. Thank you."

Count and Countess, husband and wife, sat for a moment quietly, looking into each other's eyes. "You're welcome, my lady Countess." A pause while she inclined her head. "Was that all the business you wished for us this evening, my lady"?

"I have had my time again, and it is passed. We may try again, please, my lord Count."

"Shall I send in Magdalena"?

Maura stood and shook out her tunic. "Lift this over my head, please." He did so, leaving her in her white linen cotte. As he laid the silk down on her chair, she took both his hands. "I was always a fat little girl, Hugh, a plain, fat little girl who grew up into a plain, fat woman. Some men find that attractive, but you are not one of them. You like your women thin like your sister. You find our lovemaking something of a chore."

Two bold topics on a single night. "My lady, you should not speak so ill of yourself. You are the Countess of Alberensa."

She smiled. "You do not find me attractive, Hugh, but I find you very handsome, most attractive." She motioned, and he lifted off her cotte, leaving her naked. "It is a sin, this lust I have for you. This craving for you that overtakes me every time I see you. A mortal sin. The Holy Church says that the wedding bed is for creating children, not satisfying our own passions. I pray to the Holy Mother of God that she forgives my lust and rewards us with children."

Their clothes lay in a heap on the floor as Hugh slid into the bed alongside her. "Either way, my lord, I certainly do enjoy the trying with you."

Until tonight, Maura's sex had been brief and mechanical. Now that she had finally confessed to the sin of lust, she abandoned her soul into its Satanic clutches. Her mouth was on Hugh's, her tongue in his mouth, pulling him to her tightly, kissing and fondling. He did enjoy the feeling as he entered her, her body closing around him, the sensations running through him, not a feeling of passion but certainly pleasant enough, until finally he delivered himself and, soon after, rolled over on his back.

"Did I please you, my lord"? She pulled the covers up around her neck. Her ample bulk lifted the fabric.

"Perhaps in these moments after we have committed the sin of lust, we can call ourselves by our Christian names, Maura. Yes. Did I please you"?

"Yes, but you always please me, Hugh. I hope that the Lord has favored us with an heir this evening."

"As do I." Now was the time for the Count to leave her room and let Magdelana come in and help Maura into her nightclothes. "I'll see you in the morning, Maura."

"No, Hugh, don't leave. Heirs are produced in only one way, and that is what we have just done. It may be that I shall feel lust for an heir in the morning, and it would be embarrassing to go in search of you, my husband."

2

Agnes sat in her room on the fourth floor of the Keep. "A quite feminine chamber, sister," Hugh assured her, "Filled with tapestries of noble ladies in the countryside. Lace fringes the canopy over your bed." Through the window slits, the Baroness heard the rain of a late September afternoon, a damp and chilly reminder of the winter to come. She smelled the extra candles, brightening the dark room in honor of the priest's visit.

A knock at the door. "Father Felipe has arrived, my lady," announced one of the guards.

"Ekaterina, please." The nun's habit swished, the door groaned on its hinges and the sound of a walking man entered the room.

"Thank you for your visit, Father Felipe. Please take that chair."

"You're most welcome, my lady Baroness. It is an honor." The chair squeaked slightly as Felipe too his seat.

"Ekaterina, cushion, smooth. Then leave us, please."

"Yes, my lady." The nun reached under Aggie's bony legs as she sat in her wheelchair and took away the lump in the cloth. The door closed behind her.

"Lisbetta, my robe, please." Agnes felt the young woman drape the cloth over her legs and pull the blanket smooth over her shoulders. She moved behind her liege, bringing the smell of the wool of her livery, Alberensa blue from the dyers woad that grew all over Languedoc. Its scent mingled with the candle scent and, Agnes thought, the breath of the priest. He had been eating onions.

"I'm sorry for the delay, Father. It can be difficult sometimes, in my condition. I give thanks to God for the many blessings he has given me, despite my disease."

"Yes, my lady." He crossed himself. "How may I be of service"?

"Perhaps first we should ask for the Lord's blessings upon this meeting, Father." She bowed her head. So did Lisbetta.

The priest blinked. "Yes, my lady, you are right. Let us pray." He took a deep breath and let it out, centering himself in the Lord. "Blessed Jesus, be with us today as we meet in Thy Name to do Thy work. May the words of our mouths and the meditations of our hearts be always acceptable in Thy sight O Lord, our Strength and our Redeemer."

"Amen." Agnes raised her head. "Lisbetta. Please take a chair and join us." Agnes inclined her head towards the sounds as the young girl dragged a seat alongside. "Father Felipe. I agree that Lisbetta should not take the Sacrament until you are sure she has embraced its meaning. I have a favor to ask as you instruct her."

"She must also be baptized before she may partake of Our Lord's most blessed body, my lady. I'm waiting to hear from the priest at Farga de sant Matèu if that has ever been done."

Our joust continues, Agnes. Through all his formal, proper and correct behavior, this Preaching Friar does not trust you at all. He visited the Sisters of Charity more than once, taking confession from every nun, trying to pry out the story. The Mother Superior allowed a novice, the daughter of a palace servant, to carry a warning to you.

"Father Felipe tells us all not to protect you, my lady. He says that God has stricken you blind and left you paralyzed for your sins. He urges us not to join you in the sins that outraged the Lord."

"Do you think God is punishing me for my sins, Aicelina"?

"No my lady. Satan creates blindness. Our Lord cures it, as He did at the Pool of Siloam."

"Thank you, Aicelina."

"Yes my lady." The novice paused. "Once Father Felipe makes those threats, his questions begin. 'Is the Count's sister a Cathar? Did she go to the Sárdalo Pass"?

He tried the convent's servants, too, Agnes, including the sexton. That you know from Giles, as well as the man's answer.

"Piss off, Your Lordship. You don't need to threaten me. I don't like these outsiders coming in, telling us what to do. They don't like our Cathars, they can piss off. Join me in a drink."

The sergeant of Jabil al-Hadid did just that. Agnes smiled at the memory, confusing the Father.

"My lady, I asked, 'What is the favor'"? His question brought her back.

"Sister Ekaterina is from the convent at Chadra, in the Lebanese Mountains of Outremer. My brother promised the Mother Superior that she would return to the convent after we found someone to replace her, someone I could trust. God brought me the Faure family and Lisbetta Deslegador, but I need your help."

"As you said before, my lady."

"You are teaching Lisbetta our Catholic Faith. Could you also teach her to read God's Holy Word? Sister Ekaterina cannot, so I must ask others for that assistance. To have an attendant who can read and write would be a great boon for me, Father."

Lady Juviler's intense look bored in on the Black Friar even though she could not see him. Lisbetta sat with her back erect and her hands folded in her lap, looking slightly down.

Felipe studied the gentle, demure young peasant in training to be a servant. Has this Agnes of Outremer really converted Lisbetta the Cathar to the True Faith? Unlikely. The trollop loudly and proudly proclaimed herself a heretic on Easter Sunday, of all days.

Agnes, her too. The blind and crippled witch was up in the Sárdalo, no matter what her brother says. The three of them are laughing at God's Holy Church. You cannot be a part of their charade.

"My lady, it cannot be me. Father Dominic's Preaching Friars are to be mendicants, poor men. I have stayed too long in the castle. I am moving to the parish of St. Luke's so that I may live on alms and preach in the city."

"Who will be our priest, Father Felipe"?

"I shall remain as your priest, my lady, but I shall no longer live here. It is too comfortable. It is distracting me from God's purpose for my life."

"That is a disappointment for Lisbetta, Father." The girl reached out and took the hand of the Baroness. The women sat together, holding hands, yes, two trollops, one charade. They should stay with their spinning, as Etienne de Metz declared.

"May I make a suggestion, Father"?

Agnes is blind. She will not be spinning, unless it is the snares of the Devil. For you. Be careful.

"Please, my lady."

"You know of my friends who meet in St. John's Church. Both Rubea, the wife of Consul Bertholmeu

Migona, and their daughter Brunissende can read and write, Father. I can ask them to teach Lisbetta. I would like her to prepare a Book of Hours that we could use in our prayers together."

"What is the work of this Bertholmeu that he has allowed his women to learn such things"? Agnes felt herself stiffening, but through her hand she felt Lisbetta actually preparing to rise. She squeezed, hard. Lisbetta stayed down.

"He is a tanner, Father. He scrapes and stretches the hides to prepare the parchment for the monks to write. In turn, they taught his family the letters." Agnes put her hand over her moth, took it away. "All five Consuls are faithful Catholics, Father. There is no mischief here."

Felipe had not missed the witch's squeeze, controlling the heretic's temper. Yet Father Dominic would proclaim that the deceitful Baroness had offered the Lord an opportunity, through him.

"I will agree to that, my lady, if I may be permitted to join your group, to teach you, to guide you away from heresy and into the true faith. I do not wish to stand outside in the rain like Sir Giles."

Agnes smiled. "You will find our discussion of the spinning and weaving you admonished us to pursue, you will find that boring, Father. The foolishness of husbands and the problems of children and the sicknesses in our families, tedious. But the women will be more than glad to welcome you for a period each time, to be schooled in matters of faith. As I said at Easter dinner, we value knowledge and learning here. We will be grateful for your help."

Silence prevailed for a moment while the priest considered her gentle reproach. *Do not engage her, for what is important here is the chance to guide. To that, she has agreed.* "Very well, my lady."

Agnes smiled. "Lisbetta. Please escort Father Felipe downstairs."

She listened as the girl led the priest away. The door closed behind them, leaving the Baroness with the sound of rain and the scent of candles.

That was brash again, Agnes, perhaps too brash. You believed that you could visit the Cathars and not be caught. You were wrong. Now you have taken another risk, letting this priest into your circle. Lisbetta will be watched, you will be watched, Hugh will be watched, Ekaterina will be watched. Now we must add lies to lies, and there are already plenty of lies. She bowed her head.

Forgive me, Lord Jesus, but this sanctimonious priest offends me, his certainty that You have revealed some special knowledge only to him. I let my arrogance overcome my humility in the yard, blaspheming with Mary and Martha and the Magdalene. He is a dangerous enemy. I must not match my arrogance against his, ever again.

The door opened to the scent of Ekaterina. "I wish to be alone, Sister. Please close the door and wait outside. No one is to enter unless I summon them."

"Yes, my lady." Agnes heard the door swing shut.

Forgive me, Lord Jesus, forgive me for not accepting Your will for me, my blindness, my useless legs. Just once I wanted to go out again like everyone else, ride a horse, feel the sun, smell the flowers, pretend that I could still swim in the pool in the little glade. I used poor Lisbetta as an excuse to satisfy my own pride, my Savior. For my own vanity, I rode up the Sárdalo Pass Road, and now we are all threatened again.

"Agnes? Agnes? Am I interrupting your devotions again? It's time for supper."

She woke up with a start. "Hugh? Hugh, I'm so ashamed, brother."

"Ashamed? Why? Father Felipe told me that he agreed to your request."

"The Holy Father awarded you a great victory on the road outside Fonta, my lord Count. The King of France is not happy, Bishop Jerome is not happy, Felipe is not happy, those Épernays are not happy. They are all waiting for an excuse to resume the Crusade. I gave them one, if they can only prove that I was helping the Cathars."

Hugh kissed her cheek again, but she didn't smile. "My victory came because Maura's cousin the Count won a greater victory. They'll need more than a story about something that never happened to get the King of France interested in crusading against us all. I'll send in your maids. You need to dress for supper. Stop worrying, Aggie."

Agnes sat on her stool while the two women undid her day tunic and put on one for the evening. Their hands moved over her, holding, pulling, tying, buckling.

Her brother, just like a man to be so proud, so assured. She remembered Jamilla's words, describing the trail above the Sárdalo Pass Road.

"The mountains are rugged, Agnes, and the road narrow, with many trees bearing in on us."

3

Count Oddo built the original St John's Church late in the ninth century as Alberensa spread to fill the space between the pilgrimage church and his grandfather Roland's castle. By the time Oddo's own grandson, Angibert the Builder, finished his new castle, St. John's had grown to be a thriving quarter of his city. A new parish church rose in the village square near the Avenue of Our Lady.

For two centuries, the Quarter's residents worshipped in the Builder's sanctuary, until fire struck during the Glassmaker's rule. The blaze weakened a wall, causing it to collapse and bringing the roof down with it. The second Angibert took the rubble as a sign from God. He tore down the Builder's brick and replaced the church with stone.

The new building could hold five hundred worshippers, far less than Our Lady of the Pyrenees. Although smaller, it mimicked perfectly the French style of the newly rebuilt cathedral at St. Denis, north of Paris, and the work underway in Paris itself. The upper wall, the clerestory, showed more glass than stone, a lightness on which the high peaked roof seemed to float. Groined vaulting in the ceiling, delicately woven with massive stone, linked the arches. Outside, bridged buttresses, flying buttresses, carried the load of the roof to the ground below.

The Norman craftsman Garnier, the Master of Alberensa, matched the soaring space of the new church's architecture with the beauty of its stained glass. He filled the windows on the main floor, the nave, with stunning depictions of the Gospel of St. John.

In the first space to the left upon entering, John the Baptist preached the coming of Christ, the opening story in the Gospel. "I baptize you with water," the Baptist said, "but one is coming after me the thong of whose sandal I am not worthy to untie. He will baptize you with the Holy Spirit." In the luminescent glass, John spilled the water of the Jordan River on the man Jesus, and the earthly ministry of the Divine Son of God began.

On the wall opposite the Baptism, the glass recounted the Day of Pentecost. The Disciples sit in an upper room, bereft and alone after the Ascension of Jesus into Heaven. The glass captured the moment when the Holy Spirit descended on them, baptizing them in brilliantly colored tongues of fire, just as the Baptist foretold.

Above the nave windows, in the clerestory, Moses, Elijah, Isaiah, Amos, prophets and martyrs looked down on the worshipers. Over the altar, the Risen Christ reigned in majesty with his right hand raised in eternal blessing.

The figures in all the windows were so delicate, the ornamentation so freighted with symbolism and the vitrine so intense in its deep blues and scarlet reds and verdant greens that the Very Presence of God found Incarnation in the glass. The Light of St John's shone in the darkness, and the darkness could not overcome it.

Of all the windows in the nave, only the Day of Pentecost did not fit the pattern. The Baptism by the Holy Spirit, the Consolation of the Disciples, is from Acts, not John. Hugh believed that the Master begged permission to create the window for some unknown reason, even though it did not fit. Count Angibert favored the Master with his permission as a man always favors an unusual request from his deepest and truest love.

The final Gospel window swept away any doubt. There, captured in the sunlight forever, the Magdalene turns from the empty tomb to speak to the gardener. He calls her name, "Mary," and she recognizes Him as the Risen Christ. Even on the coldest days, the affection between Jesus and Mary warmed the glass.

■ ■ ■

Lo Cercle de San Juan, St. John's Circle, sat in their circle in the crossing beneath the high altar. "Perhaps I am vain, brother," Agnes told Hugh, "but I don't want to be pushed there in my wheelchair." Hugh directed that his men carry the Baroness to the church and place her in a chair before the others arrived. Sister Ekaterina sat at her side as another woman, not a servant. Sir Giles and his men always waited in the street, although after a time, the women let them inside when it was raining. That boon was the only deference that the Circle gave to their noble companion. No one bowed towards her as they entered, kissed her ring or addressed her by her title. In this place at this time, she was Agnes Alberensa, nothing more.

No real agenda marked these informal meetings, although a collection was always taken to alleviate the suffering of the poor. Some women brought craft work, sewing and knitting, to busy their hands while they chatted. Julia Teissendièr, the wife of a weaver and a weaver herself, led the Circle with the consent of the others.

"Our sister Agnes asks permission for the Preaching Friar Felipe to join us, sisters. He worries that we are discussing sacred matters without proper guidance. Agnes promised him that opportunity if he allowed us to teach our sister Lisbetta to read and write."

The plump older woman looked around her flock, waiting for Martha Legros, the baker's wife, to object. She was not disappointed.

"Lisbetta does not need the permission of some priest if she wishes to learn to read and write."

Julia said nothing, waiting for Rubea Migona.

"We all know the problems that this priest can cause to Agnes and her brother. If Father Felipe tells the Holy Father that Alberensa is led by heretics, France will arrive to claim our County as his own. Louis the Lion will not be interested in the rights of our Count, or of our *Capitolum*, or of the Consuls themselves, or of our *Cercle*, or of the protection that we offer to those who are Good Christians. My husband Bertholmeu asks that we let him preach to us, for our own good. Then Brunissende and I can teach Lisbetta, as Agnes wishes."

Murmurings followed, and agreement.

"Ekaterina, please ask the Father to join us," Julia said. The fifteen women sat quietly while the nun made her way to the door. In a moment, she was back, leading the Black Friar to his chair. He looked around his congregation, sat and arranged his papers.

"My lady the Baroness of Juviler, I thank you for this opportunity…." Julia surprised him when she cut him off.

"There is no Baroness of Juviler among us, Father Felipe. Here we are a group of friends, equals, who have asked me to lead them. Which I will do until they ask someone else. Our sister Agnes told us of your desire to guide us, and we have agreed."

The blind Baroness sat with her hands in her lap, looking towards Julia. She wore a tunic of dark red wool, a girdle of simple leather. Plain, like the commoners she was with. Something is different, and then Felipe noticed that she was not in her wheelchair.

"My name is Julia Teissendièr, Father."

The woman's words brought Felipe back. "Equals? That is the Cathar way, *Dòna* Teissendièr. They have no respect for title, for station."

"'There is neither Jew nor Greek,'" the young Brunissende Migona replied, "'There is neither slave nor free, there is neither male nor female, for you are all one in Christ Jesus.' The words of Saint Paul, Father, not my words." Brunissende's dark eyes took the blue of the Preaching Friar, challenging him, waiting for his rebuttal.

"Brunissende, was that you Brunissende"? Agnes asked. "Should we not let Father Felipe guide us, sister? He may want to begin somewhere other than Paul's Letter to the Galatians."

"I agree with Agnes," Julia said. "We have asked the Father to join us. Let us listen to him, not argue with him."

Yes, Felipe realized, knowledge without faith can be a dangerous thing, leading men to sin. Some in this Circle must be heretics. They deny our Lord's Incarnation, His Resurrection. How does Satan work such evil, causing people to believe falsely?

God came to earth as a man to bring mankind to Himself. He could not do that unless He came to earth. The ancient witnesses, the Creeds are all clear that Jesus was born from the Virgin Mary, died and was raised again from the dead. He was not a vision, a thing of air, as the Cathars believe.

The priest bowed his head. Lord, give me the strength to be patient. Give me the patience to persevere. Give me the perseverance to fight this battle until Your victory is secured. Yours, O Lord, is the kingdom and the power and the glory for ever and ever!

Amen.

Felipe looked up at the Circle, all middle-aged women, mostly plump from motherhood. The young ones were this Brunissende, the Maronite who speaks no French and Baroness Trollop.

Begin.

"The glass in this church is most remarkable. I don't think I've ever seen any as beautiful, even in Rome."

"It was executed by a northerner we call the Master of Alberensa, Father," Julia said, "perhaps fifty years ago. This church is a place of great beauty, and a place where all in our Circle can feel secure."

All? In John's Gospel, there is no Nativity story, no story of the birth, the Incarnation of Jesus. He simply appears as an adult with John the Baptist at the River Jordan. The Pentecost window, that is the Baptism by the Holy Spirit, the only sacrament of the Cathars, their *Consolamentum*. Felipe wondered if this Master of Alberensa was a heretic himself. He looked at the Resurrection window, a most beautiful Mary Magdalene with the Risen Lord. Perhaps not.

"Let us begin with this strange notion of re-incarnation. The Albigensians do not believe that death is followed by the resurrection of the just into Heaven and the descent of the condemned into Hell. They believe that we live in Hell here, in Satan's realm, on earth. The punishment for sin is that a man, after he dies, is reborn again on this earth, this world of evil. The only way to escape this Hell is by prayer, by sacrifice and suffering, until one has made oneself worthy to be admitted to Heaven."

"I have always wondered about that," Julia volunteered. "We all know that a person, having died, stays dead. Certainly if we had all lived before, we would remember something of it. At least that is my view, Felipe."

She dropped his title, but at least he had their attention. Strength, patience, perseverance. "That may be true, Julia, but even more importantly, there is nothing in Holy Scripture that speaks of reincarnation."

"I wonder, Felipe," Agnes said. "Can a man really try hard enough to find God on his own? Don't the Scriptures teach that it is only through Jesus that we can find God"?

"Yes, my lady…. Yes, Agnes, very good. 'I am the Way, and the Truth, and the Life,' Jesus said. 'No one comes to the Father, except through me.' Let's talk about what that means."

Agnes sat quietly after that, letting the priest lead his flock. All went well until Julia thought to ask,

"Why do they believe these things? They are not in the Scriptures."

"They have false books," Felipe answered. "Books that the Holy Church has rejected because they are not from the time of Our Lord. Books that are filled with lies." The priest swept the air with his arm, as though he was pushing the false books from a table. "Twice Father Dominic put his own writings and the Albigensian books into a fire. Once at Fanjeaux. Once at Montréal. Both times Father Dominic's books flew up, spared from the flames, while the false Cathar books were consumed by God in the conflagration."

"Is that your breviary, Felipe?" Martha asked.

"It is."

"I have a copy of the Gospel of Thomas. I will throw that Gospel on a fire, right here, right now, if you will put your breviary there, too."

4

Father Ricartz prayed the Mass alone on a Monday morning. At the Offertory, he gave thanks to God for all the gifts that followed the truce in June. Baron Ferrandos replaced Sir Martin in Fonta castle. The Faure family returned to build the Count's new iron-works in the Trysting Glade. Workers and men-at-arms flooded the village, too many for this old stone rectangle.

"I'll build you a new church, Father," Baron Ferrandos announced, "A beautiful building like sant Sernan in Tolosa, like the Cathedral in Compostela, brick with rounded arches and large windows and beautiful glass." Ricartz spent his days imagining the dancing rhythms of red and green and gold that would soon illuminate his new floor.

"Accipite, et manducate ex hoc omnes," he recited. He elevated the Host.

"Hoc est enim Corpus meum."

The priest took the cup of wine. *"Accipte, et bibite ex eo omnes."* He lifted the chalice.

"Hic est enim Calix Sanguinis mei, novi et æterni testamenti: mysterium fidei."

Ricartz set the cup on his altar.

"Are you finished yet, priest"? Ricartz turned around to find Sir Arnald leering at him. The knight must have listened at the door, waiting to ensure that he arrived at the most sacred moment in the whole Mass. "Am I interrupting"?

"Not me, my lord, but our Heavenly Father."

"I'm sure He will forgive me, because I bring you important news." Arnald's serfs knew their liege as a bully and a coward, a man who avoided every fight. If the Lord awarded fiefs only to the worthy, Arnald would never have inherited Brassat and Ganat. "You are honored by an important guest today, Father."

"Has the Baron brought the Count"? By awarding Fonta to Ferrandos, a man who was worthy, the Count made him Arnald's master. Arnald protested to the Count about his decision to set a commoner over a family long noble. The Count ignored him.

"Not him, Father Ricartz," with more leering. "No, an old friend, Father, an old friend."

The Evangelist Door banged open. Sir Charles of Épernay strode in, accompanied by a Black Friar. If Arnald was a trained fighter who never fought, Charles was a trained fighter who never stopped fighting. He was a terrible disease in winter, a pestilence spreading death wherever he went. And he was in Brassat again despite the truce.

"What can you tell us of the serf girl Prisca Formatgièr, priest"? In Brassat again with the same threatening, arrogant tone that lacked any respect for the work of God's Holy Church. Ricartz turned to the Preaching Friar.

"Sir Arnald arrived just as I consecrated the elements, Father. As the Fourth Lateran proclaims, the Very Body and Blood of our Lord Jesus Christ now lie on the altar. Help me complete the Mass, please."

The itinerant preacher genuflected, crossed himself and stepped to the stone table with Ricartz. The temporary delay while the parish priest finished the Canon brought Ricartz no enlightenment, no ideas on how to avoid the double plague of Arnald and Charles.

The Mass ended. "Thank you, Father...."

"Felipe." The Preaching Friar rose to his full height. "The Holy Father has charged me to root out this Cathar heresy in Alberensa, Father Ricartz. I am about that business in Brassat."

Charles repeated his question. "What can you tell us of the serf girl Prisca Formatgièr, priest"?

"She is the Baroness Prisca of Fonta now, my lord, married to Baron Ferrandos in the Cathedral of Our Lady of the Pyrenees three months ago. Her family departed on pilgrimage for Santiago de Compostela right after the service. Others in Brassat are tending their strips at the order of the Baron."

Charles shoved Ricartz into a chair and glowered over him. "Why do you always try my patience, priest! I know where she is. Is she a heretic, Father, an Albigensian, as Sir Arnald claims"?

"When they are here, her family faithfully attends services every Sunday."

The Black Friar pulled at his black cape. "Is that really true"? His tone knew it was not. "What of their home, their behavior? There are rumors they go to a secret meeting place in the hills above this village. It's said that your church steeple is a landmark showing the way for those hell-bound atheists."

"I know nothing of that, Father Felipe."

"Then you are the only one in this hell-bound village who does not, Father Ricartz"! Passion brought fire like the new furnaces in the Glade to Felipe's eyes. "This heresy threatens Christ's One Holy Catholic and Apostolic Church, Father! Everywhere I go in this accursed Languedoc, I find clergy like you, clergy who look the other way. Who let the Cathars promise to build a new church if the priest pretends to know nothing! The Holy Father has given me authority to punish priests who shield heretics, Ricartz, and I will do it"!

All the beautiful stained glass to come dissolved into Arnald's smirk. Charles licked his lips and breathed harder, carnally passionate at the promise of violence. "Do you remember what happened to the heretic Alass, Father"? Épernay leaned over the priest and pulled him up by his cassock. "Don't make his mistake and force us to burn you, too." A shove, and Ricartz was in his seat again.

"I will stay with you some days, Ricartz," Felipe announced, "living on the alms of the people of Brassat and Ganat. I will find this secret hiding place. I will preach to your Cathars and save their souls from this heresy. Show me where I might sleep."

Arnald, Charles and now the Preaching Friar, three plagues descending upon Brassat. It made no sense to protest.

"This way, Father Felipe."

Ricartz took the Black Friar through the small door in the apse that led towards his humble serf's cottage.

■ ■ ■

Charles stopped Arnald in the square before the church. The villagers remembered Épernay's many searches for the Mark of Satan. They stayed inside.

"Best if we leave for my manor before the Count's men pass by again, Sir Charles." The knight bristled at the idea of retreat. "We are two. Ferrandos has many."

Charles did not reply. He simply mounted his horse and started for Ganat, forcing Arnald to trot quickly after him.

"This new ironworks of Alberensa is most intriguing," Charles said once Arnald caught up. "The men at

Farga de san Matèu say he is building something new, something different."

"Then the Count of Foix confirmed your ownership, my lord"?

"No. The Papal Legate confirmed it as forfeit under the Third Canon, but he awarded it to Roger-Bernard." They rode a few steps further. "Without the heretic Deslegador in charge, no one seems to know exactly how to bring the iron from the rock. Roger-Bernard has let most of the men return to farming. The remaining few run nothing more than a black-smith shop for their count."

Arnald grew wary, cautious. "I know nothing of ironmaking, Sir Charles."

Charles glared at him, scorn for the coward. "No, but we can find men who do. You can shelter them, protect them, help them find work in the Brassat foundry. If there is new magic, we will learn what it is."

Arnald grew silent at the fear he was being drawn into a dispute that had not ended with the agreement on the road. "To go against my new liege or his liege, that is felony, Sir Charles. The penalty is forfeiture of my estates and death."

Arnald received the fury last directed at Ricartz. "My father will have Fonta back, Sir Arnald! It is not a large fief, or rich, but this new foundry is turning it into a prize. The weakling Count will build it and we will take it, because Hugh has granted Fonta to a commoner married to a heretic."

"Will it not then be forfeit to the Count"?

"You test my patience, Arnald"! Charles took a moment to regain his patience. He needed this coward. "Help us by concealing these men, my lord, and you may receive Fonta yourself."

"What of Sir Martin? Will he not want it back"?

"Sir Martin feels that his insults against the blind and crippled heretic shamed his honor. He apologized to her champion Sir Giles and his apology was accepted. Sir Martin believes himself honor-bound not to molest the Count or the Witch Agnes over the matter of Fonta. He even argued against my visit today, but Baron Henri lacks an arm because of Brassat. He will have his vengeance."

"The Baroness of Juviler is a Catholic, Sir Charles, from the County of Tripoli."

Charles shook his head. Land and revenge mattered, not truth. He had forgotten how cowardly and stupid this man really was.

"You are wrong, Sir Arnald. Father Felipe received a holy vision of Satan's Baroness Harlot taking the *Consolamentum* in the Sárdalo Pass." Charles grinned at the insulted Friar's convenient theophany. "Agnes is a heretic. Her brother shields her. Serf Prisca of Fonta is a heretic. Ferrandos shields her. Watch Prisca. Find witnesses. Prove that she is a Cathar and Fonta could be yours."

Arnald shrugged. "Find witnesses? No one is willing to talk."

Charles galloped ahead a moment, turned and rode back to Arnald, drawing up face to face. "Everyone talks on the rack, Sir Arnald, everyone"! Arnald tried to look away from the violence, and failed. "Rack your Brassat serfs! Find someone who says what we need said, and soon"!

"My lord, Ferrandos will…"

Charles drew his war sword and place the point against Arnald's coif. "Send word to us in Limoux once you have extracted a suitable confession, one that is satisfactory to the Black Friar. The Blind Cripple played him for a fool, so that won't be very hard."

"Yes," Arnald said, his eyes fixed firmly on the steel at his throat.

"Good." The sword disappeared. "I'll ride with you to Ganat before I leave. The second cottage on the right, I think that girl actually enjoyed me."

5

Maura leaned towards Hugh at the supper table and whispered in his ear. "I am very late, my lord. My desire for you has produced the desired result. I am with child."

He turned and whispered back, "Are you certain, my lady"?

She leaned away from him at the supper table with a broad grin, a smirk, a face filled with happiness and satisfaction. "Yes." Hugh, too, felt happiness at the surprise news of his coming heir, someone to assure the line of Julian and Monica, of Count Roland the Founder, of Ermessenda of Juviler.

"That's wonderful news, Maura, wonderful. I'm happy for you, happy for us." They smiled at each other while he looked out at the Great Hall where the household was dining. "Do you wish for me to announce…."

She shook her head vigorously, no. "No, my lord, it is too soon. Things can still go wrong. Perhaps in a month, but not tonight. I would like to send word to my parents first."

The Count looked at his sister, further down the table. Sister Ekaterina busied herself as she always did, cutting morsels for Agnes and placing them on her trencher. "May we inform the Baroness of Juviler? She'll be very happy, too."

Maura looked at the ground, embarrassed. "Forgive me, Hugh, but I told her first. I don't know why, but we were talking this afternoon in her room, and I told her. I wasn't going to tell anyone for another month, but once I told her, I had to tell you." She drew herself up now, a Countess, not a confidante. "Only one thing mars my happiness at such happy news, Hugh. Which is why I told you down here, not in my bedchamber."

"What is that, Maura"? He was confused, or maybe not.

"The purpose of the wedding bed is procreation, my lord, not lust. I still desire you, but Our Lord requires that I contain myself, and that you do so as well. Our heir is in my womb." She took his hand and placed it there, for just a moment. "It is a great burden, I know, for both of us, but we can bear it together. Bear it, and receive God's most beautiful gift when the snows melt from *Lo Grandautar* next June."

■ ■ ■

The candles bounced delicately off the stone walls, as if they knew they were in a woman's room. The air held a scent of perfume from the Orient, from the bazaars of Damascus. The Maronite sister waited on her bed in a thin and gauzy black gown, not her habit. The candlelight flowed through the Damascene fabric to reveal the fullness of her breasts and her slender waist and her shapely legs. It glinted against her dark hair and shined off her tumbled tresses.

The door opened, and the Count of Alberensa entered the room, and her heart leaped for joy.

"God the All-Compassionate has answered my prayers, my husband." Jamilla walked towards Hugh with her body silhouetted in the light, pleased to see that he was excited by the sight of her, just as she was excited by the sight of him. He pulled her softness close, feeling the Saracen melt against him as her arms went around his back. "Kiss me, my beloved." Her face turned up, eyes closed, and he did as she asked, embracing, as they stumbled back towards her bed.

"Your spirit and your beauty never fail to amaze me, Jamilla. Your father did not know it, but he brought me a gift from God." He was undressing now, lifting off tunic and cotte, pulling down his hose. She sat, entranced as his nakedness grew. "Or maybe he did, the wily old fox."

Her breath quickened. "You are the victor, beloved, and tonight at last I shall have you for my own." She put her hand lightly on the side of his face. "You have protected our people from the King of France and from the Leader of the Infidels." She kissed him now, her hands on the side of his face, her lips soft and full against his. "And you have built your beloved furnace in Brassat, my darling."

Hugh lifted the gown over her head, watching her breasts rise and fall. She leaned her full hips back onto the bed, waiting. "We call him the Pope, Jamilla, the Holy Father, His Holiness."

"I am calling you to this bed, now, my husband. Your devotion to your first wife's needs has deprived me of your affections for too long." She had the most sensual and seductive pout that he had ever seen on any woman, ever. "One night without you is too long, and it has been months, since the Infidel Easter, when you left to besiege Fonta." He lay down alongside her, their bodies melting together, embracing, touching.

"It has been far too long indeed, my love."

Within seconds, they clung together, mouth on mouth, their bodies desperately trying to join two into one. Hugh felt her soft Arabian hand reaching to his groin, finding him beyond firm, placing him in, oh!

"Ahbak ya, Hugh, 'ana 'ahbik"! Her wonderful scent flowed over him as his passion grew, their bodies moving together, *"Nem! Nem! Akthr'! Akthr'"!* Yes, more indeed as he felt himself rising rising rising.

"AAAAAHHHHHHHH"! They exploded together, Hugh delivering as Jamilla closed upon him in a rippling surge that brought screams from her throat, "AAAAHHHHHH"!

Their passion spent, they lay side by side, satisfied lovers, satisfied friends. "Aggie told me about the Gravid Cow of Tolosa and my heart filled with joy, Hugh. I was sure that meant we would finally be together again. I want you for my own, and now I have you for my own."

"Why is that"?

She rolled and knelt up over him in the full bloom of her youthful beauty. Her full black hair, dark eyes alight with fire, her brown skin still soft and fresh at nineteen. The nose of the Syrians, not so large on her, the high cheekbones of the inhabitants of the Holy Land. Her breasts hung near his face while she leaned over to pin his wrists.

"Because I love you, you fool. I want you all the time, day, night, winter, summer, all the time always forever."

"You are a shameless Saracen harlot."

"I am not, my precious Infidel." Her pout brought forth guilt at a comment so cruel, a knife to his heart, as she intended. "I am your second wife, in the way of our people." He put his hands on Jamilla's sensuous thighs while she squeezed them in, riding her Frankish Arabian. "Do you love me, my noble lord? I love you more than I could ever love anyone. Tell me you love me and only me."

"I love you, Jamilla bint Hassan al-Haddad. As you well know." He leaned up and kissed her. "I thought you told me that we could have a relationship like in Syria. Your father has four wives. You are only my second."

He felt the fullness of her breasts on his chest as she buried her face against him and kissed his neck. "That does not mean that the wives are not jealous of each other, Hugh. The old of the young. The ugly of the pretty. The Saracen Harlot of the Frankish Countess. They all wait for the call to the harem, to see who is the favored wife for the night."

"Tonight my beautiful Arabian, tonight it has been you."

"Yes." She sat back up over him again and smiled. "What do you think the real Ekaterina is doing tonight, Hugh"?

"Praying, of course." He reached up to fondle her breasts. "I promised your father to take care of you, but a Saracen would not be safe inside Jabil al-Hadid, or perhaps even with the Maronites. And a Saracen would not be safe in Europe, either, unless we traveled to *al-Andalus*."

"Clever of you, my love, realizing that my abaya and hijab and niqab meant that no one had seen anything but my eyes. I entered the Chadra convent as Jamilla bint Hassan al-Haddad and emerged as Sister Ekaterina, just as Agnes emerged from the Sisters of Charity as the Leper Boy of the Sárdalo Pass."

"The real Ekaterina accepted it all as the Will of God."

"Yes." Jamilla pinned his wrists again. "When did you know"?

"That we would fall in love"?

"Yes."

"When we looked into each other's eyes while you held the reins."

At first, Hugh and Ekaterina held their impossible feelings even from themselves, to say nothing of each other. They strained to make polite conversation in the presence of Agnes. Until the day a year ago when Hugh reached up, pulled off her nun's cowl, and told her she was beautiful. Two months later, sitting with Agnes on the roof of the Keep, Jamilla removed her habit and dropped it to the ground. Underneath, she was wearing his sister's red tunic with the red and black silk panels, the one that was tighter and showed her shape in the bodice. Her passion, her fire, her fully revealed Syrian beauty stunned him. Her intention was clear, in case their conversations had left any doubts. This was the permitted look of the bridegroom before the wedding, so that he could see what he had negotiated to marry. That night, they consummated their union. Jamilla became his second wife.

"You have gone silent, my noble lord. Are you pining for The Cow? Tell me no, no, no." More pouting as he rolled her over and kissed her.

"No. I was thinking about the bolt that struck us both outside Jabil al-Hadid."

Jamilla propped herself up on her elbow and drew circles on his stomach. "I told you I could share, because I thought I could. I thought I understood, but I'm jealous. More jealous than I ever thought. My father put me under your protection, and I accepted his command even though you are an Infidel."

She lay back down and put her face against his neck while she wiggled and snuggled closer to his body and pulled the covers over them both. "Now I find that I never want to be away from you, Hugh, ever. It was God's will for me. It was why He let that man attack me, in Homs. So that I would be with you." A pause while she kissed his neck, ran her finger over his chest. "In Homs they would say I'm a harlot and a fornicator, and they would be right. But I'm sure that the All-Merciful God plans for us to be together as a proper husband and wife, someday."

Hugh lay on his side holding her while Jamilla drifted off. She gave one more little wiggle, pulling herself even closer, so that he felt her breasts rising and falling against him. She might awaken in an hour or two, and they would make love again. And perhaps again in the morning. As they did every time she received the call to the harem. As she had almost every night for a year, until Maura informed him that she might feel the lust for an heir in the morning.

The morning after that night a month ago, his beautiful Saracen appeared as Ekaterina with a most un-Christian pout for a woman of the cloth. "Wait upstairs"! she hissed in barely comprehensible French. "All night! Alone! Without husband"! The Cow of

Toulouse had triumphed over al-Haddad and she did not even know it.

Clever Agnes had known all along. She shrugged her shoulders on the morning after Hugh's second wedding night.

"What do you think Guilhabert was doing with Mariam before they were married, Hugh? I'm blind, but that doesn't mean that I can't see that you two have been in love for a long time." She pushed her finger into his stomach, surprising him. "It's another place where men have the advantage over us, my lord Count. You are a man with a mistress, but Lady Saissouq is a harlot."

"There is a…"

"Difference"? *Al-Zarqa'* flared and snorted. "I will not bless it, but Jamilla bint Hassan is most helpful to me, Hugh, most helpful. I will have her happy. And you are most loving to me. I will have you happy. Just be careful."

Yes, it was unfair, Hugh thought as Jamilla began to move against him again, and he against her. If Maura discovered his sins with Sister Ekaterina, there would be a tantrum, followed by a reminder to do his duty to her and to Toulouse. To sleep with her and produce many heirs. If Father Felipe could prove that Agnes had gone to the Cathars, there might be war. Which was the greater sin?

6

The Baroness of Fonta sat beside Guilhelms on the wagon. The Baron rode alongside. Sunlight glistened from the first snow on the distant Pyrenees and colored the changing leaves of the trees, yellows and reds mixed in with the browns and pale greens. Although quite beautiful, the cold late October day only made Guilhelms feel the approach of winter. He pulled his cloak tightly around his neck. At least winter will freeze the road hard, making it easier to bring heavy loads down from the furnace. As long as there was no snow.

"Do you like my new tunic, Guilhelms"? Prisca wore a deep green of fine wool with a matching surcoat. The fabric caressed her shapely hips. Her leather girdle with its silver buckle revealed her slender waist. She topped her new clothes with a winter cloak of red fox fur. Deerskin gloves covered her hands.

"It's very nice, my lady."

Prisca's green eyes kept flirting as she turned her lissome beauty towards her driver. "How come you didn't accept a title from the Count, Guilhelms? He believes that you are of his family. You could have anything." The deerskin pulled at the edge of the fox, adjusting it against the wind, delicately, like a lady. A family of Brassat serfs on the road bowed as they passed by. She waved them on their way.

The smith's guilt burbled up again. O Lord my God, when Henri of Épernay drove my family from Brassat, I was only a village blacksmith. Time and chance has made me the Count's most trusted commoner, in charge of his most important smelter. Others may starve, but Aenor and Tibaut and Isabèl will never be hungry, never be wet, never be cold. This is how Satan the Evil One works his evil ways among men, stealing their souls with wealth and power. It is the way of the world, but it troubles my soul, O God.

"I asked you a question, Guilhelms."

Time and chance made Sir Ferrandos the liege lord of three knights. Time and chance straightened the bent back of the serf Prisca Formatgièr. Her family received the produce of their own strip but no longer worked the fields themselves. Instead, they went on pilgrimage to Santiago de Compostela while others harvested their crops and stored them neatly away.

"Guilhelms"! Both seductive and petulant at the same time.

"Do not trouble the smith with that, my lady," Ferrandos answered. "Guilhelms has taken many risks for the Count, but he is not a warrior. So he does not have a title."

The mule stopped on its own in front of the blacksmith shop. "Here we are, my lady. Aenor is inside with Eva. They will be honored by your visit." Guilhelms climbed down from the wagon and walked around as his front door opened. "Our lady of Fonta is calling, Aenor."

He lifted Prisca to the ground. She clung to him just a little longer than was necessary to regain her balance, feeling the strength in his arms. A mischievous smile crossed her face as she laid her gloved hand against his face. "I had a great desire for this smith, my lord, two years ago. I was jealous of Aenor. I even cried when he disappeared. How foolish of me."

Aenor and Eva curtsied in their coarse brown as she swept into the house. The door closed behind them. Guilhelms smiled at the sight. "Her new estate becomes her, my lord. She is more spirited and more beautiful than ever."

Ferrandos frowned. "Indeed."

Knight and smith rode slowly through Brassat, past the village church and up the new road above the Barièja. The serfs had cut a path away from the river, through the trees, along the side of the hill. Noise joined the ever-present plume of smoke as they climbed, a rush of wind that overwhelmed the gentle

gurgling of the stream below and the roar of the waterfall above the Trysting Glade.

"Just a few minutes more, my lord," Guilhelms
said as the edge of the Glade came into view. No more
infants would be created in that pleasant green on
starry summer nights. Packed dirt replaced soft grass,
filled with the Count's ironworks and guarded from
spies by the Count's men-at-arms. Brush obscured the
path uphill to the old mines. No doubt a new route
led from Brassat to the Cathar hiding places, but
Guilhelms would not be told where it was. He was too
close to Their Lordships.

"We are here, my lord Baron."

No smelter ever built by Jabil al-Hadid looked like
the one at Brassat. A second furnace of brick and stone
stood alongside the smelting furnace. Water flowed
down a wooden aqueduct, a flume, from above the
waterfall. A wheel turned in the falling stream from
the flume, cranking a huge bellows that fanned the
flames of the second furnace. Its chimney came out
the side, not the top, so that the hot smoke from the
fire could enter the bottom of the smelter furnace.

"It is loud here, Guilhelms."

The smelter roared like a town set on fire during
a siege, the noise of whole buildings burning at once,
the rush of smoke pouring out of the top of the tower
like air whistling through a giant cave. Guilhelms
had named this creation well. They had built a blast
furnace.

Work stopped as the Baron rode into the space. The ringing forges fell silent as the smiths bowed to the lord but the roar of the furnace went on. The flowing water and the turning wheel and the pumping bellows did not bow to a mere mortal, not even a knight.

Ferrandos motioned before he dismounted. The hammers began ringing again.

"Have you ever seen us charge the smelter, my lord"? Ferrandos shook his head, no, as he opened his cloak. They were quite some distance from the blast furnace, but its heat was apparent, and he was feeling warm, even on a cool day. Dead trees lined the hillside across the Barièja. Smoke curled among the trees at the edge of the glade, poisoning them.

"Rothan, lead Sir Ferrandos' mount downstream. The flames discomfit him." The worker covered the eyes of the nervous animal and led it away.

"The tipple is bringing a fresh charge to the top of the smelting furnace, my lord." A cart rolled along an angled track from above the waterfall, climbing as it was pulled by ropes from the ground. A shout, a tug, and the hopper flipped up, dumping ore and limestone and charcoal into the top of the smelter. The heat sent the cold fear of damnation through Ferrandos. Hell must be like this, he thought, as fresh flames roared in a plume into the sky. This witchcraft kills the trees and poisons the ground and blots out the sun.

"Time to add wood, Guilhelms"! a fireman at the furnace called.

"Go ahead"!

Shouts and waves. Boards dropped in to block the water's entry to the flume. The wheel slowed as the full force of the stream surged in a wave over the waterfall. The roar in the furnace died. The workers flung open the Gates of Hell to receive a charge of timber. The firemen stayed to the side, cringing away from the fresh wave of heat as they threw in the wood.

The door slammed closed. "Finished"! the leader called.

"Open the flume"!

The boards went up, flooding the conduit, turning the wheel, starting the roar again. The falls dropped to a trickle, leaving glistening damp rock at the lip. The plume from the smelter puffed, then rose into the sky in a fresh wave of heat and stench.

Yes, my beloved Prisca, my Lady of Brassat, you are right. We need this metal, but this is Satan's work on his Satanic earth.

Guilhelms lifted a piece of the ore from a cart. "We are mining a rich vein, my lord," he said, pointing to the rusty color. "It seems to go on for quite a way, and it smelts into the pig iron very well." He pointed to another cart. "Come over there with me."

At the second car, the smith lifted a rock. "Some of the ore is lodestone." Guilhelms brought his rock towards a chunk of ore still in the cart. An unseen hand moved them together. Guilhelms lifted his rock and the other rock clung to it, hanging in the air.

"The ore does not cling to other ore, unless it is lodestone"?

"Unless it is iron. Lodestone does not draw tin or copper." Guilhelms reached into his pocket for a small chunk of metal. "Touch that with your sword." The chunk leaped up to the blade, clinking as it fastened on. "Careful, my lord as you pry it away. Don't cut your fingers."

Sir Ferrandos fingered his iron mail and looked at the rock in the cart. "I tried burning some of this ore on my hearth, Guilhelms. All I got was a hot rock."

The smith laughed. "Yes, my lord. It takes more than that. A lot more, actually."

Yes, it did, the knight knew. That was why the Count had ordered that this man's life, and his health, and his happiness be protected above all others. "Treat him as my son, Ferrandos."

"Yes, my lord Count," the knight had replied, "it shall be done as you command."

He must chastise his wife again about her behavior, as he had last night. "You should act as a noblewoman towards the serfs, Lady Prisca, to remind them who we are now, but treat the smith and his family as you would your liege. They have no titles, my love, but their station is higher than yours. You are not descended from Jabil al-Hadid, and you cannot make the iron."

Germain, the smelter foreman, approached at a quick pace. His obeisance towards Ferrandos was more of a nod than a bow. Sweat glistened on the man's brow even this cold day. The Count's pay fed Arnald's serfs well, making Germain freshly heavy from beer. With so much cash in the village, the ironworkers paid the farmers to perform their feudal obligations and went home to their cottages after work.

"It's time to tap the pig iron, Guilhelms."

"Pig iron?" Ferrandos asked as they walked towards the smelter.

"We let the molten iron run in this sand channel and then turn it into these separate sand squares. The flowing iron looks like piglets suckling at the mother." Guildhelms pointed towards the anvils and fires of the forge. "When the ingots harden, we teem them, that is, re-heat them in the blacksmith's forge, keep them soft and hot until we want to work them."

"Time, Guilhelms"! Germain called. "Now"!

"Step back now, my lord," Guilhelms said. "Go"!

Shouts, more shouts, the taps opened and the iron flowed out, coursing into its channels, scorching anything in its path that could burn. Living metal more white than red shimmered the air above it and puddled like water in the sand.

Always heat and now more heat. Ferrandos decided to spend his winter right here in the Trysting Glade. This infernal machine would keep the whole canyon warm, even on the coldest days. And there wouldn't be any smoke in his eyes. "Is it steel, Guilhelms"?

"No, my lord, we haven't done that, except by accident. There are too many variables, we think. We do get the metal hot enough to melt, even though there is less charcoal in the bloom. It's easier to make what comes out into steel, if we need to. Or to work the hot iron into shapes."

Guilhelms paused to look to the edge of the clearing, at the men cutting wood. "Germain. The man on the far right. Who is he"?

The foreman looked back from the molten metal, now cooling to red-hot. "Not sure. New today, from Ganat. We needed more help cutting wood."

"My lord. Have him brought here." Ferrandos merely moved his hand and three of Hugh's men-at-arms started over. The man looked up as they called, saw Guilhelms and ran for the stream. "Stop him. Don't kill him." Three crossbows launched and two bolts took the man in his left leg. He shrieked from the sudden pain and tumbled into the Barièja. The water tinged red from his blood as he struggled to climb up the far bank. "Bring him here."

The wheel turned and the furnace bellowed, but all the workers turned to watch as the soldiers dragged the wounded man to the Baron. Fear was the only emotion on the man's face, overwhelming even the rising pain as he was dragged over.

"I know this man, my lord Baron." Guilhelms laid his finger on the man's chest. "You're Izard. You worked for my cousin at his forge on the Ariège."

"No! No! I'm Ponce from Ganat! Help me! I'm bleeding to death"! Ferrandos motioned and one of the soldiers handed him a piece of wood. The knight dipped it into the molten iron and it burst into flame, flame that Ferrandos pushed into Izard's belly. The smell of burning meat joined his screams.

"Bring him along." The Baron and two men dragging Izard climbed the hill towards the clearing where the flume began.

"Back to work, Germain," Guilhelms said. "Épernay will get no secrets from him." The solid iron darkened in the pigs, but it was still far too hot to touch.

■ ■ ■

"I ordered the smelter shut down, Aenor, and the blast furnace disassembled, right away. Izard was the fourth spy from Épernay that we've caught up there. I don't want to be responsible for killing everyone in Farga, and I don't want the Count's secret to get out. Tibaut, stop teasing Isabèl."

"I'm not teasing, Papa. She likes this." Indeed, it did appear that the little girl with the white hair and the chubby arms was having a good time, as Tibaut dangled things in front of her and she tried to grab them. Squeals of delight could turn into shrieks of anguish so quickly, but not right now.

"So you're moving the mill to Petrousset now, not next Spring"? Aenor stood in her larger kitchen, built in the place that the forge had been. She stirred the broth and turned the pork. Cash was not in short supply in this house either. The daily pottage of the serfs, mostly vegetables and grains, that was behind them now.

"I surveyed the Alberensa below Petrousset before we came up here. There's a lake above a waterfall not far from the original smelter. We'll use the waterfall to run our wheel. A greater drop, a greater flow, we can build a more powerful furnace. Tibaut, careful. Let her catch one."

Aenor stirred. A whine became a squeal, and the game went on.

"It's unfortunate for Prisca and Ferrandos, love, but we have to move deeper into Alberensa. We won't be back to Brassat again. Isabèl. Hug for Papa, please, hug."

His arms went out and the little girl squealed even louder, toddled over, arms up, and waited to be lifted. "The workers, all of them, we have to take them to Petrousset with us. Their families, too. They all know the secrets. We can't leave them here. Isabèl, kiss." They smooched. "In three years, the Trysting Glade will be fit for trysting again."

"What happens to the fields"?

The little girl squirmed in his arms and snuggled into his lap. "It's Sir Arnald's right to distribute them among those who stay. The Count will be sure that Eva and her husband receive a big share. Sir Arnald will no doubt please Sir Ferrandos by giving other strips to Prisca's brother."

"She has definitely learned how to behave like our cousins the Count of Alberensa and the Baroness of Juviler, Guilhelms."

"Yes, but she's spending everything Ferrandos takes in on those clothes. He's living off rents and services from his vassals, and we're earning five times as much. Just don't let her know."

"Everyone in Brassat is laughing, because under her expensive clothes, she's a peasant with dirt between her toes."

"Whose newly ennobled husband can have a man whipped for saying so." He put Isabèl on the floor so that she could toddle around. "Their children will be in the nobility from the moment they're born. No one will laugh at them. They'll grow up thinking that the family has been noble back to the time of Charlemagne."

Aenor laughed, showing she was part of Everyone. Tibaut stretched up to look in the pot. "While your family stopped being noble right around the time of Count Roger-Bernard the Fat."

"Which is what our beloved Lady of Fonta aims to be, and soon, my love." Aenor stopped her stirring. Guilhelms looked up, stunned. A sheepish grin slowly crossed his face while a smile crossed hers. "Aenor"?

"Yes, my love." Tibaut moved out of the way as husband and wife embraced. "Three children, My Lord the Iron Maker of Petrousset, three children. We shall build a large stone house there, my love, a fine stone house, a manor house fit for a descendant of the Count of Foix."

7

Sister Ekaterina sat with Brother Marot in a little grove back from the Sárdalo Pass Road. A beautiful sunny day filtered down through the leafless trees, very warm for late November.

"You're distracted, husband. You're not enjoying this glorious day."

"I am." This little grove of trees has become our own special place, an earthly taste of the Paradise that awaits the true believers of her faith and mine.

"Why is that"?

Hugh did not want to leave, a thought that always brought to mind James, the James of Compostela, and his brother John, and Peter, with Jesus on the Mount of the Transfiguration. Moses and Elijah appeared with the Lord that day, in a burst of heavenly glory beyond anything that the disciples could ever imagine. "Let us build booths for Moses and Elijah, Lord," Peter said, "so that we may dwell here with them forever."

It could not be. An earthly ministry awaited Jesus as an earthly rule awaited Hugh. Neither man could stay.

The Count gathered Jamilla's softness closer as they sat among the fallen leaves. The bare branches of their tree overhead filtered the late autumn sunlight, but on the ground, the Sárdalo Pass Road could be seen through the trunks. "After today it will be too cold for Brother Marot and Sister Ekaterina to meet by accident in the churches and leave for prayerful walks up the Sárdalo Pass Road. Where they can now be seen by travelers who look this way, passing by."

"No more reading to each other, and talking, and then making love in the woods, you mean"? Jamilla knelt up over Hugh's outstretched legs, facing him, her favorite Arabian. "Lisbetta will be happy. She wonders why Agnes lets me go to pray so often, leaving her as the only maid."

"You are so clever, love."

The Second Countess favored her Count with a kiss. "My mother would be happy to hear you say that. That's what she said to my father."

Years ago in Homs, Safiya the maid had taken four-year-old Jamilla to see Hassan. "Your daughter will be beautiful, a prize for a great nobleman, Hassan," the one-time servant said. "She is bright and clever. You are wealthy. She will bring a large dowry to an important husband. She must be educated for her role."

Hassan looked at his beautiful Safiya. He looked at the little brown-eyed vixen holding her hand. "Yes, my love, she shall be taught to read and write and figure."

Hugh took Jamilla's hands and twined his fingers with hers. "You thought up that automatic feed for the new furnace. We made Guilhelms very happy."

Another kiss. "Thank you, my lord. Women can have good ideas, even if men don't think it's possible." She moved her habit a little on the forest floor, keeping Aggie's tunic from picking up too many leaves. "How is Maura"?

Hugh winced and wiggled against the tree. "She lost our infant again. Her mother had much the same problem at first. We will try again." A pout. "Yes, now she will want me again, all the time."

Hugh had found Maura's pregnancy a double gift. An heir, and liberation from his duty to his first wife. Day after day, he found ways to be alone with Jamilla, to talk, to read, to enjoy the warmth of being together. Night after night, they slept together, enjoying each other, over and over, two bodies becoming one, as though their union had been written in the stars by the Great I Am at the moment of Creation. Now the First Wife would be back, demanding her due in accordance with a union that had been written in a contract between Jabil al-Hadid and Tolosa.

"I have enjoyed your calls to the harem, husband," Jamilla said, laying her seductive pout on her Count. "Must they really stop"?

"For the moment, yes, my love."

"Well, my lord, we certainly know that you are fertile." Jamilla stood up and bent over to pick up Ekaterina's habit. Her lovely hair tumbled across her face. "Perhaps we should be getting back to the monastery, Brother Marot. It's getting late."

"Jamilla"?

"Our baby will come in June, Hugh. You've made me the happiest woman in the world."

8

With December, the chill of winter set upon Alberensa. The shops fell silent along the Highway of Santiago de Compostela, along the Avenue of Our Lady. Behind the shuttered stalls, their owners stretched the earnings of eight months to cover twelve. Rain fell almost every day now, cold rain and sleet. When the weather cleared, fresh snow extended down the slopes of the Pyrenees. A glorious frontal of white decked *Lo Grandautar* while drifts blocked the way through the Sárdalo Pass.

Yet hope and joy prevailed, even in these short and darkening days. The hope of Christmas, that through the Incarnation of God made Man, His saving Word would reach all peoples. The joy of Christmas, that the darkest time of year was past, that the days would grow longer, that the cold of winter would yield to the warming bluster of spring. First Lent, then Easter, the Resurrection of Christ from the Dead, bringing with it the resurrection of the pilgrimage along the Compostela Road.

Bishop Jerome sent his messenger on the first day after Epiphany, at the end of the Christmas season. The low clouds were lightening before sunrise when Father Johans, Sir Gautier's third and youngest son, appeared in full clericals at the castle gate.

"A cold morning, Father, January cold," the guards said. "Come in and warm up while we send word to Peter." They waved the priest into the guard hut. A man so thin, almost skinny, took up little space as he warmed himself among the armored soldiers around the fire.

Peter arrived. "I will tell our lord the Count that you are here, Father Johans." He escorted the young priest through the yard to the Keep. "He will certainly want to see you. Have you broken your fast this morning"?

"I have not."

"I'll send in some food immediately."

The Father entered the Reception Chamber through its arched wooden door. Just as at his father's castle at Moustalon, men-at-arms stood guard over the entrances to the room. The priest looked up at the ceiling arches where the guerdons of Alberensa, of Juviler, of Moustalon and Fonta and Sarlant and Arguenos hung in brightly-colored array.

Two servants brought in plates of meat and cheese and bread and put them on the table along the wall. Johans said a blessing, ate some bread and cheese and sat himself in one of the chairs before the Count's dais. He was barely finished thanking the Lord for his meal when he heard a knock on the tower stairway door.

"Rise for our liege, Hugh, Count of Alberensa." Which Father Johans did, and bowed as Hugh entered the chamber.

"Please be seated, Father Johans. It's good to see you." The Count took his own seat in a heavy wooden chair with lion arms. Legend held that a knight of Juviler offered the gift to Angibert the Builder when Juviler became a fief of Alberensa. "So early on a Tuesday morning, though, Father, is something of a surprise. I apologize for the cold, but there was no time to make a fire."

"No fire is necessary, my lord. I strive to live a simple, devout life." The priest rose again to deliver his message.

"Before you start, Father Johans. May I ask how you are? I value your father's friendship highly, and your brother's, and yours. Is there any way I can be of help to you"?

The priest bowed his head, earnest, sincere. "That is most gracious, my lord. I am very satisfied with my place."

Just as Gautier's second son had welcomed the opportunity to join the Templars and fight in Outremer, Father Johans had welcomed Holy Orders. Unlike many younger sons, he did not find the Church to be a burden at all.

"Then me hear your message, Father."

"Bishop Jerome has received word from the Holy Father. He is sending a Papal Legate, Bishop Angelo Donato, a member of the College of Cardinals. Cardinal Donato will be in Alberensa at the beginning of February, three weeks from now. The Cardinal will be joined by emissaries of the King of France. Both the Holy Father and the King wish to assure the support of Alberensa against the Cathar heretics."

"Who is coming from France"?

"That has not been decided, my lord."

"As a son of Sir Gautier, Johans, you will understand that I prefer not to meet the Cardinal or the King's envoys in the Bishop's palace. Nor do I suspect that the Cardinal wishes to visit me here. Has the Bishop a proposal?

"The parish church of St. John's. Convenient for you, but still a place of faith."

"Your saint's name, Father Johans. Excellent."

■ ■ ■

Father Johans departed. Hugh summoned Sir Giles to take his place. Two men from Outremer, where the main threat was the Saracens, sat in Europe, where the main threats appeared to be the French and the Church. The same Church they were fighting to protect in Outremer. Giles did not exactly long for his days as a sergeant, but they certainly were simpler.

"Build up the fire and leave us," the Count said to the men-at-arms. "Sir Giles will tend to it."

Hugh stepped off the dais and sat in one of his visitor chairs, alongside Giles. The Count always marveled at the calm exterior on a man of such strength. Perhaps that was because he was simply waiting for instructions, but Hugh did not think so. The troubadours loved Giles of Tripoli and his sacred oath of devotion to the Blind Baroness, and with reason. If Giles thought the Count was doing something that might threaten his sister, he would say so. Hugh took it as a compliment that he never had. The knight had confidence in his Count, and confidence in his own skill and determination.

"Sir Giles. Countess Maura continues to urge the message sent to me by Count Raymond of Toulouse. It is time for the County of Alberensa to join the battle against the northerners." Giles nodded, understanding, not agreeing. "We know that King Louis VIII has promised to renew this Albigensian Crusade if the Pope taxes the clergy to pay. The Montfort claims against Toulouse which Simon granted to Louis's father King Philip will be renewed by Louis. There is talk of a new Council to excommunicate Count Raymond and give the King a reason to conquer Toulouse."

Giles crossed his arms over his tunic, leaned back and breathed out. "This never seems to end, my lord. Toulouse killed Simon de Montfort in battle and drove his son's men back into a small part of Trencavel. Count

Roger de Trencavel rules again in Carcassonne. The northerners are defeated, but they will not go away."

Yes, in that way it is just like Outremer. The Saracen pressure never ceases. If they see an advantage, they seize it. If the Christians gain an advantage, the Saracens simply wait. And so it is with the northerners in Lengadòc.

"I, too, was hopeful that the battle had ended, Giles. Father Felipe has moved on, preaching in the north, in the County of Toulouse."

"And the Bishop has reported that Alberensa is free of the heresy." The two men exchanged a conspiratorial smile. "That should have been enough." He shook his head. "Apparently it is not."

"Maura attacked me about the Bishop's report, Sir Giles. 'Has the construction of his new palace in the St. Matthew's Quarter, has that distracted Bishop Jerome very much from his duties, my lord Count? I'm told that he spends much time there, supervising the construction, often accompanied by a lady who formerly passed many nights in the company of your soldiers.'"

Giles smiled. "A harsh accusation, my lord Count. It is her relationship with Count Raymond that allows the woman to be so bold."

"Indeed. I explained that in thanks for success with the blast furnace at Brassat, I offered a gift to the Church. All the nobility do that when they have good fortune."

"She found your gift of a new palace too generous, my lord"?

"I explained that the Bishop is called upon to entertain many important people as they make their way over the Sárdalo Pass. His current palace is little changed since Count Angibert built the Cathedral in 950."

"And her reply, my lord"?

"That he seems to spend all his time entertaining his new constant companion. She accused you of introducing them, Sir Giles."

The knight put his hands together under his chin. "I must admit I was there when they met, my lord." He poured out some wine for the two of them. "I had no idea that the Bishop would devote so much of his time to the saving of her soul."

Laughter followed, a moment of mirth that quickly passed.

"We are in a difficult position, Giles. My uncle Count Jacme protected our people from this madness. The Montforts had no direct support from King Phillip. Their army consisted of vassals performing their feudal duties over limited periods of time. To achieve any results at all, they were forced to choose their battles carefully."

Giles nodded, "Count Jacme convinced them to choose someplace else."

"Exactly. Alberensa lies in the far south of Lengadòc, beyond Trencavel, Fois, Tolosa. It poses no threat. The Montforts fought in Toulouse and Foix and left Alberensa alone." Giles nodded again, understanding, again. "If King Louis comes himself, he will have enough men to fight us all."

Giles frowned, deep in thought. "What does my lady the Baroness of Juviler think, my lord"?

"Aggie says that I am the Count of Alberensa, not Toulouse. Count Jacme did not grant his lands to Montfort as Raymond of Toulouse did. Louis wants all of Languedoc, but unlike Toulouse, he has no claim here." Hugh waved upstairs towards the Solar. "In fact, Aggie thinks the Pope may like it this way. We are a piece of Languedoc that stays free of the heresy and free of France and so in a way within his domains. We should not give the Holy Father reason to think otherwise."

Giles nodded as he imagined Agnes delivering her advice, the hand to the mouth followed by the finger pointing upward. Of the women of Alberensa, he found Maura stolid and Ekaterina loyal. Lady Juviler was brilliant.

"What does she say of Ponset of Arguenos"?

"With Aggie as she is," Hugh answered, "He is our Phillipicus of Nicaea, the man who stands to inherit if I have no heirs. Better for him to take over an independent Alberensa. He will remain loyal." Hugh smiled. "Remember, he warned us that Godfrey of Sarlant contemplated treason after learning that his son was mining iron in irons."

Giles smiled, then became serious.

"Alberensa is small, my lord Count. Toulosa, Fois, Trencavel, they are larger, and they have all offended the Pope. If King Louis attacks them and they cannot stand, the addition of our few men will not help. You must do as Count Jacme did, for the benefit of our County."

"Thank you, Sir Giles. Agnes and I knew we could count on you."

9

After supper, the Count and the Sister managed to escape undetected to the roof of the Keep. Hugh told Ekaterina about his plan. She sank to the stones, bawling. He found her difficult to understand through all the choking and tears, even after they switched to her own language.

"Don't send me away, Hugh! I don't want to go to Tripoli! My family will kill me or your men in Jabil al-Hadid will kill me! I want to live here, with my child and my husband, not in that convent in Chadra"!

Hugh sat down beside her. The wind dropped away, cut off by the battlements. "Once everyone here realizes what has happened, Jamilla, they will call you my mistress."

"I am not your mistress. I am your wife"!

"Christians do not have second wives, Jamilla."

"Ours is not a Christian marriage! It is a marriage in accordance with the True Faith, with Islam, the

Faith revealed to the Prophet, may the blessings and peace of God be always upon him"!

"Not only will you be my mistress, you will be my harlot Saracen mistress. The Saracens are the enemies of the Church, just as the Cathars are its enemy. We will risk Alberensa under the Third Canon."

"The words of the Roman Infidel blaspheme the One God, the Eternal Refuge! The Fire waits for him"!

Hugh took her hands. "Even worse, we will risk your life. Our child and you must get to a place of safety. I have a plan for that, in Outremer, and I will take you there. It will not be Chadra."

Jamilla shook her head and pushed her finger against his chest. "You are the Count! No one can threaten you, certainly not that stupid Three-Gods Priest Felipe"!

Hugh put his hand under her chin and turning her sobbing face towards his.

"That's not true. I'm certain that my great-grandfather Angibert II faced the same threat. He, too, was forced to yield. At least he had a son and heir. Agnes and I will be forced to give up the County to the next in line."

"Who is that"?

"Baron Ponset of Arguenos. He is descended from a brother of my great-great-grandfather Bernat. There may be a claimant from Aragon, too, descended from one of Bernat's sisters, but Ponset would have precedence even though we do not have the *loi Salique*."

Jamilla shook her head, setting those dark tresses glowing in the light of a half moon. "Angibert must yield, even though he was the Count"?

"Yes. We are surrounded here, Gascony and so England to our west, Tolosa and beyond that France to the north, Aragon to the south. Dynastic marriages have always been part of our family's strategy to balance those threats."

"And Angibert's wife was from…"?

"Bernart arranged his marriage to Rixen of Tarba, that is, Tarbes in Gascony. Like Maura, she was the cousin of a ruler, in this case Eleanor, the Duchess of Aquitaine and Queen of England."

"The marriage went poorly."

"There is no way to know directly, Jamilla. I suspect that to be true because, after the couple produced my grandfather Roland and two daughters, Rixen retired to the Benedictine Convent of Couserans on the Tolosa Road."

"She became a nun"?

"No. Noble women in unhappy dynastic marriages have been known to do that, retire in quite comfortable seclusion to a convent, leaving their husband free to pursue his lust."

"And Angibert"?

"Do you remember the Sárdalo Pass Road, the shrine to Saint Mary of Egypt"?

"Yes."

"Mary of Egypt was a prostitute who lived while the Roman Emperors of Constantinople still ruled Jerusalem. She traveled to the Holy City and tried to enter the Church of the Holy Sepulcher. An unseen hand barred her from passing through the door. She repented of her sins and lived out her life as a hermit, in the desert beyond the Jordan. She died on April first in a year when that day was Holy Thursday."

"An old monk in the Pass told the story, at the shrine."

"Think of the window of David and Bathsheba in the chapel, Jamilla. And the Resurrection Window in St. John's, Jesus and Mary Magdalene."

"They are the same people, Hugh. I have noticed that."

"In the Cathedral, too, the upper window of the Virgin Mary and the Risen Christ looking down on the Sons of Zebedee. I was not certain, so I climbed up to look."

"The same"?

"Yes." He gazed for a moment into the cold starry night. "It is not uncommon for the people who pay for a religious object to have themselves portrayed in that object."

"As you did with Agnes in the Pool of Siloam window."

"With all of the glass paid for by the Glassmaker, I decided that he must be the man in all three windows.

The woman, though, she was a challenge. Less than fifty years have passed, yet no one has any idea. One clue and one clue only, Garnier's mark. Do you remember it, the upside-down-and-backwards 'L' with a small stroke on the left"?

"Yes."

"When I climbed to Garnier's mark on the Cathedral window, high up and masked from below by the frame, I found something different. That mark has four characters."

Hugh pushed loose grit and mortar and dirt to make a writing surface. "The first is the upside-down L with a stroke," marking the sand with his dagger.

ה

"Then an 'O, like this."

ס

"Then an upside-down L without a stroke, like this."

ד

"Then the last letter, same as the first."

ה

Jamilla gazed down on the writing.

הדסה

She pushed her hand into Hugh's side. "Consider that you meant that the first was as same as the last, my noble Count." She smiled and waited.

"Are you always so clever, Jamilla? Because you are right."

"In Hebrew as in Arabic, my lord, the letters go from right to left."

"My thought exactly. The abandoned synagogue in the St. Luke's Quarter has such markings. Father Johans knows the Hebrew writing, so I went to him."

"And it says"?

"'Hadassah.' 'Hadassah,' or 'Esther,' the Hebrew woman who charmed the King of Persia and saved her people." Hugh pointed towards the Cathedral. "That is not Garnier's mark. It is Esther's. All the glass in the Cathedral, in St. John's, the David-and-Bathsheba Window in the chapel, all of it was done under her guidance. She is the Mistress of Alberensa."

"And the mistress of your ancestor, my lord Count." Jamilla leaned over and kissed him. "This is not so long ago. Even my father would remember that time, although he would be a small boy. Yet you have this story of Garnier, the Master of Alberensa."

Hugh reached over and put her hand on Jamilla's womb, feeling the growing life beneath her cassock. "The Mary in the window also has her hand on her womb, Jamilla. And she is looking at Jesus and he at her, ignoring the Sons of Zebedee as they gaze up from below."

"The pregnant Mistress of Alberensa, then, a mistress made pregnant by her Count."

"Yes." Hugh took a deep breath. "The Jews suffer in Europe, Jamilla. They are subject to oppression and terror. That was the meaning of Esther's sorrowing face in the Bathsheba window, sorrow at the pain of her people. King David, her Count, could not prevent it, and he could not console her."

"You are saying that she was barred from the church like your Mary of Egypt"?

"Unlike many other towns, we have no Jews in Alberensa, Jamilla. The small synagogue in the St. Luke's Quarter is a shambles."

"Christians do not build synagogues. Where did they go"?

"We know that Rixen of Tarba emerged from her convent just after Christmas in 1175. Soon after, Angibert abdicated in favor of his son, my grandfather Roland. He signed the instrument of abdication before the entire church and nobility of Alberensa in the Cathedral on fourth of April in 1176."

"Easter Sunday."

"Nothing is written, Jamila, but it is not hard to figure out. The town learned that their Count had a pregnant mistress, a Jewess, perhaps because he sought a divorce from Rixen so that he could marry Esther.

Countess Rixen and her son Count Roland forced Angibert to abdicate. They sparked a rampage against the Jews. 'Murderers of Christ,' the townspeople must have screamed, beating them and looting their shops and driving them out of town."

"The Count could not stop them."

"Angibert knew he could not protect his darling Esther and their child from Aquitaine, from the Church, from the town, from his wife. He sent her to the Saracens in Iberia, over the back trail that leads past the Cathar village. The shrine where you took my sister, that is most certainly where Angibert and Esther said goodbye, on Holy Thursday, 1 April 1176."

"No one has broken the Jewish windows, Hugh."

"No. Perhaps their consecration to the church protected them."

"Perhaps their beauty protected them." Hugh's Esther kissed him. "Clearly Roland watched them come into being and marveled at such works of genius."

Hugh shook his head. "He never said anything about that to my mother, Jamilla. Rather, I now realize that Roland and Rixen conjured up the Master of Alberensa, the Norman craftsman Garnier from Paris, to conceal their Jewish origin."

"The inscription on the shrine says something about dying in the same place."

"On the morning after Easter, Angibert left on a pilgrimage over the mountains to Spain. He died on the road to Santiago de Compostela."

"No, my lord Count, he did not die on the Compostela Road, you may be sure of that! He died many years later in *al-Andalus*, in the arms of his beloved Hadassah. You have cousins there even now, cousins who have embraced Islam."

Suddenly Jamilla broke out in sobs, shaking while tears flowed down her cheeks.

"What's wrong"? trying to wipe the tears from her eyes.

"You now see, Hugh, why God's Holy Angel revealed to the Prophet, may the blessings and peace of God be always upon him, that a man who is able may take up to four wives. In the *Dar-al-Islam*, Angibert could have married his Esther without breaking his covenant with Rixen, bringing justice to them both."

"We are in Christendom, Jamilla."

"So we are. If you acknowledge me, Maura of Tolosa and Ponset of Arguenos and the Roman Infidel and the King of France will seek to drive Agnes and you over the Pyrenees to *al-Andalus*. You may prevail, but to protect Agnes it is better if we withdraw."

"You are a saint, Jamilla bint Hassan al-Haddad."

"If The Cow died, beloved, would you marry me in the Christian way"?

"If you would have me, yes. And I would to bring you here, or live with you in Outremer. And I would marry no others, even if I could do so."

Jamilla rose to her feet and squared her shoulders. "Then Bathsheba will go to your Outremer, my lord Count and husband, go to protect our child, go to protect my friend Agnes, go to wait for God the All-Merciful to bring us together as husband and wife."

10

A heavy man like the Papal Legate always appeared warm, even though it was February and St. John's was cold. "Angelo Cardinal Donato is the scion of an ancient family of the Eternal City," Bishop Jerome advised the Count. "His roots go back to the Roman Senate in the time of the Caesars."

Donato's dark eyes remained bright, although after his years of work in the Curia, they seemed crafty and calculating. Hugh thought he looked tired, tired from his journey, tired from the burden of so much weight, tired from the burden of so much craftiness.

"The Cardinal is *papabile,*" Jerome added, that is, a man who might be elected Pope. Perhaps the Roman's craftiness would earn its reward. When Pope Honorius died, Angelo Donato might rule as Pope Leo or Pope Gregory or Pope Urban, and by that name be called by Christ Himself to Paradise on the Judgment Day.

Servants from Alberensa Castle had pushed the chairs of St John's to the side and set up a large table under the crossing. Moses and Elijah gazed down from the clerestory as the participants gathered in midmorning. Bishop Jerome brought Father Johans and four other priests. Cardinal Donato brought even more priests and scribes from Rome, uniformly young and uniformly thin. They arranged themselves on the side of the table facing the altar so that Christ in Majesty could regard their sacred work. A black-robed army, an army for Christ busied itself while it waited. A different army than the one that Julian of Blagnac, Baron of Jabil al-Hadid, had joined, but an army nonetheless.

So many men, from Rome and from the Cathedral of Our Lady of the Pyrenees. Even more were coming from the King. Hugh decided to match their many with few. He waited with Giles, with the Baroness and with her ladies-in-waiting, Sister Ekaterina and Lisbetta Deslegador. The men wore only the blue of Alberensa, without armor. Agnes put on blue silk, Lisbetta, brown wool and Ekaterina, her habit. Heavy woolen cloaks covered all five.

Father Johans returned from a summons to the front door. "The King's men are coming, Eminence. They will be here shortly."

"Very shortly, I hope, Father Johans," Agnes said. Cardinal and Bishop and priests and scribes started up in shock to hear a woman speak, unbidden. "It's cold in here. I'd like to get back to the Keep." She pulled her cloak around her slender body and touched her Juviler tiara. "The rest of you can enjoy The Master's glass while we wait, but Our Lord has decided that I don't need to see it."

The door to the street opened. A herald called out, "Henri, Baron of Épernay. Sir Charles of Épernay. Sir Martin of Ablois. Felipe Vilalba of the Order of the Preaching Friars." Épernay green over chain mail marched across the stone floor as Hugh felt Giles adjust against the menace. The King had designs on Alberensa, that Hugh knew. That was his message in sending Henri. The Pope was not certain he wanted the King to have Alberensa. That was his message in calling this meeting.

A Roman priest guided the newcomers to their places. Cardinal Donato began as soon as they seated themselves.

"My lord Count, the Holy Father...."

"With your leave, Your Eminence, with your leave, my lord Count." Sir Martin spoke without leave from his Baron. Hugh was not surprised. This man was Henri's Giles, the friend to whom he turned for counsel and in need. His hair was freshly cut today, his gray beard trimmed, his Épernay tunic cleaned.

"You certainly have my leave, Sir Martin," Hugh replied.

The Cardinal sucked in his bulk. Bishop Jerome fretted. "Your knight is full of surprises, my lord Baron of Épernay," Jerome proclaimed. "Do I not recall something like this during our parlay before Fonta"?

Henri placed his one hand on Martin's shoulder. "Martin of Ablois is my most trusted friend and advisor, Your Eminence. We have been together many years. I rely on him in everything. Pray indulge him, as the Count has done." He motioned with his hand towards Agnes. "He has a gift for the Baroness of Juviler."

The Cardinal resigned to the inevitable. "Proceed," he intoned, as though he had a choice. Hugh watched him calculate what might be happening, but he was dividing by zero. Every answer was nonsense. He would have to wait and calculate again.

With all eyes turned to Sir Martin, all ears were surprised to hear a woman speak again. "A gift? We have never met, yet I like Sir Martin already." She turned a mischievous smile in the direction of his voice. "Please approach, my lord. A woman is always eager for a present from a man."

Sir Martin limped around the table and knelt beside the wheelchair. "My lady, this golden cross was made in our cathedral city of Reims, where all French kings are crowned. It is a reliquary. In it I have placed an ancient piece of wood from Limoux. It is part of the cross of an early martyr to the Faith, here in Languedoc. I pray that this gift comforts you and brings you Our Lord's protection against all threats to your immortal soul."

Agnes closed her hands around the gold and touched it to her lips. "This is a most gracious gift, and I accept it with thanks." She held it up. "Lisbetta, please place it around my neck." In just a moment, the cord was tied. "Does it suit me, Sir Martin"?

"Yes, my lady."

"My lord Count." The sightless eyes smiled in his direction.

"Yes, my lady"?

"Please seat Sir Martin next to me at dinner, so that we may learn more of each other."

The Cardinal, Felipe, Sir Charles, all shuffled impatiently during Martin's presentation. Yet it was Henri who noticed first, sitting quietly as his knight returned to his side. "That lady-in-waiting to the Baroness of Juviler. I know her. I've seen her before." He glared at Lisbetta. "Yes, yes. Sir Martin. You were close to her, too. That's the heretic daughter of those heretics in Farga. She's the one who ran into the woods where the smith of Brassat was waiting for me. What is she doing here in your sister's service, my lord Count? You should burn this heresy from your midst, not protect it"!

"Lisbetta Deslegador is of our family," Agnes answered, "Of Jabil al-Hadid, my lord Baron, and of Foix. She and the blacksmith Guilhelms Faure, they are both related to us. With the help of Sister Ekaterina, I rescued Lisbetta from the heresy and brought her to the True Faith."

Sir Charles sneered in his anger, "Are you calling my father a liar, woman"? Hands went to swords but Agnes spoke before anyone moved.

"I am sorry, my lord, but when you address this woman for the first time, you must tell her who you are." Ice in the room, ice in the sightless eyes, ice in the soft low voice. A sensual voice, seductive in its anger, daring the lustful to sin. "By your rudeness, I deduce that you are Sir Charles. No one will be burned here today, my lord, certainly not by the likes of you."

The cold room froze as Cardinal Donato shifted his bulk towards Agnes, studying her with his dark eyes. He shifted to the Count, not quite in pleading, but at least in hope.

"My lord Count, I must ask, who rules this place, your sister or you? She is doing all the talking, my lord, insulting Sir Charles, who cannot demand satisfaction."

"On behalf of my lady I will give Sir Charles satisfaction, Eminence, if that is his wish"!

"That is not my wish, Sir Giles," Donato answered. "I have a message for the Count of Alberensa from the Holy Father, but I cannot deliver it through all this womanly prattle."

Agnes turned towards the Cardinal's voice. "Let us proceed then, Your Eminence. I will cease my prattle if there is no further interest in Lisbetta Deslegador."

"A moment please, Your Eminence, Sir Charles." Hugh leaned over to whisper in his sister's ear. "What are you doing, Aggie? This meeting is important to us. Your sharp and clever tongue is threatening Alberensa."

She hissed into his ear, softly, "He made me angry with his......"

"He meant to, so that you might give King Louis cause to attack even though this Cardinal does not want that. You're smarter than these people, sister, so act smarter. Apologize to the company for giving offense."

"What"!? Her body started, then froze.

"Do it, now." Even sightless eyes could rage in fury. "Control yourself, look up and apologize. Do not force Giles to fight for you. Do not give Louis the Lion and his most devout Lioness Blanche of Castile grounds to seize our fief."

Agnes' shoulders shook, her chest heaved. A moment more and her control returned. The ice melted and modesty appeared, the purity of the virgin that she was.

"Your Eminence, I have offended many here. I have interfered with the Holy Father's work. I pray that all accept my apology for the slights I have given." She looked into her lap while her brother turned towards the offended.

"Sir Charles, do you accept"? Charles glowered at Hugh while the Cardinal's eyes pleaded with Henri.

"I find the lady's apology to be most sincere, my lord Baron," Martin offered.

"I agree, Sir Martin. Charles, there is no dishonor in accepting a woman's apology for her vain and foolish chatter. A valiant knight dying over a woman's meaningless drivel, it's a waste."

Hugh put his hand gently on Aggie's quivering shoulder. Charles recognized that, once again, he was the only man wanting to fight.

"I accept Lady Juviler's apology."

"Good," announced the Cardinal. "Let's begin." He waved. One of the clerical soldiers lifted a parchment from the table. He began to read, in Latin. Hugh put up his hand.

"Your Eminence." The Latin stopped. "Eminence. So much Latin, it can be a challenge. Perhaps you could simply summarize the message from His Holiness."

Jerome had been waiting for a moment such as this. It had taken less than a year to realize he was no longer from Quillan in Languedoc. He wished to get back to Rome, away from the coming war, closer to the men who would choose the Pope of his generation. These butchers from the north and this Preaching Friar of Dominic de Guzmán were dooming him to a life of blessing pilgrims under the Sárdalo Pass.

"Your Eminence, might I make a suggestion"?

"Yes"?

"Father Johans is quite skilled at Latin. He is a son of one of the Count's barons, much trusted by him." And by Jerome as well. The priest had heard his bishop's confession about the loose woman. He had helped him win his struggle and send her back to her men-at-arms.

"Yes"?

With his sins absolved, Jerome wanted to make a good impression on this *papabile* Cardinal. Donato was his Path to Rome.

"Allow Father Johans to read the document in the language of Lengadòc, freely translating from the Latin."

Jerome watched with his heart in his throat as Cardinal Donato calculated the possibilities, the best way to give least insult. He decided.

"Father Giuseppe, please give the Holy Father's message to this priest," motioning towards Johans. "He will read it in translation."

Jerome regarded the Master's window. Glory to God in the Highest! The Risen Lord stood on *Lo Grandautar*, pointing the way to the Seven Hills of Rome.

Gautier's son began reading. The usual expressions of respect droned out first. The building creaked from the wind as he began the message itself. The sun moved along the life of Jesus as the long text continued, brightening each window for a time and then leaving it duller while it moved to the next. Colors played on the stone, lighting the dancing motes. In July this would be a cool place of refuge from the hot sun outside, but today they were in a cave of ice somewhere in the mountains. The sun reached the Raising of Lazarus from the Dead in the southern transept as the document closed with the usual expressions of respect. "That is all, Your Eminence."

"Do you understand the Holy Father's message, my lord Count"?

"Yes. The Holy Father states that the Third Canon of the Fourth Lateran Council does not apply to Alberensa, on two conditions. First, that we not permit anyone in the County to shelter heretics. Second, that we do not assist the Counts of Toulouse, of Foix, of Trencavel to resist the King of France's claims to their lands. In return for these undertakings, the Holy Father confirms that Alberensa is not forfeit for heresy."

Hugh turned towards the King's one-armed emissary. "Have you brought the King's agreement to the same conditions, my lord baron"?

It took a great deal of effort, Hugh thought, for the lord of Épernay to respond. "I have. His Majesty accepts the position of the Holy Father, under the same conditions. Your rights will not be challenged or disturbed by France."

The arrangement confirmed Hugh's thoughts. The Sárdalo was an important pilgrimage route, a gateway to Aragon, a source of revenue for the Church. The Pope did not want control in the hands of the powerful King of France. His Holiness was an ally, but only in the sense that they had the same enemy.

"We are grateful for the Holy Father's message, Your Eminence," Hugh said, "And for His Majesty's."

"And what is your reply"?

"First, please assure the Holy Father of our adherence to the Catholic faith. Second, regarding

Toulouse. I am wed to the Count's cousin, yes, but she is of Alberensa now, not Toulouse. We have no interest in the competing claims to that County, those of Raymond and those of Louis. That is an issue between them. As the Holy Father requests, we will neither take sides in, nor participate in, the resolution of that issue. Do I express myself clearly enough, Eminence"?

"Yes." The clerical army nodded in agreement.

"My lord Baron"?

"Yes," Henri answered.

"I will ask Father Johans to prepare a formal reply acknowledging our agreement. We will complete that before I depart for Outremer."

"Excellent," said a very pleased Cardinal Donato. A long journey for a short meeting, but a successful one, one that rendered him even more *papabile*. "I believe this conclave is concluded. Bishop Jerome, please give us all a blessing."

"Before that if I might, Eminence."

"Yes, my lord Bishop"?

"My lord Count. Your departure. Will Sir Giles be your Viscount in your absence"?

"No, my lord Bishop, it will be the Baroness of Juviler." Hugh lifted her hand and kissed it. "It is an old agreement between us, one we made at Jabil al-Hadid. That is why she is with us today. That is why she was so bold to speak."

"With that, then," Donato said, "Please give us...." Charles rose to his feet again, interrupting the Roman cardinal.

"You cannot put a woman in charge, my lord the Count of Alberensa! Such a thing is impossible"!

Agnes turned her blonde head towards the angry sound. "Is that you again, Sir Charles? Perhaps you forget your own queen, Blanca de Castilla, aiding King Louis in all his affairs of state."

Charles waved that away, unseen. "Her Royal Majesty Blanche of Castile is the daughter of the King of Spain and the granddaughter of the King of England. Eleanor of Aquitaine was her grandmother. She has a powerful will and offers great wisdom. It is her right to be close to His Majesty."

Very close, Hugh thought, given the continuing supply of heirs that she produced. Step in. "My sister offers great wisdom, Sir Charles. I consult with her in all things. We do not have your Salic Law here. Unlike Queen Blanche or her daughters, Agnes can inherit. It is her right to be my Viscountess."

The Viscountess pointed her finger at the ceiling. "I, too, am descended from Aquitaine nobility, Sir Charles. My mother the Countess Marguerite ruled Alberensa. My ancestor Monica of Ronzières made the pilgrimage to retake Jerusalem. I am not unequal to the challenges met by Queen Eleanor's granddaughter"!

Charles snorted, raising his arm to point, rattling his mail. "Such impudence! You are blind and crippled, woman, struck down by our Lord for your sins...."

"OOOHH"! Sister Ekaterina gripped the side of the wheelchair. *"ana bialdawar"!* Her body weaved, *"sae-iduni"!* She slumped to the floor before anyone could catch her. Only God the All-Compassionate saved her from cracking her head on the stone. The Majestic Christ reigned over a heap of fabric while Lisbetta knelt down, listening to Ekaterina moan. "My lord Count, my lady Baroness, forgive me. I cannot understand her."

"I can," Henri said, standing up and pointing his mailed hand in Ekaterina's direction. "Your Eminence, I have campaigned in the Holy Land. She spoke the Saracen tongue. She said, 'I am dizzy. Help me.'" He put his mailed fist against his mailed chest. "That is no sister from some convent, Eminence! That is an enemy of Christ's One Holy Catholic and Apostolic Church! That is a Saracen"!

11

In the silence that followed Henri's declaration, Father Felipe came to his feet. He raced across the space, the only one of the religious to move to Ekaterina's aid. He knelt on the other side of the fallen Sister.

"Sister Ekaterina, it is Father Felipe." Moaning followed. He looked up towards the Cardinal. "I, too, cannot understand her, Eminence."

Cardinal Donato's brow furrowed. His meeting was over and now it was not. This fallen sister threatened all his craftiness, all his calculations.

"Sister Ekaterina has been ill, Your Eminence," Hugh offered. "Her French can be hard to understand. Let me attend to her." The Count of Alberensa knelt beside the pale face of the Maronite nun. "Sister," he said in French, "What is the problem"?

"That's a stupid question," she hissed in Arabic. "Our child has made me ill. He grew sick of this Infidel nonsense and I fainted. Help me into a chair."

Ekaterina gagged, put her hand to her mouth and fought it down. Her cold sweat joined the fresh sweat on the Cardinal. "Now"!

Hugh looked up. "I, too, am having trouble understanding, Eminence. I think she wants a chair."

"What language did the Sister speak, my lord Count"? Jerome asked. "It is certainly neither French nor Occitan."

"It is Our Lord's tongue, my lord Bishop, Aramaic. It is the tongue of the Maronites of the Lebanese Mountains. I'm not sure I understood her completely, but she has been sick. A chair, please."

Felipe and Lisbetta helped Ekaterina into a seat. She bent over with her head between her legs. Her light brown skin flushed red while Felipe looked over at Lisbetta. He drew himself up and then pointed at Agnes.

"This cannot be, Eminence, it cannot." Everyone was shivering in their warmest clothes but small beads of sweat broke out on the Cardinal's upper lip.

"What cannot be"? Donato said.

"This woman cannot be Viscountess in Alberensa"!

Donato's thick neck moved back with Felipe's vehemence. The Preaching Friar's passion and dedication unnerved a *papabile* dedicated to calculation and craftiness.

"Why is that, Father"?

"I now recognize this serving girl. She is the Cathar harlot who ran off from Easter dinner last year. The

Baroness of Juviler and this Maronite sister followed her to the Cathar camp some days later. While they were there, all three took the *Consolamentum*," pointing to the Master's window of the Descent of the Holy Spirit, from Acts. He crossed himself at the memory, the sounds of many rushing into the woods. He felt pain again, the pain of the branch that whipped back hard against his cheek.

Hugh shook his head, befuddled. "You confuse me, Father. Did you not meet with them in this church? With the women of St. John's Circle"?

"Yes, my lord Count, I did. Met them and preached God's Holy Word. Heard that it was impossible for the Baroness to take the *Consolamentum* because she was born on Easter." He looked towards Agnes. "An interesting assertion, but without logic. Easter is not Easter to a heretic." He waved at the three women. "You know the Holy Father's desire, my lord Count. Even if these three Albigensians have repented, they must enter a convent." Felipe turned to the Cardinal. "That is why Count Hugh cannot name this heretic as his Viscountess, Eminence."

Henri and Charles beamed with pleasure, great pleasure. This arrogant bitch had doomed her brother. Sheltering her, sheltering heretics, probably sheltering a Saracen, the Pope's first condition, broken already. Charles felt himself aroused at the thought of raping the blind cripple and leaving her naked in the woods, begging for mercy. Henri imagined seizing Alberensa under the Third Canon and presenting it to the King, as Montfort had done with Toulouse. He considered how he might dissolve his agreement with the Picardy baron and marry Charles to a royal princess instead.

"Fear not, Sir Martin," Agnes said, snapping Henri from his reverie. She kissed her new cross and held it up. "I am a faithful Catholic and I am grateful for your gift."

Jerome, Johans, the other priests, the scribes, all crossed themselves. The Épernays flared, but Sir Martin looked quietly at the table, suppressing a grin. Blanca de Castilla was not the only woman in Europe with a powerful will.

Hugh faced the Cardinal. "Your Eminence. In the presence of Father Felipe, I sent Sir Giles to the Sisters of Charity. He found Lady Juviler and Sister Ekaterina there, preaching the words of Father Felipe, converting Lisbetta to the Catholic faith. Lisbetta"?

"I, too, am a faithful Catholic, Your Eminence." She crossed herself. "I am thankful to the Sisters of Charity for giving me sanctuary when I foolishly ran away. I am thankful to my lady Baroness for her efforts on behalf of my soul."

Hugh bowed gently towards the mound of Roman flesh. "My sister was not in the mountains with the Cathars, Your Eminence. That would be impossible. She cannot walk and she cannot see."

Felipe drew his cloak around, the way he had in the chapel on the morning after Easter, the way he did when he was preaching. "Then why do I hear your troubadours singing of the event? How the Baroness dressed herself as a leper boy and rode into the Sárdalo Pass, led on by Sister Ekaterina. How animals carried her away from me and hid her in their cave. How she made a fool of the Black Friar."

Hugh raised his hand softly, in protest. "Eminence, Father Felipe, please. The troubadours sing of courtly love, of mythical people, of ancient times. They sing of the unicorn, which no man has ever seen. All in Alberensa knew why you were riding to the Pass that day, Father. The rest comes from their clever imaginations."

"Or it does not," Charles said, rising to his feet, leaning against the table. "If your so-called Viscountess has taken the *Consolamentum*, my lord Count, then the King's agreement is void. We will go into the Pass, find these heretics and question them. If heresy is proved, Your Eminence, Épernay claims Alberensa under the Third Canon."

Hugh stood and leaned against the table himself. "My sister is a Catholic. Your claim is denied. You may travel through the Pass as the pilgrims do, Sir Charles. Anything else violates the King's agreement with the Holy Father."

Now Henri stood and swept the air with his only arm. "What of the Sister, Eminence? She spoke the Saracen tongue"!

"With my respects, my lord Baron, but Aramaic and Arabic sound very similar. We fetched Sister Ekaterina from a convent in the Lebanese Mountains. A Maronite convent." He smiled at Father Felipe. "We must be careful that the troubadours do not sing that you followed a Saracen Nun of Outremer into the Sárdalo, Father."

Felipe glared, but Henri resumed speaking before he could reply. "You are a fool to shelter this Saracen witch, Count Hugh! The Saracen holy book tells them that they may appear friendly to Infidels to protect themselves, but they are not to be friendly with Infidels. Your Syrian harlot will betray you, my lord Count, she will betray you as soon as she has the chance"!

The harlot responded to Henri's blast, to his pointing, by crossing herself.

"Don't be fooled by that, Eminence! The Barons of Jabil al-Hadid have always traded with the Saracens. They all speak the Saracen tongue. That Sister is a Saracen unbeliever in disguise, a Muslim." Henri turned to approach the seated Cardinal. Donato's eyes narrowed, his calculations sped up. "The Count shelters our mortal enemy from Outremer and he shelters the Cathar serving girl, our mortal enemy here, Your Eminence! Alberensa is forfeit under the Third Canon"!

Charles pointed towards Lisbetta. "Father Felipe, I can…"!

"Stop"! The Cardinal's voice resounded from the high ceiling, disturbing a bat, although Moses remained unmoved. Sweat gathered around his collar. "Enough"! only loud enough this time for Jesus and Mary Magdalene. He needed time to think.

Hugh put his hand on Agnes, a warning, say nothing. Wait. Angelo Cardinal Donato did not come all the way from Rome to give Alberensa to the King of France. He came to protect Alberensa from all those surrounding threats, to preserve the flow of cash from Jerome's alms box to the Holy See.

"The Cardinal does not believe the strange rumor that your sister is your concubine," Johans told the Count before the Cardinal arrived. "Nor the rumors that the Maronite is a concubine either." By his look now, Hugh could tell that he was no longer sure. Even a fat old Roman bachelor recognized the signs of a gravid woman in the morning. Ekaterina's language, if she was a Saracen, that would explain the inexplicable, a devout bride of Christ giving her body to another man.

No one moved while the calculations continued. Frozen people in a frozen room, waiting while the sun warmed the affection between Jesus and the Magdalene. Donato thought, pondered, grunted. Hugh could almost read his thoughts.

The Count is taking his Saracen harlot to the Holy Land. The Count's lawful wife, Maura of Toulouse, appears barren. The Count's sister, his Viscountess is a hopeless cripple. In His own way, the Lord has offered Alberensa to the Holy See. Once Hugh and Agnes are gone, I will declare the fief forfeit for heresy and award it to another man, an ally of Rome, a man who is not subject to the French king.

Donato took a deep breath. "The Holy Father's message is clear. The King has agreed. The Count of

Alberensa has agreed. My lord Count, you may make your planned journey to the Holy Land with the assurance of the Holy Father that your lands here shall not be molested as long as you adhere to the agreement. You may make that trip with the assurance that the Holy Father recognizes the Baroness of Juviler as your Viscountess."

"Thank you, Your Eminence."

"Father Felipe."

"Yes, Your Eminence."

"Please remain in Alberensa, Father. Lodge with Bishop Jerome and preach the True Faith in the city. If there are signs of heresy here, report to me directly."

"Yes, Your Eminence." The Preaching Friar gloated in triumph. Hugh was grateful that, through God's unfathomable mysteries, the Heretic Leper Boy of the Sárdalo Pass had been denied the opportunity to see his face.

"My lords, this Council is ended," the Cardinal announced. "There will be no further business. Bishop Jerome, please give us a blessing."

It was a solemn moment, outwardly. Priests, scribes, knights, servants, all got to their knees on the stone floor and bowed their heads.

"We give thanks to Our Lord for the work done here today. May the blessing of God the Father, God the Son, God the Holy Spirit be with us all this day and forevermore."

12

After Sir Frederic's meeting with Anne, Elizabeth became even more direct. "Lady Saissouq agrees with our plan, my son. Only Fat Baudoin the Lover of Boys stands between Jean and this fief. The heavens cry out for the earth to be rid of that pervert's presence." There remained the issue of Hugh, but that was waved away, as always. "He is bedding the Cripple in Alberensa. They will never be back. The Count of Tripoli, the Prince of Antioch will award you the fief. All you need to do is ask."

Frederic grew tired of explaining that he could not simply denounce Baudoin, based on claims made by the man's wife. The Hospitallers had great respect for the knight, as much as they had for Frederic. Saissouq supported Krak with money. And with arms. Baudoin liked to fight, and the warriors of Tripoli welcomed his military ardor. Leviticus or not, Baudoin was too valuable to sacrifice over a matter of little boys.

And then the Lord Himself intervened to carry out the Biblical sentence. Baudoin went hunting. His horse stumbled under his weight. He fell off and broke his neck. His burial took place before the news reached Jabil al-Hadid.

■ ■ ■

Sir Frederic ordered his men to wait in the Great Hall while he went to fetch Sir Baudoin's widow. The servants appeared very nervous, and with good reason. Since their liege had no heirs, the Count of Tripoli would award the fief. Rumors were that it would go to the Hospitallers. They would occupy the fort. Family life would cease. Military monastic life would begin. The departure of Lady Saissouq was only the first step in the servants' journey from a world of degenerate pleasure into one of rigorous discipline.

Frederic reached the top of the stone staircase. He knocked on Baudoin's bedroom door.

"Come in."

The knight opened the door to pale candlelight. Perfume, a scent of the Orient, of the bazaars of Homs. Anne stood up from the bed as he entered and closed the door behind him. What she was wearing must have been from Homs as well, a thin gauzy dress that allowed Frederic to see her arms in the sleeves, her legs under the skirt. Even at thirty-seven, the shape of her body still looked like twenty. Frederic remembered this sensual walk, her hips swaying as she approached him. He was instantly aroused, even though he expected that something like this had been waiting.

"You don't appear to be filled with grief at your loss, Lady Anne."

"No. Take off that foolish armor, Frederic. I've been waiting months for this moment. I don't intend to delay our renewed acquaintance until we are wed."

He could not believe how excited he grew with her skillful touching and rubbing and kissing. She instructed him in the midst of her own passion. "Here," she gasped, "like this, here." When they were finally together, he was lifted once again into a physical union beyond any he had ever known. His love with Sophia had been deep, eager, satisfying, but nothing like the carnal animal pleasure he experienced with Anne of Jabil al-Hadid once Sophia was gone.

The lovers lay side-by-side, embracing, exhausted. Anne leaned over and kissed Frederic. "We've loved each other for a long time, my lord." She kissed him again and smiled, like a mother smiling at her little boy. "Mariam and Elizabeth and I talked about you after I returned from Homs."

"You did? About what"? He shivered as her finger ran along his spine and her hand gently took him again.

"We are two of a kind, my love. We are ambitious and talented, but put to the side by those weaklings Hugh and Agnes. We are a powerful couple now,

Frederic. We, not Hugh and Agnes, we hold Jabil al-Hadid for the Christian cause." She was ready to start again, but he held her away.

"Hugh is still the Baron, Anne. I agree that I should be entitled to the fief, that Jean should be entitled to the fief, but we are not. We are a long way from ruling Jabil al-Hadid. And I swore a holy oath."

"You need not break your oath, my love, because I will deal with our problem. I am the sister of Baron Joscelin, the daughter of Athèné on whose behalf that foolish agreement was made." She leaned forward as she massaged him. "Hugh is in Languedoc for good, Frederic. He needs to protect the Cripple and fuck his fat Toulousian countess. We'll never see them again. Here. Like this. I'll petition the Count of Tripoli and he will…..Ohh yes! Yes! Jabil al-Hadid will be yours"!

She rolled up on top of him and he was lost. Again. And, he realized, so was she. He guessed that the servants would put out food for his men, because they would not be coming downstairs for quite a while.

In the name of the Eternal Triune God, Father, Son and Holy Spirit, Amen.

> I, Bohemond, fourth of that name, by the Grace of God Prince of Antioch and Count of Tripoli, have considered the petitions of Anne of Jabil al-Hadid and Frederic of Jabil al-Hadid concerning the succession to the fief at Jabil al-Hadid in my County of Tripoli.
>
> Whereas dispensation has been granted by Christ's One Holy Catholic and Apostolic Church, in the person of Pons, acting as the Latin Patriarch of Jerusalem, and petitioners are now husband and wife.
>
> Whereas Sir Frederic lies second in succession to Jabil al-Hadid were it not for the Agreement made in 1166 between Amalric I, King of Jerusalem and Guilhabert, Third Baron of Jabil al-Hadid concerning the succession to said fief.
>
> Whereas the Agreement was approved by Amalric of Nesle, Latin Patriarch of Jerusalem.
>
> Whereas Sir Frederic is a valiant and chivalrous knight who has nobly served the cause of Christ in the Holy Land for many years, as attested by Stephen of

Orcival, Grand Master of the Sovereign Military Order of the Knights of the Hospital of Saint John in Jerusalem.

Whereas Isabelle Queen of Jerusalem is in Palermo with her husband the Holy Roman Emperor Friedrich and has not responded to our inquiries.

Whereas Pons has given us leave to determine the fate of the Agreement.

So be it decreed that the Agreement between Amalric I, King of Jerusalem, and Guilhabert, Third Baron of Jabil al-Hadid, concerning the succession to the fief at Jabil al-Hadid is null and void.

By this deed we confirm that Hugh, now Baron of Jabil al-Hadid, also Count of Alberensa, is rightly seized of the fief of Jabil al-Hadid and is entitled to all the rights and preferences accorded to his status. All heirs male of his body shall precede Frederic of Jabil al-Hadid and the heirs male of his body in succession to the fief of Jabil al-Hadid.

Done at Tripoli in the County of Tripoli, on the fifteenth of April, in the Year of Our Lord Twelve Hundred Twenty-Five.

Bohemond, *Princeps Antiochenus, Comes Tripolitanus*

PART FIVE

Jabil al-Hadid
May – July 1225

1

The captain of the <u>Salvatore</u> rolled gently with the waves, arms across his chest as he stood atop the aft castle of his two-masted lateener. Even after six weeks at sea, his companion, Don Diego de Alarcon, leader of the Hospitaller knights, still needed to grip the rail of the rocking ship. Don Diego found the Genoese mariner in a good mood, smiling broadly for the first time since they had beaten the storm into Sicily, and survived. Finally this morning after weeks of struggle, the wind came around into a fresh quartering breeze.

The captain ordered the triangular lateen sails trimmed out over the gunwale. The helmsman maneuvered the steering oar in the fresh breeze, leaving a straight wake behind. The rippling of the wind and the hiss of the water and the creaking of the tackle all spoke of the fastest speed they had made since battling the headwinds out of Barcelona on March 31, the day after Easter.

Don Diego came down the ladder from the castle and made his way amidships. "We're close, my lord Count. Those boats we passed through two days ago were the fishing fleet from Cyprus. If the wind doesn't shift or slow, we should reach Tripoli no later than tomorrow. Six weeks, a very good passage."

"Time enough for us all to be ill, my lord," said Maura from her own seat by the rail. Count and Countess had quarters in the aft castle with the captain, but in a cramped and foul-smelling place. They passed all sunny days on the deck, where the warm sun and the chill rising from the water helped to control their lingering seasickness.

"Yes, my lady. My lord Baron. Don Sébastian and two squires will ride ahead to Jabil al-Hadid. You should be met at the Krak turning when we arrive. What of the Maronite"?

"She'll come with us until we reach the Chadra turnoff. I'll take her to her convent myself."

"Very good. Go with God, my lord Count."

"Go with God, Don Diego." The Hospitaller walked towards the forward castle where his ten men were gathered. Twenty paces and he had covered the full length of the deck. Beyond Diego's men, Maura's two young maids, Louisa and Esmeralda sat in their livery, surrounded by the sailors, again. Esmeralda was a prize, very attractive, but even the heavy and plain Louisa was of interest. The two women lost count of how many times they had been offered the opportunity for pleasure and sin by the crew.

Maura followed Hugh's gaze, and snorted. "I hope they have kept their virtue, my lord." It had been her constant concern on the voyage, even though her maids were only commoners. While the <u>Salvatore</u> waited out the storm in Sicily, Maura insisted that Hugh complain to the captain, but he told "Your Lordship" that if "Her Fuckin' Ladyship" didn't want her maids hazed by his crew, maybe she should tell those maids to find another place to sit. From which Hugh concluded that the two women were enjoying every minute of the voyage.

Without Agnes to attend, Maura saw no reason for Sister Ekaterina to stay with the nobility in the after castle. She was a servant on a voyage home and could stay forward, with the crew.

"Is good, lady," said the Sister. "Alone. Prayer. With God. No earthly duties." The captain ordered that a hammock near the forward castle entrance be curtained off, and told his men to leave the Sister alone, on pain of eternal damnation. Ekaterina took an oath of silence and repaired to her cloth cell, where she remained for the entire voyage, taking even her meals within her narrow space.

Had the Countess asked the Sister, she would be pleased to learn that Esmeralda the Prize was still a virgin. She would not be pleased to learn of fat and ugly Louisa, who took the only chance she feared she would ever have to learn about this mysterious carnal love. Sister Ekaterina heard her through her curtains, grunting in the hammocks. Nightly the men plighted their troth, and morningly, they forgot. After a week, Louisa no longer asked for the plighting, as long as she had a hammock and a man.

The wind backed around to the bow. Hugh looked to the aft castle and watched the captain swear. Orders were given, the course changed, the sails re-trimmed.

Hugh smelled Tripoli. The sewage, the cooking smell, the animals. Maura wrinkled her nose. Could it be? The captain was wondering, too.

"Paolo, sale l'albero!"

Paolo climbed the foremast.

"Vedo la terra, capitano!" The crew erupted in cheers. *"Si, Tripoli, capitano!"*

The men leaped to their feet, cheering, shouting. Louisa and Esmeralda were forgotten as the crew rushed to the top of the forward castle.

"Gloria al Dio! Gloria al Dio"!

Hugh wasn't sure if they were giving praise to God for surviving the hazards of the sea or for reaching the brothels of Tripoli. Twenty men needed more than one willing Alberensa maid to satisfy their lust.

■ ■ ■

"Let me see if she will talk to me, Captain." The Genoese nodded, *si, si.* The crew had already gone ashore, except for the watch. The ship's cargo stood on the pier. The Hospitallers stood there, too, lined up with their baggage loaded onto their wagons. Don Sébastian and the two squires had already left, riding through the town at a trot. Maura sat with the driver on a wagon, waiting.

Hugh pulled the curtain aside and found Ekaterina curled up in a ball, moaning. "Sister Ekaterina. Sick"?

"Yes. Bad." She moaned again. "Very sick. Help. To Sisters."

"Captain. She must rest here a while. A convent of her Order is nearby. I'll go arrange to move her there." The Genoese looked at the curled-up woman, moaning and sweating, and at the Frankish Crusader Count, standing beside her in his armor. He looked at the two gold coins in the knight's hand. "She will be off by sunset." The coins disappeared, and the captain, too.

The Baron of Jabil al-Hadid strode down the gangway into the County of Tripoli. He walked to Maura's wagon. Diego de Alarcon quickly joined them, still mounted.

"Don Diego. Sister Ekaterina is sick. She was the Baroness of Juviler's lady-in-waiting for three years. I must stay with her for the sake of Agnes. Leave without me, my lord. I will follow tomorrow, once I get her safely into the convent."

"Six weeks, my lord Count," Maura says, "and she gets seasick now"? An imperious wave, a wave of annoyance. At least it meant that the sulky, gloomy, irritating nun was already gone. Gone into her convent to spend her sulky days in gloomy prayer. They wouldn't have to ride, side by side, to the Chadra turnoff. "I never understood what your sister saw in her, why she cried so much when they parted." She looked back towards the ship. "Could not someone from the crew take her"?

"You know Agnes would never accept that, Countess. I must bring her to Chadra when she feels better."

"She is so strange, with her strange airs and her strange speech. Do what you must, but then let's be done with her." A nod, and Don Diego set the wagons and his column into motion.

■ ■ ■

It took Hugh an hour to find the Maronites, explain about the very ill sister on the <u>Salvatore</u>, and find three men to carry a stretcher and her baggage. The captain waited at the gangway.

"She is still crying, my lord. Please, you must get her off. I want to set the watch and get into the Genoese Quarter before dark."

Hugh led the young men into the forward castle.

"Sister Ekaterina. Help. Stretcher. Must leave."

Ekaterina moaned as the men eased the crumpled black fabric ball from the hammock onto the hard wooden pallet. A cry of pain as two men lifted her stretcher, while the third put her clothing chest on his head.

They started along the pier as Hugh paused on deck for a brief word of thanks to the captain. They had spent six weeks in close and continuous contact, yet in all likelihood they would never see each other again. Even as Hugh made his way down the gangway, *Il Capitano* was giving his orders, setting his watches, freeing his men. His last voyage was already forgotten as he prepared for his next.

Mild attention accompanied the procession as it made its way off the pier. A nun on a stretcher was unusual, not impossible, noticed and quickly forgotten. Even after three years, the smell of the Lebanese cooking was familiar as they left the wooden dock and turned into the city, the spices, the bean paste and baking bread. The Baron walked on solid ground for the second time in six weeks, with the rocking motion essential to balance on the <u>Salvatore</u>'s deck quickly forgotten.

Paved streets of worn stones that might have felt the sandals of the Apostles passed under Hugh's feet. Stone buildings covered with cracked stucco crowded in at first, and then they came into an open market, a *souk*. The setting sun stretched across the open ground. Some merchants were already preparing to close for the night while others remained hard at work. Women in abaya and hijab haggled, walked away, came back as the vendor called after them with a new offer.

A continuous din of Arabic, the language of coastal Lebanon, assaulted Hugh's ears. The sewage in the drains running down the middle of the street assaulted his nostrils.

Hugh's goal came into view beyond the *souk*, a high stucco wall pierced only by a single wooden door. The walls and roofs of the convent buildings climbed above the enclosure, with the chapel the highest of all.

Two minutes more, Lord, please, two minutes. Two minutes to sanctuary, from the Franks, from her family. Two minutes.

Hugh waited for a donkey and cart to pass in front of them, then crossed over and rang the convent bell. Two minutes became four, and another ring, until the view port slid back. And closed, and the door opened immediately. Stretcher, clothing and Baron passed through.

"Leave her there now," Hugh said to the porters, in French. They didn't really speak the language, but his hand motions made the meaning clear. Coins were produced and pressed into waiting hands. "Thank you, thank you," sending the men back into the *souk*.

The door closed. The sound of the street faded away, replaced by a murmur from high up, as the noise filtered over the top of the wall. Birdsong in the green cloister replaced the tumult outside.

"Welcome home," Hugh said in Arabic. "Welcome home, Jamilla bint Hassan al-Haddad."

The moans stopped. Jamilla uncurled and sat up. Her habit might be loose, but not loose enough. With their bulk, Maura or Louisa could conceal even a late pregnancy, but not Sister Ekaterina. Jamilla's condition blazed out like sunlight glinting off polished steel.

"Thanks be to God the All-Compassionate that we arrived in safety, my beloved husband." She stood up, removed the Infidel's cross from around her neck and handed it to Hugh. Her habit tented out over her treasure, and she laid her hands to its bulk, smiling as she winced through a kick. Hugh turned to the astounded gatekeeper.

"This woman seeks sanctuary. Please let me speak to the Abbess."

2

The sister at the gate led them through the little garden to an enclosed corridor. They walked through in an ancient place, where buildings constructed for different purposes in different times were finally surrounded by a single wall and turned to the work of God. In some rooms, they passed over mosaic floors with figures in togas that dated back to the time when the Romans ruled their Empire from Rome.

The Maronites arrived in Tripoli when they came down from the mountains after their discovery by Raymond of Toulouse a century before, but no one doubted that the convent had long been used as the center of a religious community. An Eastern complex, ornate, dark, enclosed and smelling of incense, its walls had held back the flood of Islam ever since the Arab conquerors appeared in the seventh century.

Jamilla and Hugh arrived at the cell of the Abbess. Sister Martha's room proved less dark, more Western, with a window giving out to a greensward in front of the chapel. The elderly woman sat at her table and waited while the nun who brought them lit more candles.

The Abbess dealt quickly with the matter of Jamilla. Martha was sympathetic to her unfortunate plight, even if she was a Saracen.

"Sister Anna. We will grant sanctuary to this woman of Homs. Take her to a cell and help her arrange her things. She will be here at least until her child comes."

Hugh and Sister Martha watched Jamilla waddle off with Sister Anna. With the woman protected, it was time for the Baron Jabil al-Hadid.

"You swore a marriage vow before Almighty God and broke it, with an unbeliever, my lord Count! You seduced a foolish young girl with these second wife lies! She cannot go back to her people, my lord Baron, you know that! What are we to do with her? What are you to do about your sin"?

■ ■ ■

"Everything's agreed, Jamilla bint Hassan. The Abbess decided that my donations were not from the Tempter, but rather sent by God for the benefit of the Order. You can wait here while our baby comes, and until I can bring you to Jabil al-Hadid." Her face beamed while he gently touched her stomach through her silk tunic. "Maura will be greatly offended, but it will not be the first time that a noble husband has betrayed his wife."

"I am your wife, too. Loving one wife does not betray the others."

"As you know, love, she will not quite see it that way. It will make no difference, because I will do what I promised despite that. As the Baron, I will declare our child as the heir to Jabil al-Hadid. Appropriate donations will induce the Bishop to confirm that declaration. I will appoint you as the regent, responsible for the child's upbringing, ruling in my place when I'm gone." He paused, reminding her again of the most difficult part.

"The baby must be baptized, Jamilla. The sisters will arrange it as soon as it is born." Her pout was positively overwhelming, her body movement alluring, even on top of a bulged-out belly. "You know it must be so. Jabil al-Hadid is a fief of Outremer. The Bishop will require that its lord be a Christian. You do not have to be a Christian, but the baby must."

Jamilla sat for a moment in her maternity clothing, feeling the kicks. Agnes ordered the tunic made for Prisca of Fonta, blue silk and a linen surcoat. Lady Fonta never knew of the order, because Agnes gave the dress to Jamilla instead when they parted. "You will have one night as husband and wife in Outremer, Jamilla, before the baby comes. He must remember you that night as the wife of a Count." At this moment, the unhappy wife of a Count.

"That is hard for me, Hugh, but I will do it for him. When he is older, he will choose on his own.

Maybe you will make the right choice with him at the same time."

"He"?

"It is a son, my love, a son. I know it. He is so eager to come out."

■ ■ ■

Jamilla had grown too large for her to enjoy comfortable love, so they simply sat up, talking. He would contact her father as soon as he reached Jabil al-Hadid. Sir Frederic would know how to reach him, or whoever was running her family business now. Hassan al-Haddad would use the blast furnace as his excuse to protect her from the family.

They opened the plans again. She looked, she asked, he answered, she understood. They rolled them up, tied them with a ribbon, and lay down side by side on the narrow bed. Neither one remembered exactly when their conversation grew quiet, but they were both surprised awake by the call to Matins.

After breakfast, it was time to part. Their walk along the narrow corridors and through the little garden brought them to the gate all too quickly. Hugh turned to Jamilla, bent over and kissed her stomach. Then he kissed her and held her. He was gentle, because she was still a Countess in silk and he wore his armor. Her dark curly hair gleamed in the sunlight and her brown eyes gleamed with tears. "I don't want you to go back to France, Hugh, I don't want that. Not if I can't come, too."

"I don't want it either. Step by step, Jamilla, step by step. First, reconciled with your family, and regent of Jabil al-Hadid. Then we'll see what can be done next." He took her in his arms, and she in hers, for one last lingering kiss while Their Son kicked at their stomachs. When they separated, Jamilla put her hands on her belly, wincing, smiling through her tears.

"We'll be together again soon, Jamilla, *inshallah*."

"*Inshallah*, my love."

He opened the door and stepped into the street. She stood briefly in the doorway even though she was uncovered, watching him walk away. Then she closed it, leaned back and began her wait.

3

Hugh left the Hospitaller caravan at the junction in the Homs Gap and rode on alone. Despite the crops in the fields, Outremer seemed barren and desolate after so many years of European green. The summertime heat felt hotter than his hottest remembering. The canyon with the glade passed by, but he would not ride up that stream again without Jamilla. He imagined her soft skin, damp from the water, glistening in the moonlight as they lay in the grass and talked and laughed and made love for as long as they were able.

Jabil al-Hadid came into view, changed in some way, but he could not decide how. His arms still flew from the tower gate. His men still moved on the ramparts. With the castle at peace, its outer door stood open.

Maura's peace is sure to be disturbed, he thought. Tonight she would learn that her husband had been bedding another woman, a Saracen hiding in their home, for years.

Many times on the long voyage the Count asked himself why he did not tell Maura in Lengadòc. Always the same answer, that the risk to Agnes was too great if Maura were left behind. Instead of accepting her lot as other noble wives did, she might urge her cousin to use the slight as grounds to seize Alberensa for Toulouse. They would order Agnes locked in her room to await her fate, unless Lisbetta could help her escape to the heretic camp.

Once informed by Father Felipe, the Pope could never allow Alberensa's iron and its soldiers and the alms of its pilgrims to fall to the heretic Count of Tolosa. The Holy Father would quickly declare Alberensa forfeit under the Third Canon, bringing King Louis and his crusade to Alberensa.

No. Better to tell Maura here, calm her anger, assure her that as the Countess of Alberensa she would be the mother of his heir. Male or female, either way her child would rule their County.

Hugh waved towards the guards over the castle gate but did not turn in. First he wanted a quick look, a moment to survey the Orontes. He remembered a narrowing spot below the forge. A small dam there would still the water and allow it to enter a flume.

Now he knew what was wrong. No smoke rose from the smelter chimney and very little noise from the forges.

The horse's hooves clacked on Guilhabert's stone bridge. The narrow gap downstream was wider than he remembered, too wide. He turned and looked upstream. Better. *We won't need to build a new smelter. We can put the wheel and the furnace right into the works.*

The Baron crossed back over the bridge and rode into his smelter's yard. He dismounted and took off his armor. He laid coif and hauberk over the saddle, hung sword and shield from the pommel.

"My lord Baron? Is that you, my lord"?

The forge fell silent as Hugh looked towards the Arabic, towards a man walking out from the forge. *That is the younger smelter worker, Aram's assistant. Mahmud. Yes, Mahmud.*

"Greetings, Mahmud. Yes, I've returned."

Mahmud turned and called back into the works. "It is our lord, Baron Hugh." Ten men came forward to kneel. *Ten? Where was everyone?*

"Who's in charge here, Mahmud? Where's Aram"?

"I am, my lord." Mahmud looked at the ground and back at the kneeling men. "Aram died two years ago," Clearly he was reluctant to speak with so many listening.

"Thank you, friends. Please return to your work. Mahmud, stay a moment, speak with me of Aram." They walked towards the cold, silent smelter.

"Aram was an old man, my lord. He fell sick the winter after you left, a fever and the coughing sickness where you cannot breathe." A pause while the younger man decided whether to go on. "He was a faithful servant of God, my lord. He is with God in Paradise."

Mahmud didn't mean in heaven with Jesus, with the Blessed Virgin. Hugh nodded. "So may it be, *inshallah.*"

Mahmoud blinked in surprise, recovered, *"Inshallah."*

"He was a good man, Mahmud," Hugh continued, "A good man with the iron. I'll miss him." Hugh looked at the smelter, at the forges, back towards Jabil al-Hadid. "What's happened here? Why aren't we smelting? How are we making any money"?

"I know nothing of the castle, my lord Baron. Sir Frederic does not come here, neither does Sir Guy, no one." His head lowered and he bowed at the waist. "Please my lord. Please stop me if I offend."

"Please continue, Mahmud." What was Frederic thinking?

Mahmud looked up furtively, then more confidently when he realized his lord was not angry after all. "Sir Frederic campaigns more with the Franks than you, my lord. A soldier comes from the castle and tells us what to make. Most of the men have gone back to farming, or run away to Homs."

"What of our customers? What of Hassan ibn Ishaq al-Haddad"?

Mahmoud smiled. "That wily fox is old but still alive, my lord. One son by his first wife and another by his second are running his business. I know this because I am told. They also no longer visit. We have nothing to offer."

By abandoning the smelting, Frederic had made Hugh's plans more complicated. Hugh's offer to al-Haddad would be less valuable now. Less valuable, but still valuable. Everyone in the forge watched him look towards the castle. He made his decision.

"Can you reach him"?

Mahmud was confused. "What, my lord? Reach who? I don't understand."

"Can you reach al-Haddad? Does he remember you? Will he speak to you"?

Confusion still flooded Mahmud's face. His eyes glanced around, seeking clarity in the sun and the ground. "Yes, certainly, my lord. What do I say? We have nothing to sell."

Hugh put his hands on the man's shoulders. The confusion in his eyes was replaced by surprise at the familiarity, and perhaps a little fear. "Mahmud, please tell al-Haddad that his daughter Jamilla is at the Maronite Convent in Tripoli. She will give birth within the month, to my child."

"Your child, my lord"?

"Yes. If they pledge to spare her life and the life of our infant, I will bring her here to live among us as a noblewoman."

"A Muslim noblewoman at Jabil al-Hadid"?

"Yes." Hugh gripped harder. "I have a most generous offer for al-Haddad, which Jamilla will explain.

My offer only stands if they pledge to spare her life and return her to the bosom of their family."

Mahmud was beyond speechless. His mouth opened and closed, but no words came out.

"We have pledged our lives to each other, Mahmud, Jamilla and I. I consider her my second wife. She will be honored as such in Jabil al-Hadid. Male or female, our child shall be its next ruler." Hugh dropped his grip. "Hassan's messenger should ask at the door of the convent for Sister Ekaterina."

"My lord, I…I…."

"Will you help me, Mahmud? Will there be danger for you in bringing my message"?

The man had heard the words, but real understanding came more slowly. Now he smiled, a conspiratorial smirk. "Yes, my lord, I will help. There will be no danger to me, my lord. I hope your offer is very good, for the sake of your second wife and your child."

"I think they will find it such." Hugh took up the reins to his horse. "I'll be back tomorrow for any news.

"*Inshallah*, my lord *Sheyk*."

"*Inshallah*."

4

Hugh decided that he needed to walk. Six weeks on the boat, all day in the saddle, he needed to walk. And to think.

Mahmud gaped behind as the Baron led his horse towards the castle gate. Hugh had not heard of any reverses in Outremer, any long campaigns that might drag Frederic from the family business. What had happened? He didn't notice that he was reaching the gate until the sentry called out a challenge.

"Who goes there"?

"Hugh, Baron of Jabil al-Hadid, lord of this place."

"Enter."

The familiar sound of horseshoes in the double-gated tower echoed in Hugh's ears, even though he had not heard it for three years. A moment of cool passed while he walked in the shade under the stone. He emerged into yard, squinting in the sun.

Once inside, he found that Sir Frederic, like Peter in Alberensa, had assembled the entire household to greet their lord. His cousin stood forward of the line of men, in his armor and wearing the sword of Blagnac. Lady Elizabeth stood behind him, with Maura. He remembered Elizabeth as an overly plump woman, but she seemed slender compared to his Countess.

In a true surprise, Lady Anne stood on the other side of Lady Elizabeth, wearing a bright red tunic. A tunic that was too tight, but not because Anne had gained weight. Hugh looked for Baudoin but did not find him.

A groom stepped up, "My lord," and took Hugh's horse. The noise from behind sounded like the portcullis sliding closed, but the Baron did not look around to check. He smiled at his cousin. "Sir Frederic. Thank you for this greeting. It's good to be back."

Frederic did not smile in reply. Four men stepped out from beside Sir Guy. Now Hugh looked behind, and the gate was indeed closed. Horseless, without weapons and trapped in his own castle yard. The soldiers had his hands behind his back, tying them tight. Their leader, the smirking young knight, that was Josse of Sarlant.

"Hugh, Baron of Jabil al-Hadid," Frederic intoned from where he stood, "We have learned that you have been seduced by a Saracen whore. You protected her, bedded her, got her with child. You have brought her back to Outremer to have that child here. Do you deny this"?

Say nothing, Hugh. Wait.

"Your silence confirms your sins! You let this Saracen harlot, this heathen enemy of our Lord and Savior Jesus Christ into your bed! You brought her here to pollute the Holy Land! You gave her a child who can make claims on Christian lands! You have betrayed the Christian cause in Outremer"!

Frederic drew his sword and pointed it at his cousin.

"You are a traitor to the Cause of Christ, Hugh! Your title to Jabil al-Hadid is forfeit"!

There were spies everywhere in Tripoli. Perhaps it was *Il Capitano*. Perhaps Cardinal Donato had raised suspicions with the Hospitallers. Perhaps it was someone at the convent, riding hard for Jabil al-Hadid. Whoever it was, Maura now knew who Sister Ekaterina really was. And had been for three years.

The sword stayed up, pointing.

"Your sister Agnes, your concubine, has conspired with you. She is a heretic witch. She has taken the *Consolamentum* in Languedoc. She has sheltered this Saracen and protected her while you bedded them both. She, too, is a traitor to our cause"!

The mysterious messenger brought word of Sister Ekaterina to Jabil al-Hadid. The Countess supplied the Heretic Leper Boy of the Sárdalo Pass. Maura's thirst for revenge had overwhelmed her thirst for dynastic advantage.

"My sister is a gentle woman badly injured, Sir Frederic. These insults to her….."

"Silence!"

Josse motioned. The two soldiers drove Hugh to his knees. If my title is forfeit, Phillipicus of Nicaea inherits. Why this?

"I have sent word to our liege lord, Bohemond, Prince of Antioch, Count of Tripoli. With your treason, the fief now falls to me. To confirm my allegiance, I have married Princess Athèné's daughter. While we wait for word from the Prince, you will wait in the dungeon."

Josse shoved Hugh forward onto his face. Married Athèné's daughter?

Dung filled the yard but Hugh managed to keep his face clear even as the two men lifted his ankles to tie them. Dung did smear his gambeson now, and his hose. Familiar shoes waddled into view while they worked, and the familiar hem of a familiar gray wool tunic. At least Maura was blocking the sun.

"You are like all the others, Hugh, you pig! You take who you want and you treat your wife like dirt. Like my uncle. He seduced the daughter of one of his lords, a woman twenty years younger."

Suddenly that piece of dung he had so carefully missed was in his face. Her shoe, miraculously, avoided any stain.

"But you, my treasonous husband, you are the worst, the worst"! Her voice rose, getting louder until she was nearly screaming. "You and that sneaky cripple, that blind witch, that Bride of Satan. You bedded your Saracen whore right under my nose, in my castle. Bedded her, got her pregnant, and then snuck her back into Outremer."

Her shoes disappeared, and then returned.

"You have cost our children this fief, Hugh, you and the blind cripple and the Saracen harlot. What was your plan, you three? To give Jabil al-Hadid to the heathen's child? Never!"

Another kick of dung.

"NEVER!"

Another. The shoes disappeared, but not the shade.

"Take him away! Get the loathsome traitor out of our sight! Let us await the righteous ruling of Antioch, and then let justice be done"!

"As you command, my lady" Josse said. "Pick him up! Let justice also be done for Sir Godfrey of Sarlant, my father"!

Manure squelched under Hugh's side as the soldiers rolled him to lift him. The sun burned down from behind Elizabeth, leaving her face outlined in a halo of light. Inside the corona, a radiance of triumph illuminated her features.

Married to Anne? Confirmed his allegiance?

Amalric's decree. What if Amalric's decree…. Frederic, then Jean.

It had taken decades, but at last Mariam gained her triumph over Athèné. Here, today, Elizabeth is wreaking her mother-in-law's vengeance on the grandson of Jerusalem.

The soldiers lifted Hugh under his arms. Anne put up her hand, wait. She was quickly beside him, letting him smell her perfume.

"Turn your thoughts to God, Hugh. Seek His forgiveness. Prepare yourself for the Heavenly Jerusalem."

■ ■ ■

Hugh had never visited his own dungeon. He didn't recognize the two men who dragged him towards the door in the entrance tower. Furrows followed his dragging feet, harrowing the dirt and the dung, as though he was a serf in Brassat plowing his strip.

The soldiers dragged him down the corridor inside the wall, head first. The bright sun disappeared but the smell of manure remained. The light through the door grew smaller and smaller, farther and farther away, weaker and weaker. Soon it was only a very bright star far off in a very dark firmament. They turned a corner and only the candlelight remained.

One soldier opened an iron gate in the corridor, then both men dragged Hugh down a flight of stairs. They emerged into a room that was five paces square, its walls hung with chains. The candles carried by his guards illuminated the only other prisoner, a dirty young man with a scraggly beard and matted hair. He squinted against the sudden light.

"Get your fucking legs out of the way, Francois," and a kick. They dumped Hugh on the far side, opposite the prisoner. They began to remove Hugh's bonds. He sat up to be shackled.

"Where's my food, Alain"? Francois whimpered. "Water, I need water"!

"Shut up, Francois! It's not time yet"!

The shackles rattled as Francois tried to stand. "Please, Alain, please! Tell Sir Guy I'm sorry"!

"SILENCE"!

Alain lifted a wooden door in the floor. He kicked Hugh.

"Get in, traitor. Climb down. Lie on your stomach unless you want to choke if you puke." Hugh took the small step down. The soldier climbed in with him, pushing the Baron down on his face.

"Where are those...here they are"! Alain shackled Hugh's wrists to the floor, and then his ankles. He climbed out. The other man let the door drop closed over Hugh's body, shaking down dirt and dust. He heard murmurs, Francois begging, and then silence.

Calm. Calm. Explore. The Count's head touched the wall at one end, his feet at the other, so he had to twist a little to let his whole body down. His eyes were adjusting to the dark, and it was still dark. Completely dark. He could see nothing. He lifted his head a little and touched the wood above. A strong stench of urine and feces from Francois and his clothes filled the chamber.

He had to go. He gave up and added to the stench. The warmth on his clothing grew cool, and then cold.

Hugh lay in his coffin, yet he was still alive. Alive, and frightened. Frightened of this hole. Frightened of the bugs and the rats that would soon appear. Frightened of the torture that must be coming. Frightened of the death that would follow. Frightened for Agnes, left alone amid the circling enemies of Alberensa.

A bright thought pierced the dark, and, like the Word, the darkness could not overcome it. Jamilla, granted sanctuary in the convent. The thought of her safety calmed him. He drew a picture in his mind, added the color, erased and drew again. Jamilla lay next to him in their bed, her beautiful smile, the warm glow of their love in her eyes.

The Baron of Jabil al-Hadid wondered if Agnes ever drew pictures like that, lying in bed, unable to move and so completely alone in the dark.

5

A Saracen woman in abaya, hijab and niqab followed her husband through the *souk*. His weight and soft jowls and clumsy walk all proclaimed that this middle-aged man was not a warrior. His billowing trousers and the quality of his wife's abaya said instead that he was prosperous in his business, whatever that business might be.

The couple made to approach the convent but saw two knights coming along the road. The woman turned back to a stall and began to haggle over some vegetables.

The Infidel warriors passed.

"Now, Khalid." She put the vegetables down. "Let's go." A brisk walk to the convent door, the walk of a leader, with the man following behind. She stunned the merchant, a wife giving orders. He meant to watch what happened, but a new customer appeared to take away his attention.

The sister who answered the bell looked out through the view port, saw hijab and niqab, and opened the door. "Come in." When the door closed behind them, the Syrians relaxed for the first time since their caravan crossed Guilhabert's stone bridge. "Sister Ekaterina told us to expect you. Please wait here."

The woman pulled off her niqab and hijab, shocking the man. "There are only women here, Khalid. It is not a sin." Wrinkles had begun to appear around her eyes, but her skin remained soft and her face not yet touched with age. As a young woman, she had been stunning, but now she was only beautiful. They sat on the stone bench in the garden by the gate.

Jamilla appeared at the end of the corridor across the garden, dressed in her blue silk gift. She took a step into the green, saw Khalid and stopped. Her arms went over her delight, her proof of God's love for her. "No, Mother, no!" she called across the garden. "Why did you bring Khalid? He will kill my baby!"

Khalid shook his head. "Umm Yusuf Safiya could not travel alone through the Infidel lands, Jamilla. Our father asked me to bring her. No harm will come to you by my hand."

"Come to me, my beautiful daughter, come to me," Safiya cried. "I thought you were gone into a brothel, Jamilla bint Hassan. Your father told me you had run away. Now you have risen from the dead like the Infidel's God."

Safiya embraced her daughter. Silk rustled and tears flowed, and then Safiya held Jamilla at arm's length, fingering the dress.

"I was a maid to Khalid's mother when I caught your father's eye. You, Jamilla bint Hassan, you caught the eye of the rich Jabil al-Hadid Baron."

She helped her daughter to the bench and sat her next to her half brother. Jamilla leaned back against the stone, late in her term and very uncomfortable.

"Khalid will join a caravan this afternoon, Jamilla, to bring your offer to Abu Khalid Hassan. Your father has given me his permission to stay until your child is born." She put her hand on her daughter's baby and smiled. "It is not long now, beloved, not long at all."

Jamilla smiled. "Umm Yusuf, Mother"?

Safiya smiled with her, and Khalid as well. "Our father is still powerful, Jamilla, and your mother still fertile. Your little brother Yusuf is almost three years old." He looked at Safiya. "My boy Da'ud and Yusuf are best friends."

Jamilla turned and hugged her mother, again. "Mother, mother, I'm so glad for you"! Jamilla felt very happy, warm, grateful to be embraced and cuddled by her family. "Tell me of Hugh's visit, Mother. How does he look"? Khalid and Safiya exchanged glances. "No! Tell me! What has happened"?

"There is trouble at Jabil al-Hadid, Jamilla bint Hassan. Give Khalid the offer so that he may be on his way. I will explain the rest."

■ ■ ■

Hugh called out to the prisoner, "Francois! Francois"! He heard no reply. Held firmly by shackles fixed to the floor without slack, his muscles cramped in agony until he finally passed out.

And woke up, in agony, with no sense of the hour. Bugs crawled on him, but so far, no rats. He heard the murmur when food was brought to Francois, later that first day. He drew his pictures in his mind and passed out and woke up and prayed.

Again he heard the thumping, the murmur as they brought food to Francois. They fed the prisoners once a day, so now he had been here a whole day, alone. He was thirsty, very thirsty, lying in his own piss, with crap between his legs, in his tunic. He waited for the door to lift, but the sounds just faded away.

When the thumping came again, Hugh was delusional. He remained sane enough to know when he was asleep, because then he was with Jamilla, or sitting on the roof of the Alberensa Keep with Agnes, or throwing little Maddie into the pool in the glade. And then he awoke in the hole, anchored firmly to the ground, a permanent piece of the foundation.

When the thumping came a fourth time, he was busy designing the blast furnace. Now he knew that Frederic really did mean for him to die down here. He was desperate for water, just a little water. He could smell a puddle nearby, but it smelled like urine, and he couldn't reach it anyway. Bugs were everywhere on his body now, biting and crawling. He would eat one, but they never went near his mouth.

How long could a man go without drinking? Five days? He was already up to three. Jamilla came to him, carrying their child, smiling, bringing him a huge flagon of cool water from the pool in the glade.

He followed Anne's advice, and turned his thoughts to God. My God, my God, why hast thou forsaken me? Hear my prayer, O Lord. Take Your servant Hugh into Your Eternal Kingdom. Do not let him linger any longer in this Hell of the Baron Julian of Blagnac.

6

Safiya and Jamilla knelt in the shade of a tree in the small cloister outside Martha's cell. Just the softest sound of voices floated in the air as the sisters prayed the office of Sext in their chapel, saying their Infidel prayers to their God who died but didn't die. Mother and daughter tried to comprehend the strange belief that the One God had begotten a son.

They failed. Instead, they faced east of south in the direction of Mecca, performed *wudu*, the ritual ablutions, and silently prayed the noonday office, *salāh aẓ-dhurur*. They finished, "May the peace and blessings of God be upon you," stood and sat down on the stone bench under the tree.

"As a woman with child, Jamilla, you are exempt from *salah*."

"I want to pray, Mother. God the Light, The Guide, the Way has brought me home."

Safiya looked at her daughter, fighting back tears of joy. "Even your father did not know that the Baron brought you to the Frankish lands, Jamilla. Once he risked a question to Sir Frederic. The Infidel told him that Hugh took you to the convent in Chadra. Hassan never told me, because he was worried about your brothers."

"By the time we reached the convent, Mother, we knew that we were falling in love. It is as though God the All-Merciful put each one of us here for the other. I am happiest and he is happiest when we are together." Sounds from the *souk* drifted faintly overhead, another world, another time. Neither woman had left the convent since Safiya arrived.

Jamilla's little son, yes she knew it was son kicked again. "Oh, Mother, my back hurts so much from him." She slid from the stone bench and lay face up in her abaya. Building walls framed blue sky, a gentle sight, but the pain in her muscles mounted before it began to ease. "Was I this big in you, mother? Were you this uncomfortable"?

"We are all uncomfortable, little one. And then the labor starts and you cannot believe the pain. I am sorry, my *amira*, my princess, but it will hurt, it will hurt more than you can imagine." She took her daughter's hand. "And when it is over, God presents you with a most magnificent gift as a reward for your suffering." Safiya leaned over and hugged her daughter, again. "I thought I had lost you, Jamilla my treasure. God the All-Merciful and your father and your *Sheyk* have saved your life."

■ ■ ■

"Leave the traitor down there, my son," Elizabeth said at dinner on the third night. "Once he's dead, he can't be the Baron of Jabil al-Hadid. It's a fitting end for those merchant cowards."

Once again, Frederic marveled at his mother's anger towards Athèné's line. Merchant Coward Baron Joscelin had treated her well, despite his own mother's anger at his behavior. Joscelin's kindness, and Marguerite's, all meant nothing to Elizabeth. That moment when the Hospitaller brought back the sword and Athèné showed no sympathy to Fulk's widow, no thankfulness, no kindness, that moment etched itself forever in Elizabeth's mind. The insult of Amalric's decree might be gone, but the insult of that moment was even now being avenged in the stone coffin under the dungeon floor.

Yet again Anne said nothing in reply at dinner, but on this third night Frederic sensed her discomfort. She proved it when he entered their bedchamber that evening to find her in her most sensual nightgown, doused with perfume. Her marriage had surprised her, finding that she loved him so much, in bed or out. His arms were around her now, their favorite place, and she knew he had grown to enjoy her constant eagerness. She began moving her mouth down his stomach, preparing to take him in her mouth and harden him for a second time. She never liked doing that, so he knew.

"That is not necessary, my ever-lustful wife and cousin. If you have something to tell me, then tell me, Anne of Jabil al-Hadid."

She slapped him, a girl's permitted little slap. "You should be kinder. My change will come, and I will be wizened and you will be lonely." She kissed where she had hit.

"Your thoughts, love"?

Anne snuggled close. "Vengeance, naked hatred, without benefit, it is always dangerous, Frederic."

"What do you mean"?

"Your mother is wrong, leaving Hugh to die like that. He is a traitor and an unbeliever, but he is the Baron until the Prince says he is not." Frederic frowned. "If he dies at our hand before the Prince decides, he may rule that we can't inherit, either. He will give Jabil al-Hadid to Phillipicus of Nicaea, someone who probably doesn't even know where it is. Even worse, to the Hospitallers." She pulled herself in tightly and rubbed herself against his hip.

"You are right, of course, my lady. It's just that will be such a pain in the ass to listen to my mother bitch if we ease Hugh's punishment."

Anne got up on her elbow and looked down at him. Her dark hair hung in his face and her breasts brushed his chest. "I have to show you the thing that the Syrian kitchen boy used to do to me."

"What's that"?

"First your mother. Ignore her. Take Hugh from the coffin and put him in the dungeon until we hear from Antioch. If Bohemond awards you the fief, my nephew goes go back into the hole and waits there to meet Our Savior."

"What of the Saracen and the child? Sophia would want no threats to Jean."

"You put your hand here, yes, yes ooooooh yes." Her hand reached down to find him, and he was ready. "Yessssss. They are….cannot….inherit….aaaaaah…. Saracens. We will…..find her and ooooh….deal with them…both…" And she rolled up on top of him and they were both lost, again.

■ ■ ■

Hugh sat in a grassy field in Petrousset while Jamilla forged a new sword for their son. Agnes held him in her arms and walked around with him and told him what lovely blue eyes he had and Joscelin and Marguerite and Roger and Madeleine were reaching out come to us now he is such a handsome boy and the sunlight was blinding blinding and something fell with a thud and he tumbled into the River Alberensa and it was cold and wet and he was in agony his muscles cramping……

"Jesus, Mary and Joseph, Ramon, look at that piece of shit. What a fucking stench. What a mess." Alain put the water bucket down on the floor and climbed into the hole while Ramon spoke to the other prisoner.

"It's your lucky day, asshole. Sir Guy says next time you get drunk and talk to his daughter like that, he'll cut off your balls." He undid the chains holding the man's wrists to the wall. "Get your fucking ass out of here before he changes his mind."

Francois cried out with the pain as he moved his legs, "AAAAHHHH"! Bent his back differently for the first time in days, "OOOOWWWW"! He knelt up, "Jesus Christ, fuck me, FUCK ME"! The prisoner kept groaning from the pain, but he didn't waste any time. His crabbed body moaned its way up the stairs and into the firmament, where the bright star in the distance slowly became the sun.

"Let me help you, Alain," Ramon said, and climbed into the coffin. Together they hauled Hugh up and tossed him on the floor. The Count shrieked as his frozen muscles cried out, except that no sound came from his dry mouth, just a rush of air. The light hurt his eyes, the single candle blazing brighter than the sun. He lay in the shit-filled straw exactly as the two soldiers had dropped him. "Wurrrrrr." He forced his thickened tongue to move. "Pluuu, wuuuurrrrrrrr."

"What's he saying"? Alain asked.

"Whaddya think"? Ramon answered. "'Wur.' This piece of shit traitor is thirsty." He picked up a bucket.

"The water is coming, my lord the Baron of Saracen. First you need a bath." Two more buckets of cold water splashed down on Hugh, freshening the smell of piss and horse manure and his own turds in his clothes. Each cold wave made him flinch and scream his soundless scream against the pain of moving. He slurped eagerly at the little water that came into his mouth, desperate for more.

"Wuuurrrr, pleeee, wurrrrr." Baron Julian would never beg, or Giles, or Frederic, Hugh knew, but he was just Hugh the Ironmaker. Please, Lord, please, I need water, please.

Ramon kicked him. "Move your ass over there." Hugh pulled himself to the spot where Francois had been, dragging his frozen legs. The shackles went on his wrists and on his ankles, but at least these chains let him move around. He could slide towards one side, letting on the opposite arm straight out, and then he could reach his mouth with his hand.

Ramon scooped water out of another bucket with a cup and held it to his mouth. Hugh pushed his whole face into the cup, inhaling the water, choking. "Easy, my lord the Baron Traitor, easy with the water. Little sips." Hugh sucked thirstily every time the cup was against his lips. "Extra ration today." Ramon put bread down, and more water. Alain dropped the door to his coffin closed and Hugh tried to stretch his legs over it. He shivered from the cold water.

"See you tomorrow, my lord," said Alain, and the two men went up the stairs. The candlelight faded to the glow in the corridor and, when the door slammed in the distance, to black.

Hugh struggled to get comfortable in the straw, closed his eyes and saw Jamilla. "Out of the depths I cried to you, O Lord," she said, "and you have heard my voice."

7

When her time came, two weeks after Safiya arrived, Jamilla understood her mother's meaning. She had imagined terrible pain, awful pain. She fell short of the actual agony. As her contractions mounted in intensity and drew closer and closer, taking away any moment of relief, she thrashed and writhed while her mother spoke calming words and told her, "Wait! Don't push! Wait! Not yet"!

"Oh God! Oh God, Hugh you bastard! Look what you've done to me! It hurts so much you dog! Oh God! Oh God"!

The Sisters increased the level of their chanting to drown out the heathen sounds.

Nine hours after it started, God had indeed presented Jamilla with a lovely gift. Her little boy appeared pink and healthy, crying loudly right away, until she placed him against her breast. He suckled briefly, calmed down against the sound of her heartbeat, and fell asleep.

Sister Martha knew when the screaming stopped and the laughter started that God in His mercy had been gracious today. She sent for the convent's priest to baptize the Baron's son. Safiya was shocked, but her daughter pushed back.

"He will be the Seventh Baron of Jabil al-Hadid, Mother. When he is older, he will make his own choice, but I will honor my husband and baptize him now, as he wished."

So it was that the two Saracen women stood and watched the Maronite priest nestle Jamilla's child in his arm and recite the ancient words, in Syriac.

"I baptize you Guilhabert," taking up the cup and dipping it into the consecrated water,

"In the name of the Father," pouring water over the baby's head,

"And of the Son," a second pour,

"And of the Holy Spirit," a third pour, three times for the Holy Trinity,

"Amen."

Guilhabert cried but a moment as the love of the Risen Lord entered him, and then he was back in Jamilla's arms, content.

■ ■ ■

Seven men reclined on cushions in a formal reception room. At the place of honor, on the highest seat, sat Hassan ibn Ishaq al-Haddad, The Blacksmith. His father Ishaq had indeed been a smith, but the son grew from forging iron to selling it, becoming one of the richest merchants in Homs.

The serving girl let Hassan run his hands inside her thigh as she bent to wait on him. She felt pleasure again in his gentle touch. He was skilled for one so old, and considerate, and she enjoyed their nights together. A woman's place was hard. To bear his child would give her an advantage granted few others.

Khalid and his five adult brothers watched and smiled. Their little brother Yusuf was among them, although he understood nothing.

"Khalid," Hassan said, admiring the girl's shape as she walked away. "Tell them."

"Our sister Jamilla is not dead. Abu Khalid gave her to the Infidels for her protection." He looked around, especially at Buran's son Sa'id. "Protection from us. It is Abu Khalid's position that our sister was attacked against her will. She committed no offense. She did not dishonor our family."

The voice of the Blacksmith followed. "Does any here disagree? Speak now"!

No one spoke. Khalid continued.

"Umm Yusuf has sent word that Jamilla gave birth to a son by our father's friend, the Infidel Baron Hugh. Our sister is now Umm Guilhabert Jamilla."

Murmurs followed. "Her child is not…" Sa'id began.

"The Baron entered into a marriage contract with our sister," Khalid answered. "Under *Sharia*, Guilhabert is their lawful child."

"A marriage contract with an Infidel? That cannot…"

Hassan raised his head and glared at his sons.

"Tell them of the prize, Abu Mansur Khalid, my son, tell them of the prize"!

Sa'id caught Yusuf and sat him down, holding the little boy. What gold or silver had Jamilla found in the far-off Infidel kingdoms?

"The Infidel Baron has learned how to make the iron flow. He can make the bloomery iron, the soft iron, run like water. It can be cast and worked and turned into steel. Steel that is as fine as the Hinduwani, perhaps even finer. No one has ever done this, my brothers, not even the fabled Men of the East. It is a prize for us, a prize of great value."

"How is this done"? Nasr asked.

"There is an extra furnace," Khalid answered. "Jamilla has seen it. She has the plans, the drawings. She knows all the details for how it works."

Hassan raised his hand again.

"My sons, this is a gift to us, to our family, from God the All-Compassionate, the All-Merciful. The secret of the flowing iron is the reward of the Great Judge for sparing Jamilla's life. God the All-Knowing knows that she is not a harlot." All the force that made Hassan a great merchant and a powerful leader flowed from him now. "Jamilla will return to us now, with my grandson Guilhabert. I will hear no talk of Hadd offenses, none. You will embrace your sister and your new nephew. You will love her and honor her for as long as she should live. You will respect her as your Princess, your *Amira*. Do you so swear"?

There was a moment of hesitation, until Khalid stood and put his hand across his heart. "Abu Khalid Hassan, Hassan ibn Ishaq al-Haddad, in the name of God the Creator of the Universe, I swear it."

Each followed in his turn. Even Yusuf squeaked out the words, *"Walli al-Khaliq,"* in his little boy voice. Laughter followed. One so young could not swear an oath, but Yusuf's pride at being a man amused them all.

Hassan rose to his feet as the laughter faded.

"You have done well, my sons, and I am pleased." The eyes narrowed. "The Messenger of God, may the blessings and peace of God be always upon him, has warned that the Fire waits for any man who swears falsely."

He looked at each son, one at a time, holding them with his eyes.

"This I promise you. Whoever goes back on this oath after I am gone will not need to wait for the Fire. Umm Yusuf and Abu Mansur will bring my vengeance down on him. Do you understand"?

A silence like death, an imagination of a Fire more terrible than the heat of a smelter, settled upon the room. Hassan nodded, satisfied.

"Good. *Al-Amira* will be among us again by the day after tomorrow. We will hold a feast in honor of her return. We will all rejoice that she is back in the bosom of her family. Good day, my sons."

Safiya had known her husband well. Jamilla was still the light of his old eyes.

8

Hugh tried hard to keep count. He thought Alain or Ramon had come seventeen times since they had pulled him from his grave. Or maybe sixteen. Or eighteen. One visit a day, and there was a rhythm to each one. A rumbling, which must be the gate moving, was followed soon after by the visit. Much later, there was another rumbling, but no visit. They fed him in the morning, Hugh guessed, after they opened the gate. He made it a point, then, to eat only half what they brought in the morning. When the gate rumbled down in the evening, he ate the rest.

Visions of roasted meat, of feasts in Alberensa with Agnes and Giles and Ekaterina and Maura joined his other waking dreams. He made himself drunk on Gascon wine and rolled in the straw, unable to get up. Sitting amidst his urine and his offal, his image of the world grew dim, as though this dark hole, interrupted once a day by a single candle, was the only thing he had ever known. He was, he realized, slowly losing his mind.

He heard the rumbling and started to count. Usually they were here before he reached one hundred. He reached three hundred before he was interrupted by Jamilla walking down the stairs in her blue tunic. No, he wanted it to be red today, red!

The faintest of faint glows appeared high on the staircase. No, stop, the light is driving Jamilla away! Voices, the footsteps of many men, not one. Many men with many candles made the cell as bright as any in the castle. Hugh's eyes hurt, but for the first time he could see the far wall, five paces away, the dirty straw, his own filth. A chair appeared, and a man with fresh clothes. And then, Josse of Sarlant.

"Unshackle the traitor and stand him up"!

"OWWWW"!

His arms tore at his sockets, and his ankles tingled in pain. He fell. They pulled him up again.

"AAAAAAAAHHHHH"!

"Shut up." Hugh looked at Josse, confused. "Undress him."

Two men ripped off Hugh's clothing, stripping him naked. Shit ran down his bare legs as they dumped his clothes into a heap.

"Put those in a bag and burn them." A guard jumped to comply.

"Give him a bath." The buckets came now, rinsing him down. And then a cloth.

"Wash yourself off." He washed, and dried, and dressed in fresh cotte and tunic.

"Clean him up." Alain shoved Hugh into the chair. He sat quietly while a man trimmed his hair and shaved his beard.

"Let's go."

The Baron crawled up the stairs on his knees, but he managed to stand at the top. His walk grew steadier as they drew near the corner. At least they were going to kill him outside, in the sunshine, instead of down in this hole.

The star's light appeared far off in the dark sky, growing brighter and brighter, too bright and suddenly he was in the courtyard with his eyes squinted down, staring at the dirt because the sky was too painful. The sun warmed him, even if he could not look. He had been cold for so long that he had forgotten that he was cold.

"Where is the Countess of Alberensa"? It was Frederic's voice, from in front.

"She does not wish to come," said the voice of Esmeralda.

"Fetch her now, girl, now! Prince Bohemond has sent a message. Even a Countess must attend its reading"! Hugh heard Esmeralda's shuffling feet and ventured a look to follow her. It still hurt, but at least he could stand it now. His balance was improving. The aches in his joints were receding. He shivered in the sunlight, shaking off the chill. He raised his eyes to look around.

Frederic stood in front of the entire household, dressed in his mail, with the arms of Jabil al-Hadid on his tunic. Sir Guy stood on his left. To his right stood another knight, a man Hugh didn't recognize. The man was Frederic's age, short and already too heavy. Even before he spoke, his arrogance could be felt in his bearing. This man would never fight, because he was related to someone important. And he had learned how to read.

Maura hurried out between Esmeralda and Louisa. Her green dress, her surcoat, her whole appearance, disheveled, distraught. Tears streaked her face.

"My lord, I….."

"Silence! You have kept Sir Fulcher waiting, my lady! Was William's message to your fat maid not clear"? Frederic pointed at Esmeralda. "Even in Toulouse a Countess does not send a serving girl, even one of such obvious charms as this wench, to attend to the embassy of a Prince"!

"My lord, my husband is not….."

"Be silent, I said! Take your place and do not delay us further with your prattle"! Hugh realized that revenge had been replaced by dynastic advantage, although it appeared that Maura's repentance had come too late.

The visitor began speaking.

"My lords. I am Fulcher, nephew of Bohemond IV, Prince of Antioch, who is also Count of Tripoli. His Royal Highness, your liege, has sent me as his envoy." He turned to Hugh. "Do you, Hugh, claim that you are the Baron of Jabil al-Hadid, rightly seized of this fief"?

It was still too bright, but Hugh looked directly at Fulcher as he answered. "I do."

"Do you, Frederic and Anne of Jabil al-Hadid, still claim that Hugh has forfeited this fief through felony"?

Anne appeared as the perfect model of a noble Christian lady. Her dark gown and surcoat, long shoes, cap and fine veil, spoke of her breeding and her good taste. Her clothes were not too tight today, no, rather they were elegant. She stepped forward, stood beside her husband and curtsied to Sir Fulcher.

"We do," they said in unison.

"What of Hugh's sister Agnes? We have heard that she is a heretic, crippled and blinded for her sins."

"No, no, my lord," Maura wailed. "That is not true. Lady Juviler was at the convent, my lord, at the convent. She is not a heretic, my lord….."

"Please, woman, cease these interruptions," Sir Fulcher replied. "Your cousin Count Raymond would not accept them in Toulouse. You are not here to speak, but to attend to the envoy of your liege." Maura stood, shocked, frightened at the violence. Louisa reached out from behind and drew her back. "Sir Frederic? What of Agnes"?

"We have heard the same, that she has taken the *Consolamentum*," Frederic answered. "It is of no matter here. Even a faithful Catholic woman cannot inherit Jabil al-Hadid."

Fulcher nodded, "Quite so." He drew himself up to his full height.

"Both Hugh and Frederic contend that they are the rightful Baron of Jabil al-Hadid," Fulcher said. "It is the decree of Bohemond, Prince of Antioch, Count of Tripoli, that the rightful holder of the fief shall be chosen by God from among the contenders." He glared at Maura, daring her to speak. Her bulk shook, frightened at what she had helped to start. She remained silent.

Hugh considered Frederic, Guy, so many men here who would have risen to his sister's defense eagerly three years ago. Today, silence.

"My sister is innocent of this claim of heresy, my lord, as Sir Frederic well knows."

"You are lying," Elizabeth blurted out, "And she is lying and God will judge it so! Our just and righteous Lord will send you both to the Pit"!

Sir Fulcher drew himself up. "That is for God to decide, my lady. In two weeks time. Our business here is finished. Sir Frederic. I gratefully accept your invitation to dinner."

Frederic turned to his wife. "My lady, will you allow Sir Fulcher to escort you"?

Anne stepped up, the Baroness-To-Be, and gave her arm to the Prince's nephew. Frederic turned to the assembly.

"Countess, if you feel unwell, you may retire with your maids. Mother, permit me to escort you. Sir Guy. You have your instructions. Follow them, then please join us with Lady Catherine."

The courtyard emptied in a matter of a few minutes. The guards walked the rampart as dust from the leaving filtered slowly to the ground. It felt good just to stand there, waiting, warming, tasting the dust, smelling the air. Hugh didn't mind the leg irons they fastened to his ankles or the handcuffs to his wrists, as long as he could stay out of the hole.

"Take him to the forge, Sir Josse," Sir Guy ordered. "Sir Fulcher has decreed that he is to work there and regain his strength for the trial by combat. It's the traitor's favorite place anyway." A final scowl, and Guy turned for the Keep.

"Let's go," Josse said, motioning Alain and Ramon to accompany them. He called up to the guard, "Raise the gate." A nudge from the guard, and Hugh, Sixth Baron Jabil al-Hadid, left his castle in irons, shuffling towards his forge.

9

The Baron of Jabil al-Hadid took his place at the bellows in his own forge. An Infidel from the castle kept the Syrians away, but their interest in talking to their lord was already limited. Either he would soon be dead, or he would again be their lord. No man wished to risk an action that might be perceived as a slight should the All-Merciful God extend His mercy to this Unbeliever. Only Mahmud hazarded any approach at all, and then only to have the guard move him from hearth to hearth.

Hugh found the labor tedious, monotonous, but at least it was the monotony of action, not the boredom of a dark hole in the ground. And it helped him regain his strength. The more they worked him at the forge, the more he built up his arms, extended the endurance of his wind, regained the flexibility in his body. They let him dine with the Syrians. He ate and drank his fill.

The Baron focused his mind on the task to come. Like his grandfather Olivier, he was a merchant with a title, but also a warrior. He worked to bring forward his warrior's mind for his own Hattin.

On his first night at the smelter, Hugh wondered if God's judgment had ever been awarded to the weaker fighter. He decided it had not. He decided that Bohemond knew it had not. All the cleaning and eating and strengthening in the world would never turn him into a warrior like Frederic. This trial was Antioch's way, Tripoli's way, of giving Frederic the fief without coming up with a justification. Instead, the Prince arranged for legalized murder masquerading as the Will of God.

■ ■ ■

Sir Frederic. Hugh had thought about him often in the dungeon. One night at the forge, he permitted himself to think about him one more time. To purge the regrets from his mind. To prepare himself for the battle to come.

They had been friends, especially after Joscelin died. Hugh concluded that no man had come between them to bring on this fight to the death. God in His infinite wisdom had chosen women as His instruments. Elizabeth championed Jean. Anne thirsted for revenge for Baudoin. Hugh protected his sister and loved his Saracen and jilted his wife. He gave Frederic all the grounds he needed to conspire with Anne and assert Jean's claims. Even gentle Sophia, watching from heaven, must be urging the Lord to take Frederic's side.

Enough. My cousin and my aunt betrayed me. They are stealing my fief. And, as he knew after Mahmud whispered in his ear, Guilhabert's fief.

Hugh smiled. His son was safe. Jamilla bint Hassan al-Haddad was safe. She would always be his Princess, *al-Amira* Jamilla, for as long as he lived. Just as he planned, Agnes was safe, far from the treachery here, protected by the agreement with Cardinal Donato, protected by Giles.

Hugh's smile disappeared. Antioch has set Sir Frederic on you. He is your enemy. Prepare for battle, without quarter, to the death. Fight him as well as you can until you no longer can, and then trust in Our Savior's merciful grace.

■ ■ ■

Two weeks after Sir Fulcher's visit, Stephen of Orcival rode down from Krak. At the Prince's request, the Grand Master would judge the combat. Sir Guy brought the news.

"The Grand Master has arrived. The combat will take place tomorrow, when the sun stands over Iron Mountain. I'll send your armor and weapons in the morning." He turned and rode away, then rode back. "No man is willing to act as your second." Turned and was gone.

That night, chained in his hut by the forge, Hugh slept very little. He tried to feel remorse for his deceit towards Maura. He could not. For that he prayed for forgiveness. He prayed for forgiveness for leaving Maura without an heir. For leaving Agnes. For leaving Jamilla. And for leaving Guilhabert.

Lord God, protect them all. Do not let my sins, my failures as Baron and Count and brother and husband and father be visited on them if I am gone.

10

Sir Josse delivered Hugh's armor and his mount. He ordered the guard to return with him. Their departure left the Baron alone for the first time since he walked into his castle from Tripoli.

He watched the guard recede. He looked towards Guilhabert's stone bridge. He understood Frederic's message, both gift and insult.

In memory of our former friendship, I offer you life, traitor. Take it. Mount up. Ride away to your Saracen whore. Spend your days cleaning the chamber pots in your father-in-law's house.

Mahmud helped Hugh saddle his mount and put its armor in place. To put on his own mail, his boots, and his tunic with the arms of Jabil al-Hadid. His sword and his dagger. Coif and helmet.

Ready.

Syrian and Frank waited silently together for the trumpet to sound. Hugh's horse pawed the ground, nervous, sensing the anxiety in the two men.

The Baron looked towards Guilhabert's stone bridge, the escape to Homs.

No.

Sir Frederic insulted the Baroness of Juviler. You cannot betray her honor. If you do that and return to Alberensa, Sir Giles will still obey you, but he will never respect you.

If you return to Alberensa, Jamilla and Guilhabert will languish in Homs, orphans in their own family.

The smelter, the iron. For six generations, your family has created the metal here. The sinful incestuous lust of your felonious cousin and your sex-crazed aunt have destroyed it all. You cannot betray the work of your ancestors.

And you cannot betray yourself. Some men can live with dishonor as long as they can live. You, the Baron of Jabil al-Hadid, the Count of Alberensa, you are not one of them.

Agnes always knew, even if you did not. "You may not be as skilled as many, but you are as courageous as any. In my nightmares you die bravely." Yes, in that, Hugh of Jabil al-Hadid, in death before dishonor, you have surprised yourself. You are not only a merchant with a title. You are a nobleman, a knight, a Crusader.

The trumpet sounded the call. Mahmud helped Hugh to mount, made sure that his feet were in the stirrups, and handed up his lance.

"You always had the respect of the men here, my lord. Aram especially. May God the Conqueror ride with you in this fight. May the Giver of Victory give you victory today. May the Exalted One bring you back from this combat as our lord, *inshallah*."

"*Inshallah*. Go with God, Mahmud, God the All-Merciful, God the All-Compassionate."

■ ■ ■

The smelter, his smelter, fell away behind him.

Hugh had not used a lance in years, since he had learned as a youth. Frederic trained on it often, participated in the jousts and in actual battles. His warrior spirit welcomed the thundering gallop that preceded the mighty collision.

Against such a threat, Hugh shaped a simple though dangerous plan. Survive the first pass of the lance, be unhorsed, and hope for Frederic to join him on the ground. Use Giles' training to seek an advantage with the sword. If his luck still held, there might be a fatal mistake from his cousin, some carelessness caused by his belief in his own superiority. Hugh might kill him, and survive.

No. He remembered his man with the guerdon before Fonta, as Giles urged him to think only of victory.

You are the Baron of Jabil al-Hadid. God will judge it so.

You will kill Frederic.

You will survive.

The Iron Mountain rose in the distance behind the fortress as Hugh approached. The castle gates stood open. Except for the rampart guard, the entire company had lined up along the Tripoli Road. His men wore their armor and carried their arms, yet a festive air filled the day. Maids and cooks and grooms mixed in with the soldiers. If a woman had a beautiful gown, one that she wore to chapel or to dinner in the Great Hall, she put it on. Ten Hospitallers, Sir Stephen's escort, gathered behind the crowd. Their black cloaks made the only spot of night among the bright colors of the day.

Hugh turned behind him. He saw his Arab serfs tending their fields, ignoring the commotion. Today's fight among the Infidels held no interest for them at all.

Hugh picked out Esmeralda in her Alberensa livery as he rode by. The arm of The Prize rested on Sir Josse and her eyes rested on his face and she had eyes for no other. Even as Hugh watched, she pulled a veil from her cap and laughed as she tied it around his arm. Bright sun and bright colors and the favor of one so noble banished all memory of her father's souvenir shop in Alberensa.

Hugh's mount grew skittish as he pulled alongside Frederic. Sir Stephen waited on foot in front of the two knights, flanked on each side by the ladies of Jabil al-Hadid. Elizabeth and Anne stood regal and elegant in almost matching tunics of red covered by white surcoats. Anne smiled at Frederic and he smiled back.

The animals snorted. The flags billowed. Everyone waited for the Grand Master to begin. From somewhere in all the color, Hugh marveled that Anne had finally found contentment with a single man.

His father's voice called, and Sir Giles. Stay hard. Do not let your mind wander. See your sword going into Frederic's throat. Make it so.

"My lords. I am Stephen of Orcival, Grand Master of the Sovereign Military Order of the Knights of the Hospital of Saint John in Jerusalem." Stephen wore his hauberk and his black cloak with its Hospitaller star, but left his head bare. "I am here to judge the trial by combat between Hugh of Jabil al-Hadid and Frederic of Jabil al-Hadid to resolve the claim of each to be lord of this place."

"My lord, if I might." Anne took a step forward, causing the Grand Master to turn.

"Yes my lady"?

"Sir Frederic rides for the honor of Jabil al-Hadid against a traitor. I offer up this token to my husband to carry, remembering the generations of Jabil al-Hadid who favor his cause." Anne removed a red kerchief from her sleeve. Frederic leaned down to take it. He put it to his mouth and kissed it, and tied it around his belt.

"Sir Hugh"?

"I am ready, my lord."

Sir Stephen drew his cloak around him. "Father Sebastian, would you grant absolution"?

Sebastian's appearance marked the first time that Hugh had seen the priest since he returned. In his memory of the man, the Father was not so heavy, or so old. Sebastian looked in despair at his old friend Joscelin's son, near tears, but he discharged his office.

"My lords," and he bowed to them. "Please lower your weapons."

Both men tipped their lances to the ground. Sebastian sprinkled holy water from the baptismal font on each tip.

"We trust that the Lord our God will judge this combat fairly and award victory to the righteous man. May our Savior Jesus Christ have mercy on the soul of the other."

"Amen," answered the entire company of Jabil al-Hadid.

The priest raised his hand, making the sign of the cross.

"O God, pardon and deliver these your servants from all their sins. Bring them to everlasting life, through Jesus Christ our Lord, who lives and reigns with You and the Holy Spirit, One God, now and forever."

"Amen."

Hugh's mount skittered at the sound of so many voices speaking at once. The priest stepped back. The lances tipped up. Sir Stephen stepped forward.

"My lords. You shall start with lances. You shall fight until one of you is unable to continue. If that man is still alive, the other shall decide his fate. Make ready now, and begin when the trumpet sounds."

Hugh and Frederic turned towards one another, held their lances upright and tipped them in salute. They spoke no words. They rode away from each other, along the road, fifty paces.

Hugh turned and drew up his mount, waiting for Frederic to do the same. A remarkable stillness settled upon him. He centered himself on the battle to come, as a monk centered himself in his prayers. He had no room in his mind for family, or smelters, or Lengadòc, only for the hundred paces of dirt that separated him from his enemy.

The trumpet floated into Hugh's consciousness, a sound from outside, from another place. Cheers rose along the Tripoli Road, handkerchiefs waved, veils streamed out in the breeze. His lance came down as he started off at a trot. The two knights angled to pass right to right, lances striking into the other man's shield, or if the attacker was good, the other man.

Frederic increased to a gallop and Hugh did the same. Weapons and shields moved, aiming, protecting, the riders leaning forward into the coming crash. Thundering hooves and cheering crowds echoed faintly in Hugh's ears as he put his whole mind into the tip of his weapon.

O Lord My God, as You gave David the victory over Goliath, so guide this lance through The Harlot's red kerchief and into The Betrayer's gut!

Suddenly, the overwhelming shock of the collision. A shout from the crowd accompanied the crash of lance into shield. Hugh held his shield exactly where it needed to be, saving his life. Instead of piercing him, Frederic's blow lifted shield, lance and Hugh straight out of the saddle. Iron Mountain turned upside down and right side up and out of sight as he thudded on the ground. He planned to be unhorsed, but a blow like that would unhorse anyone, even a man trying to stay mounted.

The hoofbeats of their animals stayed loud, strangely loud amidst all the confusion of his fall. Hugh knelt up, still dazed, and turned to face his enemy. Frederic turned his mount back for another pass, then realized that his lance was broken. Hugh's lance was not, giving him the advantage if his opponent tried to charge. Frederic fell into Hugh's plan, sliding from his horse as both men drew their swords.

They heard hoofbeats again, the sound of their animals running away.

No, the hoofbeats were getting louder, louder. Hugh realized that the cheers of the assembly had become screams. Arrows began falling into the bright and festive crowd.

Frederic stopped. Hugh stopped. Everyone else was running for the castle.

The hooves are not here, they're beyond the forge. Yes, yes, as Syrian warriors poured out of the slag gulch and across Baron Guilhabert's stone bridge, swords out, yelling the *takbir*.

"ALLĀHU AKBAR"!

Hugh turned the other way. More men thundered from the canyon with the glade.

"ALLĀHU AKBAR"!

God is Great! The call sounded from two hundred throats.

Waves of hoofbeats, waves of sound, waves of arrows. The serfs tending their fields had become archers, and been joined by other archers, filling the sky with deadly missiles. Christians fell, pierced through the back as they tried to run for safety.

A lone woman walked steadily through the fields, wearing abaya and hijab and niqab. The archers rushed past her, and the horsemen, even the real Syrian serfs brandishing their hoes and scythes, but she kept her steady pace. Only one woman in the whole world walked like that, only one.

Suddenly Jamilla began running, waving at him, yelling something that he could not hear. He felt an incredibly sharp pain in his back, through his chest.

"You have betrayed us, Hugh, you traitor! Roast in hell with your Saracen Witch"!

The Count turned and looked behind. He saw Frederic let go of the hilt of Julian's sword, the sword brought out from Blagnac. The tip, he realized, extended from the front of his chest, lifting his coat of mail. He took a step forward, holding out his hand towards his bride.

11

The Christians ran for the castle as hard as they could, but the rampart guard knew that the charging horses would get there first. The iron portcullis crashed down even as the crowd cried out to leave it up. The guard moved to close the solid gate, securing the fortress.

Sir Stephen joined his knights, shouting at them, moving towards their horses to mount up for the attack. Sir Guy did the same, but the civilians mixed in with his soldiers hampered his efforts. Women cried and screamed and crouched behind the men, trying to hide from the storm of Saracen arrows. Guy stood firmly upright, a rock of Christian strength. Men and women fell all around him as he shouted out his orders.

"Form up! On me! We must fight together to the gate! To run is to die"!

The knight cursed to himself as the Saracen cavalry swarmed around the Christian host. He warned

Frederic to patrol in case of ambush, but his liege found it unnecessary. Instead, he spent the morning in bed with Anne the Whore.

Guy felt someone clinging to his leg. He looked down. His wife?

"Catherine. Lead the women to the castle while we make a stand here. The Saracens want the men, not you. If we draw them off, they will not molest you."

Another wall of arrows swept through the Christian mob, slaying the man next to Guy. "No, no, I can't, I'm afraid, help me, Guy, save me"!

He pushed her down behind him. "Then let go! Stay down and get the women together"! He looked to his men. "The gate, men, the gate! Shelter the women and make for the gate! This battle is yet ours to win"!

From Guilhabert's bridge, the Syrian leader surveyed his threats. Deal with their cavalry first, the Black Knights. Do not let them get on horse.

Shouted Arabic, more shouts. The archers turned their attention to the Hospitallers. Riders from the gulch reached the small band of knights, *"Allāhu akbar"!* swinging and slashing with swords of Damascus steel, cutting down the Infidel Three-God polytheists as they tried to mount.

Four men managed to hang onto the pommels without mounting, turn their mounts and make for Krak. Sir Stephen watched in amazement as the cowards raced away. He stood among his six dead men, put his sword to the ground, and waited.

Across the Tripoli Road, a woman in black walked slowly towards the battle. Stephen's spine chilled and tingled. The Saracen god had sent his Angel of Death to claim the Grand Master's soul.

The Syrian leader turned his attention to the fray before the castle. By concentrating on the Black Knights, he had let the leader there form up his men and women and move them in steady motion towards the castle gate. He must organize a final assault before they made it inside.

"Keep moving," Guy shouted. "Get close enough for the rampart guard to use their crossbows"! Bolts began passing over his head now, striking the ground in front of the Syrians. Their leader held back, surveying, drawing his horsemen and his archers together. "Steady, steady, keep moving"! Sir Guy shouted. "We're almost there."

"Allāhu akbar! Allāhu akbar"!

Guy looked towards the fresh sound. No so fresh, actually, just missed in all the noise of battle. The Saracens from the glade were not making for the battle but rather for the rear of the castle. *"Allāhu akbar"!* Ropes, grappling hooks, even ladders rode with the shouting Saracen warriors as they disappeared from sight.

Like Sir Guy, the rampart guard realized too late what was happening. They raced the Saracens to the far side along the wall but arrived too late. Fifty Syrians broke both ways as they gained the ramparts, killing each Christian they reached until the rest surrendered. They left the inner wooden door closed, mounted a watch and began to search the outbuildings and the Keep. The crossbow bolts ceased. A moment later, the guerdon of Jabil al-Hadid fluttered from its mast to the ground.

With the falling guerdon, the Syrian leader ordered the charge. His archers unleashed a final volley at Guy's assembly. The riders came forward in line, swords out.

"Allāhu akbar"!

Guy turned to meet them, forcing back the thought that his cause was forfeit.

"Fight until the victory! It is the Will of God"!

The Syrian cavalry smashed through the Christian foot. From horseback, they cut down any man who stood to fight. Men who tried to run met the same fate. After the first pass, the survivors put up their hands and surrendered.

The shouts of battle ended, replaced with the moaning of the wounded and the dying. The Syrian leader drew up his mount and raised his sword to the heavens.

"Allāhu akbar"!

His men responded, lifting their swords, pounding their shields, stamping their feet.

"ALLĀHU AKBAR! ALLĀHU AKBAR! ALLĀHU AKBAR"!

In the span of ten minutes, the army of Jamilla bint Hassan al-Haddad ended one hundred and twenty-five years of Christian rule at Jabil al-Hadid.

■ ■ ■

As the battle raged, Frederic climbed onto Hugh, both feet, trying to work free Julian's sword. The victory cheers reached him just as he succeeded. He looked up to find ten Saracen warriors surrounding him. He raised his sword to attack one, but the man fell back. Frederic turned to attack another. He, too fell back while the first closed in behind. The Syrians would not fight, nor would they let him escape.

The woman in black arrived. "Take him alive." She knelt down beside Hugh as Frederic attempted battle again. One Syrian baited him forward. Three men jumped on him from behind, forcing him down on his face. He lost his weapon, his helmet and his coif.

The woman stood up from Hugh's body. "I will carry the sword."

A warrior presented the weapon, hilt first. She turned the bloody steel in her hand. Not since Hattin, before Fulk took it from his dead enemy's hand, had a Saracen touched Julian's sacred weapon.

"Carry my husband to the yard, with honor." The tip of the sword pushed against Frederic's armor. "You. Move."

God had judged the combat fairly. If the righteous man was no longer alive, at least he had been awarded the triumph.

12

With their victory chant concluded, the Syrian leader shouted at the Christians.

"Drop your weapons! Everyone into the castle yard"!

The survivors needed no Arabic to understand. All around them, bodies lay crumpled on the gentle slope between the Tripoli Road and the castle, women as well as men. The fallen traced out a colorful pyramid, wide along the Road and narrow as the runners were cut down before they could reach Jabil al-Hadid. None of the fallen could hear as the sound of battle gave way to smaller sounds, hooves here, voices there.

The Saracen leader broke his men into small groups, rounding up stragglers, ordering the healthy Christians back to assist the wounded. Within minutes, the chaos of little movements became a steady flow towards the castle, men and women and horses piling up near the re-opened gate like water at the precipice of a cataract.

A horseman swept up Sir Stephen and marched him toward the entrance, with the Saracen riding behind. Behind them, Death's Angel knelt over the ironmonger's body while Saracens fought Sir Frederic above her head. One of Sir Guy's soldiers cried out to the Hospitaller as he passed, "We have been betrayed, my lord"!

"Yes, we have," Sir Stephen answered, "but by whom"?

■ ■ ■

Anne waited until the shouting Saracens moved away before she stood up, slowly, carefully, so as not to attract an arrow.

"My lord. My lord, please get up." Anne saw Guy's wife, wailing as she tried to pull her husband to his feet. Blood from the stump of his severed arm covered her dress and face.

"Frederic!" Anne turned to the new sound and saw Elizabeth standing nearby. "Frederic!" Anne followed her gaze, to the place where the Saracen woman pushed her husband forward.

"Lady Elizabeth. Let's go inside, my lady."

"Is this what they were like in Homs, Anne"? Anne lifted Elizabeth's arm and put it around her shoulder. "They are murderers, these Saracens."

"Let's go, Mother." Elizabeth didn't seem to notice the arrow point protruding from her stomach. Its shaft pinned her surcoat to her back, high up. A circle of red slowly spread into the white. More red trickled from her mouth. The arrow had dealt a mortal wound, with death only a matter of hours, no more.

"Did he kill him? Did Sir Frederic kill that filthy Athèné's filthy grandson"?

"Yes, Mother, he did."

Elizabeth smiled, a smile of great satisfaction. "Then I greet you as my liege, Baroness Anne of Jabil al-Hadid."

They stumbled towards the gate, past Sir Josse, run through the neck by a Saracen blade. Fat Maura's beautiful maid lay nearby, her Alberensa tunic torn and her face crushed by an Arab horse. A Saracen knelt to cut a lock of her straw-white hair. Anne guided them around, away from his reach.

The cool of the entrance tower passed by. They entered the heat and chaos of the yard. Shouting in Arabic, lots of shouting as the Saracens divided their captives, separating the men-at-arms from the few knights. Other soldiers scoured the buildings. Piles of Christian armor and Christian weapons grew steadily, the chain mail mounding up like haystacks after the fall harvest.

"Sir Frederic is your consort, Lady Jabil al-Hadid, and Jean shall inherit and Fulk is avenged. It is a great day for Jabil al-Hadid. We shall toast your success tonight, at dinner."

Anne marveled that even now the pain of her wound had not reached Elizabeth. Dampness stained the red of her dress, darkening her stomach. Finally she winced. "Help me sit down, my liege. I ran too hard. I need to catch my breath." She looked around. "My liege, you should order the gate closed. The Saracens are getting in."

Anne turned towards the clamor by the chapel, as a dozen women and children were driven from its sanctuary into the yard. Immediately after, an apparition in nightclothes waddled through the door of the Great Hall. Knots filled Maura's hair. Offal stained her gown. Tears filled her red eyes as she surveyed the chaos before her.

Anne looked at her with contempt. This so-called Countess hasn't even dressed since Sir Fulcher left.

A shriek from behind and Louisa ran out naked, clutching her cotte, followed by the cook, clutching his. The Saracens all laughed, but the Christians were too stunned to enjoy the humor.

The Syrians led Frederic in, hands tied behind his back. Two boys broke from the chapel, "Papa, Papa," and ran towards him. Anne winced as the Saracens caught them and dragged them to stand with the nobles.

Six men carried Filthy Athène's Filthy Grandson on their shoulders and laid him gently on the ground. A bolt of fine black cloth floated in behind them. "All Hail *al-Amira* al-Haddad Jamilla bint Hassan," a Syrian called, followed by laughter. The Princess of al-Haddad knelt down, put her hand to her mouth through her *nikab*, and touched his lips.

"No!" Maura ran and threw herself on Hugh's corpse. She caught the Saracens by surprise with her speed, a cow that moved like a deer. Her arms clutched her Count. Her weight gave her an advantage now as a Syrian tried to pull her off.

"Leave her," Jamilla said as she knelt alongside, stunned at The Cow's sorrow.

Hugh and I were each that perfect star in all the firmament, the one star that shines through eternity only for the other. He was her star, too, if she was not his, and now we have both lost him.

"Leave her. Maura is his first wife. Let her have her grief."

"Hugh, Hugh. I'm sorry Hugh. I was so hurt that I loved you and you didn't love me.....I never wanted this...." She looked up. "You! You! You're that filthy lying bitch Sister Ekaterina! You killed him, Ekaterina you witch. You killed him, you Saracen whore from Hell"! Maura tried to slap the Sister, but Ekaterina no longer existed. Jamilla caught her hand, put it back on Hugh, and stood.

"Not me." She looked towards the nobles. Stephen of Orcival saw Death again through the slit in her *niqab*. He crossed himself.

"They pray to the Infidel god, Umm Guilhabert," the Saracen leader said.

"Yes, Ya'qub *al-Tayyib*, my Generous One," she answered, "they do." She put her hand on his arm. "God the All-Compassionate, the All-Merciful has truly been generous to us today, *al-Tayyib*. It is time to bring His worship back to this place."

Julian's sword shot into the air over Jamilla's head.

"I testify that there is no God but God"!

Her countrymen answered, one voice, their chorus reaching to the heavens, to the glorious Paradise of the All-Compassionate.

"AND I TESTIFY THAT MOHAMMED IS THE PROPHET OF GOD"!

They repeated the prayer, Jamilla leading, the others responding.

"La illah illala Allah"!

"MUHAMAD RASULU ALLAH"!

And again.

"La illah illala Allah"!

"MUHAMAD RASULU ALLAH"!

"ALLĀHU AKBAR"! The Syrian host shouted after they finished the *Shahada*, shouts that shook the *kafir* dust from the once-Christian stones of the castle. *"ALLĀHU AKBAR! ALLĀHU AKBAR"!*

"What's that, Anne"? Elizabeth spoke as the Arabic died away. "What are they saying"? She moved again, and cried out. "It hurts more, Anne, it hurts more, not less. Is it bad"?

Elizabeth put her hand gently on the blood-stained arrow point, as though noticing it for the first time. "Frederic! Help me! It hurts, my son, it hurts"!

She leaned forward and her hands went in the manure. Blood poured from her stomach, dripped from her mouth. The back of her surcoat flamed red in the sunshine. "My tunic. My nicest gown." Her words came out with a spray of blood, frothy and pink that splattered onto the ground. "Why"?

The yard grew silent, respecting her death agony, giving her the space for her final thoughts, her final words. "No." She knelt up, weaving, and found her son again. "Sir Frederic. Did you did kill that filthy….." and tumbled onto her back. The point of the bloody arrow surged above her stomach, a red flag of steel to salute the moment of her death. Louisa broke the silence with a long moan of despair, as she sank, naked, to her knees.

"Stand up," Jamilla said to Anne. "Leave her and stand up." Anne rose from the dead as she had outside, very carefully. "Nasr."

Nasr gripped the red cloth of Jabil al-Hadid. "Kiss me, my Infidel." He grabbed Anne's hair and forced her mouth on his. "That was a greeting from your husband Hassan ibn Ishaq, with his love." He turned to his sister. "This is her, Princess Blacksmith. It's Lady Anne the Slut."

Anne flared in anger. "Princess? You're the daughter of the peasant Safiya. Safiya, a common maid who seduced an old man and took him from me."

"Oh? That from the daughter of a baron who married the grandson of a maid"? Jamilla spoke to Nasr while her eyes locked with Anne's. "Tie up her hands so she does not bother us." She turned to leave, and turned back. "Put up and cover her hair. Who are these boys"?

They did not answer. Nasr drew Anne to him again, grabbed her breast, and squeezed. "My sister asked you a question, Lady Anne the Slut. Who are these boys"? He released her while she gasped for breath, and then put his hand back.

"Stop! Stop! They are my husband's sons, Jean and Luc"!

The yard grew silent, imagining their fate. The boys looked through the slit, but they did not see Death. Rather instead, the eyes of a mother, softer somehow, kinder.

"I do not make war on boys. Take them to the chapel and hold them." She looked around as they were led away. "Is there a man here who speaks French"?

"I do, lady," said one of the men-at-arms. Meaning that he spoke Arabic in addition to French.

"Tell the Infidels that I am Jamilla bint Hassan al-Haddad, the second wife of Hugh, Baron Jabil al-Hadid. Tell them that our son Guilhabert now holds this fief as Baron of Jabil al-Hadid for the Emir of Syria, and that I am his regent. Offer life to all who will swear allegiance to the Emir and take up the True Faith."

The soldier repeated it all. Murmurs followed in the yard, shuffling among the men-at-arms. Jamilla stepped up to the Hospitaller. French came from her mouth, her impenetrable French with its Arabic accent. "Accept True Faith"?

Sir Stephen barely understood the words, but it was enough. Yes, the Saracen god had sent his Angel of Death today. The Grand Master remembered Grand Master Roger de Moulins after Hattin, lifted his thoughts to his Savior and prepared himself for the Heavenly Jerusalem.

"No, you Saracen whore, I do not. A Hospitaller gladly dies as a soldier of Our Lord and Savior Jesus Christ, sure in his own salvation. Roast in Hell, witch of Satan"!

Jamilla looked for confirmation from the soldier. He trembled as he spoke. "He says no, my lady."

As it always was with these Infidel Hospitallers. Jamilla nodded. The man behind her swung his sword, a strong clean stroke. Sir Stephen's head rolled into the dust. She did not even glance at his falling body as she turned again to the soldier.

"Tell the old priest to take six Christians and prepare my lord the Baron for the Christian burial. Carry him into the chapel. Tell the priest to go now or I will ask him the same question. Hamid."

"Yes, *al-Amira*"?

"You go with them, make sure they treat my husband well." She turned to another brother. "Sa'id. Take two Christians and make them dig a grave in the glade."

Maura rose up as the men lifted Hugh's body from under her. Not just her offal, but his blood was on her now, her hands, the arms of her gown, her bodice. She stood to follow, stumbled and curled up in a wailing ball on the ground. Jamilla waited as she passed through the sharp point of her despair, just as she had waited through the death agony of Lady Elizabeth. Only after Hugh's body disappeared through the chapel door and Maura's wails receded into sobs did she speak again to her translator.

"Tell Sir Frederic that he has tried to steal my husband's fief. He has murdered my husband, a foul murder. He has tried to hide it behind this trial by combat, to use the Infidel God as an excuse. That is blasphemy. We have a punishment for such crimes, and all here will witness it."

Anne shrieked, "No!" Running awkwardly with her hands behind her, "Not that! No!" tripping and tumbling to the ground. "Please! No"!

Terror and panic appeared in Frederic's eyes. Terror and panic that no one had ever seen before. He struggled against the Syrian who forced him to his knees. A quick vertical slice, the Syrian using Frederic's dagger, cut open his tunic and through his gambeson and into his stomach. Blood flowed down on Anne's kerchief, brightening it. The defeated knight screamed with the sudden pain as the man reached in, found the intestine, and pulled.

Jamilla handed over Julian's sword, "Here." The soldier wrapped the gut twice around the blade and shoved the tip into the earth. If Frederic moved, he would draw out more bowel, but he could not stay motionless forever. It was said that it sometimes took hours for a man to die this way.

Nasr walked up to stand beside Anne, pulling her to her feet. "No, stop!" she screamed. "It's not too late, let him go, please let him go"!

Anne's eyes darted around the yard, seeking help for Frederic, begging, pleading, but no one moved. She took in the Hospitaller's body sprawled on the ground, his head nestled under Elizabeth's arm. Her husband knelt nearby, screaming as no one had ever heard him scream. The whole castle yard reeked of blood. Just as Elizabeth finally acknowledged the arrow through her body, and its meaning, Anne now acknowledged that she was the only Christian woman whose hands were tied behind her back.

"No! Please, no!" It could not end like this, no. "Take me to my husband, to Hassan. I always gave him great pleasure." She pushed herself against the Syrian, letting him feel her body. "Don't take me to him, then, Nasr. Keep me for yourself. If you have me once, you will want me again and again."

"Be still," Jamilla said. "You plotted against my husband, Lady Anne. He is your nephew, your brother's son, and you worked to kill him."

Frederic lurched and shrieked again. Anne struggled in Nasr's grip, trying to break away.

"You swore to the True Faith when you married my father, Anne of Jabil al-Hadid. Swore, and then renounced. Renounced and returned to your Infidel god. You are an apostate, and you will pay the penalty of an apostate."

A soft wail now, "Please, no." Nasr was on his knees, holding her tightly around the back, pressing his head against her breasts. She smiled down at him, her final seduction, as tears filled her eyes. "I testify," she sobbed, "I testify that...."

The sword swished through the air. Anne's head followed it. Blood fountained from her neck, showering Nasr as he let her body slump to the ground.

Jamilla pointed towards Louisa next, panicking her. "*Al-Tayyib*, that fat one slept with every sailor on the boat. You like them that way. Ask nicely and I'll bet she'll be your concubine." The Syrians laughed as Louisa trembled for her life.

Now Maura cowered away as Jamilla approached.

"Please, Sister Ekaterina, please. Don't kill me, please." She tried to push away without standing up.

Jamilla knelt down. "No kill. When blood"?

"What"? Maura was ready to shove with her legs again, but didn't. "What"?

Jamilla pointed to Maura's womb. "Blood. When blood? Blood since boat"? Maura tried to think. Yes, she must, because it was too embarrassing to.....with so many people....

"Yes, I think so."

"Good. No blood, come Homs. Blood, go home. You stay here until blood again. Then home."

"What"?

Frederic's screams of pain distracted them. "Stop this, please stop! Let me go"!

Jamilla pointed. "Stand up, Maura, Countess of Alberensa. Stand up. We go funeral, our husband. He die as he live, a *Sheyk*, a Count, a nobleman."

Jamilla pulled off her *niqab* and smiled. In her calm face, in her dark eyes, Maura found her place again, her role, her duty. She watched as Jamilla put her foot against Frederic's shoulder and shoved him over, ripping his guts from inside his body.

"The sword, Nasr, give me the sword."

Nasr lifted the weapon from the quivering gore even as Frederic shrieked in his death agonies.

"We go."

Jamilla slipped her arm around Maura's waist. Maura did the same. *Al-Amira* lifted Julian's blade above her head while the Saracens and the Christians bowed. Side-by-side, heads held high, the wives of the Baron entered the chapel to join their husband.

13

The escaping Hospitallers brought back news of the castle's loss, but Simon of Apamea found their accounts, although consistent, confused. He waited a week and then rode alone through the Homs Gap. He approached Jabil al-Hadid under flag of truce, very carefully, very slowly.

While understandable, he found his caution unnecessary. Guilhabert II, Baron of Jabil al-Hadid, was most pleased to receive the Hospitaller in his Great Hall. The audience had barely begun when the Baron cried out in hunger. His Regent took him to the Solar so she could feed him. She left the Countess of Alberensa behind to convey the Baron's offer.

"Her French is poor, my lord. You would not understand her anyway."

"Yes, my lady."

Maura looked up the stairs, to the place where the Regent vanished.

"It is as though the world has ended for her, my lord. I had a great infatuation for my husband, a lust for his handsome body, but it was not true love. Their love was the love of which our Lengadòc troubadours sing, deep, respectful, affectionate beyond imagination. In their lives together, the sun and the moon and the stars rose only to make the other happy."

Little expression marked the Hospitaller's face as Maura spoke, but she was not surprised. A man who spent his life only among men, making war on other men, that man would not understand.

"At least she has his child. Guilhabert, Baron of Jabil al-Hadid, will have all the love that she brings as a mother, and all the love that she would have brought as a wife. He will be very loved."

"Yes, my lady."

Maura gave up and moved on. Sir Simon learned of the bravery of Guy and Stephen and the cowardice of the four who returned. And of the witchcraft of Hugh, who could make the bloomery iron flow. Jamilla offered the Infidels the same terms that the Barons of Jabil al-Hadid had always offered the Saracens. Access to the products of the forge and smelter would be assured in all times of peace, on commercial terms.

Sir Simon resolved not to lose men trying to retake this frontier outpost. The acting Grand Master reported back that the new Baron was a baptized Christian. He acknowledged that he had accepted a truce on favorable terms. He sent word for the Bishop of Tripoli to excommunicate the four runaways. He expelled them from the Order.

The day's business concluded, Simon sat in the chapel, lost in thought. He tried to understand, yet again, how affectionate-beyond-imagination love had left Sir Stephen's head separated from his body in the Jabil al-Hadid castle yard.

■ ■ ■

A month later, Jamilla rode at the head a small group of men, a column of twos, on the road to Krak des Chevaliers. Countess Maura of Alberensa sat in the wagon they escorted, together with Jean and Luc. Her brother Sa'id argued on the day of the battle that the boys should be sold into slavery. That was all it took to convince Jamilla to entrust these two to the Hospitallers. Sa'id had argued that she should suffer the Hadd penalty, too. His judgment was poor, and she did not follow his advice.

Al-Amira al-Haddad rode astride the horse like a man, dressed in the garb of an Arab warrior. Her flowing trousers revealed her ankles above her shoes and a small bit of leg. Her quilted armor displayed the curve of her breasts while her tunic showed her wrists and arms. Sunlight lightened her dark hair and blazed from her dark eyes. It was difficult for the men to keep their eyes from her beauty and the lust from their eyes. Now she understood why God the All-Knowing had decreed that women must always protect men from temptation by keeping their bodies covered.

Another meeting of the brothers had preceded today's ride, one called by Khalid.

"The Emir has accepted that Jamilla can keep Jabil al-Hadid for her son and bring us the magic iron," he announced. "Our father has accepted that *al-Amira* may show her body as the Franks do, one time. She wants the Hospitaller to see her face, as she will see his. She will return from Krak and return to our ways. One day soon she will make someone a fine wife. We already know she is fertile."

The column stopped on the road below the fortress and waited. It was midsummer, and hot, with no clouds in the steel blue sky. The horses grew restless, waiting, wanting to go forward or turn back.

The gate opened. Two men rode out. Before long, Simon the Hospitaller reached them, together with another young knight.

"*Salaam aleikum*, Sir Simon."

"*Aleikum salaam, Sheyka.*" Jamilla nodded towards Maura, begin.

"These boys are Jean, ten, and Luc, eight. They are the sons of Sir Frederic, a Christian knight, and of his Christian wife, Sophia. Their parents are both dead. They bring nothing but themselves to your Order, but they are noble, descendants of Julian and Monica of Blagnac, first Baron and Baroness of Jabil al-Hadid. We commend them to your care."

"It was always the wish of Sir Stephen that they join us. I am sure that he is rejoicing at this moment."

"As am I, my lord."

The two boys sat, quiet, in their Jabil al-Hadid tunics. Maura pointed behind her, where one of the Saracens was tying a horse to the wagon.

"That is Sir Stephen's mount, Sir Simon. Umm Guilhabert wanted you to have it."

Simon bowed towards Jamilla. "Thank you, my lady." Jamilla bowed back from horseback, and motioned toward the wagon. The Syrian driver stepped down from the bench and mounted up behind another man while Simon's young knight climbed up and took the reins.

"Countess. Safe….." Jamilla paused, full of emotion, so full that she was having trouble recalling the French words she had practiced. "Safe trip home. Tell Agnes all. Tell her Guilhabert is beautiful. Tell her I love Hugh. Tell her I love her." And? Yes. "Hope you find happiness, Maura." Yes. That was all. "*Ma as-salaamah*, Countess. Goodbye."

"Goodbye, Countess," Maura answered, while Sir Simon added, *"Ma as-salaamah."*

Jamilla nodded to the man next to her, and the column turned. She led them down the hill without looking back, towards the castle at Jabil al-Hadid.

Hugh, my love, she thought, her hair streaming in the breeze, I miss you, I miss you so much. You came back to Syria for me, to protect me, and you paid with your life. I am so grateful, my love, grateful beyond imagining. We covered our charge with the hoofbeats of your joust, giving us the surprise, but it made us too late. I could not apologize then, my love, but it will not be all that long in God's time before I join you in the glade, and in Paradise, and I can beg your forgiveness. While I wait for that happiest of happy days, these are my promises, Hugh my darling.

We are nearly finished with the blast furnace, built from the plans you drew. The smelters of Jabil al-Hadid will return, better and more profitable than ever before. You have given our son Guilhabert and me a prize of great value, and the Emir has honored it, and we will learn and experiment and make it better and better, all for you, my love.

We embraced each other as equals, beloved, each seeking only to make the other happy. In our way here, Hugh, a wife must submit to her husband, and I will never submit. So you are the only husband I will ever have, and Guilhabert will be my only child. I will raise him well, my child, your child, our child, my love. He will make the iron as his father did and his father's father and their fathers before that. He will be kind and brave and strong. He will make you very proud.

And if it is the Will of God, he will see the Christian Infidels, your murderers, my love, he will see them driven from the Holy Land of Islam.

PART SIX

County of Alberensa
November 1225 - April 1226

1

Advent's first Sunday fell on November 30, the same day as the Feast of St. Andrew. Andrew was the *Protokletos*, the First-Called, for the Gospels recounted that he was the first to lay aside everything and follow Jesus. The Master's window in St. John's portrayed the moment, Andrew and his brother Peter bidding farewell to the Baptist to take up following the Messiah.

Yet it was not just his role as *Protokletos* that made Andrew so important. He was the one who prepared the way for a great miracle by announcing, "There is a lad here who has five barley loaves and two fish; but what are they among so many"? From those five loaves and two fish, Jesus fed five thousand, with food left over. Afterwards, in the mountains, the disciples sat with their leader and professed their faith.

"You are the Christ," they proclaimed, "the Son of the Living God."

Sunday Mass honored the Resurrection. It always took precedence over the celebration of a saint's day, even one as important as the *Protokletos*. But the Bible speaks often of Andrew, together with Peter, the first Pope, and John, the Evangelist, and James, of Compostela. Father Duran declared that Andrew's feast was too important to be ignored. He announced that a Mass of the First Sunday of Advent would be offered in the chapel one hour after dawn. A time of silent prayer and contemplation would follow. When the sand ran out on the hour, Duran would celebrate a Mass of the Feast of Saint Andrew.

A woman accustomed to sitting and not seeing always had the advantage during these times of silent devotion. For the others, the shapely waist of a young maid distracted, the shoulders of a groom, the color through the glass as it played against the stone. Nothing drew its attention to the eyes of the Baroness of Juviler, nor was she inclined to move about. Wrapped in her wheelchair, sitting on a soft cushion to protect against sores, she wore the penitent clothing appropriate for Advent, dark, simple and, most especially, warm.

Yet today, even with the advantage of her disabilities, Agnes had difficulty in centering herself in the saint and the season. Politics intruded on her contemplation of the faith that had moved Andrew to stand up and follow God. Certainly she would not be moved to stand up and follow Pope Honorius, even if she could. His endless quest against Lengadòc threatened their liberties and their way of life. Even now, fresh danger rose from the north, at Bourges, where the Pope's council had summoned Raymond VII of Toulouse.

The mountains are indeed rugged, Jamilla my friend. The road is narrow, with many trees bearing in on us.

Commotion filtered in from the yard outside. The chapel door flew open and a messenger stepped in. He mistook the meaning of the silence, and spoke. "An urgent message for the Baroness of Juviler from Sir Gautier." Agnes raised her hand, knowing that Father Duran would be most distressed at the intrusion.

"Who speaks"? Her voice remained soft and low, but it had become the voice of a Viscountess. A still, small voice filled with authority, like the voice Elijah had heard on Mount Horeb. "Is that you, Sir Laurent, my friend"?

"Yes, my lady. I have….."

"Sir Laurent." The Voice stilled the wind that passed before Elijah, and the earthquake, and the flame. "If a building is on fire, or has collapsed, pray continue. If you wish merely to inform of Bourges, then we are at God's work here, my lord, at prayer. It is the penitential season of Advent, when we contemplate the Second Coming of Christ, the Judgment Day. Join us."

The knight's armor rustled and clanged as he sat. That was clever, Agnes. Isn't Bourges supposed to be God's work? Lisbetta, sitting beside her, touched her gently on the shoulder, a mark of congratulations. Yes, her cousin was clever, too.

Father Duran began the Mass for Saint Andrew. The Invocation, and then the Collect, the prayer for the day. The priest raised his voice steadily as he prayed, trying to overcome a new rumbling in the yard. The chapel door flew open again and the sound of many boots thumped against the stone.

"Amen," said the Baroness, and her hand went up, again. "Whoever is here, we are celebrating God's Holy Mass. I wish no news of Bourges until dinner. Join this service and worship our Savior."

"My lady, I….."

"My lord, I said…." Who was that? "Is that you, Sir Rodrigo? You did not travel to Bourges."

"No, my lady." Agnes felt the distress in his voice, and made a small hand movement, continue. "My lady, I have received word from Barcelona. The Countess is there, my lady, arranging passage by ship to Narbonne, around the Pyrenees. She does not wish to come over the Pass in the snow."

"Sir Rodrigo, that cannot be so important that we….." Lisbetta's hand rested on her shoulder again, gently, lightly, comforting. "So my brother the Count is not with my lady the Countess? He has remained behind in Tripoli"?

"Yes, my lady." She felt Rodrigo's hand resting gently on her other shoulder. The Earthquake that came before the Voice rolled over her, even as she struggled not to believe. "Our liege lord Hugh, Count of Alberensa, Baron of Jabil al-Hadid, has been slain. He is buried with your fathers in Outremer."

■ ■ ■

Agnes never paid much attention to the weather. People who could see the clouds or walk in the rain would tell her, it's a lovely day, my lady, or it's pouring down rain, Baroness. Yet that December she did remark often on the dampness, on the constant sound of rain sluicing off the rooftops and splashing into the yards. In the city, she was told, families hung black cloth from their windows. The fabric, soaked through from the storms, clung to the wood, sucked against the mortar, and dripped steadily into the streets.

Sir Gautier confirmed the news of the Council of Bourges. The Holy Father, Pope Honorius III, had excommunicated Count Raymond VII, just as Innocent III had excommunicated his father. The Council decided that Raymond VI had indeed ceded Toulouse to Simon de Montfort in 1214 as the price of a truce, and of his life. Montfort's cession to Philip II passed his claim to the French crown. It was the right of Philip's son King Louis VIII to rule Toulouse.

Raymond did not agree. The Lion sought financial support to press his cause. Eager to stamp out the Cathar heresy, the Council levied a tax of ten percent on all church revenues to support a renewed Crusade against the Cathars, the Albigensians.

Agnes received that news quietly, commented little, and asked to be taken to the chapel. Sir Giles sat quietly in back while she prayed. On the morrow, she asked for the same, but this time Giles sat with her, answering "Amen" to any prayers she recited out loud. On the third day, she gave him leave to go.

"No, my lady," he answered, "I would either be dead or a Saracen slave had your brother not brought me here. I will keep the vigil with you." She nodded without speaking, and he stayed. Day after rainy day passed as the troubadours added to the Legend of Giles of Tripoli and his faithful devotion to his Lady.

In the evenings, Agnes stayed in her room. Giles or Peter or a vassal invited for the evening took her place in the Great Hall. Sometimes she asked Lisbetta to read, or converse, or tell her of new songs. Other nights, she asked to be put in bed early and left alone.

Lisbetta remembered her own loss, sudden sharp, swift. One morning she was a young peasant girl, that night an orphan. Now she was becoming a woman, groomed for a court marriage. The memory of her old life, the life of her childhood, was fading, yet she could still conjure up the sight of her father and her mother and her sister lying in the blood-red dirt as though it was happening now.

You suffered one sharp, fierce blow, Lisbetta, followed by a life that has grown better and better.

For Agnes, one sharp blow has followed another sharp blow, drawing out her agony, over and over. Her younger brother and sister taken by the crippling disease. Losing her own legs and her sight. Her mother and father, dead of a fever. Her friend Sister Ekaterina, returned to Syria. Now this final blow, this final loss, the brother who was her friend and her strength and who encouraged her independence and her spirit.

Sister Ekaterina. Maura had not yet arrived, but the whole castle knew the story. Guilhabert's mother was a Saracen. She held Jabil al-Hadid in his name for the Saracens. The illegitimate son of a Saracen could not rule in Christendom. Agnes, with her broken body, bereft of everyone she loved, lonely beyond imagination, was the Countess of Alberensa. Paralyzed, blind, unmarried, without children, the last of her line.

Word reached the castle just before the Fourth Sunday in Advent. Maura would arrive in time for Christmas. That night, Agnes asked to be put in bed early. Lisbetta complied, but this time climbed in after her.

"What are you doing, Lisbetta"?

The thirteen-year-old girl pulled her Countess to her breast as Jamilla had done in the mountains. "Aenor Faure did this for me, my lady, and I will do it for you." Lisbetta let her Countess cry, cry some more and still some more until finally she fell asleep. A maid found them lying together in the morning when she knocked on the door, looking for Lisbetta because she wasn't in her room.

Agnes presided at breakfast that morning. And at dinner. And at supper. She thanked Peter for his assistance in these recent days, and complemented his preparations for Maura's arrival.

The Voice had returned.

2

Agnes decided that she would meet Maura alone. Completely alone, with no one else in the room. On Monday, three days before the happy Christmas feast, she sat in black in her wheelchair, waiting for her sister-in-law. She had the men-at-arms set her on the Reception Chamber floor, not the dais, so that they could sit as equals, Countess and Countess.

"The Dowager Countess of Alberensa has arrived, my lady."

"Thank you, Peter. Send her in. You may all leave." Shuffling. "You know my wishes, my friends. Please do not make me command."

Agnes heard doors opening and closing, and the familiar heavy tread of Maura. "Are we alone, Maura"?

"Yes."

"I am glad you have returned safely, my lady. Say what is on your mind, now. Let us be done with that, because important matters are at hand."

Maura sucked in a breath, waiting, pondering. Agnes inclined her head and motioned with her hand, please begin.

"Very well, Aggie. Yes, I was very angry with you. It's bad enough when a woman finds out that her noble husband is sleeping with some knight's daughter or the milkmaid. It's another to find that he's bedding a Saracen upstairs and that her sister-in-law was helping them. Did you know that she called me The Cow"?

"Yes, I did." She raised her hand, wait. "I do not excuse what they did, but I understood it. We were spoiled, my brother and I. Our parents were in love, and I rejoiced in the love between Jamilla and Hugh. We did not expect you to fall in love with him, too."

Agnes heard sobbing, and suddenly Maura grabbed her hands. Agnes did not hear it coming, and had no way to prevent it if she had. Her heart missed a beat as fear gripped her, the worst fear since she had lain abandoned in the cave.

"I have heard of lust, Aggie, but Lady Anne, that aunt of yours? All she ever wanted to do was… was…. fornicate like the animals. Frederic's mother Elizabeth, she killed her son to settle some ancient grudge. I don't think she even cared that she got killed herself, as long as Hugh was dead." The sound of a runny nose drawn in. "A just God has sent them to Hell, my lady, to Hell"! More snurfling, and a wail. "I helped them to kill him, Baroness"!

"Countess, please, Maura, it's Countess Agnes now. And let go of my hands."

Maura's words tumbled out in a rush as she ignored the request. "I loved Hugh and I was so angry about his deceit and your deceit that I helped those incestuous bastards to kill him. I fear for my own soul, Aggie, my own eternal soul"!

Maura squeezed even more tightly now. She posed no threat, but Agnes decided that even so she would never again receive a subject alone. It was not worth the risk, no matter how trusted the person might be.

"Did you really know this Sister Ekaterina, this Jamilla, Agnes? Did you really know her? She is a Saracen, Baroness... Countess, a Saracen. You would not believe her in the yard...." Agnes heard more tears, and fought back her own.

"Maura. Maura. Let go of my hands, Maura." Agnes pulled hers back, into her lap. "Start at the beginning, my lady, the beginning. Tell me what happened to our liege."

3

Vassals and servants filled the Reception Chamber, Maura, Giles, Peter, Lisbetta, the men-at-arms at their stations. Agnes sat on the dais, on the Count's carved chair.

"Peter."

"Yes, my lady."

"There is a shop, a big one, on the south side of the Avenue of our Lady, just west of the Compostela Road. They sell religious articles and food and tools and everything our summer guests require. And there is a butcher shop in the St. Luke's Quarter, on the square."

"I know them both, my lady. The maids whom the Dowager Countess took to Outremer came from those families."

"Be sure you get this correctly, Peter. Put on your finest and visit the shop on the Avenue. Inform them that their daughter Esmeralda died in a Saracen attack on…...what day was that, my lady"?

"19 June."

"Yes, 19 June. She has been given a Christian burial in Outremer and awaits her family in Heaven. We will say a Requiem Mass in her memory in the family chapel on Wednesday morning, Christmas Eve. They should join with us. On Christmas, they will be our guests for dinner. Do you think that will be acceptable to them"?

"Yes, my lady. They will be consoled in their grief by your respect for their loss, by your kindness."

"Good. Next, the butcher shop. Their daughter Louisa found favor with an important general of the Emir of Syria, a man known as 'The Generous One.' She has been taken to Damascus and has joined his harem."

"'Found favor,' my lady? 'Joined his harem'"? The Seneschal was not a young man. This news sounded most scandalous.

"Yes, 'found favor.' Make something up. Tell them that she sacrificed her virtue to save the lives of many Christians." Peter shuffled. "She went willingly, Peter, glad for her station to be so improved! This *al-Tayyib* is an important man. Louisa will live her life in luxury. She will never want for anything."

"Yes, my lady."

"Sir Giles. My compliments, as you knights are so fond of saying, to my barons, Gautier, Rodrigo, Bertrand, Ponset, the others, and to my *Capitolum*. I will have them here for dinner on the Tuesday following Christmas, 30 December."

"Yes, my lady."

"Send word to Jerome, our Bishop. I will meet with him Monday at ten."

"The Bishop will ask the purpose of the meeting." Agnes stiffened, without speaking. "It is a reasonable question, my lady Countess."

"My lord, I…" If she could not trust Giles, if she did not have his full support, she could not survive. He must be an exception to her new rule, that she never meet anyone alone. "Everyone leave except Sir Giles."

■ ■ ■

The door closed, the sound faded. "Are we completely alone, Sir Giles"?

"Yes, my lady."

"The mystery of my life continues, Giles. To give hope to the hopeless, Hugh named a blind and crippled woman as his Viscountess. It was a boon, a present, never serious, something to amuse me while you and the *Capitolum* and Peter ran Alberensa in his absence."

She felt one hand taken, softly, and then the feel of his lips on it.

"You are wrong about that, my lady. This broken body holds a powerful mind and a powerful will. Your brother trusted you and relied on your judgment above all others. The best decision he ever made was to grant you the barony of Juviler and make you his Viscountess. You have ruled wisely in his stead."

"Thank you, Giles, but will that continue, do you think"?

"You mean, are you threatened"? Once again he kissed her hand and released it. Agnes felt the movement, the pause as he framed his thoughts. "Yes, the wolves are circling, my lady Countess, waiting until Christmas is past to put their fangs in the neck of the lamb. They forget that I have pledged my life to protect your honor. I have never regretted that, and I never will."

Agnes gripped his hand and squeezed as Maura had done, holding on. "Thank you, Sir Giles. It is a great gift, for which I thank Our Savior daily." She put her hand over her mouth, took it away. "What should I do with Maura? At least the Prodigal Son admitted his sin when he returned to his family. She has not."

"What does she wish, my lady"?

"To live her life here as the Dowager Countess. She feels it is her due, especially since Hugh made Jamilla his mistress."

Silence. The sound of the wood crackling on the fire.

"Does she realize that she is only here because Jamilla needed a messenger? If Umm Guilhabert had a better way to send word, Maura would be a servant of *al-Tayyib,* waiting on Louisa."

"Maura does not realize many things. She does not realize that her plotting with my cousin and my aunt caused Hugh's death. The death of many of our friends,

Giles, yours and mine, people who served my family faithfully. The loss of a fief that we have held through six generations. The sale of all its Christian survivors into slavery. And yet she expects to live among us and be treated with respect. She should take herself into a convent and spend her life in penitential prayer"!

"Will you send her there, my lady. I thought…"

"Whatever she does, convent, brothel, home, I want her gone"!

Silence. The fire crackled. A thump, "That's me tossing on a fresh log, my lady."

Calm down, he means. Use that so-called powerful mind, he means.

Yes, he's right.

"I understand, Sir Giles. We are threatened from many sides. Toulouse is one possible threat. Sending Maura packing to Colomiers puts her in a position to plot. Better to keep her here where we can watch her."

"Yes, my lady. The time will come for her to leave us. It is not now."

Again the fire crackled as her faithful Giles waited.

"What of my barons, my *Capitolum*"?

"Women do not usually inherit in the Frankish lands, my lady. Your mother never lived in Alberensa during her rule, leaving Gautier and the barons in charge. Before then, no woman has ruled Alberensa since…. since…"

"The Countess Harildis in the last half of the ninth century."

She heard Giles take a deep breath. "Three hundred fifty years, so far back that no one is sure if she ever lived or ruled."

"She lived and ruled, my lord, on that our chronicles are clear"! Calm, Agnes. "As I asked, what of my barons, my *Capitolum*"?

"Alone, who knows, Countess, but you are not alone. You have Lisbetta as your eyes and your hands. You have me as your arms and legs. You have Guilhelms as the guardian of your most valuable secret and the source of your immense and growing wealth. You have the townswomen from St. John's Circle who consider you a friend. Their husbands in your *Capitolum* will agree. They will support you."

"My barons"?

"Gautier is the leader among them. He was loyal to your mother. When your Uncle Jacme died, he insisted that she had become the Countess."

"Why would he do otherwise"?

"All the barons in Europe prefer an absentee lord, my lady, particularly if that absentee lord is a lady. The legend that the Salic Law does not apply here enabled each of your barons to pledge allegiance to the Countess Marguerite and then do as he pleased."

"Once again, my lord, it is no legend"!

"At this moment Gautier and the others, having accepted that your mother was the Countess, cannot easily claim that you cannot be the Countess too. However, your mother was absent. You are not.

Your brother insisted on receiving his feudal dues. So will you."

"Of course! They are my rights, granted to me by our Lord in Heaven"!

"Yes, but who knows what Sir Ponset might be telling them, what relief from their obligations he might offer in return for supporting the position that Harildis is a myth, Marguerite was an error, the Salic Law does apply and he is the Count."

Agnes thought to protest, again. Instead, she took a moment to calm herself, to think clearly. "Ponset is my...." Bernat's brother... "My fourth cousin, Giles. A man that far removed from our common ancestor should no longer have a title, much less be a landed noble in this county. He should be a soldier or clergy-man or bureaucrat in some town."

"Or own an ironworks like Gervais Deslegador or be a blacksmith like Guilhelms Faure."

"Exactly." Agnes tapped the arm of her chair. "Hugh suspected that Rixen of Tarba gave Ponset's grandfather the Arguenos border fief. It was a pay-ment to her husband's nephew for his help in ousting the Glassmaker."

"He told me the same thing."

Think, Agnes, think. "Without heirs, his line inherits anyway. Why stir things up? His line may ben-efit in future generations from the absence of the *loi Salique*."

The Countess heard her Marshall pace and then turn back. "He may not be prepared to wait, my lady Countess. The Church may not be prepared to wait. King Louis. The English. The Aragonese. The…"

The hand waved, the Voice spoke. "Thank you, Sir Giles, I think I have the picture, even though I cannot see."

"Yes, my lady."

"I will have the Bishop here on the 29th, at ten. I will have the barons and my *Capitolum* here on the 30th. Make it so."

"Yes my lady."

"In the future, Sir Giles, when I give you a command in public, you will respond, 'yes my lady Countess,' even if you disagree. You may raise your objections later."

"An excellent idea, my lady."

"I did not ask for your opinion, Sir Giles."

"Yes, my lady."

"Summon the others back in."

4

Sir Gautier's son, the kind and faithful Father Johans, helped Giles convince Bishop Jerome to attend upon the grieving Countess. Jerome came at the appointed time, ten in the morning on the Monday after Christmas. As declared by the Bishop when he consented to the meeting, Father Felipe, not Johans accompanied him, "to guard the honor of Rome against any heretical plots."

"Sir Ponset of Arguenos is with them, my lady," Peter said when he announced the arrival of the bishop and the friar.

To meet Rome's emissaries, Agnes planned to sit as she had with Maura, humbly in her wheelchair on the Reception Chamber floor. No longer.

"Giles. Lift me into the Count's chair. Lisbetta. Dress me properly. Get my wheelchair out of here."

Bishop, priest and knight entered the Reception Hall to find the Countess of Alberensa seated on the dais in her lion-armed chair. Her silk tunic of Alberensa blue covered her shriveled and bony legs. Over her shoulders she wore a cloak of white ermine, the animal's winter coat. The Juviler tiara rested on her blonde tresses.

To one side of the Countess, Lisbetta sat below the dais at a small table. Her maid added a sash of yellow silk around the waist of her blue tunic, matched by a cap of the same color. "She is at that strange age, Countess," Giles told his liege. "All awkward, a woman on top as she fills out, hips and waist still a girl's, with a face that grows more attractive every day."

Her informative Marshal stood to the other side of his Countess, wearing his own Alberensa tunic with the County's coat of arms. He wore no armor but did have his sword buckled around his waist. His men-at-arms stood guard along the walls, neither moving nor acknowledging the new arrivals. The servants bustled around the room, stoking the three fireplaces, keeping them roaring.

Agnes listened as the three men marched across the floor. Bishop and Friar no doubt wore their clericals under cloaks against the winter cold. The swishing metallic sound on the third man meant that Ponset must be in his armor.

Lisbetta stood and whispered in Aggie's ear. "In his early thirties, my lady. Not so bad to look at, but rather rough in his behavior." The Countess nodded. Wife dead, sons to hand, just like Frederic with Jean and Luc.

Unlike you.

Begin.

"Thank you for the courtesy of your visit, my lord Bishop. I wish to speak of my brother, but it is difficult for me to leave the castle. Would you all please be seated."

"Yes, my lady," the rustling armor, the soft swishing cloth sound. Felipe must be fuming, but the Heretic Leper Boy remains unmentioned.

"The prophet Samuel says that when a man rules justly over men," Agnes began, "He dawns on them like the sun shining forth upon a cloudless morning, like rain that makes the grass sprout from the earth. My brother was such a ruler."

Jerome crossed himself, "Yes, my lady."

"Count Hugh's body lies in Outremer. Like our mother, the stone over his space in the cathedral crypt shall be carved with his name and his dates as though he was buried there. With this inscription: 'A Faithful Soldier of Our Savior Jesus Christ, fallen in battle in His Name and buried at Jabil al-Hadid, 19 June 1225 *Anno Domini*.'"

"Very well, my lady."

"Thank you, my lord Bishop. Now…"

"One moment please, my lady," Felipe interrupted. "I recognize the wench to your side. She is the Cathar heretic Lisbetta Deslegador. What explains her presence"?

Rudely interrupted. The holiday from the Heretic Leper Boy did not last very long.

"Lisbetta is a faithful Catholic, Father Felipe. Can you not accept that our Lord and Savior, through the passion and grace of your own teaching, has rescued her from the pains of Hell"? Agnes pointed towards his voice. "Have more confidence in your gift, Father! Trust in the Lord's power as He guides you"!

Silence. Continue.

"I have appointed Lisbetta as my personal secretary. To her I confide everything that concerns my County. Please treat her with the respect due her education and her station. Bishop Jerome, I..."

"Thank you for your kind words, my lady. My purpose for attending is to urge your acceptance of Sir Ponset's petition."

"Father Felipe," Giles began, "That is the second time that you have interrupted our liege."

"Stay, my lord," Agnes said, raising her hand. "Sir Ponset. I invited you to a meeting of my barons tomorrow afternoon before dinner. I had not expected you here today."

"Father Felipe urged me to join him, my lady. He wishes to assure a Catholic succession to the County."

"That succession is a topic that I planned to discuss tomorrow, my lord."

"Why wait"? Felipe responded. "Sir Ponset is a faithful Catholic, a supporter of the work of the Holy Father and of the order of Preaching Friars, both with his words and with his wealth."

"Father Felipe, I..."

The Friar's voice rolled in from the darkness again. "Are you concerned that you are too closely related by blood, my lady? Sir Ponset and I have calculated that you are full fourth cousins."

"That is correct. Count Joris was the father of the grandfather of the grandfather of each of us."

"Canon 50 of the Fourth Lateran Council reduced the prohibited degrees of consanguinity from third to first cousins. Our Holy Mother the Church has never prohibited fourth cousins from marrying."

Ponset joined in. "In your condition, my lady, our marriage benefits our County. I pray that you look favorably on my petition."

Your brother Hugh let Frederic in, Agnes, lulled from the risk by Amalric's decree. You have no such advantage. Once you wed this knight, you will lose power immediately. You will never have a baby that can threaten Ponset's children. You will be sent to Rixen's convent in Couserans to live out your days.

That will not happen while I still breathe, Mother! It will not!

"Again, my lord, I prefer to discuss this topic tomorrow. It is not the purpose of my invitation to the Bishop."

"Father Felipe thought we should discuss it today. The Bishop agrees. After we finish, we may turn to the matters that impelled your invitation."

The Countess sensed her Marshal's movement, reached out, found his hand over his sword and pushed down. "Stay again, I pray, Sir Giles."

"Yes, my lady."

They plan to pound you to their will as though you are a piece of red-hot bloomery iron under their hammers, Agnes.

"Very well, my lord. We shall discuss the topic today."

Fortunately, you are the only one here who knows anything about making steel.

"Betta, please."

Agnes heard her cousin rattling her parchments. She heard her three visitors drawing in their breath, astonished that they must listen to the insolent Cathar wench.

"Our liege the Countess Agnes of Alberensa has received three offers of matrimony." A sweet voice, very disarming. "There is yours, Sir Ponset." Rustling. "There is one from Pascual, a knight in the service of Aragon."

"He is only a fifth cousin," Ponset offered, "Descended from a brother of Count Joris. His fief is on the other side of the Pyrenees."

"And he descends from an illegitimate union in his grandfather's generation," Felipe added. "Our Holy Mother the Church would raise objections to that marriage under the Fifty-First Canon of the Fourth Lateran Council."

"Lissie, the last."

"There is one from James, the Baron of Guildford in the County of Surrey, England."

"Who"? Felipe said in amazement. "From where"?

"Betta."

"According to his petition, Sir James holds a fief in the Duchy of Aquitaine, closer to Alberensa than the city of Tolosa. As well as his fief in England."

Agnes nodded. "I confess that I find myself rather intrigued."

That produced the result you expected, Aggie. Felipe exploded from his seat and began pacing. "Does he know you are blind, my lady? That you cannot walk"?

"Liss"?

"He does not say, my lady."

"Thank you, Lissie-Bet."

"Of course, my lady."

Now Agnes heard Ponset's armor moving. "One suitor ineligible. The other, there is no chance he will consummate that marriage! He simply seeks to seize the County of our ancestors as his own! I renew my petition, my lady. Our marriage will add my strength to yours."

Agnes drew back, sat straight up. "As your liege, Sir Ponset, I trust that I can depend on your strength whether we are wed or not."

She heard not only Ponset's deep breath, but those of Jerome and Felipe.

"You may, my lady. I only say that our marriage will strengthen you even more."

"On that position the Church agrees," Felipe added. "It looks most favorably on this union."

The rugged mountains, the narrow road, the trees bearing in, this loathsome Friar is all of them.

"Do you not have another petition, Lisbetta"? Giles asked.

What?

"One from a man perhaps closer to our liege"?

What?

"Closer"? Felipe said. "Angibert's two daughters died without issue. Roland's…"

"Ah! How careless of me, Sir Giles"! Agnes heard Lisbetta rustling her parchments. "Yes. Here it is." She paused.

What is going on?

"Our liege has received a petition from Giles of Jabil al-Hadid, a knight in her service and Marshal of her County."

Silence. More silence.

Be bold, Countess, be bold. "Pascual is eliminated, my lord Bishop. Do you see any impediments to the other three"?

"I know nothing of this James."

"The other two, then, Sir Ponset and Sir Giles."

"No my lady."

"My lady, I must protest"! Ponset exclaimed. "This Giles does not come from a titled family. He was a sergeant, a man-at-arms in Tripoli"!

"That is true, Sir Ponset. In that capacity he fought battles in the Holy Land, protecting it from the Saracens. He is well-respected by the military orders, especially the Hospitallers."

"He is a commoner"!

"Have you ever fought in a battle, Sir Ponset? Stood face-to-face with your enemy amid a hail of arrows? Driven your sword into his throat before he did the same to you"?

Silence, finally broken by Felipe.

"A commoner is not a suitable consort for a Countess, my lady."

"He is not a commoner, Father Felipe. My brother knighted him while we were still in Tripoli."

"My lady, I…"

"Sir Ponset. Please stay any further remarks concerning Sir Giles. I need the help of both of you to guide this County. I do not wish that my fourth cousin forces my Marshal into an affair of honor."

"Yes, my lady."

"Sir Giles."

"Yes my lady"?

"Your petition is accepted. My lord Bishop."

"My lady," Felipe began, "Our Holy Mother the Church…"

"I did not address you, Father Felipe! If you plan to protest my decision, let me say only this. With so many real problems besetting our Lengadòc, I cannot imagine why the Holy Father should spend any time worrying about my marriage arrangements. My lord Bishop."

"Yes my lady."

"We shall mourn my brother until Easter. The Saturday after is the feast of St. Mark the Evangelist.

At noon I shall come to Our Lady of the Pyrenees and be acknowledged as the Countess of Alberensa in accordance with the ancient rites of the County."

Agnes heard Felipe draw his cloak around him. "You mean you'll come to seek the Holy Church's blessing and consent to your rule, its acknowledgment that you did not take the *Consolamentum* in the Sárdalo Pass."

A soft white hand brushed that away. "I am the Countess of Alberensa, Father Felipe. I do not need the Church's consent to occupy that position." The white hand waved again. "About your oft-repeated and ridiculous lie concerning the *Consolamentum*, let me say only this. You might induce the Holy Father to issue a papal bull declaring that I have taken the Cathar sacrament, but that would not make it true."

Silence, shocked silence no doubt. Then, "My lady, the Fourth…"

"What ancient rites, my lady Countess"? Jerome asked, cutting off further protestations from the Preaching Friar.

"If you have no record of the rite, my lord Bishop, our chronicles here do. You may send Father Johans to copy them out."

5

Once her visitors departed, Agnes cleared her reception chamber, leaving only Sir Giles behind.

"Sir Ponset and the Friar and even the Bishop plot against me."

"They do, my lady."

She waved her hand towards the entry. "From now on, if someone appears without an invitation, have him sent away. I will not allow myself to be pushed around like that ever again."

"Yes my lady."

"I very much appreciate your petition, Sir Giles. You caught them by surprise. You caught me by surprise."

"Their plan seemed quite obvious, my lady. Force a marriage and then dispatch you to some convent while Ponset took over for his sons. No one from Jabil al-Hadid has ever gone to a convent against her will. I decided that you would not be the first."

"Thank you, my lord. Did Lisbetta know"?

"There was no petition until that moment, my lady, but I thought she caught on rather quickly."

"Yes. The troubadours will sing of clever Lisbetta while they sing of your valor."

The Countess sat in the dark amid the smell of the fires.

"Did you welcome my petition, my lady"?

"Of course. It was an honorable, selfless act in support of a helpless…"

"You are blushing, my lady."

"And you, my lord"?

"Smirking."

"Smirking, my lord! Smirking at your liege? I…"

"Perhaps I should explain, my lady. When a sergeant is assigned by his commander to be the personal bodyguard for his liege's elder daughter, that sergeant is wise to ignore her quite blatant flirtations. She is, after all, betrothed in matrimony to the eldest son of the Prince of Antioch. Her destiny is to be the Princess consort of a most important ruler in the Holy Land."

"Was I that obvious"?

"You caused me to be the butt of many barracks jokes, my lady, with your constant requests to be taken here, taken there, taken everywhere. You are blushing even harder, by the way."

Agnes put her hands to her face. Yes, warm. "Did you not enjoy our company, my lord"?

"Oh, I enjoyed it very much, my lady. You grew into a quite beautiful princess-to-be, and yet without hauteur, without arrogance. As a sergeant, though, I turned my thoughts to the quite lovely daughter of one of the workers in the foundry."

"Felise."

"You know her name"?

"Men"!

"Then tragedy fell, Countess. All those deaths, your sickness, and then your Aunt Anne trying to murder Hugh and you. I went to the chapel. I prayed. One never knows, but I believe that Our Lord ordered me to defend you with my life. I swore an oath to do so. A monastic oath, of poverty, chastity and obedience to your needs."

"Chastity? You mean..."? Agnes blinked in the dark, in the silence.

"What I mean, my lady, is that I swore that I would never wed if that would take me from my place as your guardian and protector."

"What of Felise"?

"We had not gotten so far, my lady."

"As I recall, quite attractive in an Eastern sort of way, dark eyes, dark hair, most alluring. Did she like you? Did you like her"?

"Yes, yes and yes, my lady."

"Do you prefer that sort to... to... am I blushing again"?

"Yes my lady, from neck to forehead. Perhaps that is because you pressed your brother so hard to bring me. To knight me. To make me his Marshal. To assure that I was always close at hand, just like those rides around Jabil al-Hadid. One might believe that, the Prince of Antioch being no longer in your future, your most obvious flirtations increased in intensity."

Men!

"My lord! This conversation is… is most unchivalrous my lord! You laugh at my love for you! The troubadours will…"

"Never doubt, my lady, that I wished back in Tripoli that you were Felise, not Agnes Maria Constansa Hélène. You are a most intriguing and beautiful woman. I have enjoyed every moment we have ever spent together. It is just that, until these petitions started arriving, I never thought that a marriage…"

"And now"?

"I am embarrassed by my failure to appreciate how truly brave you are, my lady, how resolved. I stand in awe."

"Then you understand my intent, my lord."

"I do, my lady."

"My parents were in love themselves, Giles, yet they sold me to the Prince of Antioch. I will not suffer that indignity again! I will not be sold to Ponset by that loathsome Felipe! I will not lie in bed with a man I do not love while he studs me like a bull! Even worse while he sends me unstudded to the Benedictines on the Tolosa Road"!

Giles laughed. "Somehow I think that the Benedictines would soon wish to be rid of you, my lady."

"It has never been my intent, Sir Giles, to live my life chaste and pure, Ever Virgin like the Holy Mother of God! It has been my intent to live that life happily married to a man I love, just as my parents did"!

"It is good that Father Felipe did not hear that last, my lady."

"I still have my flow, Giles. I have feeling down there. I get the cramping every month that we women must endure, for reasons known only to our Lord. I believe that the things I need to deliver a baby still work. I need the assistance of a husband whom I love to see if that is true."

Silence. He felt his hand on her cheek.

"I am no longer smirking, Agnes. I am thanking Our Lord and Savior for His gift of knowing you. I do not think that anyone truly appreciates how bold and resolute you can be."

She took his hand and held it, firm, rough, a man's hand. "Is it hard, Giles"?

"Hard, my lady? Is what hard"?

"Having a baby, of course, Giles! Having a baby"!

He squeezed her hand. "There are two parts, Aggie, the getting and the birthing."

"Yes"?

"The getting with child can be quite enjoyable, especially if the couple enjoy each other as we do. You will not know at first when you have gotten, so..."

"Does it hurt, Giles"?

"You mean the getting"?

"Yes." He let go. Silence. More silence. "Well"?

"For the woman, the first time in her life, a little painful. After that, with some experimenting given your condition..." He stopped. "Did not your mother ever discuss this with you, Agnes"?

"No. The birthing"?

"Very hard, my lady, but then you have seen that for yourself. I really do not think..."

"Stop! We will know for sure if things work when the time comes. If they do, good. If not, the surgeon must cut the baby from me and hope that we both survive, as Caesar's wife and baby survived."

She felt his hands caressing both cheeks. "It's too great a risk, Agnes, too great a risk. Live your life fully, govern your County wisely and trust to Our Savior's merciful grace that Ponset's heirs will rule well when your time is accomplished."

She shook her head. "Please, Giles, please! I want to be a mother, to have a child of my own, a baby to hold and to love. Can you understand that"?

Silence again. "Certainly my mother enjoyed us, Agnes. Aenor Faure enjoys her children."

"I want Alberensa to have an heir in my own line, an heir that descends from my mother Marguerite, from the Glassmaker loved by Hadassah. I must give birth to that heir to honor them, to honor my father, to honor my three dead siblings, to honor all of my own ancestors."

The Countess heard her Marshal pacing. "Should I get you with child, Aggie, and you die, I will feel a great guilt for my part in it."

"I absolve you of any guilt, Giles my love."

"That absolution is not yours to grant, my love. In getting you with child, I will have ignored my own good advice to myself. I will have made the choice that kills you and no doubt enjoyed myself in the process." She waited in her darkness while Giles pondered his choice. "Should that happen, I shall return to the Holy Land and join the Knights of the Hospital."

My darling, my beloved Giles, he will do it! "So then you will help me"?

She felt him move. "I am kneeling before you, Countess."

Her hands came out and found his head, just as she had found Hugh's head on that visit to the glade.

"When I swore my oath, Agnes, I knew it was because I loved you, but I also knew that, in your condition, my love must remain chaste and pure. If you are willing to risk carnal love, then my love also extends there."

"Even as I am, blind and crippled"?

"We mean so much more to each other than just your unfortunate condition, Aggie. We both know that. It's why your brother brought me. It's why he knighted a sergeant. It's why we're here right now. I would be honored if you would have me for your husband."

The Countess put down her feet, stood up and reached out to take her beloved around the neck and smother him with kisses. Except that she still could not stand or see. Instead, she fell forward, knocking Giles backward, causing them both to tumble off the dais.

"Are we on the ground, Giles"?

"Yes, Aggie."

"Kiss me."

The door crashed open as he did.

"My lady"! The feet of her men-at-arms froze. "What is…" and then silence. A moment later, Peter's voice emerged from the darkness.

"What is happening, my lady"?

"What does it look like, Peter? What does it look like"?

"Yes my lady."

"Sir Giles and I are to be wed."

"My lady this…"

"It will be a private affair. Inform Guilhelms and Aenor Faure of the event. They are to attend. Lisbetta. And you, Peter. Father Duran will perform the service."

"My lady, I…"

"Peter." The Voice, again, speaking even though it was lying helpless on the stone floor. "Really, Peter. I plan for us to be together for quite some time. When I ask you to do something, just do it."

6

Tuesday evening, the Countess of Alberensa sat on her lion-armed chair in her Reception Hall, arrayed in her silk tunic, ermine cloak and jeweled tiara. Giles and Lisbetta framed their liege in their own tunics of Alberensa blue. The banners of Alberensa's vassals hung from the arches overhead. Her men-at-arms stood guard along the wall. Her fireplaces blazed hot against the winter cold and the permanent chill of the stone building.

One-by-one, the herald announced the arrivals. Gautier. Bernard. Rodrigo. Ferrandos. Ponset. Her *Capitolum*, First Consul Garcias Lana, Anton Legros, Anfos Lodet, the others. To each Agnes held out her large comtal ring, feeling each man's breath as he lifted her right hand to kiss it.

"My lords, members of my *Capitolum*, I thank you for joining me today. It is unusual for my nobility to meet at the same time as my trusted advisors from the city, but we live in unusual times."

A chorus followed, "Yes, my lady Countess."

"The woman to my side is Lisbetta Deslegador. I have appointed her as my personal secretary. To her I confide all matters concerning the governance of this County. Please treat her with the respect owing a woman so trusted by her liege."

"Yes, my lady Countess."

"I have received many petitions these last days. Today I shall inform you of my decisions. First, however, we must deal with external matters, things far more threatening than our own affairs."

"Yes, my lady Countess."

"The Holy Father has long sought an opportunity to charge my family with heresy and open Alberensa to a noble of his choosing. My brother has given him an excuse. Fortunately that excuse came before His Holiness and Cardinal Donato were prepared, before they had located the Frank or Italian outsider they could trust to rule in my place. Now, after Bourges, they are busy with Louis and Toulouse. Liss."

The young girl rose and handed up a parchment to her lady. Tall, the men realized, slender, a girl wearing the clothes of a woman.

"This document petitions the Papal Legate Cardinal Donato to affirm Hugh's agreement from last Spring, immediately. Bishop Jerome joins his own petition to mine. We expect that the Pope will assent to purchase time. That will keep us away from the coming war." She put her hand over her mouth and took it away. "Does anyone here see a reason to participate in that war"?

Silence.

"Good. Lissie." Lisbetta stood to retrieve the parchment and resumed her seat.

"Internal matters. Sir Giles shall remain Marshal of Alberensa. In addition, we shall be wed." Murmuring arose, stilled when Agnes raised her hand. "The banns of matrimony will be read in accordance with Canon 51 of the Fourth Lateran Council for the next three Sundays. On the Monday after the third Sunday, the twentieth of January, Father Duran will marry us in the family chapel. Given my condition, it will be a private affair." More murmurings. "Lissie-Bet."

The young girl rose again from her table with a parchment in hand.

"In the Name of God, Father, Son and Holy Spirit, Amen."

"Amen," answered all the men."

Agnes sensed the shock in the room, shock of which her beloved Giles had warned. Not Sir Giles the Marshal, not Peter the Seneschal, but rather this slip of a girl, this child named personal secretary, this thirteen-year-old baby in expensive silk would be the one to convey the wishes of a twenty-two-year-old blind cripple to the powerful men of the County. A woman reading the decree given by another woman, that had never happened before, even in the time of the fabled Harildis.

"I, Agnes Maria Constansa Hélène, by the grace of Almighty God Countess of Alberensa, Baroness of Juviler, Baroness of Sarlant, Lord of Mayrènge, hereby confirm that, in default of my own issue, Sir Ponset of Arguenos and the heirs male of his body shall succeed by right of primogeniture to all my titles and to all the lands, fiefs, estates, rights, honors, dues, fees and profits appertaining thereto."

Agnes imagined her young cousin standing straight and tall, looking over the parchment she had memorized, taking in the eyes of the astonished men while her sweet yet deepening voice rolled out over them.

"In default of heirs male of the body of the said Ponset, heirs female of his body shall succeed by right of primogeniture to the said titles, lands, fiefs, estates, rights, honors, dues, fees and profits, it being clear from our ancient chronicles that the *loi Salique* does not apply in Alberensa.

"Copies of this document shall be deposited in my Treasury and in the Treasury of the See of Alberensa in the Cathedral of Our Lady of the Pyrenees,. A further copy shall be presented to the said Ponset of Arguenos.

"Done in the City of Alberensa in the County of Alberensa this thirtieth day of December in the Year of Our Lord One Thousand Two Hundred Twenty-Five, and of my rule the First."

Lisbetta lowered the parchment. "Their follows the signature of our liege and her seal impressed in wax on all three copies."

"Sir Giles, please offer Sir Ponset his copy humbly on my behalf."

"As you command, my lady Countess."

Agnes listened as the footsteps moved and the cloth and armor rustled. She felt her beloved Giles retake his place beside her. May he always be so close, dear Lord!

"Sir Ponset, please know that I was deeply honored by your offer of matrimony. I respect the loyalty to our ancestors with which it was given. In all likelihood your heirs will inherit this County without the need for you to wed a blind cripple and pretend you love her. Until then I ask for your loyalty and support, as I do of all of my barons here assembled."

Only one answer would serve, and he gave it. "You have it, my lady Countess."

Good. You have thwarted his plans, and Felipe's. For now.

"Betta."

Lisbetta rose again, holding another parchment, again rolled open so that she could read it aloud.

"Let all who hear this decree obey its commands"!

In the name of God, Father, Son and Holy Spirit, Amen.

Whereas, it has been the custom in this County of Alberensa since the time of the Countess Harildis that each new Count or Countess be recognized in a Service of Acknowledgement,

Now, therefore, I, Agnes Maria Constansa Hélène, by the grace of Almighty God Countess of Alberensa, Baroness of Juviler, Baroness of Sarlant and Lord of Mayrènge, decree that a Service of Acknowledgment shall take place in the Cathedral of Our Lady of the Pyrenees at noon on the Feast of Saint Mark the Evangelist, Saturday the twenty-fifth day of April in the Year of Our Lord One Thousand Two Hundred Twenty-Six and of my rule the First, and

I further decree that the nobility of this County of any rank or station shall attend this Service and shall swear their fealty to me as their liege lord before Almighty God and in the presence the assembled company, and

I further decree that the members of my *Capitolum* shall attend this service and pledge their lives and their honor to support their ruler before Almighty God and in the presence the assembled company,

I further decree that any nobleman of this County of any rank or station who fails to attend this Service and swear fealty to me as their liege lord shall be guilty of felony, shall forfeit all holdings to their liege and shall be banished from this County forever.

Witness my hand and seal in my City and County of Alberensa this thirtieth day of December in the Year of Our Lord One Thousand Two Hundred Twenty-Five and of my rule the First.

Agnes Maria Constansa Hélène, *Per gratium Deo, de Alberensa, Comitissa*

7

On the day of the Service of Acknowledgment, Lisbetta supervised the maids as they dressed their Countess in a tunic of blue, the blue of the Virgin Mary's purity, the blue of the winter sky against the Pyrenees, the blue of Alberensa. Delicate small flowers embroidered her waist, neck and hem. Open sleeves flowed from the elbows, with ruffles at the end. A clasp in the shape of a Compostela seashell kept her blonde hair neat as it hung down her back from her bare head. Lisbetta's fingers tickled against the bare skin at her neck they fastened a full cloak of plain black wool around her body.

"Do you like the dress I ordered for you, Lissie-Bet"?

"Oh, my lady, the blue silk, the embroidery, it makes me cry." She took her liege's face in her hands as Jamilla had done that night in the forest and kissed her on the lips. "Thank you for everything, my lady, for everything. We have come far from the sadness of your brother's death to this day, this most happy day."

■ ■ ■

The household cheered as Sir Giles carried their Countess into the yard. Lisbetta's friend Guis, the groom from the stables, waved at her while she waited for Agnes to be loaded. She favored him with a coquettish curtsey and waved back. She should blush under his admiring glance, but instead she filled with pride, pride at how beautifully she filled out her silk, how lovely the tunic made her look.

"Are you coming, Lisbetta? Our Countess is ready. Guis will still be here when we return."

"Yes, my lord." She climbed up as Giles smiled. Today he did not wear armor, but a tunic of Alberensa blue, fine linen, and a sword belt of tooled leather. He closed the door to the new enclosed wagon and leaned in. Lisbetta never failed to marvel, as Hugh had marveled, at his strength, his calm yet intense dedication to his lady.

"It is an honor to serve you this day, my beloved liege. Your mother and father, Baron Joscelin and Countess Marguerite, they must be most proud." He mounted and drew his sword. "God protect our Countess, Agnes!"

"God protect our Countess, Agnes!" from the assembled household and the escort.

"Open the gate for the Countess of Alberensa!"

A roar like their blast furnace blew in from the street as the door swung open. Every throat in Albersensa was shouting her name, asking God to protect her, wishing her good health and a long life. The weather smiled on her, a warm sun for late April, no rain in the sky, a gentle breeze.

"Every window is open, my lady, with people leaning out and waving. It's hard for the carriage to push through the crowds." The shouting overcame even the sound of the hoof beats and the rumbling of the wagon wheels. "They are all cheering for you, my lady."

"They are cheering for themselves, Lisbetta. I am their liege, but they are Alberensa. If it were not for them, I would have nothing. My father said that to us many times in Outremer. It is something that I must be sure to remember, always. You will help me to do that, always."

"Yes, my lady."

"He also told us that we might rule them here on earth, but that in God's eyes we are all equal. We will all stand together before Him on the Judgment Day. At that most awesome moment, all shall be revealed to us, as Bishop Thomas reminded me that night."

"You mean that night when we were not in the Sárdalo Pass with Sister Ekaterina, my lady"?

"Yes, that night. When we were at the Sisters of Charity. Otherwise Cardinal Donato might not have confirmed my brother's agreement."

Lisbetta touched her liege's hand. "He must want someone closer to Rome than Ponset, my lady. A marriage to him would not have protected either of you from the Papal scheming."

Agnes nodded. "For now, that scheming is ended. The Holy Father recognizes me as the Countess of Alberensa. Let us work to keep it that way."

The carriage drew up to the cathedral. The Bishop and the priests appeared as a snowdrift on *Lo Grandautar* as they waited on the steps in their white surplices, a blizzard blown up against the cathedral's face. The Bishop stood before the others, with Father Johans beside him holding his shepherd's crook, the emblem of Jerome's role as the shepherd of God's flock on earth.

Sir Bertrand and Sir Gautier reached in and lifted Agnes into a waiting sedan chair. Sir Ferrandos and Sir Rodrigo joined them in carrying the chair into place at end of the clerical procession.

"God bless you on this most wonderful day, my lady," Jerome said. He wore a gold-colored stole over a surplice embroidered around the neck with gold threads. More gold hung around his neck, a large golden cross on a golden chain. A cross of golden thread was embroidered on his miter. A resplendent figure gleamed in the sun, shining his gold on the severe black of the Countess.

"Thank you my lord Bishop."

Jerome turned and called to the front of the procession, to a clerical army formed more precisely than any band of yeomen about to advance across a muddy field. The full dignity of the Holy Catholic Church, of God Himself, would descend upon this ceremony. It must please the Lord.

"This is the day which the Lord has made," intoned Jerome.

"We will rejoice and be glad in it," the priests responded.

Crucifer and thurifers lifted their cross and candlesticks and led the way into the church, chanting the canticle "Come Creator Spirit." The Bishop followed, then Giles to lead the Countess.

Male voices echoed off the brick as the column of white followed cross and candles down the center aisle. To either side, the nobility, the guilds, the common people who had arrived early filled every seat. Even those with dresses and tunics of brown homespun had found some item of blue to wear, around arm, or waist, or neck.

"Come Creator Spirit," Agnes prayed to herself, "Enter our hearts. Bring your heavenly grace to fill the hearts that you have made."

Agnes knew that the cathedral was full, but all she heard were the monks chanting the *Veni Creator.* "We are passing the transept, my lady," whispered Sir Ferrandos, "under the windows of Saint James. The Throne of God is aflame from the sun."

Bertrand and Gautier lifted their Countess into a wooden chair set before the altar. The end of the canticle, "And to You, O Holy Spirit, the Comforter, while endless ages run," died away just as the two knights faced the chair to the nave. On the high altar behind them, golden chalice and paten and chrism glowed in the candlelight. The golden color from Hadassah's Throne of God washed over the front of the assembly.

Sir Giles, consort to the Countess, stepped forward.

"My lords and people of the County of Alberensa, our Countess Agnes Maria Constansa Hélène has arrived to receive the fealty due her as the liege lord of her County."

"God protect our Countess, Agnes"!

The force of so many voices thundering from the darkness surprised the Countess. She felt Giles removing her plain black cloak. She bowed gently from her seat.

"My lord Bishop, God in His infinite wisdom has given me rule over this County of Alberensa. I humble myself before Him, a man like all men, a woman like all women, naked and weak and a sinner. I ask the help of Our Lord and Savior Jesus Christ that I rule justly in His name."

Father Johans lifted the Coronet of Alberensa from the altar. Legend held that Lothar and Bedolf discovered the thick gold band with its single blue jewel buried beneath the altar of the sixth century wooden church. "A talisman, perhaps," Hugh once said, "Assuring that Belenus blessed Our Lord's work."

The priest held the ancient gold of the ancient Gauls over Agnes's head while the Bishop spoke the ancient words.

"Agnes Maria Constansa Hélène, in the Name of God, Father, Son and Holy Spirit and by the power vested in me by Christ's One Holy Catholic and Apostolic Church, we acknowledge you to be the honorable, noble and rightful Countess of Alberensa." Johans lowered the golden ring onto her head. "May the Lord bless you in your work on earth, and when that work is done, may you enter with joy into His Heavenly Kingdom."

The "Amen" from the congregation came as a thunderclap in a clear blue sky, a shock of sound that overwhelmed the quiet. Giles stepped up beside the Countess as the thunder echoed away.

"My lords of Alberensa, come forward and pay your homage to our liege."

Sir Giles knelt before their Countess first, kissing her ring.

"My lady Agnes, I acknowledge you as the Countess of Alberensa. I pledge my life and my wealth and my honor to your service."

There followed Ponset, Rodrigo, Bertrand, Gautier, Ferrandos, even young and landless Laurent.

"My lady Agnes, I acknowledge you as the Countess of Alberensa. I pledge my life and my wealth and my honor to your service."

The five Consuls stepped forward, one at a time.

"My lady Agnes, I acknowledge you as the Countess of Alberensa. I pledge my life and my wealth and my honor to your service."

The monks chanted psalms while men ten, fifteen, twenty years older than her pledged their lives and their wealth and their honor to a twenty-three-year old woman from Tripoli who could not even see them. It must indeed be God's will that you rule, Agnes, because no man would ever think that such a thing made any sense at all.

Bertrand and Gautier came forward again, lifted Agnes from her chair and held her standing as Giles spoke. "My lords and ladies, members of the *Capitolum*, masters of the guilds, people of the County, greet Agnes Maria Constansa Hélène, the Countess of Alberensa"!

A wall of sound erupted in the cathedral, a pulse that raced forward and pushed against her. Agnes was not certain, but she thought it might have actually moved the fabric of her clothing. She stood amidst the cheering, enjoying the feeling of being upright, trying to imagine what her cathedral must look like, her vassals, her people. It was strange to be locked in her own darkness and yet know that she had never before been together with so many.

Her knights carried Agnes to her seat in the front row. They sat together, the Countess and Giles and Lisbetta and Maura, Guilhelms and Aenor. The monks chanted and Jerome began the Mass. Agnes lost count of how many times the Bishop said all four of her names, asked God to grant her long life and health, to rule wisely over her people. She tried to concentrate on the sacred words of the readings, but she was constantly distracted by the difficult task that God had set for her.

The Lord has given you these people, Agnes Maria Constansa Hélène, to defend, to protect. Their whole trust is placed in His trust in your judgment, your wisdom, your skill.

God has given you Louis the Lion and Blanche the Lioness and Pope Honorius, too. What would Queen Blanche whisper in her husband's ear after Louis had just gotten her with child for the tenth time?

Gotten. You are quite late, Countess. Your breasts are quite tender. Sometimes you are queasy in the morning. We do enjoy it, Giles, but now you have gotten me, my love, well and truly gotten me. Agnes rested her hand on her womb. My love for you drives away the fear, my darling little one. I cannot wait to meet you.

Be the best mother you can for as long as you can, Agnes, and then trust in our Savior's merciful grace.

Blanca. Her advice. Yes, Blanca, yes, reward those most faithful to you. Your consort must be a baron, especially if he is soon to be the father of your heir. Elevate Giles to the vacant fief at Sarlant.

Jamilla could pretend to be a nun, but your new lady-in-waiting must be a noblewoman. Knight Lisbetta and award her the fief at Mayrènge on her fourteenth birthday this summer.

Guilhelms and his family must never want for any-thing. Grant him a tithe of all your income from iron-working. Make him wealthy beyond anything he could ever imagine.

Those are easy. They are friends. The wolves still circle, still plot, still work to remove the blind cripple struck down for her sins.

The Pope, his Legate and Father Felipe might plant lies that the Dowager Countess Maura was plot-ting with her cousin the excommunicated Raymond of Toulouse to draw Alberensa into the heretic orbit. The disappointed Ponset might plot with Felipe to use Maura as a spy, even get her to swear that I confessed to taking the *Consolamentum* in the Sárdalo Pass.

Maura has betrayed us once. She could do it again. She must be married off again, and quickly.

Agnes's inspiration for Bishop Jerome came just as he was elevating the Host, the moment it became the Body of Jesus, His flesh. He ruled his diocese from an ancient cathedral, dated in style, a brick embarrass-ment compared to the stone of Notre Dame de Paris. Alberensa has more than enough money to build him something better, a grand building in the Northern style, a proper place of rest and refuge for the pilgrims of the Sárdalo. The Bishop will be remembered for generations as the creator of a masterpiece.

You must set only one condition, Agnes, only one. The glass of the transept, the glass of Hadassah of Alberensa, that must remain.

The Black Friar Felipe Vilalba himself, you have no solution for this most dangerous enemy, this passionate Catholic priest made a fool by the Saracen Nun and the Leper Boy. Felipe decided that God had called him to live on alms and preach His word in the villages of Fonta this week, avoiding this service. And no doubt meeting with the Épernays at Farga, passing information that Henri could use to gain favor with King Louis.

Brother, Mother, Father, I miss you and the counsel you would give. Husband, beloved husband, help me to do my duty. Help me to preserve my County and my people.

In Thee, O Lord, have I placed my trust. Let me never be confounded.

PART SEVEN

County of Alberensa
April 1231 – May 1231

1

Vanity of vanities, says the Preacher, vanity of vanities, all is vanity. It is certainly vanity that I wish no one to see me crippled. And so I must always be first into my Reception Chamber, to sit alone, waiting for my first visitors of the day. The King of France can make his entrance after leaving his subjects waiting for as long as he likes. My pride requires that I wait on them instead.

Four steps after the Keep tower door, Agnes reached out with her hand, feeling for the arm of her carved chair. "Yes, you are at the dais, my lady." She moved her wooden crutches under her left shoulder.

"Help me up, Little Lisbet." The twist, the pushing up with her arms to get herself over the chair, the sitting. The Countess reached down to unlock her braces at the knees. Guilhelms invented this marvelous iron device, holding her shoes and strapped to her calves and her thighs.

Five years ago, as soon as Agnes delivered her beautiful little Madeleine, she enlisted Lisbetta's help to master the braces, to get back on her feet for the first time in years. Week after week, stumbling, falling, learning to keep her balance with the crutches while she walked in the dark. Tumble after tumble but she forced herself to go on. It was vanity, yes, but a Countess could not be carried everywhere in the arms of her loving husband, to say nothing of the servants.

"Remove these," Lisbetta said. A man-at-arms took the crutches from the room. Agnes wiggled on the chair while Lisbetta arranged her legs and straightened her tunic and re-tied the ribbons under her cap.

"Am I looking at you, Lissie"? Agnes practiced every day, focusing her sightless eyes where she thought the others were, looking at them as though she could see. A Countess could not rule from a vacant stare.

"Yes, my lady." Lisbetta walked into the room. "The Bishop will stand here, my lady." Another move, "And the King's man, here."

"Will he be one of those disgusting Épernays"?

"I'm more down and right, my lady. No. The French mean to insult you by sending only a commoner. Yes, I'm right there. Rather handsome, I'm told, dark hair and dark eyes and olive skin and broad shoulders. Confident that all women are eager to be seduced, to lose their virtue just for one night in bed with him."

Agnes heard Lisbetta walking back to her desk. "How do I look, Liss"?

"You're wearing red for this meeting, my lady, not Alberensa blue."

"Maddie picked my tunic for me." Agnes conjured up her image of the little girl behind the voice in the dark, so huggable and cute as she tried so hard to be a woman. You imagine her as your sister Madeleine but Giles says her hair is darker, a reminder of his own mother, and her eyes more hazel than blue.

"A familiar tunic, my lady, one you often wear when we sit to do your correspondence. Wool, not silk."

"Do you think our guests will note the subtle slight in that choice, Betta"?

"No. They are men." Agnes felt a hand on her shoulder. "We will, though, and that is what matters."

The door opened. "The King's Herald has not arrived, my lady," Peter announced. "The others have been out there for thirty minutes. Shall I invite them in"?

"No. Have Maddie and Hugh brought in while we wait. We'll talk with them until the Herald arrives. The conversation might not be very informative, but it will certainly be enjoyable."

It took but a few moments for the door to the tower staircase to open, "Mommy"! The Countess heard the patter of her children's feet and the deeper step of a maid.

"You look pretty, Mommy"! She felt Madeleine's hand on the fabric, adjusting the skirt. "Can we stay when the King's man comes"?

"What do you think, Hugh? Should you stay to meet the King's man"?

"King"? Not quite two, her little toddler's vocabulary was just beginning to grow, faster than Maddie's had, but then Maddie thought of Hugh as her favorite doll. She talked to him all the time. "He will look a lot like me, Aggie," Giles said. "He's a brash little man, the future Count Hugh II of Alberensa."

Agnes felt her son come close and grab her tunic alongside Maddie. "See King Mommy? See me"?

A sudden pang of guilt swept the Countess. "No, my precious, but I can hear you and feel you. For that I am very thankful to our Lord."

Indeed you are thankful for these two. As for this coming meeting, that is another story.

It took four years after Bourges for the French crusade to reduce Tolosa, Fois and Trencavel. Hugh was right, and Giles, all those years ago. Alberensa's modest contribution against the might of France could not have turned a battle that was lost before it began, despite all the fighting.

Two years ago, on Holy Thursday in April 1229, Raymond VII of Toulouse signed a treaty with Louis IX at Meaux near Paris. Raymond agreed that he held Toulouse as the King's vassal. A dynastic marriage assured that the French royal line would inherit the

County in the next generation. France controlled all Lengadòc now, except Alberensa.

The door opened. Agnes recognized the footsteps of her Seneschal. "The King's Herald has joined the others outside, my lady."

"Show them in, Peter."

"Gracia," Peter said, "Take away the children first."

A proper order, because children never attend a formal reception, but these children are my heirs. Let the Herald see that they exist.

"Have them stay."

"My lady…"

"Maddie, stand beside me where Daddy does. Hold Hugh's hand."

Peter turned for the door. "I'll bring in your guests."

The Countess felt the breeze in her face as the door opened. She heard it flutter the banners overhead. She reached down and fingered Sir Martin's cross while important footsteps made their way across the stone floor. The knight's gift helped her to remember that at least one Frenchman was a chivalrous gentleman, a man of honor. She had little expectations of chivalry at this meeting.

"*Un, deux, trois,*" Maddie counted aloud. "*Un, dos, tres.* Three men, Mommy."

Peter stopped in front of her chair.

"His Grace Bishop Paul Genet. Father Felipe Vilalba of the Preaching Friars. *Monsieur* Etiénne

Charpentier, Herald of His Majesty King Louis IX of France."

"My lord Bishop, Father Felipe, *Monsieur* Charpentier, may I present my children, Lady Madeleine and Sir Hugh. Help Hugh to bow, Maddie, then curtsey yourself, then go with Gracia."

"Hello King man," Maddie said, giggling. "It is nice to meet you."

"Yesh," Hugh added.

"The Baron of Sarlant is not joining us"?

"Father Felipe? No, Father, he is in the town on my business."

"Mommy is the Countess, not Daddy," Maddie added helpfully. "Everyone talks to Mommy."

Agnes felt the three men struggling, cleverly insulted by an innocent child.

"Thank you, children. Take them, Gracia."

Babbling, giggling and the sound of footsteps followed by the closing door.

"Well," Agnes said, "That is that. Shall we begin"?

2

Chairs squeaked and rustled as the three visitors sat.

"*Monsieur* Charpentier, your name says that you are a carpenter."

"As was our Lord." The Carpenter spoke with a smooth voice, calm, assured and embarrassingly not exactly where Agnes thought it should be. "I'm just a herald, sent from Paris to deliver His Majesty's message and carry back your reply." The insult from King Louis, sending a commoner, it was just as she expected. Or perhaps the insult came from his mother Blanche, since Louis was barely seventeen years old. "May I present His Majesty's message, my lady"?

"First we must welcome our new Bishop." Agnes held out her hand, but it was not taken. "My lord Bishop, it does not lower the place of the Holy Church for a gentleman to favor the hand of a lady with a kiss. Bishop Jerome always did so."

"The Holy Father Gregory, ninth of that name, has sent Jerome to be the parish priest in his home village, Quillan." Agnes put her hand back in her lap. "All this talk about building a new cathedral instead of rooting out this awful heresy."

It had started as a ruse, but Agnes had grown to like the idea of replacing the Builder's cathedral with one of her own. Agriculture, the pilgrims in the Sárdalo, Petrousset and the blast furnace at Pont de Moulin made Alberensa rich, richer than it had ever been. Her new cathedral would be a fitting tribute to the Lord's grace in shining such favor on her County.

"Your accent, my lord Bishop. You are not from here."

"No, from Paris."

Instead, the Lord's grace had only attracted the northerners to afflict her people, yet again. Instead of a building a cathedral, the Holy Father demanded that Jerome help fund the French war against Lengadòc.

"Please fetch the messages, Liss."

Lisbetta stood up from her small writing table next to the dais. "She's grown up tall and slender like her sister Andreva," Guilhelms told the Countess, "But much fuller, like her mother Petrona. Her face looks like the goddesses in the statues left behind by the Romans."

Lisbetta's wool swished gently as she walked with erect carriage towards the visitors. She favored yellow, a subdued yellow in the style of Provence, as she had that Easter when she challenged the Black Friar. The three fingers of height added to her heels at her request made her taller than most men who called upon her liege. The little pieces of metal in the soles clacked against the stone floor and allowed Agnes to follow her with sightless eyes.

The secretary's long fingers reached for the King's parchment. The Carpenter took her wrist, regarding her with an insolent, even leering look. "Your maid is a most attractive creature, Countess. I am constrained by my liege not to tarry, but I could find excuses to delay and savor all the pleasures of this delightful *loriot.*"

Lisbetta froze, not deigning to struggle. She let her blue eyes go cold with contempt. A man-at-arms started over from the wall, but the secretary shook him off with her head.

"The Baroness of Mayrènge is not our maid, Etiènne," Agnes answered. "Nor is she a golden oriole, or yours to savor. She is our personal friend and confidant, one of the most important nobles of our County. She will be wed this Midsummer's Eve to Godafres, son of Rodrigo, Baron of Sárdalo. Unhand Lady Mayrènge and give her His Majesty's message or we shall have you put to carpentry, repairing our castle gate." In but a moment, a clack signaled that Lisbetta was free. "Do you have a message, my lord Bishop"?

"I carry one from Cardinal Donato, the Papal Legate. It is in Latin but I will explain it to you."

More insults. This middle-aged cleric had no interest in building a cathedral he would never live to see. Like Pope Gregory, he was interested only in ending the Cathar treachery and their treason against God. He would succeed where Jerome had failed, be named a Cardinal, and become *papabile*. Vanity of vanities, Paul Genet, vanity of vanities.

"The Baroness reads and speaks Latin and French, my lord Bishop, in addition to her native Occitan. She is most accomplished for someone who is only eighteen." Agnes waited for Lisbetta to seat herself. "Start with the Cardinal's message, please, Betta. I imagine that the King's message assumes we have heard the Pope's." Agnes turned towards Charpentier, getting it right, looking exactly where he was. "That order should not make you tarry from your liege that much longer, *Monsieur* Charpentier."

Lisbetta studied the parchment so that she could avoid Etiénne's glare. It was dangerous, the way her lady used her station to challenge arrogant men like these three. Well, maybe she challenged them, too, with her little trick of the heels.

"It has the Holy Father's seal, my lady." A pause and a snap of the wax and a rustle of the taut skin. "Yes, Latin. The usual greetings. The Holy Father says that you have not been diligent in rooting out the heresy, my lady. The agreement between Alberensa and the Holy See is ended. The Third Canon "On Heresy" applies in full here. Nobles who fail to hold to the

Catholic faith shall forfeit their lands. All forfeited lands in Alberensa shall fall to King Louis of France, who has the Holy Father's blessing in his work."

Agnes turned towards Genet. "Always the same nonsense, my lord Bishop. 'Rid Alberensa of the stench of this heresy,' yet nowhere can we find any heretics. We have no idea what we are supposed to do to rid our County of a problem that it does not have. We have kept the agreement with Cardinal Donato faithfully. There are no lands to forfeit."

Felipe's familiar voice responded, "That is not the report that I have given His Holiness Pope Gregory, Countess. He believes…" Agnes raised her hand.

"Is there more, Lisbet"? The Black Friar stopped.

"Yes." A rattling of the parchment. "The Holy Father has proclaimed a bull, *Excommunicamus*. The Preaching Fathers have been empowered to conduct an Inquisition to root out the Cathar heresy. Persons found guilty of heresy by ecclesiastical courts shall be turned over to the secular authority for punishment. For those who recant, prison, and for those who do not, death by fire."

Lisbetta stopped, her mouth trembling. A deep breath, you are a lady, a Baroness. Regain your composure.

"The Holy Father places great confidence in the Black Friar Felipe Vilalba, who has preached in Alberensa for many years. He shall lead the Inquisition in the County." A pause. "Then the usual closings. The Papal seal is in wax at the end."

Agnes said nothing. Lisbetta sat poised, the message in her hand, not moving. Both women waited for one of the men to grow impatient, as Hugh and Giles had done in the yard before Gethsemane.

The Bishop cracked. "Countess, I plan to excommunicate you in accordance with the Canon when…."

"My lord Bishop. Please. I was thinking. I must still hear His Majesty's message. Now, please, Lady Mayrènge."

"It is the King's seal, my lady." The snap and the rustle. "After the usual greetings, His Majesty states that Alberensa is forfeit to him under the Third Canon, because you are a heretic and you shelter heretics. You are to proceed to Paris where a treaty to that effect will be signed, similar to the Treaty of Meaux. If you recant of the heresy and return to the Catholic faith, you will remain Countess, as his vassal."

Months of talk, but now it is ended, Agnes. Hugh my brother, our worst fears have come to pass. The Church abandoned Amalric's agreement in Tripoli. Today they abandon Cardinal Donato's agreement in Alberensa. The Lord is faithful in all his words, the Psalmist says, and gracious in all his deeds. This Church is neither.

Agnes could hear Queen Blanche and Bishop Genet pressing on the Cardinal. The Kingdom of France wants Alberensa. After Meaux, France has earned Alberensa. If the Holy Father wants the help of France in the future, he must allow the King to

pick the last piece of rich and ripe fruit that lays below
the Sárdalo Pass, to push the border of France to the
Pyrenees and to Gascony.

Blanche and Louis assumed that I was blind so I
would not see them coming.

I did see them coming, even though I cannot see.
Now I must stop them.

"My lady," Charpentier said, "I…."

Her hand went up, silencing the Herald. She
counted to twenty, then spoke.

"I am sorry, gentlemen. I must compose myself.
After our many communications, I had expected better of the Holy Father and the King." Agnes put her
hand to her mouth and took it away. "Our answers
today are these."

She turned to where Genet was.

"My lord Bishop, this message for Cardinal
Donato. We are unaware of any threats to the Holy
Catholic Church from the Good Christians. In fact,
we know of no Good Christians in Alberensa, none
at all. We will not accept excommunication by you
without an appeal to the Holy Father. We wish to
know what more we must do here to avoid that most
awful and awesome penalty. Is that clear, my lord
Bishop"?

"I understand what you say, Countess."

"This new bull, 'Excommunicamus,' was that it?
No Roman priest will descend on my people, Father
Felipe, and threaten them with an Inquisition. I rule

Alberensa, not Gregory. Your Inquisition will await a response from His Holiness to my appeal."

"My lady, it is not your place…"

"Mr. Charpentier. For His Majesty. As you can see, we are not able to travel so far as Paris. Alberensa has been in our family since ancient times. It has never been a holding of the French crown. We reject His Majesty's claim that it is forfeit to him under the canon on heresy. It is not forfeit. His Majesty has no right to it. Lady Mayrènge."

"Yes, my lady Countess"?

"Put that in writing, add the usual greetings and the usual closings, and we will present it to these gentlemen tomorrow."

"Yes my lady."

"My lord Bishop, Father, Mr. Charpentier," Agnes continued, "We have others waiting for an audience with us. I am constrained not to tarry longer with you."

At first, a stunned silence, broken by the Bishop.

"No heresy? What of the events that occurred here seven years ago, while Count Hugh was making his agreement before Fonta? Father Felipe believes that this maid of yours, this Lisbetta Deslegador from Farga de sant Matèu, is a Cathar and remains a Cathar. And that you, Countess, took the *Consolamentum* in a Cathar village near the Sárdalo Pass. You are a heretic. Alberensa is forfeit, save on the King's most gracious terms. You are called to recant or suffer the penalties."

Agnes looked directly towards his voice, and actually pointed her finger.

"It is most unchivalrous of you, Bishop Genet, not to respect the title and the station of the lady we have chosen as our closest confidant. She is of our family, descended like ourselves from Sir Julian of Blagnac, Baron of Jabil al-Hadid, a soldier for Christ against His true enemy, the Saracens."

Agnes turned, moving her hand in dismissal towards the Preaching Friar.

"One tires of this endless obsession of yours, Father Felipe. As you well know, I converted the Baroness of Mayrènge to the true faith in the convent of the Sisters of Charity, many years ago." Lisbetta of Mayrènge looked down demurely and fingered the wooden cross on a leather strand that matched her leather girdle. "The only person in the Sárdalo Pass with the heretics was you, Father Felipe."

"Was the Maronite Sister who helped in this conversion the same Maronite Sister who ordered the beheading of the Grand Master Stephen of Orcival at Jabil al-Hadid"?

"No Maronite Sister would order the beheading of anyone, Father." The Countess pointed in the direction of the door. "Gentlemen. Good day, gentlemen."

3

The Countess reached down to straighten her legs and lock her braces at the knees. "Bring my crutches, Lissie, and help me down." Lisbetta held Agnes by the waist as she slid from her chair. "The arrogance." The Countess put her crutches under her arms, took one tentative balancing step and stopped. "Such arrogance. We must be clever, Lissy-Bett."

"Yes, my lady."

"At first, after Toulouse surrendered two years ago, the French respected Cardinal Donato's agreement. I had hope, Little Lisbet, but it was a false hope. Blanche and Louis only left us alone last year because Henry III of England attacked them in Gascony." She waved towards the west, beyond Alberensa, where Gascony lay between the Pyrenees and Bordeaux. "Henry is back in England. These gruesome northern bandits are free to turn on our County."

"Yes, my lady."

"If we seek aid from Aragon or England against France, we will just end up as the vassals of a different monarch."

"Yes, my lady."

"With Hugh dead and me…..as I am, Bishop Jerome brought the Pope's proposal. Bequeath Alberensa to the Church in my will, make it an episcopal fief ruled by the Bishop after I die. That would put the Sárdalo pilgrimage route and its tolls and the wealth of our smelters directly in the Holy Father's hands. I asked, what of my little Hugh, my Maddie"?

"For Hugh, the right to inherit Sarlant from his father, with the Holy Father as his liege. For Madeleine, betrothal now to a suitable marriage."

Agnes crutched forward two steps and turned back. "That last is the most annoying! I was sold to the Prince of Antioch when I was five! I am not selling my daughter to anyone"!

"Yes my lady."

"Jerome carried my proposal in response. Continue our family's rule of Alberensa as it has always been, but accept the Holy Father as our liege. He received a favorable reply from Cardinal Donato. I thought we were negotiating my feudal dues. It appears I was wrong. Jerome is gone and there is no further word from Cardinal Donato."

"Yes, my lady." Lisbetta had learned that it was best to let the Countess pour it out. Then it was time for conversation.

"Know this, that I have no plans to make it easy for Gregory or Blanche or her charming stripling Louis, ninth of that name."

"The troubadours already call you by Jamilla's name for you, my lady, *al-Zarqa', Sheyka al-Hadid,* 'Lady Blue-Eyes, the Baroness of Iron.'"

"Too much iron for the Lioness Blanche. She thinks she's the only woman who can be both clever like a woman and tough like a man." Agnes stopped and turned towards Lisbetta. "She is wrong! There are many of us, is it not so"?"

"Everyone in St. John's Circle agrees."

"No doubt our friends the Épernays plan to be close to hand when the looting starts."

"No doubt." Lisbetta walked beside her liege as she always did while the Countess thought on her feet, ready to catch her if she faltered.

"*Excommunicamus* indeed, sending that wretched Felipe Vilalba to take away everything that is Lengadòc."

"And to burn us alive, my lady."

Agnes nodded. "He will order us tied high up on the stake to prolong our agony. We will make a fine shrieking couple as our blonde hair burns away and we roast slowly to a crisp." The sightless reached out to embrace the sighted. "It seems a poor reward for all your hard work, Little Betta. Let us see how we avoid it. More importantly, how we protect the people of our County."

Lisbetta opened the door into the waiting room. "Peter, we are ready. Show everyone in."

■ ■ ■

Giles, Baron of Sarlant, Lisbetta, Baroness of Mayrènge and the Five Consuls of the *Capitolum* sat in a circle with the Countess. Each commoner wore his finest tunic and the surcoat known as the Consul's Robe. Count Jacme created the garments, fine black wool lined with a fringe of fur around the neck and along the open edges down the front. By custom, each outgoing Consul placed his coat on his successor. The new man then knelt before the Countess to swear his allegiance.

"Gentlemen, our visitors brought the messages we have long feared. Please read them to us, my lady Baroness."

It did not take Lisbetta long to translate again the messages from Church and King. The Consuls looked to Garcias Lana, their First Consul, to speak.

"What of your barons, my lady Countess, of Ponset, Gautier, Bertrand, Rodrigo"?

"If I might, my lady Countess," Giles said. He received an approving nod in the correct direction. "They are all threatened. The fiefs of Alberensa are rich and fertile. There are many nobles in France with second and third sons in need of lands. If the Countess falls, then the King and the Pope will apply the Third

Canon to each of us. Our lands will be forfeit for failure to root out the heresy."

"If the King attacks, I will levy on my barons as is my right," Agnes said. "They will answer my call unless they are besieged themselves." She spoke with certainty, assurance, her soft, low, firm Voice. She prayed that she was right.

"With your leave, my lady Countess, another question to my lord the Baron of Sarlant. In the time of Montfort, the plague of these northerners came and went. The campaign season opened, men served their forty days obligation to their liege and left. Once Montfort's force was reduced in the fall, the nobles of Lengadòc were usually able to regain their lands. Simon's control, and Amaury's, was never secure."

"Yes, First Consul," Giles answered, "but now we face the King of France. The Holy Father put the wealth of the Church behind his campaign against the other counties, giving Louis and his mother far more money than the Montforts. Now the Pope will pledge that wealth against us. Some in the King's army serve as vassals, but for others, it is their only work. He does not have the problem of the forty days."

Consul Anton Legros, the baker and master of the numbers, spoke next. "What of our defenses? Can we hold long enough for them to decide it is not worth the cost"?

"We can hold the city through this summer, yes. When the weather turns foul, they may break off their siege. Or Henry of England may raise a threat, or the Holy Roman Emperor, someone else to draw their force away. We will not break their siege, but we might wait them out without a great cost in casualties. Then we may be able to secure a treaty with the King and the Holy Father on the more favorable terms that our liege has proposed."

"That is our best hope," the Countess said. "Aragon, England, France, we are between them all. None of them wants the others to have us. But it is a difficult business to thread between powerful kingdoms without becoming subject to one of them."

"Should we choose one," her Marshal added, "One of the others might attack them here. In that war, Alberensa will be looted, pillaged and destroyed."

In the following silence, the Countess raised her hand, index finger pointing to the ceiling. Everyone present recognized the gesture that meant she was changing the subject.

"I will soon be excommunicated. I will be cut off from the Sacraments of the Church, from the Mass. I was raised as a faithful Catholic in Tripoli, gentlemen, so this excommunication will be most distressing to me, most distressing. I fear for my immortal soul, but I comfort myself that Our Savior knows that this excommunication is unjust."

The room remained silent while the Countess crossed herself, then resumed.

"That Frenchman Bishop Genet abuses his power for the benefit of France. I will not give in. I will remain faithful in my heart. I will fight for Alberensa as well as I can for as long as I can and then I will trust in Our Savior's merciful grace."

Even the air, the candles in the Reception Chamber grew still, for all knew the words of Christ in Saint Matthew, his commission to St. Peter to lead his Church on earth. "I will give you the keys of the Kingdom of Heaven," Jesus said. "Whatever you bind on earth shall be bound in heaven." The Holy Father, not the Countess of Alberensa dispensed the Savior's grace.

"Forgive me for asking, my lady," Consul Lana said. "What of the city"?

"The canon on heresy calls for the ruler to be excommunicated. It does not require the Holy Father to place the County under the interdict, removing the comfort of the Sacraments from every Christian. The churches will remain open, First Consul." She paused. "That is a benefit. Otherwise we might suffer unrest in the city."

"Yes my lady." Another pause.

"Well, my faithful *Capitolum*. What is your view? Should I resist the King, or should I join Toulouse, Foix, Trencavel and bow to his might"?

"If I might, First Consul."

"Consul Legros, please."

"The King will not honor our *Capitolum*. The King will think little of the ladies of St. John's Circle. The King will unleash this Black Friar on our Good

Christians. The King will tax us far too much. The King will take our men for his wars with King Henry. The King will declare that after you are gone, my lady, some member of his family will inherit, as he did with Raymond of Toulouse. I say we fight, we resist. We buy time and we see what we can negotiate."

"I agree," said Consul Anfos Lodet.

"I agree," said Consul Bartholmeu Migona.

"We all agree, Countess," said First Consul Lana. "If you are willing, we will fight with you. We will fight for our rights and for our freedom."

4

After supper, Lisbetta sat with Agnes in her bedchamber and wrote out the formal replies. For dinner the Countess wore a silk tunic of Alberensa blue, matched with embroidered shoes and a girdle of silver links. Lisbetta worked steadily away while Anniken and Gracia bustled around, hanging up the evening clothing and unbuckling the leather straps that held on her braces.

"The children must know none of this, Liss. It will frighten them."

"Yes, my lady."

Lisbetta looked at her naked Countess. Still slender and small-breasted, still those bony and shriveled legs, now joined by a little pot and stretch marks from her two babies. That, and the beginning of wrinkles around her eyes.

"Yes my lady." She pointed downstairs, foolish since her liege could not see the movement. "The Baron of Sarlant is below in the Great Hall, instructing the messengers who will ride through the County tomorrow. The children are upstairs, in bed."

"Excellent, Betta, excellent." Agnes held her arms over her head so that the maids could drop on her nightgown.

Lisbetta put down her pen. "Done, my lady Countess."

"Seal them, Lisbet."

Lisbetta poured candle wax at the bottom of each parchment and pressed it with the Count's seal. She had worn the State ring ever since her sixteenth birthday, when the Countess announced at a dinner in her honor, "Vesting great confidence in our beloved friend and cousin, Lady Lisbetta of Mayrènge, we name her Keeper of the Count's Seal." To balance the Count's ring on her right hand, Agnes gave her a beautiful ruby of Saracen design for her left.

That sixteenth birthday dinner followed the pattern that began when Agnes knighted her on her fourteenth birthday, a fief, a title, a piece of Jabil al-Hadid jewelry. On her seventeenth birthday, she became the Baroness of Mayrènge and the owner of "This golden Saracen necklace and bracelets once worn by my grandmother, Princess Athèné of Jerusalem." Lisbetta woke up the next morning as the ruler of eight villages, with three manor houses and a small castle. Among her mills and her ovens was a blacksmith shop.

"All sealed, Countess." Lisbetta turned towards the maids. "I'll wait for Sir Giles with our liege. Tell

Mabila and Docina to prepare a bath for me. I feel dirty from the touch of that French peasant."

"Yes, my lady." It was an unusual request at an unusual time, but the maids had learned that the Baroness of Mayrènge often made unusual requests. She was much beloved of their Countess, but they found her a difficult charge, moody, mercurial, often lost deep in her own thoughts.

"I'm putting the messages in your strongbox, Countess," Lisbetta said once the maids left. "Sir Giles can take them from there."

"Good, Betta." The telltale hand went to the mouth. "Do you know what I worried about during supper tonight, Lissie? That Wretched Louis and Awful Blanche will ruin your wedding. I want a festive affair, a special day only for you. I don't want it ruined by those arrogant Frenchmen."

Her wedding, that was Lisbetta's eighteenth birthday, last summer. "We are most pleased, most happy to announce the betrothal of our beloved friend and cousin Lisbetta, Baroness of Mayrènge, to Godafres, son of our most trusted friend Rodrigo, Baron of Sárdalo." Lisbetta did not think the troubadours would ever sing the legend of their love as they did of Giles and Agnes, but she was a most suitable dynastic match for this son of an important baron.

"That is kind of you, my lady." Lisbetta had almost forgotten her handsome friend Guis the stable boy, with his strong shoulders, his lovely eyes, his kind way of speaking. Agnes apprenticed him to a weaver in the St. Luke's Quarter soon after knighting her. Her maid Mabila said he was married now, to the weaver's daughter. "I'm more worried that you still be our Countess on my wedding day."

The blue eyes sparkled with laughter. "That could be a problem, yes, Betta." Her finger pointed towards the ceiling. "By all reports Queen Blanche is very devout and her son Louis is very devout. I'm sure they believe that their battle against us is the Will of God."

"Julian and Monica believed that they were carrying out the will of God in their battle, my lady."

"Yes, but our ancestors were fighting the Saracens, freeing the Holy City from their yoke. Conveniently for the French, God calls them to free rich and Christian Alberensa with its pilgrims and its ironworks, completing their control of Languedoc."

"And rescuing the County from Agnes Her Brother's Concubine and Giles the Common Sergeant who both defy the Holy Father by sheltering the heretic Lisbetta Deslegador, the Conjured-Up Baroness of Mayrènge."

"That summarizes the essence of the Pope's message nicely in one sentence, Liss."

Silence followed, as it often did when one thought reminded the Countess of another.

"I feel like I've been in a battle of wits with Queen Blanche ever since my brother died, Lisbet. She maneuvers and she fights. She takes to the field herself against any challengers to her son the King. One winter when the cold set in, her knights wanted to break off a siege. She made them cut down the forest, build fires and stay." Her hand went to her mouth. "What of Lo Cercle de San Juan, Bet? Would they agree with what I did today"?

Lisbetta smiled, "They send their greetings to Agnes Alberensa. They miss her."

"They still have Lisbetta Deslegador. It was one thing to be Agnes when my brother was the Count. It is another thing when I'm the Countess."

"The Teissendièrs were grateful that you came to Julia's funeral. Rubea is doing a good job as leader, but of course it's different from Julia. Your question? I think they agree with the Consuls. The Baroness of Juviler said it best, at Easter dinner on the day we met. 'We are more open to learning here, to knowledge and education among our women. We would not want that light taken away from us.'"

Agnes nodded, slowly. Lisbetta waited, knowing her liege, giving her time.

"When the battle comes, Lissie-Betta, I cannot take the field like Queen Blanche of the Cut-Down Forest. That does not concern me, because our men do not need me to tell them how to fight. Giles and Fulques and my barons and the others, they will make the right decisions, but the siege will occupy all their thoughts, all their time."

"Yes."

Agnes reached out and found Lisbetta's hand. "Our role is different. Like Blanche, we must think beyond the battle, away from the battle. We must search out other alliances, other strategies, other ways to defeat Louis and save this County. What do we have besides our vassals and our soldiers and how can we use them? You are clever, Lisbetta of Mayrènge. Help me think."

Lisbetta remembered the greed of the Épernays that left her family lying in the dirt. "The French do not know the secrets of the ironworks at Pont de Molin, how we make the soft iron flow."

The hand on the mouth and a slow smile. "Good, Little One, good. My family in Outremer used their smelter to keep peace with the Saracens. I'll have Giles send for Guilhelms."

"Why don't we all ride out there together, my lady? Let the men of Petrousset and the Pont see their Countess, talk to her."

Agnes clapped her hands, surprising Lisbetta with her glee. "You were born to be a noblewoman, a ruler, Lisbetta Deslegador, Lady Mayrènge. A person of learning and breeding who speaks and reads three languages and knows numbers. It was the Will of God that we met, my lady Baroness, the Will of God"!

■ ■ ■

Lisbetta's father would never agree that anyone was born to be a ruler. Under Christ, he said, all men were equal.

"For you are all one in Christ Jesus," as Brunissende Migona reminded Satan's foul priest Felipe Vilalba. Her father warned her against what she had become, against the Evil One who created this Evil Earth, who stole people's souls with wealth and power.

The Baroness of Mayrènge passed the servants' bedroom on her way to Maura's former bedchamber, now hers. The Dowager Countess departed within a year after she returned from Tripoli, newly married to a forty-year old nobleman with a fief near Acre on the sea below Jerusalem.

"I thought it best for Alberensa that a close relative of the excommunicated Raymond of Toulouse not remain among us," Agnes explained on the day Maura left. "We might be accused of sheltering heretics. I paid her dowry on behalf of Colomiers."

"Yes, my lady."

"Once Maura learned of her father's new arrangements, she begged me to stop them, to show mercy, like Joseph showed to his brothers after they sold him into Egypt or the Prodigal's father showed to his Son when he returned."

"You helped them send her to Outremer, my lady, like Lucratz of Alberensa in the chapel window"?

"I found myself less forgiving than the Prodigal's father, Liss. I imagined my brother shackled to the floor of the death chamber. Buried alive, with her help. I told her there was nothing I could do. She hates Outremer, but she will be well cared for."

On the day that Maura left for her living grave, Agnes moved her Little Lisbit downstairs, nearby, within the hour.

Lisbetta found her own maids waiting when she opened her door. Redhead Mabila with her curly hair and green eyes came from the family of a seamstress in the town. Two years older than her charge, she stood a hand shorter but still maintained the slender shape of youth. Plump and pleasant and deferential Docina acted as the Mother Superior for all four maids.

"We are ready, my lady," Docina announced. Mabila removed her jewelry, took off her evening tunic and silk cotte and helped her sit in the tub. The hot water felt good, relaxing, comforting. Bathing so often, her maids found that strange, but the Baroness enjoyed being clean. She closed her eyes and let her servants wash Satan's Pawn.

On her fifteenth birthday, after the dinner in her honor, Lisbetta went to the Faures' room, wearing her new green Damascene silk tunic and Saracen necklace.

"The life of a commoner is not hers to lead, my lady of Mayrènge," Guihelms told her. "When you came back from the Sárdalo Pass with our distant cousin the Countess, your life passed into her hands. Now you have wealth and title, but she will always direct your way. And you will never know her full purpose, her full intent."

Lisbetta shook her head, no, no. Guilhelms reached out and lifted the young woman's chin, treating her as a cousin and not a noblewoman for the last time.

"Little Lisbit, with your hard work and study, you have made yourself very special to our liege, just as the Saracen did. She knows you are a Good Christian, and she does not ask you to change. She is protecting you, my lady, and you are protecting her." He took his thumbs and wiped the tears from her cheeks, for his cousin Gervais. "Sit up and comport yourself as a noblewoman, Lady Lisbetta. It is the life that you must lead."

The lady of Mayrènge ran to the roof of the Keep, alone. She heard Satan speaking through the men who told her how lovely she looked in her pretty clothes and fancy jewelry. Through Peter, too, when he complimented her on how skillfully she had mastered French and Latin. Her serfs labored in Mayrènge and she did not know the face of a single one.

You must leave, Lisbetta. You must run away to the mountains, join Bishop Thomas and take the *Consolamentum.*

The roof felt cold that night. The cold and the thought of Thomas reminded Lisbetta of the cold night in the Sárdalo while Agnes lay deserted in the cave. The thought made her angry. God did not cripple the Countess for her sins, as the filthy Catholic priests constantly muttered. The God of Light would never do such a thing. No, the Evil One mangled a virtuous woman. A determined woman. A clever woman. Her beloved friend and cousin.

"That cannot be, Lord," Lisbetta cried aloud into the dark night. "I cannot let Satan defeat Agnes"!

A vision in Damascene silk stood in the darkness with her hand over her heart. "I will battle Lucifer in the company of my liege," she swore. "Together, we will fight. Together, we will lead Alberensa as well as any man, nay, better. Together, we will triumph over Satan's Evil. Together, we will defeat Satan's Henchmen, Louis, Blanche, the Antichrist Pope, Felipe, the loathsome Épernays."

Lisbetta looked up at the blaze of all the stars of Creation, to Heaven where Andreva and her parents looked down. "Mommy, Daddy, Sister, I must submit. God calls me to help this woman. Forgive me, but duty requires me to live as the velvet-chained slave of a Countess, not as a *Parfait* hiding in the Pyrenees."

Lisbetta came down from the roof a noblewoman. She accepted the respect and the deference due her station. The right to wear fine clothes while others wore rags, to eat while others went hungry. The silence and deep bows when she entered a room. The power that came from being so close to the powerful. The fear that one so young could provoke with a single glance. The responsibility that confined her life to a few small rooms and the desires of a single woman.

Through some holy mystery that you cannot fathom, Lisbetta, your Satanic life of sin is the Will of the God of Light, the True God, the Creator.

"My lady? My lady? We're done, my lady." Lisbetta returned from her memories. "Please stand up so we can dry you." Mabila dried while Docina held her nightgown.

"You seem concerned, my lady," the older woman said. "Are you worried about your wedding"?

"Our liege has much to worry her, Docina. I am worried for her, for us all."

"Yes, my lady," Mabila said. "It's just that we're so excited about your wedding….."

Lady Mayrènge didn't feel like tittering about losing her virginity. That was a sin, too, and Agnes had explained the whole thing. "I know. Please take out the tub, and leave me." She got into bed and rolled to the wall.

"Good night, my lady."

Her door closed. The Baroness remembered too late that she had forgotten to say good night.

5

When Sir Ferrandos started uphill with Sir Raolf and the lookout's relief, showers threatened. Now they had become steady rain, soaking his wool cloak and the tunic beneath it. Water dripped from the front of his hood and ran down his face. At least his chain mail remained dry back in Fonta, making the climb from Ganat easier.

The little party reached the outcrop over Farga to find the lookout hiding just inside the trees. "I'm sorry, my lord, with this rain, I couldn't see very far and there was no dust. That group surprised me when they rode into view." Ferrandos watched as a scouting party of about a hundred mounted men, all in mail, turned north from the Lavelanet Road towards Foix.

"Anyone ahead of them"?

"No, my lord, they're the first."

The lord of Fonta lay down on his belly and slithered out onto the rock. He watched while the leader sent outriders into the fields, scouts to scout the perimeter of this scouting unit. The column paused, the leader gave orders and four men rode back the way they had come.

A whole army must be in motion behind them, Ferrandos thought. It was too far to see the guerdons at the head of the column, but there could be no doubt. The messenger from Sir Giles had been right. King Louis was coming to seize Alberensa.

Ferrandos crawled back into the woods and stood up. The dripping from the trees had not abated, but the knight no longer noticed. He turned to the lookouts.

"You two men stay here. As soon as a large body of foot appears, one of you run down and report. Or if anyone turns the other way, towards Tarascon, planning to work through the hills and come down at us that way. When I get to Fonta, I'll send back two more men as extra runners. Understood"?

"Yes, my lord."

"Good. Sir Raolf, they're coming. And we're first. Bring your levy into Fonta, now. Tell Sir Gaucelis to come with his full levy. I'll inform Sir Arnald on my way back."

A stunned old man looked back at Ferrandos. The climb had been difficult for Raolf with his weight. With two daughters married away and a son waiting to inherit, he thought himself well past the age for fighting.

"My lord, they will be too many. We cannot stand."

Certainly Raolf hadn't stood for Sir Alass when the Épernays seized this fief nine years ago, Ferrandos knew. No doubt he planned the same this time. Survive at all costs as the lord of the manor of Cazac, a petty knight, nothing more. Survive if necessary by swearing allegiance to the French lord who took Fonta after the battle, and hope not to be replaced.

"We must yield, my lord."

"You will not find that advantageous this time, Sir Raolf. The Holy Father has declared all of Alberensa forfeit. These dogs have come for the spoils. If you don't fight for your land, some French knight will have it, not you."

Raolf did not appear convinced. He shuffled his feet, he looked out over the hillside, he looked back. Ferrandos pushed against his chest with his full hand.

"Do you and your son want to muck out your own stables for these heathens? Where is your fighting spirit, my lord? Yes, they will besiege us, and we will kill some. The Countess will attack them and kill more. We will break their siege. We will hold this fief for Agnes of Alberensa. Get your levy and your people inside Fonta, and prepare."

■ ■ ■

Once she passed the Trysting Glade, it took Prisca but twenty minutes to reach the small camp above the Barièja. She lined up the Bear's Tooth with the tower of St. Gregorio's, picked up the skirt of her fine green tunic with one gloved hand and pushed aside the bushes with the other. This dress, surcoat, gloves, had always been her favorite, and she would wear them, one more time. Just as, one hour ago, she had made love with her handsome Ferrandos, one last, deeply satisfying time. She allowed herself a feeling of pride at still fitting into the gown, even after two pregnancies. The relative poverty of their fief after the blast furnace moved to Pont de Molin had helped to keep her thin.

Like her husband on the outcrop that morning, Prisca was soaked to the skin, but the warm spring rain gave way to drizzles as she reached the clearing. Her father was the first to leave a cave, but soon after, the forest began to fill with villagers from Brassat, Ganat, Fonta, Cazac, Guzet. All wore the brown wool of the indentured farmer.

"I didn't think you would make it, Lady Prisca. We will leave at first light tomorrow. We should be in Aragon in a few days."

Prisca hugged her father. His quiet understanding had been important when her first baby was stillborn and the other died after just a few days. "Think how many evil people have healthy children, daughter," he said after the second death. "You are not being punished. Tested, perhaps, but not punished. Your mother and I lost children, too."

Perhaps it was God's will, God's plan, for her losses had freed her for this moment. Certainly if she was a mother, she could never do it.

"I'm going to stay with my husband, Papa. He is brave and confident and bold, but I don't think Fonta will survive this battle."

The smelter worker Rothan joined them as shock filled Papa's face. Rothan made to bow, but Prisca reached out and stopped him. He was confused, half-way between up and down, until Lady Fonta reached out and pulled him to his feet.

"Not all of the Good Christians managed to get up here, Bishop. There are many in Fonta Castle, but all of us are *Credentes*. There are no *Parfaits*." She knelt and bowed her head. "Bishop Rothan, I wish to take the *Consolamentum*."

Lady Prisca had not bowed her head to anyone in Brassat since her wedding day. She had not been alone with commoners, unguarded, for seven years. Still, she felt strangely calm as she knelt amidst people who had curtseyed to her, kissed her hand, worked hard so she could afford these deerskin gloves and this fine wool dress. Was their silence surprise, or disbelief, or were they only waiting for their Bishop to speak?

"Lady Prisca, have you considered what you are asking? You have not followed the way of the Good Christians for a long time. We do not eat animals, or eggs, or cheese, because they come from fornication. We eat of the water and the wood, only fish and vegetables. You relish your place as a noblewoman, yet all are equal here, men and women. It is hard even for a Good Christian to stay chaste, but you, my lady, enjoy your time with your Catholic husband, very much. These are things of Satan. A *Parfait* of our Church does none of them. We require a *Credente* to undergo a long period of preparation before taking the sacrament."

Prisca looked at the mud as she spoke, in a whisper. "Baptism in the Holy Spirit can come only from the laying on of hands of one so baptized, Bishop. You are that man here. Men have laid the hand of the Spirit on you, and others on them, and still others, back to the time of the first Apostles. There is no such person in Fonta, Bishop, and yet at the end, many will wish the Sacrament."

A gasp of understanding now, especially from the women. Prisca raised her hand to stop the Bishop from speaking.

"There is no time to prepare me for the Sacrament. The French are here." She pulled the gloves from her hands and dropped them to the ground. "If Fonta is to fall, I will lay my hands on all who desire it, before the end comes." She untied her cap and dropped it on the gloves. Her surcoat followed. "Many Good Christians will die, Bishop Rothan. I have been their master. Now let me be their servant. I beg you, perform the ceremony and let the Holy Spirit descend on me, as it descended upon the Disciples in the Upper Room on the Day of Pentecost."

Rothan stood for a moment, trying to decide. Prisca was boisterous as a little girl, flighty and flirty as a teenager, imperious as their master. Now she was choosing her duty as their lady over her life. Such a choice could only be the Will of God.

The Bishop nodded at a villager. In a moment, the man was back, with a Bible, a cord and a simple black robe.

"Kneel down, Prisca Formatgièr." The ground soaked through Prisca's tunic, wetting her knees. Rothan held the Bible over her head and recited the Lord's Prayer.

"Amen," said all the *Credentes* as he finished.

"Remember, Prisca," Rothan continued, "That we have received this prayer from Our Lord himself, as is taught in Matthew's Gospel. Remember that if you do not forgive men their sins against you, the Heavenly Father will not forgive your own sins. We pray that you receive the grace to follow this Our Lord's prayer steadfastly for all the days of your life."

"I receive this prayer of you, and of this, God's Holy Church."

"Prisca, our Lord Christ was not born as a man, as the harlot Church of Rome vainly teaches. He came to us as Spirit, as He breathed fire into His disciples in the upper room after His Ascension. As John the Baptist said, 'I baptize you with water, but one is coming after me who shall baptize you in the Spirit, and give you everlasting life.'"

The Bishop reached down to take her hands.

"I stand before you, baptized in the Spirit through the laying on of hands. The Holy Spirit dwells within me and sets me apart from those not so consecrated. When I lay my hands upon you, you shall receive the Spirit, as from Christ Himself, and you shall also stand apart."

"May it be so, Bishop Rothan."

Rothan's wife Francesca took a place at the side of her husband. Like her husband, she wore the simple black robe of a *Parfait*.

"From this time forward, Prisca," Rothan said, "You will not eat of any food not from water or wood. You will not lie, or swear, or kill, or give up your body to any form of luxury. You will never go alone when you may have a companion. You will never abandon your faith for fear of water, or fire, or any manner of death. Do you understand these commandments"?

"I do."

The woods seemed strangely quiet, after the rain. Prisca's rain-soaked dress felt cold now, and she shivered.

"My sister, do you desire to give yourself to our faith"?

"Yes. Bless me. For all the sins I have ever done in thought, word and deed, I ask the pardon of God, of the Church and of you all."

Rothan placed the Bible on Prisca's head with one hand, and put his other on her shoulder. Francesca laid her hands on her other shoulder.

"Prisca, do you wish to receive the spiritual baptism whereby the Holy Spirit is given in the Church of God by the laying on of hands of the Good Christians"?

From somewhere deep inside her, from a place she had never known before, Prisca felt the sure certainty that it was her duty as the Lady of Fonta to stand up for her people. Whether it was truly the flowing of the Spirit or simply the vital presence of these two *Parfaits*, she could not say. She knew from the Catholic priest Ricartz that Christ's work had advanced by sacrifice and witness such as hers, over and over through the centuries. She would hold to that thought at the end, until the agony of the flames drove everything but the pain from her dying mind.

"I have this will. Pray to God for me that He will give me His power."

The moment had arrived to receive the Consolation of the Holy Spirit.

"Good Christians, we pray by your love of God that you grant this blessing of the Holy Spirit, which God has given, to this, our friend Prisca, here present."

"Let the Spirit be with us," said Prisca's neighbors.

"We worship You, Father, Son and Holy Spirit.

"We worship You, Father, Son and Holy Spirit.

"We worship You, Father, Son and Holy Spirit."

Francesca extended her hand to help Prisca to her feet. Rothan tied a cord around her waist and placed a black robe, like the habit of a nun or a monk, over her green dress.

The new Parfait made it back to Fonta before dusk. Behind her, in the camp, her gloves and surcoat and cap burned in the fire made for the evening meal of wood and water.

6

The French army stopped for the night outside Foix. They would advance and besiege the castle in the morning. Ferrandos brought in the lookouts from the outcrop and took thirty men to wait on the road between Fonta and Foix.

As he expected, a small unit of the French came along the road in the dark, reconnoitering. They yielded after a quick but fierce fight. The lord of Fonta left three wounded enemy to be recovered by their own men. He took the others into the castle and questioned them. Their knight resisted the torture, but two of the men looked at the hot irons and babbled out everything they knew. It was not much, but it was enough.

Ferrandos selected three different farmers from the levy inside Fonta, men who could ride, men without families.

"Make your way to Alberensa. Hurry. Inform our liege and Sir Giles that we face at least ten thousand

French. A thousand knights, siege machines. We will hold here while the water lasts, but we cannot stand. Do you understand"?

"Yes, my lord."

"They will only leave a small number to besiege us. The others will go on towards the city. Ride quickly. They will be right behind you."

■ ■ ■

The French arrived early the next morning. Sir Ferrandos walked the entire circuit of his rampart wall, picking out their dispositions. They had drawn up, as Count Hugh had done all those years ago, just outside of crossbow range from the walls. Foot soldiers gathered all around his small fort, on the best ground, with knights racing back and forth giving orders. Most of the French army passed by on the Foix Road, headed further into Alberensa.

"My lord, they are leaving behind a trebuchet," Izarns, Ferrandos's Marshal said. The lord of Fonta looked at the field towards Brassat, where French men-at-arms were rolling a large triangle of wood on wheels into place. A shaft at the apex of the triangle held a long wooden arm, with a sling at the end for holding stones. A short extension of the arm continued beyond the other side of the shaft. A large weight was attached there, on its own shaft, so that it remained below the arm as it fell.

Ferrandos imagined the cursing now as the soldiers struggled to adjust the machine. They pulled down the long arm with a rope, lifting the weight. They loaded stones into the sling. When they released the latch, the weight would drop, swinging the long arm up. At the top, one side of the sling released and the stones flew to the target.

Of the artillery used in a siege, the trebuchet was the most accurate of all. Assembling the weapon meant that the French did not plan to wait for Ferrandos to run out of water. They would pound the same spot on his wall with their infernal machine, over and over, until it weakened and collapsed. Then they would surge into the yard. It could be over in just a day or two.

"Another one over there." Ferrandos turned towards where young Izarns pointed, near the joining of the Fonta-Brassat track. Indeed, there were two now, as far apart as they were from the wall.

Ferrandos looked to his own artillery. He lacked the space inside to set up siege engines that could lob stones back at the trebuchets. He did have twenty of the giant crossbows called arbalètes mounted along his ramparts, each capable of launching several arrows at a time. At close range, the iron bolts, as long as a man's arm, could penetrate the wood of any shield used by advancing attackers.

"We have no chance, my lord," Sir Gaucelis said. "Two trebuchets and thousands of footmen. We must yield, my lord, yield to the King and hope to keep our fiefs."

Gaucelis stood to the other side of Izarns in his hauberk and chausses, without coif or helmet. These so-called knights, his vassals, were growing tiresome with their whining. Ferrandos turned on Gaucelis and let his voice rise, so that no one in the yard mistook his intention.

"Get your coif and your helmet on, Sir Gaucelis. Otherwise you might get a very large headache from that trebuchet."

The men-at-arms, the yeomen of the villages, all laughed at the discomfort of His Lordship. They watched as Gaucelis finished putting on his armor.

""'That's better." Ferrandos pointed outside. "In an hour, most of these Frogs will be an hour down the road. On their way to besiege, perhaps, Roncis, the castle of our most beloved Baroness of Mayrènge."

"Please, my lord," Gaucelis answered, "You are confusing me."

"They think we are easily defeated, my lord. They are dividing up, trying to do everything at once. They have left behind too few, and we will break their siege. Break their siege and wreak havoc on their supply trains. We will leave them weak and starving, and then drive them from our County."

Ferrandos turned and strode away. After a moment, he realized that Sir Gaucelis was not behind him.

"Look to your dispositions, my lord! We sortie tonight against those machines! Prepare your men"!

■ ■ ■

Ferrandos skipped quickly down the rampart stairs and entered his Great Hall. Prisca waited at the head table of the dais in her black robe. The green dress was gone from underneath now, he knew, although he had not seen her body since yesterday afternoon. She had been crying, indeed was still crying.

"Be of cheer, my lady. All is not lost. We shall break this siege."

"We have made our mistakes, my husband. We have been arrogant and full of pride, but I have loved you from the first moment I saw you in the field. I pray that in your next life, you are a Good Christian, and that we meet again, in Paradise."

■ ■ ■

Ferrandos re-mounted his rampart and studied the milling French as they set up their defensive positions.

"The Frogheads are testing their machines, my lord," his Marshal said. The knight nodded as he looked to his own dispositions. His men and the yeomen had spread out along the wall, hiding with their crossbows behind the crenellations. Long poles lay by them, ready to resist an escalade, to push away any scaling ladders.

"I see no reason for further delay, Izarns. Let's give them something to think about. The arbalètes."

Izarns raised and dropped his hand. With a twang of straining steel, twenty waves of bolts went on their way. Shouts of fear and panic rose in the French line as most of the arrows took some target.

"Again."

More shouts, and some of the French began running back. "Can we reach the trebuchets"?

Two bows twanged again, sending several bolts into the artillerymen before each weapon. They quickly began untying their machines from the ground pegs they had driven.

"Again"!

More artillerymen fell, but now the French leader ordered his foot soldiers to step in front, to shield the artillerymen from the arrows' path.

"No more. Save the bolts."

A cheer went up around the walls of Fonta as the French backed out of range. Ferrandos turned towards his yard.

"Good work! They aren't so tough, these Northerners! Be of cheer, men! This battle is still ours"! He spoke to Izarns. "Now we'll be able to sortie quietly tonight and reach those machines without going through their lines."

The drizzle of the day grew heavier, afternoon showers. The soft ground of springtime grew muddy after three days of rain. Good. The muck will slow down any French advance, giving more time for Fonta's archers to take a toll.

"What's this, my lord"? Ferrandos followed Izarns' gaze. Three riders approached.

The Lord of Fonta spoke to his Marshal in a whisper. "One of them is our Most Traitorous Vassal, Sir Arnald, running off to save his ass again. Keep a bolt in an arbalète on him, Izarns, and watch for my signal." He turned into the yard again. "The Frogs are sending someone to surrender! I'm going out to accept"!

He enjoyed the laughter as he walked down the stairs, through his yard, and out the sally gate, alone. Keep their spirits up, Ferrandos, keep yours up, and believe.

The drizzle turned to rain, rain heavy enough to hiss as it fell. The falling droplets re-arranged the little craters that they made in the mud. Ferrandos stood with his sword sheathed and waited for the three riders to draw near.

Yes, the coward Arnald. A week ago he was kissing Prisca's ass, hoping for some boon. Now he's gone over to the French. Not even wearing his armor. Second man is just the guard, carrying the truce flag. Could the third man be….?

"Good day, my lord. I am Sir Martin of Ablois, in the service of the Baron of Épernay. I remember you, Sir Ferrandos, from the treaty discussions that day."

"And I remember you as well, my lord. I was obliged to stand in the rain, but you had the benefit of shelter."

Martin smiled, just a brief acknowledgment of his opponent's bravery. "I will have my fief back, my lord. As the Baron of Sarlant once said to me before this gate, you cannot hold. Yield my castle and your weapons, and you may ride out with honor. All who are not Albigensians may return to their fields."

"And those who are"?

"Must recant or face the fire."

Sir Ferrandos turned towards Arnald and gave a little bow. "And you will help them know who is who, Sir Arnald? Is that your arrangement? Help the French find the Good Christians, and keep your fief"?

Arnald drew himself up to his full importance. "I will aid the King in many ways, in return for my fief. You should accept Sir Martin's gracious offer, my lord. He is offering to let you live."

Ferrandos shook his head. "My wife has taken the *Consolamentum*, Sir Arnald. She will not be recanting, and she will not be burning. As for you, please give my compliments to the traitor Judas Iscariot when you join him in Hell."

Ferrandos dropped his hand. Two seconds later, the arbalète bolt entered Arnald's shoulder and drove out low on his back. The steep angle carried him from his mount and pinned him to the ground. Blood poured from his mouth, his shoulder, his back as he writhed in desperation on the shaft. Sir Martin motioned to his man, put up your sword. Ferrandos gave a slight bow to the mounted knight.

"My lady Agnes, Countess of Alberensa, favors your cross, Sir Martin." Ferrandos had to raise his voice to overcome the screams of Sir Arnald. "It is a treasured gift, one that she wears all the time."

Sir Martin looked towards the shrieking Lord of Brassat as he choked in his own blood. "My compliments to your lady, my lord. I am glad that my poor gift has been so well received." Ferrandos handed the reins of Arnald's mount up to the guard. "I shall carry your reply, Sir Ferrandos, to my liege Henri, Baron of Épernay."

Two men and three animals rode swiftly away as Ferrandos walked back towards his gate. Arnald's shrieks became moans, weak and feeble, near the end. Stone splinters rained down on the Lord of Fonta as the first salvo from the trebuchet hit the wall beside him. Sir Raolf and Sir Gaucelis looked at him in horror as he came through the sally gate. There would be no quarter granted to Fonta or anyone in it, not now. They must break the siege, or die.

7

"The Pont," the workers called it, the blast furnaces that Count Hugh built at Pont de Molin, just downstream from Petrousset. The Brassat men built flume and wheel and furnace just as they had in the Trysting Glade, except that here, everything was larger, and they built two of them. After the first year, Guilhelms added a small dam to quiet the water as it entered the flume. The smoother flow raised the volume. He redesigned the wheel to take advantage of its greater power.

When demand was high with both furnaces running, their sound could be heard a thousand paces away. On a clear day, the plumes of smoke were visible in Alberensa. A green and verdant river bank, a narrow spot with a lovely waterfall, had become hardpacked dirt bordering a sullen pond. Yet although the furnaces had ruined the spot, the workable soft iron they produced made Alberensa even richer. Certainly none of the men earning wages here worried much about the birds or the fish or the trees.

"My brother would be most proud of what you've accomplished, Guilhelms," the Countess said. "He would want you to have this." Agnes handed her foundry master a chunk of rusting iron. "This comes from Monica and Julian's smelter on the Orontes, from the first time Jabil al-Hadid made the iron flow. The Men of Lengadòc have indeed bested the fabled Men of the East."

The master of Pont de Molin lived in a big stone house on the other side of the Tolosa Road. He planned to build directly across from his works, but his wife, the farmer's daughter, remembered the noise and smell of the Glade and told him no. Instead, she spent two days on a pillion behind Sir Giles until she found her perfect place on a hill ten minutes from the mill.

"The Countess shall make it so, Aenor," and indeed she had. Two stories, with a kitchen and two rooms on the ground floor and three bedrooms upstairs. Aenor laid it out so that the smelter could be seen from the kitchen. From the rooms up front where guests might sit, her house looked down on a little creek and a forest and, in the distance, *Lo Grandautar* and the Pyrenees. She hired a widow from Pont de Molin as a maid to help with the house and the cooking. The mistress herself spent hours in the garden, keeping hold on the skills she had learned as a little girl.

Guilhelms was just preparing to leave for the works when Sir Laurent of Burgalays, the knight from Moustalon, stopped at the house.

"I'm on my way to Alberensa, Guilhelms. It's begun. The French are coming south along the Tolosa Road. They will reach the border at Arguenos today." He mounted up again and rode off. Aenor came out into the yard.

"Does this mean…"?

"It does." She struggled in shock to hold back her tears.

"Will the Countess…"?

"She will." He took her and held her. "It's time to prepare."

"No"! Aenor cried. "You are a commoner, Guilhelms, and a free man. Our children are free. Let the nobles fight, that's what they like to do. They are part of Satan's evil. We don't…"

"Aenor, Aenor, if you say what you just said to that Black Friar, you'll be at the stake within the hour. Our wealth and our freedom depend on Alberensa."

"Our wealth and our freedom depend on what you know, Guilhelms, not on Alberensa! Do we care if we work for the Countess or the King, as long as we earn a fair income"?

"Aenor, it's not that simple."

She started to cry. "Look at our house, Guilhelms, look at it. We've made it lovely, a home for our children. Little Melisende knows no other place. Our furniture, our kitchen things, all of it can't go to Alberensa. The French will burn it. It's a lovely home and I've worked hard and…..and…."

He took her into his arms. They were rich now, and she dressed as the nobles did, and ate as they did, and talked about travel as they did. Four children had made her thick around the middle, but her face was still lovely even when it was upset.

"We own The Pont, Aenor, because the Countess gave it to us. She honors Foix's grant of my freedom. The King may not think we own Pont de Molin, and he may not think we're free. A few beatings, a little torture and I will be building blast furnaces somewhere up north."

"Beatings? Torture? Why"?

"Remember what the Countess and I discussed when she visited."

Aenor remembered the visit, Agnes and Giles and Lisbetta and a small column of soldiers visiting from the city. "We've learned much about how to run a blast furnace, Countess," Guilhelms said that day. "And how to judge the iron, how to work the metal. There is more to it than just lighting a fire and throwing in the rock."

"As we both know well, Guilhelms," the Countess replied.

"The French need what we know to make the iron flow. If they have the furnace but not us, it will be a challenge for them. If the works have been destroyed and we are gone, they will have nothing. Once peace comes, we can rebuild the smelters in a few weeks, maybe less."

"You mean in return for concessions," Baron Giles said, "we show them how"? The Countess had put her hand to her mouth and shook her head no, quietly.

"Possibly, my lord Baron," Guilhelms answered. "Better, not show them how, but promise that if they leave Alberensa, we will rebuild and keep the iron coming, meeting all their needs. As the Barons of Jabil al-Hadid did with the Saracens. What's up here" – he tapped his head – "is more valuable than the works themselves."

"Yes," through the hand, "As Jamilla is doing with the Hospitallers, even now." The hand came down. "I'm glad we met, cousin Guilhelms, I'm glad we met."

8

The messenger from Fonta brought bad news. Lisbetta sat with Agnes and Giles and Fulques in the Reception Hall while he described the arrival of the French. The Baron of Sarlant pressed him hard, how many men, what arms, foot, mounted, artillery. Could he see any coats of arms, describe them. Lisbetta sat at her little table, listened carefully and made notes.

"Why did it take you so long to get here? The ride is not that long."

"There are French scouts everywhere, my lord. I could not keep to the roads. It took all night and half of today. They must have caught the other two men."

Or perhaps the other two went up to the Good Christian camp above the Trysting Glade, Lisbetta thought.

"Is there anything else"?

"You have done well, Guigo," the Countess said when Giles was finished. "You have my thanks for your bravery and your loyalty."

"It is an honor, my lady."

"Fulques, see that Guigo is well fed. Have Peter give him a guardsman's wages, two months. He may stay here or return home, as he wishes."

"Yes, my lady." If Alberensa survived, the serf would have more coin than anyone else in Cazac.

Lisbetta had grown steadily more impressed by Fulques as the crisis grew. Young, tall, with strong shoulders and auburn hair and wonderful hazel eyes, he was handsome in the way Lisbetta remembered Sir Ferrandos. His imperturbable calm in the face of danger matched that of Giles.

No sooner was Guigo dispatched for a good meal than Sir Laurent arrived.

"My liege Sir Gautier must concentrate his forces in his castle at Moustalon, my lady Countess." He bowed gently towards Lisbetta. "I'm sorry, Lady Mayrènge, but he thought it best to abandon Roncis." Lisbetta merely nodded as she drew a rough map of the County and marked the French positions. She caught the Marshal's eye and tapped the bridge across the Salat at Arguenos.

"Any word from the north, Sir Laurent"?

"We have learned that Sir Ponset is with the French as they come down from the north, my lord. I think we will learn that Louis has promised him our lady's titles for his support."

"If Arguenos does not resist, my lady Countess," Giles said, "The French will easily cross the natural river barriers at our frontier. They will be deep inside your lands quite quickly."

"Liss."

"Yes my lady."

"Sir Arguenos is a felon. His fief, his titles, his fees and profits are forfeit to me as his liege. He and his whole family are banished from Alberensa forever. Prepare the document and seal it."

"Yes my lady."

Agnes pointed her finger towards the ceiling. "A large force of the enemy is coming from the east, from Limoux. Another large force is coming from the north, from Tolosa. The Sárdalo Pass is quiet, and the border with Gascony. We face only the French, not Aragon or England."

"Correct, my lady," Giles agreed.

"Ferrandos will hold as long as he can in the east and Gautier in the north. Eventually the French strength will overcome them. Sir Laurent."

"Yes my lady."

"My compliments to Sir Gautier. It is my view that we should concentrate everything here. We need every man we can get to sustain the siege. Men killed in a failed attempt to protect Moustalon will help neither Gautier nor me. If your liege is not already besieged, ask him to join us here as soon as he can."

■ ■ ■

Ferrandos left his whining knights Gaucelis and Raolf behind as he sallied forth with Izarns and two groups of men. He set Prisca and the women to guard the gate, to ensure that his knights did not lock him out, light torches and yield his castle to the Frogs.

Men carrying crossbows, swords and daggers moved quietly across the still-barren fields. Some carried jars of oil as well. Ferrandos sent Izarns to take the trebuchet near Brassat. He took a larger group of men towards the road junction, where both trebuchet and supply wagons created a tempting target. Only the stars shone overhead at this phase of the moon, masking their movements in deep darkness.

Slowly, carefully they approached the Frogs without encountering any kind of picket line to guard against intruders in the night. Our Savior favors our enterprise, Ferrandos decided as he brought his fifteen men within twenty paces of the trebuchet. The smoke of the French campfires wafted over his group, the smell of roasted meat, the jesting and laughter as the enemy drank their wine. The green of Épernay marked the soldiers near the wagons.

"Now," Ferrandos whispered. Fifteen men rose from the dark, suddenly visible as specters in the flickering firelight. The twang of bowstrings, the swish of the bolts, the sudden screams as at least a dozen arrows found a home in the waiting Frog flesh.

"Forward"! The knight led his men towards the trebuchet, swords and daggers out. Two of them poured oil on the machine. Another lifted a log from a French campfire and tossed it on. Around them, shouting, yelling, the screaming of the wounded men, the confusion of those not injured giving way to understanding, to order.

"At the wagons"!

Another volley of bolts soared across the open ground to the supply train. One of the trebuchet's engineers rushed at Ferrandos with a sword in hand. The knight sidestepped the rush, pushed his own sword into the man's side and dumped him, screaming, into the rising flames.

"With me"!

The last oil carriers followed their liege towards the wagons. Arrows were beginning to come their way, the French shouting taking on order, only one or two voices yelling now, giving commands. The oil bearers, Ferrandos and four men carrying burning logs rushed the wagons.

"Now"!

Oil here, oil there, burning logs following. Flames leaped up in the fabric, the nearby tents, the wood of the wagons.

"Back! Back now, into the dark"!

Fifteen men, no one yet injured, darted off into the darkness. Crossbow bolts began to fall among them.

"To the castle"!

Ferrandos turned as the French officer shouted, "After them! After them"! Flames from two burning trebuchets and the burning wagons backlit the charging French. Its flickering light exposed the Fonta men too. Cries of pain, of anger rose in the darkness as the French volleys began finding targets. The French officer waved his sword, pointing, urging, forming up his men for the advance. "Their gate must be open to receive them! After them"!

Ferrandos drew careful aim. The first arrow from the former archer took the officer in the stomach, doubling him over, leaving him to die in agony from a mortal wound. His next took the man who raised his own sword to take over. One more arrow, another hit. The Lord of Fonta turned and raced off into the darkness, praying to the Good Lord Above that he not stumble or fall.

"We thought you hadn't made it, my lord," Izarns said when he regained the safety of the yard. Ferrandos turned and looked back before his men closed the gate. The Brasset trebuchet lofted a column of flame into the heavens above. The junction trebuchet's arms had already burned in two and dropped to the ground. Men ran around in the flames surrounding a dozen wagons, trying to save what they could. The charging French had stopped, realizing they would only suffer casualties while finding the gate already closed.

Thanks be to God, who has given us the victory through our Lord Jesus Christ!

"Our casualties, Izarns"?

"Two missing, four wounded, one mortally." Ferrandos nodded. "And then there is the matter of Sir Gaucelis."

■ ■ ■

"Gaucelis and these two men attempted to overpower us at the gate," Prisca said. "They did not succeed. Some of the men helped us subdue them."

Ferrandos looked at one man lying dead on the ground with his head bashed in. His blood still oozed into the dirt of the yard. Another sat with his back against the wall, dead from the knife sticking out of his chest. He turned to Gaucelis, standing with two of the older Brassat farmers holding his arms, his hands tied behind his back.

"Arrest Raolf, Izarns. Put him in the dungeon."

"Yes, my lord," Fonta's Marshall said. "You and you," pointing to two men, "Find him and do it." They trotted away across the torch-lit yard.

"Put Gaucelis there, too," Ferrandos ordered.

The felon stood slightly bent over, still trying to recover from the struggle of his capture. "Don't be a fool, Ferrandos! You have no chance! Surrender! Save your fief, and mine, and Sir Raolf's"!

Ferrandos put his sword against his prisoner's throat. "With vassals like you, Gaucelis, it's no wonder Sir Alass found himself burned at the stake"! He took his weapon away. "Remove this coward from my sight! He is an insult to knighthood"!

9

Lisbetta awoke late and stared at her ceiling in the darkness. Sleep did not return. She should give warning, but that would require taking advantage of her liege.

You must do it. You are only taking advantage a little. Remember that terrible Black Friar, all his justifying, reconciling, explaining. Your excuses are no worse.

The Baroness of Mayrènge tiptoed into the maids' room just as light began to filter in through the slit windows of the Keep. "Mabila," she whispered, holding her hand over the woman's mouth as she frightened her awake. "Bring your tunic and cloak and shoes." Mabila stumbled out of bed in her linen cotte and dragged her clothes behind her.

"My lady, what is….."

"SSShhhh." Lisbetta pulled her into her own room and closed the door. The Baroness was already naked. "Give me your cotte. Dress me in your tunic."

Mabila struggled to fit her lady into the garment. She gave up. "It's too tight around the top, my lady, and too short." She brushed out Lisbetta's hair and tied on the maid's cap and veil. "It makes you look….."

"It will do. Stay here and wait for me." She waved towards her bed. "Get under the covers to stay warm. I won't be gone long."

Now Mabila understood why Lisbetta didn't want to talk about her wedding. "My lady, you are betrothed." Her lady was moody and mercurial, but if she lost her, her next mistress could be even worse. "An assignation is most dangerous, my lady. Your lover will be considered a traitor and…."

The Baroness smiled as she wrote out a gate pass, dripped wax on the parchment and pushed the Count's seal into it. "You listen to the troubadours too much, Mabila." She rolled the ring around her finger to hide the seal in her hand. "Say nothing to anyone."

Her pass opened the castle gate. Outside, a simple maid walked in the morning twilight along the Avenue of Our Lady. The sound of the common people starting their days in the buildings around her filtered into the street.

You have not walked alone, unguarded for a long time, Baroness. You feel exposed, naked even despite your warm cloak. You can be approached here without your permission.

The commoners walk out here all the time, Lisbetta. Even you did it, before. You'll be fine.

The secretary followed the sweet smell of yeast and wood smoke to a bakery on St. John's Square. A push and the heavy door opened, letting her into a low-ceilinged room. To one side stood a rectangular table where the apprentice mixed and kneaded the dough. In the back, a large brick oven, fed by wood faggots underneath, where the baker turned the dough to bread. Lisbetta taxed the owners of eight or nine bakeries just like it out in her villages.

It was still early. The maid was their only customer. The warmth and the aromas reminded her of mornings with Aenor in Petrousset. She stood for a moment to enjoy the smell.

The young apprentice, a man her age, turned around. The flour and clumps of dough speckled his brown woolen clothes. Surprise at her arrival moved to annoyance, then delight.

"Eh, girl! Somethin' go wrong at Their Lordships? Cain't get the fire started"? He leaned forward. "Nice ankles, lass." Lisbetta's tunic was indeed much too short and much too tight around the top. The apprentice puckered up his lips. "Give us a kiss, cutie."

I should have him whipped, the Baroness thought. Maria the Maid smiled and answered, "A slap is more likely, you scoundrel. Does Berengar still own this shop"?

"Here, missie." The beefy older man appeared from behind the oven, munching a chunk of his own bread. He stopped and smiled. "You're a delight for me old eyes, tall one."

He tore off a piece for Lisbetta and she ate it. It tasted warm and fresh, very good. She remembered her mother's bread and fought back her tears.

"You here for the castle, or are you just Phelip's latest"? He looked at her smooth hands and brushed hair as she ate the bread. "Tunic's a little small. You look a fancy lady, not a maid, missie."

Lisbetta put her hand on his arm, gripping it.

"Berengar, I'm Lisbetta Deslegador, the daughter of the *Credentes* Gervais and Petrona Deslegador, from Farga de sant Matèu. A Good Christian myself. Guis, a boy from the castle, brought me here years ago when I was being chased by a Black Friar. Don't you remember"?

"No."

Of course not. Back then you were an awkward peasant girl, now you are a full-grown pampered woman.

"I'm the one that our Countess fetched from the mountains. I serve her now, her correspondence, her accounts. I'm here with a warning."

Berengar smirked as he kissed her hand.

"Phelip, missie here says she's Her Royal Majesty Lisbetta, the Baroness of Mayrènge."

Phelip laughed. "You mean she's *La Conglaçada*, 'The Frozen One' of the troubadours"? He looked Lisbetta up and down. "This pleasant tidbit is Miss Frosty? Hardly likely."

"I agree." Berengar dropped Lisbetta's hand and put his own to her cheek. "Stop trying to fool us, lass.

That *Conglaçada* bitch is as cold as the snow in the Sárdalo. I put myself in her, it'll freeze up and break off. She's in her bed in the castle now, fingering herself, 'cause that's all she's ever going to get."

Now Lisbetta did slap him for his insolence. He took it with a smile, and she did it again. He caught her hand and pulled her close, feeling her warm soft body through the fabric. "See? Too much passion for the Ice Lady. You're here for Phelip, is all."

Noise filtered in from the street outside, growing louder, the sounds of horses galloping along the Avenue, into the square. Men dismounted, shouted, banged on doors.

"They're looking for me, Berengar."

Berengar released the tidbit as fear came into his face, and Phelip's. Lisbetta rolled the ring back around so that the men could see the seal.

"Berengar, listen, we have little time. The Satanic King Louis is marching here with his mother the Witch Blanche. The Countess will try to stop them, but they are very many. War and pestilence and the Inquisition are coming, far worse than the time of the Montforts. Get word to Bishop Thomas in the mountains. Spread the word here. The Good Christians are threatened as never before. I'll come again as I learn more."

Berengar and Phelip bowed deeply. "Yes my lady."

"And learn some manners."

They bowed again. "Yes my lady."

"Is there a back door"?

The soldiers charged into Berengar's shop just as a maid emerged from an alley several doors away, next to the church. She walked calmly through the square on her mistress's errand, ignoring a commotion that was not her affair. Hoofbeats, closer, closer, stopping.

"Here she is." She looked up to find Fulques looking down. The soldiers all turned towards him while he glared at her.

Of course Giles would send Fulques. He has no reason to fear you, Ice Lady. Put on your best smile and try charm instead.

"Fulques, good morning. What's this all about"?

The glare did not waiver, nor did he answer. Instead, those strong arms reached down and lifted her straight up as though she weighed no more than the veil behind her cap. She was Charpentier's *loriot* for just a moment, her legs dangling in the air until he set her in his lap across the saddle.

"You're a selfish spoiled baby, *Conglaçada*," he whispered. "You deserve a spanking. Instead, good people will be whipped because of this little walk of yours. You, of course, will be welcomed home like the Prodigal."

"I wanted to warn….."

"The Countess needs a loyal servant who believes we will win, not one who runs off to warn her friends that we might lose. Try to remember that."

He raised his voice. "Thanks be to God that we have found our liege's most beloved friend and confidant, the Baroness of Mayrènge, safe and sound! Hold on, my lady, while we ride to the castle"!

When they got there, she slapped him and went inside. Her hand stung from so much slapping.

■ ■ ■

Complete panic enveloped Lisbetta's bedroom, indeed the whole second floor. Agnes stood in the center, already dressed in dark red wool for her morning audiences. *Al-Zarqa'* leaned on her crutches as the four maids stood trembling in a row along the wall. Mabila shook from the cold, naked and crying.

"Is that you, Lady Mayrènge? Come here."

Lisbetta approached as the Countess reached out and found her tunic, feeling the wool. "That's a maid's dress. You're a Baroness. Get it off"! Mabila leaped forward, dressing herself but leaving Lisbetta naked. "You four, leave us"! They were gone so fast that Lisbetta wasn't really sure she saw them go. She was cold. Her robe was lying on her bed, but there was no maid to put it on her.

"My lady, I….."

"Stop! You did not have my permission to leave the castle, Lisbetta of Mayrènge! You used my seal without my permission! You took advantage of my condition, of my trust in you"!

For the first time in years, Lisbetta slipped the ring from her finger and pressed it into her lady's hand.

"Did I ask for that, Lady Mayrènge? Put it back on! You are my Keeper of the Seal until I say you are not! I decide, not you"!

Lisbetta knelt and kissed Agnes' hand.

"I'm sorry, my lady Countess, the Good Christians, I…."

The anger in Agnes' face softened and the Voice disappeared.

"I know where you went, and why, Lissie-Bet, but you scared me to death. I was so frightened that I didn't even think about how you used my ring. There are guards you can trust. Next time, send them in your place." The Countess started to sob. Lisbetta looked over to be sure the door was closed all the way. "Liss, Liss, you're very special to Giles and me. You're part of my family, a descendant of Julian and Monica. We love you as we love our own children. I need you as much as I love you. Stand up, Lissie, please. I'm sorry I shouted at you."

Lisbetta stayed on her knees, shivering in the cold.

"Fulques called me a spoiled baby, my lady. He said I need a spanking."

The eyes of *al-Zarqa'* flared. "I will have him…"!

"No, my lady, he is right. I am a brat, spoiled, pampered, given anything I want. I took advantage of you because I know that this brat is never punished, no matter what she does."

"I love you, Liss, I want you…"

"No, my lady. With the French out there, that cannot be. A servant who did such a thing would be punished."

"Liss, no, I can't do that to you, I can't hurt you, you are my closest…."!

"You must, my lady. You cannot let me do what I did and not be punished. You will lose the respect of your people. As you always say, they are Alberensa, and you need them now."

There was a long silence. "Stand up and hug me." Lisbetta stepped forward and the Countess leaned into her. Her hands ran down her back, on her stomach, and she laughed. "You're naked, Betta"!

"Yes, my lady. Mabila took her tunic back."

Agnes nodded. "You are right, Liss. Thank you."

10

Ferrandos and Izarns and Prisca stood on the ramparts, looking towards the Fois Road. They surveyed the still-glowing embers of the two trebuchets. They watched men busy removing the rubble from the French wagon yard. They watched the column of Frogs marching back to Fonta along the road from Alberensa.

"I count eight trebuchets, Izarns. They mean to make us pay for last night."

"They do, my lord." The young man looked along the road towards Foix. "They're setting up a large camp. They must have stopped their advance into the County."

"The outcome is clear. We should let the people who want to leave, leave. Will there be many"?

"I don't think so," Prisca answered.

"Why, love"?

"Most of the people in here are Good Christians, my lord. We know what waits out there."

"So I am the lord of a Cathar castle"?

"Indeed you are, husband, but you've known that for a long time."

A voice called from the yard, "Sir Ferrandos"! The threesome looked down to find Gaucelis between two men-at-arms. The lord and the marshal moved quickly from the ramparts.

"Open the gate. You three men come with us."

Ferrandos, Izarns, three guards and the lord of Guzet stepped from the castle onto the ground in front. The buzzards flew off as they stopped beside the rotting corpse of Sir Arnald. Shouts began from the French, calls of alarm, quickly subsiding once they realized no attack had begun. A stillness settled over the land as hundreds of the enemy checked their weapons and turned to watch what was coming.

"Your fief is forfeit for felony, Gaucelis. You are sentenced to death."

Gaucelis struggled to escape, failed and turned to argument. "Look around you, my lord! We are both Catholics in a castle filled with heretics! Let me go to the French! We can still save ourselves"!

Ferrandos shook his head. "Izarns, pull that bolt from Arnald's body. Drive it into the ground. Make Gaucelis kneel before it."

The knight looked up in panic from his knees. "What are you doing"!

"You are a traitor to your liege, Gaucelis. You will die as a traitor dies in the Holy Land, in the Saracen way"!

■ ■ ■

Ferrandos mounted his rampart. Outside the wall, Gaucelis knelt beside Arnald, still alive, screaming in agony as he slowly drew his bowels into the dirt. All around Fonta, the French resumed their preparations for the siege.

Hold as well as you can for as long as you can, Ferrandos. Then take council with Izarns and Prisca, and decide.

■ ■ ■

Hour after hour, the view of the St. Luke's Square before Lisbetta remained unchanged even as people came and went. That view would never change, in fact, until the city watchman removed her from Alberensa's town pillory. Since first light, she had been standing on a wooden platform, each wrist and her neck locked into its separate hole, all three immobile. The heavy wooden beam that held her in place was a little too low for her to stand up. Her back screeched in louder agony with each passing hour.

"Ain't never whipped a woman afore," the city watchman announced at Terce. He lifted her tunic and hooked it on the stock, baring her bottom. "Not sure I like the idea."

Swish.

Thwack!

"AAAAHHHHH"! The Square disappeared into a blackness of pain and stars.

Swish.

Thwack!

"AAAHHHHH"!

Ten blows, the agony of the last never dying away before the next arrived, a mounting crescendo that took at least an hour to fade. Lisbetta wondered how badly it would feel if he had liked the idea.

"This maid lied to her mistress," the watchman called to the watching crowd as he dropped her brown wool tunic back over her bruised buttocks. He put a sign, "Maria, A Liar," over her place. "Sentenced to a day in the pillory. See you in the morning, missy."

Lisbetta turned her head left, right. The Spirit of Jesus hung on the Cross with thieves to either side of him. You have only some sullen drunk locked in beside you, recovering from his hangover in a pillory that can hold five.

I thirst, as the Spirit of Jesus thirsted.

The foolish Black Friar claims that Jesus actually suffered the thirst, the heat, the pain of the nails, the death, suffered as though he was alive in Satan's world.

Lisbetta moved, trying to relieve the ache. She succeeded only in putting her bare foot into her own turd on the ground.

It must be after noon. It must.

Someone passed by, pouring the whole contents of a chamber pot over the prisoner's head. Urine dripped from her nose.

After the sun sets, I'll be out here all night. Cold. Lonely. Frightened.

"Have some of this"! a man called from the square. Yet another piece of dung splatted against the sinner's face. She blinked her eyes to clear her view. Tears ran down her cheeks. Her rear end still ached.

The Black Friar lies. Satan's Church always lies. The True God would never allow his own Son to suffer like this.

"Liar"! A rotten egg this time, another square hit, releasing its foul aroma to cover her face. Her coarse wool stank of her own urine.

Lisbetta blinked away the rotten egg. She opened her eyes.

Thank you, Lord! The square is empty except for this moaning idiot beside me.

Not for long.

"Liar"! Andreva stood there, throwing more of the endless supply of horseshit at the Silken Pawn of Satan. Their mother watched from behind her, urging her on.

11

When Sir Giles and fifty men rode into the Pont's yard with a train of empty wagons, Guilhelms knew. He called his men together. To the ones who were single, "Shut down the smelters. Let the iron and slag harden inside." To the married, "Go home and bring your families for the trip to Alberensa. Be back within the hour."

The sun shone around puffy clouds as Guilhelms reached his own house. A beautiful day, unfortunately, because a rainy day would have made it easier to leave. "Aenor, Aenor darling, it's time. Sir Laurent's news is confirmed. The French are coming. We're going to destroy the works and retreat into Alberensa."

Aenor put on one of her older tunics, something to wear while sitting on a wagon. Tibault, Isabèl and Melisende wore old clothes too. Everyone's old clothes were nicer than anything owned by anyone else in Pont de Molin.

Guilhelms looked at his three children, drawing slowly closer together, clustering into a single defensive tower against whatever was going on. "Tibaut, come here, son, come here." The dark-haired boy took a tentative step, and then a firmer one, remembering that he was almost a man now, at twelve. "You, too, Ebel." The eight-year-old Isabèl bristled at being called by Tibaut's baby name for her, but she walked over, too. Melisende didn't want to be left out, so soon all five of them were gathered in a circle.

"Yes, Papa"? Tibaut asked.

"We all have to live in Alberensa for a while. I must stay here and help the soldiers prepare, and then I will come, later today. Tibaut, you are the man now until I get there. You help your mother with everything."

Isabèl and Melisende spoke quickly, saying the same thing, making Guilhelms think that nuns were chanting. "Papa, no, he's a boy, he doesn't know anything. You come."

"I'm a boy, too. Do as I say, unless you think you can lift the boxes into the wagon, Meli." She sulked and pouted in her little girl outfit. "Better. That's what boys are for, Melita, to do the heavy work for you. When you get older, you'll see what smiling at a boy can do for you. Ask your mother."

■ ■ ■

With the families gone, Guilhelms gave his instructions. He had worked hard on the size of the water wheel, the shape of the buckets, the number, so he had a man cut out a section as a template for a new one. His men dragged the rest of the wheels from the stream, demolished the flumes and set all the wood on fire.

"Take apart the bellows and the furnace plenum and load them on the wagons," he called. "We've made big improvements there. I want to keep them as a model."

After that, the men knocked the blast furnaces and smelters to the ground and left them in a heap of brick and frozen slag. Guilhelms mounted the hill above the dam and watched as the workers finished and scrambled up to join him. He turned to his foreman, the incorrigibly urinating Bernart.

"Did you do a count, Bernart? Is everyone up from the works"?

"Yes, all here," his foreman answered. Guilhelms turned to the Baron of Sarlant.

"Open the dam, Sir Giles."

Ten men quickly carved a deep channel in the earthen dam, working as quickly as they could, even as the water started to flow. "Back, get back, it's enough." Within minutes the flowing water pushed the rest of the dirt over the ledge. A waist-deep wall of muddy water poured over the original brink of the waterfall. It flooded the smelter ground below, washing away the ashes from the flume and the loose brick from the chimney. It buried whatever did not flow away under a steadily growing blanket of silt and mud.

"We can leave now, Sir Giles." It had taken two hours.

A small unit of French horsemen scouting south of Arguenos saw the smoke from the burning wood on the southern horizon. When they arrived to investigate just before dark, they found a waterfall and a field covered with brown ooze and slime. Boots and hooves sank in, ankle deep.

They rode back to the large stone house and moved in for the night. They soon found the wine. They drank it all while they sat with their muddy feet on the furniture.

■ ■ ■

Lisbetta was not quite sure where she was, but it sounded like the wagon was rolling through the gate and into the castle yard. She wasn't quite sure how she ended up in the wagon either, although in the delirium of her endless agony she had felt a different agony as her body moved differently.

She opened her eyes and looked up. The walls of the castle framed the stars in the black sky above. A head looked down at her.

"You're a tough one, *Conglaçada*. You took that like a man."

"Fulkes? Is it over"?

"It is."

"Am I still alive"?

In reply, he poured a bucket of cold water over her face and chest.

"Stop"!

Another bucket, rinsing turds and piss and eggs into the wagon's bed.

"STOP"! She flailed at her tormentor as he stepped back.

"I'd say yes, Your Majesty. Soon the whole town will know they were throwing rotten eggs and horseshit at Aggie's Pet." He leaned over. "You served our liege well, Frozen One. People never thought their Iron Countess had that much iron."

"I worried, Fulques. What if someone… lifted my tunic… tried to…"

He laughed. "Our Iron Countess isn't that tough, Frosty. I spent the whole day in penitential prayer just inside the church. It was a challenge, really, not to come out and beat some of those people to a pulp."

"Thank you, Fulques."

"An honor, princess. Can you sit up"?

Lisbetta felt his hands behind her back, lifting her upright. "AAAHHHH! That hurts"! She rolled on her side. Fulques lifted her tunic, "What are you doing"!

"Those are some welts, Your Highness. Easier if you just stand."

Fulques lifted the Baroness of Mayrènge to her feet. She shuffled for a moment, urine-scented water dripping from her filthy hair. He caught her before she fell.

"Docina," Fulques said. "Mabila. Come help your liege." The two maids stepped from the darkness, one to each side, arms around her waist, holding her up. They took a step and stopped. Lisbetta turned them around.

"Fulques. My punishment is now over. I am once again Lisbetta, Baroness of Mayrènge, Keeper of the Count's Seal, Personal Secretary to our liege Agnes."

He laughed. "So you are, Lissie-Bet, so you are, despite how you look."

"I am not 'La Conglaçada' or 'Frosty' or the 'Frozen One'"!

More laughter. "Be sure you tell Sir Godafres, Betta. He has heard otherwise from our troubadours."

Such impudence!

"I did not take it like a man, Fulques! That whining drunk beside me took it like a man! I took it like a woman"!

12

The solid thunk of stones against the walls of Fonta had become so regular that it seemed natural now, like the noise of the wind. The trebuchet swinging around its shaft in the distance came first, and then those standing on the ramparts could watch the boulders arching through the sky. The castle shook with every blow. Dust flew and rocks dropped into the heap in front of the wall. It had been going on for five days now. This morning the defenders realized that the castle wall was finally coming apart.

Another trebuchet released as Ferrandos watched from his ramparts. Oh, very clever, they've changed the aim of that machine to hurl stones into the yard, a surprise.

"Watch out! Watch out"! he shouted down.

The men scrambled to find a place to hide. The load flew long and crashed high against the wall of the Keep. And a second load, and a third, and then back to the outside wall. The knight looked into his yard. Two men were lying on the ground, not moving.

"Izarns, our Countess can't relieve us and we can't hold. One by one, they'll kill us, like they have just killed those two men." They looked over the wall, where the vultures had picked most of Arnald and Gaucelis clean. "Perhaps we should release Raolf. He'll run for it. We can put an arrow into his cowardly back, like Prisca's lord out there."

Izarns laughed, a hearty laugh, sincere. A laugh that said justice had been done to Sir Arnald and Sir Gaucelis. A man could feel comfortable, very comfortable, being led by Ferrandos. He was personally courageous. Unrelenting in his optimism. Merciless, completely merciless to his enemies. The Baron of Sarlant gave up a valuable officer when he accepted Count Hugh's decision to award Fonta to this man. Even now, hard pressed, perhaps even doomed, his lord was planning how to make his efforts bear the most effect.

"Indeed they are wearing us down slowly, my lord. Everyone is growing tired, very tired." With the advantage of numbers, the French launched sortie after sortie, testing the defenses. Fonta always killed or wounded a few, but they could not let down their guard.

"Yes, Izarns, if we just sit here, this siege is a trap of death for us. We have done all we can for the Countess. Now we must save as many of our own as we can. Follow me."

The two mail-clad warriors ducked from battlement to battlement as they made their way to the wall opposite the Foix Road. "There. They have no natural defense there, no hill, no stream, just the low earth they piled up. We can ride downhill through them, back into the woods on the far side and join the Countess in Alberensa. It hasn't rained in two days, so the ground is hard enough for a fast ride."

"What of the women, the older men"?

"Any who wish to join us can do so. We'll ride two, even three to a horse."

"The others"?

"The French are thin against the steep hill towards Guzet. We can't ride up that way, but people on foot can sneak through and scramble into the woods. From there to the Trysting Glade, the Cathar camp and over the mountains into Spain."

"Sir Raolf"?

"The Frogheads will find him in the dungeon. Who knows, Sir Martin might make him his personal manservant."

Izarns smiled. It was not likely that they would succeed, but some would certainly escape. Everyone would not die like rats under a wall of trebuchet stones.

■ ■ ■

The crashing of French-propelled Lengadòc rocks against the castle covered the noise of moving all the arbalètes to the wall facing the Foix Road. Six volunteers, older men and women, would let fly as the charge began, then try with the others to get past the uphill French in the commotion. If their bolts thinned the French line, the riders might make it through. Not all of them, perhaps, but each one who did was another defender for the siege of Alberensa. And, Ferrandos admitted, each one who did was another Cathar heretic spared the flames.

Darkness brought the trebuchet bombardment to an end for the night. The waxing half-moon cast its blueish glow on the scene. The first nightly French test of the castle's defense would come once it set, sometime after midnight. Ferrandos decided that Fonta must strike first, in the moon's last glimmer through the trees.

■ ■ ■

The knight left his Great Hall for the last time. His own men lined up with the horses, not yet mounted, waiting.

"Izarns."

"Yes, my lord." A whisper.

"Sir Arnald's fief at Brassat is forfeit through felony. I am sure our lady Agnes will welcome my decision. Kneel."

Izarns knelt.

"Izarns, I dub you a knight in my service. I award you the fief at Brassat."

Ferrandos tapped Izarns on each shoulder with the flat of his blade.

"Rise, Sir Izarns. If you should arrive in Alberensa before me, please inform the Countess of your new station, and your fief."

Sir Izarns was surprised, still recovering from what had just happened.

"My lord, you can…."

He stopped as Prisca came from the Great Hall in the black robe of a Parfait. She stood, quietly, waiting.

"Lady Prisca has given the *Consolamentum* to six people who wished it, Sir Izarns. Her work here is finished. I've convinced her that I won't leave unless she does, so she's coming." Astonishment and doubt flooded the face of his new vassal. Ferrandos lowered his voice. "We must try, my lord, we must all try. Better to die in a fight with the enemies of our liege than be burned at the stake."

Izarns nodded, slowly.

"Be of good cheer, Sir Izarns. You are a nobleman now. I will greet you as such in Alberensa, and if not there, in Heaven."

■ ■ ■

Twenty horses, all with two riders, waited behind the castle gate. Prisca straddled the horse like a man, behind Ferrandos on the animal's bare back, with her calves and ankles showing below her robe. Her husband's body would protect her until they were through the French line, and then hers would protect his. She felt a strange tingling in her back, imagining the sudden feel of the arrow as it struck.

"Are you ready, my lady"? Sir Ferrandos whispered.

"I have made a very poor *Parfait*, my lord, for I cannot get my love for you out of my mind. I want you again, even now."

"You have done all that our God could expect of you, Lady Prisca, everything and more. A former serf has served her people as a noblewoman in this siege. And you have done everything that I could expect of a wife. I am only sorry that I have failed to protect you. I will say it, I do love you. Are you ready"?

"Ready, my lord. And I love you."

"Sir Izarns. Now!"

The gate swung open with a loud crash. The column began to ride, swords drawn. Izarns with a woman took the lead and Ferrandos and Prisca, the rear. The fading moonlight guided the way, but they knew the way even in the dark. The sudden thunder of hooves brought shouting along the French line as the soldiers came forward to see what was happening.

The Lord of Fonta paused one last time in his gate as his column turned left and rode along the wall towards the road.

"Now"! Sir Ferrandos shouted, his last command as lord of this place, unless his Countess defeated the French and he could win it back.

The steel of the arbalète bows rang out above the noise, sending bolts into the same small part of the French line. Six launched, a count to five, six more, another count, the last. Cries of pain and fear went up, shouting, fading away from directly in front as the arbalète bolts killed every man for a width of twenty paces.

Ferrandos had timed his command perfectly. The last bolts arrived in the French line mere seconds before Sir Izarns. The shouting grew on either side of the gap as the French realized that the thunder of hooves was bearing down on them. Ferrandos heard an arrow sing by in the night, and then another. Sir Izarns was through the French line, but just like the night of their trebuchet sortie, the jumbled shouting from the enemy on either side was subsiding into a single voice giving orders.

Sir Izarns was away, up the road in the dark, at least a dozen horses with him. Ferrandos and Prisca plunged through the French position. More arrows, striking the couple in front of them. Suddenly the knight found himself on the ground, his horse bellowing in pain, thrashing in agony. Prisca had fallen free as they went down. She was trying to stand up.

"Prisca, to me, darling, to me"! swinging his sword at the nearest man while he ran towards his wife. Someone punched him in the stomach, in the chest, in the back as he reached for her outstretched hand.

13

The French soldiers held Prisca as their commander stood over Ferrandos. In the distance, she heard the French shouting warnings, trying to catch the people running for the woods. "Let me see him." The commander held a torch close to Ferrandos's face. "Who is he, you heretic witch"?

"My husband."

"I thought you bastards didn't have husbands, get laid, none of that shit." There was more noise now, nearby. An older knight walked up.

"How many got out, Sir Jean, do you think"?

"Ten, maybe fifteen horses this way, Sir Martin. We killed everyone on the last four except her." Martin took the torch himself and looked at Ferrandos while Jean went on. "His Majesty will kill the rest before they get very far."

Martin stood back up. "This is Sir Ferrandos, the Baron of Fonta. A chivalrous knight, a warrior and a gentleman. Treat his body with respect. Bury him with honors."

■ ■ ■

Lady Prisca sat on the ground with her hands tied behind her, next to one of her new *Parfaits*, a man. Five *Credentes* sat with them, one a mother with two small children. It was still dark, yet bright around the large campfire in the midst of the French camp. The fire felt warm, uncomfortably warm for a May evening.

Prisca remembered that the Catholics always offered the Good Christians a chance to repent, yet no priest came forward to make that offer. She had wondered if she would recant in the face of the flames. Now she would never know.

She recognized three of the French standing together, although she had not seen them since she was a serf. Sir Martin, defeated here by Count Hugh in the siege that made her a lady. Henri, Baron of Épernay, now without the arm he lost to Guilhelms. And Henri's awful, sinful, lecherous son Charles. Constantly threatening, constantly raping. If Satan walked this earth as a man, that man was Charles of Épernay. Even now, he was proving his Satanic spirit.

"My lord, we must check the women for the Mark of Satan." He used his broadsword to lift the tunic of a young woman of Cazac. "And this one, too," poking Prisca's robe and lifting it.

"My lord Baron," Martin interjected, "this heretic is the wife of Sir Ferrandos." He gestured at all of the Cathars. "They are on their way to Hell soon enough. They need not be checked for any marks."

Henri stood, impassive, and waited while his son gave up his search. Then he motioned towards Sir Raolf.

"What of this knight of Cazac, Sir Martin? Our men found him in the dungeon. Will you have him back again"? Henri put his one hand on Martin's shoulder, as he had that day in St. John's. "It's up to you, my lord."

Fear lit up Raolf's eyes. He had donned his armor and tunic and buckled on his sword, but he made no move to defend himself. Too old, too fat to run, a defeated man waited at the mercy of the Épernays.

"As you know, my lord Baron," Martin replied, "I did not object when Sir Ferrandos killed the traitor Arnald. No doubt Ferrandos locked this man in the dungeon to guard against another betrayal." Martin pointed into the darkness. "Sir Jean has performed well in all our campaigns, my lord. You should award him Cazac. I have no need for this coward."

"I agree, Sir Martin."

"Then what of this oaf"? Charles asked. "This Fonta is shot through with heretics." He turned on the knight. "What of it, Sir Raolf? Are you a Cathar heretic"?

"No, my lord, I am not." The old man's voice trembled. "Ask the priest of Cazac."

"I'm sure he's sleeping now, my lord. We should not disturb him." Charles gripped the stunned Raolf by his tunic. "What of it? Everyone we captured from that castle is a Cathar. You are a Cathar heretic, a pawn of Satan, you fat old man. You will pay the price of your heresy now. Do you wish to take the heretic sacrament, this *Consolamentum* before you die"?

Old Raolf was near tears. "My lord, no, no, it's a mistake, I'm not……"

"No? Excellent. We need waste no more time with these Cathars, Father."

Henri turned to his soldiers. "As required by the Holy Inquisition, these heretics are to be put to the stake. Take them now to the field before Fonta and burn this heresy from our midst"!

Prisca stumbled to her feet as Raolf shouted, "No! No"! She turned to the Baron.

"The children, my lord! You cannot burn children! They are too young to understand"!

Charles slapped Prisca across the face. "Shut up, witch"! The iron on his glove scored her flesh. She tasted blood on her lip. Her broken nose bleed freely. "They don't need to understand! They just need to burn"!

The cruelty of this Charles stunned her, and she had learned cruelty while she was the Lady of Fonta.

"My lord Baron! Please! No"! The little boy and his sister looked up at all the grown-ups, completely unaware. "They are not old enough to become *Credentes!* Send them to the Benedictines at Couserans"!

Henri stood, immobile, uncertain. Sir Martin reached down and took the two children by the hand, leading them to the side. He said nothing, standing with them, waiting. Henri nodded and turned to his son.

"Get on with it, Charles. We must re-join His Majesty."

"Put the wife in the middle," Sir Martin said to the Épernay soldiers. "Bury her in the wood and start the flame near her so that her time is brief. Let her rapid trip to Hell be a tribute to the bravery of her husband. And to her own courage on behalf of these children."

Thanks be to God on High, my beloved husband, for chivalrous men such as Martin and you!

Prisca's stomach knotted and her bowels cramped and her broken nose oozed blood while her legs moved her forward, guided from her unseen place. A hand too close to a fire smarted for days, and yet that burning would be multiplied now, a thousand-fold. From a distant corner of her mind she heard Raolf wailing, begging, pleading, crying as the soldiers marched them to the large woodpile near the remains of Arnald and Gaucelis. One shrieking knight and five quiet Cathars, each trying to center on God to prepare for what was to come. Old Raolf might be pitiful, but so was she as she gave up to her fear and let her turds and her urine run down her legs.

Prisca's guard separated the logs so that she could stand on the ground, surrounded by wood up to her waist. He did the same for the young mother, standing them back-to-back against the stake and using one line to tie them both together. To Prisca's right, the begging knight crashed through the woodpile from his own weight. The guards tried to haul him back on top, failed, shrugged their shoulders and left him standing on the ground. So much wood, so many stakes driven in, so quickly.

"Ready"? asked the sergeant as his men finished tying everyone up.

"Ready," said Prisca's guard.

"Begin." The torches came forward.

Like the ancient martyrs, O God, let my sacrifice speed the coming of Your Kingdom. Thy Kingdom come, O Lord, Thy will be done, on earth as it is in heaven. As St. John said, love not the world, neither the things that are in the world. If any man loves the world, the love of the Father is not in him. For all that is in the world, the lust of the flesh and the lust of the eyes and the pride of life, is not of the Father but is of the world.

The flames licked at the dry wood. Still not very warm but the smoke was rising, blinding Prisca, choking her. Through its haze she saw the sky growing light. Growing light on Sunday, Pentecost Sunday, the day of the Consolation, when the Holy Spirit descended on the Disciples in the upper room. The flames rose, hotter now, clearing the smoke, hot, too hot, making the sunrise waver in the heat.

When the Day of Pentecost had come, they were all together in one place. And suddenly a sound came from heaven like the rush of a mighty wind, and it filled all the house where they were sitting. And there appeared to them tongues as of fire distributed and resting on each one of them. My robe is on fire the pain the pain tongues of fire my skin is burning, turning black. And they were all filled with the Holy Spirit and began to speak in other tongues as the Spirit gave them utterance Ferrandos beloved Ferrandos my

"AAAAAAIIIIIIIIIYYYYYYYYYYYY"!

PART EIGHT

County of Alberensa
June 1231

1

The frontal of white snow disappeared from the High Altar. Sunlight danced amid white clouds without the plumes of Pont de Molin soiling the blue sky. The Sárdalo Pass shimmered in the distant haze with the fresh bright green of early summer, but the Compestela Road remained empty. Religious articles, tools and supplies gathered dust in the shops. The Throne of God shone down on empty chairs in the Cathedral.

Two days after Pentecost, the newly-knighted Sir Izarns entered the Reception Chamber with word of the fall of Fonta. As he recounted the gallant death of Sir Ferrandos, *La Conglaçada* surprised the room by crying. "He brought us here that first Easter, leading the wagon train."

A few days later, Sir Laurent rode in with the report of his reconnaissance towards the north. Ponset had indeed yielded up Arguenos and allowed a French scouting party to cross the bridges into the County.

"What of his people"? the Countess asked.

"The Preaching Friars have been busy, my lady. The French soldiers burned eighty heretics in the fields before his castle."

"And Ponset"?

"Is with the French in Arguenos, together with his levy. His family is with him."

On the third of June, the first Tuesday of the new month, Sir Izarns returned from his scouting trip to the east. "The fields of Fonta are empty, my lady, weeds growing everywhere. The village of Ganat is burned, the others abandoned. Most of the people are hiding in the Pyrenees."

"What of the castle"?

"Father Ricartz says that Henri of Épernay, an old knight with one arm, took it after the siege. The Épernays burned Sir Raolf and Lady Prisca and four others as heretics in front of the walls. The others escaped into the mountains during the chaos."

"Was Raolf a heretic"?

"No, my lady, just a coward, old and fat and weak. His son Charles urged them to it, for sport. He even wanted to burn two children, but Sir Martin would not let him. He took the children and gave them to Ricartz, knowing that the priest would get them to their family."

Agnes reached down and found her cross. "You met Sir Martin"?

"He came under flag of truce, early in the siege. A valiant and chivalrous knight, my lady, the only decent man among the Épernays."

Agnes broke the silence. "Once again, Queen Blanche shows her contempt for Satan's Whore, Crippled by Our Lord for Her Sins. She sends us the Épernays, Satan's Army on Earth."

■ ■ ■

The Countess ordered the room emptied except for Giles and Lisbetta. She listened for the closing doors, then spoke. "What do you think, Giles"?

"When this began a month ago, Aggie, the King did not send a large army. He expected you to yield, save your title and let him move in. He sent the Épernays while he kept most of his men in the north to guard against his other threats, his other enemies."

"As Simon de Montfort did two decades ago."

"Exactly. No doubt Ponset assured His Majesty that your barons would come over, eager to depose the Heretic Witch Who Took the *Consolamentum*. Henri from the east, Ponset from the north, it would be enough. Instead, Rodrigo, Gautier and Bertrand remained loyal."

"Better to be an important man in a small place than a small man anyplace."

"Indeed. They do not trust a traitor like Ponset. He says they can keep their fiefs, but they know there is some third son of an important knight in Picardy seeking to become the Baron of Moustalon." He paused. "The Épernays reduced Fonta, but Henri needed all his men to do it. Ferrandos kept him from an easy victory over the County."

"Ponset"?

"He let Henri do the work. Except for the scouting party down from Arguenos, the French molested no other place during the week it took to reduce the fortress."

"And now"?

Giles smiled and shook his head. "Blanche and Louis must have decided to finish it quickly. Lots of Frogs out there, coming from the north and the east. No individual castle will stand long, so your barons are riding into Alberensa with their levies. We'll be besieged within the week."

The Countess sighed and turned towards Lisbetta.

"Well, Little Lissie, did my….my….what is it that the troubadours call you"?

"La Conglaçada, Countess."

"Yes. Did the spoiled brat *Conglaçada* learn anything in her rounds"?

"Peter believes that the servants are loyal, my lady. The women of St. John's Circle prefer our Lengadòc the way it is."

2

Giles and Fulques rode onto the Alberensa Bridge. Agnes rode behind her husband on a pillion. The two men studied the place on either side of the city where the wall arched across the stream. Grates could be lowered into the water in case of attack. Murder holes in the ramparts allowed the defenders to attack those trying to enter on the river. Still, the spot remained worrisome.

"There's no way for the French to divert the river and dry it up," Fulques said. "They might try to dam the downstream side and cause flooding in the city. And float dead animals against the upstream grates, to taint the water that does get through. We must fill every cistern, my lady, and watch that the wells do not become polluted."

Agnes nodded. They rode across the span to the St Matthew's Quarter.

"The trebuchets are ready. We have tested and noted the fall of rock. We can adjust and get on target on the first or second try." The two animals trotted around the machine in St. Matthew's Church square, next to the Sisters of Charity. "This one will clear the buildings to the east. It will engage their artillery there. It's one of many, sited in all the open places, hidden from the view of those outside the walls."

"Very good, Fulques," Agnes said.

Giles looked at the eastern gate, along the eastern wall. "The arbalètes and catapults seem well situated on the ramparts."

"Let's go up and look, Giles." The two men exchanged a glance. "I do not feel you dismounting, my lord."

Giles let Agnes slip into his arms. Fulques handed her the crutches and pointed her towards the wall. Blue silk tunic, blue cap, silver girdle and embroidered slippers started down the manure-filled street. First singly, then in couples and finally in groups the townspeople came out to watch their Countess maneuver through the barricades of barrels and wagons blocking the gate.

"Let Fulques carry you up, Aggie."

"No."

Both men followed behind as their liege worked her way up the steps. She reached the top, feeling for a step that was not there. "Turn right, my lady," a man said, taking her arm and guiding her to the battlements.

"Thank you, my friend." Soft, low and yet the Voice.

The men on the ramparts watched as Agnes looked east towards Foix. The view remained unchanged. Serfs worked in the fields of the first village. They labored on, even though, within days, those crops might be crushed under the French army.

"You have done well, Fulques," the Voice announced when she turned back. "We are well-prepared and well protected."

"We are, my lady." He turned to the officer at the gate. "Do you have any problems seeing the signals"? Both men looked up at the cathedral tower.

"No, but the French will try to chase them away with their siege machines. The building will be damaged."

"It's too old anyway," Agnes replied. "I want to replace it with that new style from up north. The Frogheads can help with the demolition." Laughter followed.

"We may lose the Master's glass, my lady," the officer said.

"That we don't want to lose. Have the windows boarded up, Fulques."

"Yes my lady."

The Countess turned towards the city, towards the sound of the crowd gathered beneath her. The breeze fluttered the ribbons of her cap as she balanced lightly on her crutches.

"Hold fast, my good people, hold fast! Hold fast and the Frog King and his Mommy will be in their Paris by autumn! Hold fast and we will win this battle! We will preserve our Lengadôc! It is the Will of God"!

■ ■ ■

Giles and Fulques rode side-by-side down the Avenue of Our Lady.

"Fulques."

"Yes my lady."

"The night when you found Liss in the St. John's square, she slapped you at the door to the Keep."

The lieutenant smiled. "She did."

"Why? She will tell me nothing other than that you were insolent. I value your service, Fulques, but I will let no man trifle with that innocent girl."

The two men exchanged a smile. "Except the watchman who stuck her in the pillory and switched her bare behind ten times. She couldn't sit without a cushion for two weeks."

"Except him, yes."

"I lifted your innocent little Baroness onto my horse. I told her she was a selfish spoiled baby, that her little walk was going to get good people whipped."

"So she told me."

"Her answer was to snuggle up against me. She whispered in my ear. 'A selfish spoiled baby doesn't work hours every day to learn Latin and French and numbers, Fulques.' Then she put her arms around me and her head against my chest." They rode a few steps in silence. "She has worked hard, my lady."

"And the slap"?

"When we reached the yard, the Baroness whispered in my ear again. 'If you put yourself in me, Fulques, would it freeze up and break off'? It took me a second to figure out what she was talking about. I'm not sure she understood herself."

"And"?

"I lifted her to the ground and leaned down. 'No, my lady, you seem warm enough,' I said, 'but I will check with Sir Godafres on the morning after your wedding.' That's when she slapped me."

3

Lisbetta sat with the Countess, reviewing petitions. "Next one, my lady, it's from my village of sant Foy." Giles and Fulques sat to the side, trying to decide what they had forgotten. Maddie and Hugh played on the floor, babbling nonsense, enjoying their freedom.

"I want them with me as much as possible, Giles," Agnes said as the crisis mounted. "If we cannot trust Anniken and Gracia to keep the secrets of our County, then we certainly should not trust them with our children." She indulged every distracting question and foolish diversion as their time together grew ever shorter.

Peter entered, a deep bow towards his unseeing mistress.

"Martha Legros and Rubea Migona are outside, my lady. They seek an audience with their Countess."

"Their Countess, not Agnes Alberensa? What do you know of this, Betta"?

"I have been a poor spy, my lady. I did not know this was coming."

The two older women bustled into the Chamber. They wore their finest tunics with their husbands' Consul Robes as surcoats. They curtseyed. They took the hand of their Countess and kissed it.

"Find them chairs, Fulques," but the men-at-arms had anticipated her command.

"Help me down, Little Lisbet." Fulques fetched a chair for the Countess. In a moment, a smaller part of St. John's Circle was assembled, although men had scandalously been admitted.

"Children, come here." Agnes tilted her head as the patter approached. "Martha and Rubea, these are my children, Madeleine and Hugh. Say hello to *Senyora* Legros and *Senyora* Migona, children."

"Hello, *Senyoras*"! followed by tittering.

"Now go with Anniken."

"We want to stay, Daddy"!

"Sorry, Maddie." The children disappeared in a torrent of giggles.

"Very lovely children, my lady," Martha said.

"Quite cute," Rubea added.

"I agree, but then I'm their mother." Agnes let the laughter subside. "Thank you for your visit. You want something big, coming here, bowing, kissing my hand, calling me by my title."

They blushed, Lisbetta reported later, and looked from side to side, but the always outspoken Martha recovered quickly.

"We do, my lady Countess. We want to help. The women cannot fight the French hand-to-hand, but we can carry supplies and water. We can man the siege machines. We can make it possible for more men to be on the walls."

"You will not be popular with the men who are moved to the walls, Martha," Fulques replied.

Martha waved the joke violently away. "We are fighting for our way of life here, Fulques, all of us! If I could man the walls, I would do it. At the end, all of us will be attacked when the French break in. Until then, each of us must do what we can."

Agnes Alberensa smiled, more a knowing smirk than a smile. "And the ladies of *Lo Cercle de San Juan*, they have a special request."

"Let us man a trebuchet," Rubea answered. "At the siege of Tolosa in 1218, a stone from a trebuchet served by women and girls struck Simon de Montfort in the head, killing him. With God's help, we will do the same to the Frog King."

"Something tells me Mommy will not let him get so close, Rubea. She fancies her little teenager too much. What do you think, Sir Giles"?

Sir Giles looked at Rubea, at Martha. He thought of the others who left him standing out in the rain. He reminded himself that Agnes fit very nicely with these forceful and forward women. He decided that it did not matter what his answer was. His job was to give Agnes Alberensa the answer she wanted.

"We can use all the help we can get, my lady. We will put them on the trebuchet in the Cathedral Square. Will that work, Fulques"?

"An excellent disposition, my lord." Agnes smiled and Lisbetta smiled. Fulques smiled at Giles, two conspirators, making the women happy. There was enough war outside the walls without starting one in here. And they could in fact use all the help they could get. "If you wish, ladies, I will take you there this morning."

"Thank you, Fulques," Martha said. The two women stood.

"We have decided to call our trebuchet 'David's Slingshot,' Countess. With it, Alberensa shall slay Goliath."

4

The waiting wore on. The Countess and her confidants spent the days in her Reception Chamber. Lady Mayrènge made notes. Giles and Fulques made plans. The children made their blind mother come down to the floor where they could talk to her.

"Sir Laurent returned from his ride to Gascony," Giles said as Agnes sat on the stones. "Nothing unusual. They do not expect a French attack and they are not preparing one of their own. The report from the Sárdalo says the same of Aragon."

"It is still just the French coming to besiege us, not the start of a general war."

"Yes," Giles answered. "We have a formidable position. We can hold for a long time. Louis cannot keep this large army in the field forever, because there are other threats to his rule. If we can hold to the winter, he will withdraw."

■ ■ ■

Agnes resumed her daily visits to the chapel, even though she had been excommunicated. Lisbetta guided her there, "Come back in an hour." Alone amidst the unseen stained glass of her ancestors, she pondered them all.

Your ancestors, Mother, now lost in the dim mists of time, who turned a tiny farming village into this thriving County.

Your ancestors, Daddy, and the knowledge of the metals that created our wealth.

Our people, all the loyal men and women through all those generations who made the Barons of Jabil al-Hadid and the Counts of Alberensa wealthy and powerful and prosperous.

You lost Jabil al-Hadid and your life through treachery, Hugh, but I helped. Your marriage to Jamilla bint Hassan, my trusted confidant, gave the traitors an excuse to make their murder legal. Somewhere deep inside, we both knew that the fief was too exposed, too vulnerable, that it might fall to the Saracens at any time. Still, we were the two who actually lost it, even if we lost it to a friend.

Now I could lose Alberensa. Yes, Giles, we can hold back the King for this season. If we do, he will only return next season. This siege will cost Alberensa a year's crops, a year's income from the pilgrimage, a year's income from the steel. That cannot continue, year after year. Nor can I sacrifice loyal men in battle this year only to sacrifice more next year.

I need something different, a different way to save my County. The mountains have never been more rugged or the road more narrow.

■ ■ ■

Four days after St. John's Circle took over David's Slingshot, the French arrived. Within a matter of hours, they surrounded the city, detaining anyone who sought to leave. A colorful ensemble indeed, Giles reported, and very large. "We are besieged, my lady, well and truly besieged."

The French spent three days maneuvering, adjusting their lines, arranging their artillery, sitting and waiting. On the fourth day, Peter admitted *Monsieur* Charpentier to the Reception Chamber.

"His Majesty has graciously offered that if you surrender the city without a battle, there will be no looting and no burning. Here it is in writing, for *ma belle fleur d'or* to read."

Fulques put his hand out for the message instead. "The Baroness of Mayrènge is not your lovely golden flower. Hand it over."

The Carpenter smirked. "I have competition for her favor, I see."

"Do not take the message, Fulques." Agnes turned towards the Herald's voice. "What of my lords, *Monsieur* Charpentier? What of Sir Gautier, Sir Bertrand, Sir

Rodrigo? What of my *Capitolum*? What of the Good Christians"?

A slight bow. "His Majesty has been most gracious with you, my lady. Your excommunication will be lifted by the Bishop. You will remain Countess and rule this city as a vassal of the Count of Toulouse. His Majesty will decide who will hold your fiefs. The smelters at Petrousset and Pont de Molin will be given to His Majesty's brother, John Tristan, Count of Anjou and Maine. You will give us the men who work there, this Guilhelms Faure who knows how to make the soft iron flow. Your heretics will be given up to the Inquisition. They can recant or be burned."

"That does not sound like much of an offer, *Monsieur*."

"You have no choice, Countess. You cannot prevail."

Agnes tapped the arm of her chair. "Our Lord God, in His infinite wisdom, has made it certain that we always have a choice, *Monsieur* Charpentier. The choice between Good and Evil stands before us, every day."

Agnes reached down to lock her legs straight, to rise in front of her chair, to point one hand at Charpentier while she held on with the other.

"Your boy King and his Mommy mistake me for a coward and a traitor, *Monsieur* Charpentier! I will not save myself and let my people suffer! I will not let

Louis burn my subjects to death, even if they are heretics! I will not betray the people who have supported my family since Paris was nothing more than a muddy village on a river island! I will die before any of those things will happen"!

"Countess, that is not a wise....."

"My compliments to His Majesty, but his offer is rejected. Fulques, blindfold *Monsieur* Charpentier and escort him to the gate."

The door closed behind The Carpenter, into silence. "Giles, please take me to the chapel."

■ ■ ■

Alone, the Countess steadied herself against the threats, the insults, the arrogance. Blanche and Louis intend no quarter at all. They will spare my title. I can collect tolls from the pilgrims. Our little Hugh will inherit nothing. Madeleine will end up a maid.

Quietly, slowly, the small, still Voice of God rose in her excommunicated mind, at the edge, nagging, drawing closer, closer until it was at the very center of her thoughts.

Only a miracle can save the Alberensa of my ancestors, of Lothar and Roland and Oddo and the Builder and the Glassmaker, of Harildis and Marguerite.

Only a miracle can preserve this place and my people, separate and apart from the growing power and wars of France.

Only a miracle can save *parainça*, Lengadòc's ancient spirit of tolerance.

Only a miracle can save the ancient Occitan language.

Only a miracle can preserve the Good Christians from a most horrible death.

Jesus, God the Son, fed five thousand people with five loaves and two fishes.

He healed a cripple and a blind man.

He raised Lazarus from the dead.

God the Father parted the Red Sea to let the Hebrew people walk across on dry land. He drowned the Egyptians when they tried to follow.

God the Holy Spirit carried the remains of the beheaded Saint James from the Holy Land and laid them in a tomb in Compostela.

Agnes pulled up her skirt, undid the straps on her leg braces and took them off. The floor felt cold underneath as she dragged herself on her elbows, reaching out and feeling her way, polishing the stone beneath her with her wool. When she found the steps before the altar, she lay down on her face.

"God of my fathers, I beg forgiveness for all my sins and failings. I humble myself before you, Lord Christ, blind and crippled as it was Your will to leave me for Your own unknowable purpose. I pray for Your miracle now, my Lord, Your miracle to save my people."

David's Slingshot. David went out before Goliath, without shield, without armor. Goliath mocked him. "Am I a dog, that you come to me with sticks"?

"You come to me with a sword and with a spear and with a javelin," David answered, "But I come to you in the name of the Lord of Hosts, the God of the armies of Israel, whom you have defied. This day, the Lord will deliver you into my hand."

Agnes folded her hands under her face. "My soul magnifies the Lord, and my spirit has rejoiced in God my Savior. In this flesh that you have given me, let me see Your miracle, O Lord my God."

From outside in the yard, she heard the rattle of the falling weight as the trebuchet launched its first load.

5

Her afflictions made their lovemaking clumsy, but Agnes always found Giles tender, gentle, caring. When he was in her, her body urged her to move in impossible ways, impossible, at least, for over ten years. She was a lump, but she was a most passionate lump, and she found her husband's passion to be a most wonderful gift. She imagined her brother in bed with Maura and felt sorry for them both.

"What will happen tonight, Giles"?

Giles leaned over and kissed her. "The King will send skirmishers forward tonight. They will try to scout our positions. Bertrand's men are waiting in a few likely locations. We'll capture some Frogs and bring them in for questioning." He kissed her again. "They'll be trying to capture Bertrand's men, because they know they'll be out there. We know the land, and we'll prevail."

"And tomorrow"?

"They were concentrating around the northern river wall as the light faded. They may bombard it, maybe even launch an attack to see if they can get into the city and end the siege quickly. We've planned for an attack at a weak spot like that. We'll be ready."

Agnes didn't answer. Giles thought he might have talked her to sleep, because she often drifted off very quickly after their lovemaking. "Giles, pull me close and hold me. Reach down and put my legs around yours." No, wide awake. "Tighter, Giles, hold me tighter." He felt her hugging back.

"My parents sold me to the Prince of Antioch. Maura's parents sold her to Hugh. I've vowed never to sell Maddie to anyone. She will marry a man she loves."

"Yes."

"I won't sell Maddie, yet I sold Lisbetta to Rodrigo, a delightful *loriot* for his son, a move to assure his loyalty."

"Yes."

A little wiggle, getting comfortable. "Do you think she loves Fulques"?

Giles smiled in the darkness at the thought of the Innocent Baroness with her arms around the soldier. "Yes, she does, very much. She can't keep her eyes off him during our meetings."

"Is he suitable for her, Giles? Clever enough? Bold enough? Gentle enough? Worthy to marry into the nobility, to be noble himself? She has become a most refined and accomplished woman, this cousin of mine."

"Isn't there another question first, Aggie"?

"Does he"?

"Yes, Countess, I believe he does."

Agnes squeezed her husband. "The betrothal was a mistake. I shall send a message to Rodrigo, begging release. We will find someone suitable for Godafres, if we prevail."

"Yes, my lady."

"Do you believe in miracles, Giles"?

■ ■ ■

Outside the Reception Chamber, the trebuchet launched sporadically. The artillerymen gathered up French stones that landed inside the city and returned them, supplemented by paving stones from the streets. Giles gave the order to conserve lest the siege reduce Alberensa to the mud that Lothar received from Charlemagne's grandson.

"Fulques, your report."

"We captured two Frenchmen last night outside the North Gate on the Compostela Road. They say that the King's tent is to the north, confirming our suspicions from what we can see of their forces. They are from the Épernays, so we'll torture them a little more before we put them in the dungeon."

"Very good. Continue."

"At least one Frog siege machine has a sense of humor. They have started lobbing our own paving stones back at us. Men are gathering opposite the wall on the north, near the river. No attack appears imminent."

The Countess put her hand to her mouth, took it away.

"I need to send an emissary to His Majesty with a message before any attack begins. Fulques, would you carry that for me"?

"It will be an honor, my lady."

"That's not a good idea, my lady Countess." Lady Mayrènge surprised them by speaking so boldly. The private secretary almost never spoke unless spoken to. She certainly never challenged their liege. A frown of annoyance crossed Agnes's face.

"Why is that, Little Lisbit? He seems most suitable, and he is willing."

"What if the French keep him? We need every man we have, my lady."

The others waited while Agnes pondered.

"You may be right, my golden *auriòl*." She looked towards the ceiling, unseeing, and back again. "Well then, as the Lord asked of Isaiah in the year that King Uzziah died, 'Whom shall I send, and who will go for us'"?

"Here am I," Lisbetta answered. "Send me."

6

Guilhelms drove the Baroness of Mayrènge towards the North Gate. Fulques and Giles rode alongside the wagon. Years ago Lisbetta Deslegador rode through this gate the other way, in another wagon, on a rainy day, in brown homespun. Today, the sun shone brightly on her muted yellow silk, her blue cap and blue sash. Shone on Alberensa's seal, and on her necklace with the blue stones, and her Saracen ring, the gift of the Countess.

David's Slingshot stood before the Cathedral where the Compostela Road joined the Avenue of Our Lady. A load of stones filled the pulled-down sling. The Circle stood away from their charge, sheltering themselves near the walls.

"Where are you going, my lady"? Brunissende Migona called as Guilhelms drove by.

"I fancy a ride in the country. It's a lovely day."

"Bring us some flowers."

As the wagon neared the gate, Lisbetta watched the men on the ramparts watching the enemy from behind the crenellations. Even from here she could hear the sounds of stones crashing into the wall by the river.

A officer shouted down from the gate tower. A woman in the street signaled with flags. A moment later, David's Slingshot rattled into life. Lisbetta looked up to see pieces of the Avenue of Our Lady soaring towards the French. Two catapults on the wall launched. Crossbowmen loosed their bolts.

In a moment, whatever it was, it was over.

Quiet returned to the gate as Guilhelms drew up. He walked around and lifted Lisbetta off by her slender waist as he had for Lady Prisca in Brassat. Little Liss had grown up a beauty as Guilhelms knew she would, ever since she stood up in her too-big tunic at the Easter dinner. And she had grown up smart, very smart. Gervais and Petrona would be proud, if they could forgive her for holding a title.

"Thank you for the ride, cousin." She hugged him. "I hope I won't keep you waiting too long." The Baroness seemed radiant, glowing, very happy after Agnes had explained the change in her wedding plans.

"Get down and kiss your betrothed, Fulques," Giles ordered. "We're at war. You may not get another chance."

■ ■ ■

Giles gave the order, the signalwoman wagged at the cathedral tower and soon white flags went up all around the walls of Alberensa. It took the French a few minutes to respond, so long, in fact, that Giles worried that they would not. Then the noise slackened and died away completely. In the sudden silence, Fulques held Lisbetta's hand for just a moment and whispered in her ear.

"You may be spoiled, *Conglaçada*, but you're clever, and brave, and beautiful. I'm going to spoil you for the rest of your life." He kissed her again, just a little kiss on her lips this time. Lisbetta squared up and stepped through the sally port, alone. The door closed behind her.

Her feet must be moving, because she was floating along the paving stones of the Compostela Road. Her hand was on her mouth, where his kiss had been. Her other hand, clutching the message, was on her tummy, which was tickling in that most strange way.

At last she noticed her silent surroundings. The Alberensa River gurgled in its course as small animals began to move around in the no-man's-land between the two armies. A light breeze from behind blew the ribbons tying on her cap before her face.

The Baroness walked through a beautiful day of sun and clouds and green and the Pyrenees, yet all she noticed was that persistent tickle in her stomach. She did not think she was a Catholic, but she was having trouble understanding how something as wonderful as Fulques' kisses could be things of evil. She would never become a *Parfait*, ever, as long as he was able to kiss her like that.

"*Arrêtez! Ne proche plus! Pourquoi êtes-vous ici"?*

The rough voice surprised her. *Qué? Francés?* It must have come from behind a barricade, because she saw no one. Off to the right, people tended to the wounded from the Slingshot's volley. The Circle had not found the King, but his men had known their handiwork.

"*J'ai dit arreter"!*

Lisbetta stopped, as ordered. *Oc, oui, la langue française*, of course, I'm bringing them this message. She held it out, away from the tickle.

"*Je suis la baronne de Mayrènge. Je porte un message à Son Majesté. Je dois lui parler moi-même.*"

The rumblings of many voices, most commenting on how nice it was that the heretics had sent out such a good-looking whore for their pleasure.

"*Bon. Venez ici.*"

As Lisbetta walked past their barricade, the French soldiers reached up and pulled her down. Her cap disappeared and hands dug into her hair. They felt around her body, squeezing her breasts.

"*Ils sont les vraie choses, mes amis,*" a soldier said.

Of course they are real, peasant. I should have you whipped for your insolence.

No time, because suddenly she was being held upside down by the ankles. Her tunic and her cotte fell all the way up, over her face, while hands felt her legs and rubbed her tender bottom and fondled her bare breasts.

"C'est le même coleur que ses cheveux."

It's always the same color as the hair, you arrogant fool.

They stood her up. They left her tunic a mess. No maid stepped forward to straighten it. She did it herself while the soldiers watched and laughed. She bent over to pick up her sash and her cap and the soldier who touched her….there…..drew close, pursing his lips for a kiss. She slapped him, once with each hand. He reeled back and the others laughed.

"Enough, lads."

Thank you, Jesus my Savior, it's their sergeant. He looked towards the wall beyond, the stones piling up by the riverbank.

"I don't think the heretics called a truce just to send out this little butterfly for us to fuck. Tie her hands behind her, blindfold her, and I'll take her back to Sir Robert." He pointed towards the city wall. "Watch out for their witchcraft." He lifted Lisbetta's silk gown and squeezed her thigh. "This tasty morsel does appear quite bewitching, I must say."

Lisbetta would have slapped him for his presumption and his insolence, except that she was already tied up with her sash and blindfolded by fastening her cap across her face. At least they were silk.

■ ■ ■

Fortunately Sir Robert did not think that the tasty morsel should be manhandled by every Frenchman between Alberensa and His Majesty. A woman as a herald surprised him, but he decided it was not impossible. Her French was good, quite good. Her clothing and her bearing made it unlikely that she was a pleasure girl expelled for her sins. Perhaps the young thing was a Baroness, as she claimed. The unseen Robert put Lisbetta in his lap and rode back, walking his horse in circles to confuse her.

"What have we here, my lord of Tourgéville"? The voice, an older man's voice. A cold chill gripped her as she heard it. Épernay's men had been captured outside the North Gate, so their liege lord could not have been far away.

"She claims to be a herald from the city, my lord the Baron of Épernay," Sir Robert answered. "I'm bringing her to His Majesty."

"You're the heretic of Farga, aren't you, wench"? Stark fear gripped *La Conglaçada*. She felt a mailed gauntlet pushing her tunic up, scratching her thigh. "The bitch who tends the Cripple." The rings of mail dug in as Charles began to tug her from the horse. "It's her, all right, Father, the one who took your arm. She should be checked for the Mark of Satan."

Unable to move, unable to see, for the first time Lisbetta truly understood the panic that seized Agnes when she was snatched up and taken to the cave in the

Sárdalo. Lisbetta's prideful move, showing Alberensa's men that Blanche was not the only woman who could fight, it seemed a vain and foolish fantasy now. She felt Sir Robert's arms tightening around her waist, pulling her back, holding her on his horse.

"She came out under flag of truce, Sir Charles. She has a message for our King."

"Leave her with us, Sir Robert. We'll bring her to His Majesty."

"I can't do that, Sir Charles. My liege the Count of Deauville would expect me to bring her myself. It will stand to his credit with His Majesty that I received the emissary from the Countess of Alberensa." The horse shifted and snorted, nervous from the tension, but Robert brought it under control. "You are of course welcome to accompany me." A long silence followed while Lisbetta's stomach churned. The digging from the rings of mail eased and the gauntlet came off her thigh.

"My compliments to the Count of Deauville, Sir Robert. Pray take the witch yourself."

You would marry this knight of Tourgéville, Lisbetta, right here right now if you weren't so happy being betrothed to Fulques.

More circles, up and down, through woods with branches whipping against her and out into the fields again. Lisbetta felt her heart slowing. "Thank you, Sir Robert."

"You heretics will be burned soon enough. It would not be chivalrous to let him rape you first."

They rode for only a minute more until the horse stopped. Hands lifted her to the ground and led her forward.

"Stand here."

7

Soft sounds surrounded Lisbetta, people moving
nearby. Her face tickled, although she didn't know if it
was really tickling, or just tickling because she couldn't
rub it with her hands tied behind her. Someone
gripped each of her arms, surprising her, making her
squeak out, "Oh." Her cry was drowned by the voice
of a familiar herald.

"His Majesty the King"!

A soft swish of fabric, His Majesty entering.

"What have you brought us, my lord the Count of
Deauville"?

"This slip of a girl claims to be a herald from the
city, Your Majesty."

"Remove her blindfold."

Lisbetta found herself inside a tent with the flaps
closed. She could see nothing of where she had been
taken, but she could still hear the river. They hadn't ridden around the city, so they were downstream. Those

woods whipping her face, that was the forest around the smelters. They were near Petrousset, Pont de Molin.

Monsieur Charpentier stood beside the King. A middle-aged nobleman flanked him on the other side with a younger knight in mail behind him. The Count of Deauville and Robert of Tourgéville, certainly.

To Charpentier's other side stood Bishop Paul Genet and Father Felipe. Advancing in front of them all, a woman glared back at Lisbetta, middle-aged like the Count and the Bishop, well-dressed with a cloak of fine wool.

Yes, it's her. Blanca de Castilla, Queen Blanche, without a doubt. For a woman who had mothered twelve children, the Queen remained remarkably thin and, for her age, attractive. Maybe the songs of the northern *trouvères*, especially Count Theobald of Champagne, maybe his songs of courtly love masked a passion between them that was more….carnal. She was devout, the *trouvères* sang, most devout. Yet something more than duty must have impelled the production of twelve potential heirs to her late husband's throne.

Devout carnal lust, was it possible? Lisbetta felt that strange tingling again, Fulques, my darling Fulques…

No! Pay attention! However this woman passes her nights, she is most formidable during the day!

King Louis, Ninth of that Name, pointed at Lisbetta. "Is this your golden oriole, Charpentier"? Lisbetta realized that Louis was even younger than she. He wore woolen hose and a deep blue linen tunic, deeper even than Alberensa. And covered with a field of lilies, the *fleur de lis*. Blond hair and blue eyes, like her. Intensely pious, they said, like the Queen Mother.

"It is, Your Majesty. Delightful to see, as always."

Some of that intensity flowed from him as he looked at her, not with lust like his men, but seeking out who she might be. Finally he sat.

"Undo her. We see no threat here." Lisbetta re-tied her sash around her waist and her cap on her head while the King watched. "Besides being Charpentier's *loriot*, who is she"?

"She is the confidant of the Countess," Bishop Genet confirmed. "Her secretary. Lisbetta, Baroness of Mayrènge. '*La Conglaçada,*' the troubadours call her, 'The Frozen One.'"

"She is the heretic Lisbetta Deslegador from Farga de sant Matèu," added Felipe with enough heat to warm up the frozen. "She lived with the heretics near the road to the Sárdalo Pass. She was there when her Countess took the *Consolamentum*. It is to redeem souls like hers that the Holy Father has sent me to Alberensa. Beware of witchcraft, Your Majesties."

Louis looked at Lisbetta again, her face, her eyes, seeking guile, seeking innocence, not sure what he found, except beauty. "Mother"?

Blanche did the same, less interested in the beauty, more interested in her dress, her poise, the intelligence in Lisbetta's own blue eyes looking back at her. A wave of the Queen's hand. "Sit down, girl."

Lisbetta knew The Voice when she heard it. She obeyed.

"Are there so few men in Alberensa that they send women as heralds? That they send a pretty young girl onto a field of battle? Should you not be tending to your husband, working on your crafts"?

Yes, Agnes, such arrogance.

"Perhaps we could work on those crafts together, Majesty." The French rustled and shuffled while the two women held each other's look. "Of course Alberensa has men, but I told my liege that I wished to meet the woman of whom your Count Theobald sings."

The rustling and shuffling grew into murmuring. The face of Blanche remained blank, a mask for a clever mind.

"I think not, Lisbetta. I think that you do not have any men to spare. Charpentier"!

"Yes, Your Majesty"? bowing deeply.

"Why is this insolent wench here? Our terms for surrender have already been rudely rejected by her heretic Countess. Tie your delightful little bird across your saddle, *Monsieur*; take His Majesty's message back to Alberensa and receive a proper answer this time"!

Charpentier reached for Lisbetta, hesitated, turned back into the glare of the Queen.

"Well, *Monsieur*? Was something I said not clear"?

"She brought a message with her from Alberensa, Your Majesty."

Blanche snorted. "We are to read a message from that impertinent blind heretic after she rejected His Majesty's message? Why is that, Lisbetta, why is that"?

"*Monsieur* Charpentier explained His Majesty's message, Your Majesty, and my lady replied. I can accept the document now, but her reply will not change. And I can explain my lady's message, even if His Majesty does not choose to receive it."

Mother and son exchanged a glance. They seemed to have a language of their own, Lisbetta thought, quiet and subtle movements like those that Hugh and Agnes shared. She guessed Blanche was signaling, you decide.

"Charpentier," the King said, "send a man for my message and bring it here. What message do you bring, girl"?

Thank you, Lord Jesus, you made him curious!

Within seconds, Lisbetta's note appeared from somewhere. She handed it to Charpentier, rolled, still sealed, and turned towards the King.

"I will leave the full reading to *Monsieur* Charpentier, Your Majesty. Briefly, the Countess of Alberensa says that your claims to her County are false. She wishes to let God be the judge of who is right."

A shocked silence filled the room as the King looked at his mother, and back. "God? You mean trial by combat? Her champion against mine, for Alberensa"?

"No, Your Majesty. She means herself, personally, against you, personally, and let God decide the outcome. She is, as you know, unable to walk and unable to see. She proposes a joust, blunted lances unable to penetrate, but otherwise full armor and shields. Whoever remains seated on their mount at the end, God has judged that person the righteous one."

Charpentier turned to Their Majesties. "Their troubadours do call her *Sheyka al-Hadid*, the Iron Baroness. It started after that trip to the Sárdalo Pass to fetch this lovely flower for her garden. But this challenge is most extraordinary."

The Herald fixed his leer on Lisbetta again, making her skin feel dirtier than when the soldiers rubbed her bottom or Filthy Charles of Épernay squeezed her thigh. "If God should judge your Iron Baroness the winner, Lisbetta Deslegador, what is the result"?

"Her excommunication is lifted. Alberensa remains free and independent for as long as the County does not take the field against the French crown. France protects that independence against other challengers, the English, the Aragonese, the Castilians. All lands are restored to my lady's barons. The Baron of Arguenos and his line are banished from Alberensa. If France has no need for him, my lady recommends Outremer, where the Christians require much help."

"And if the King prevails"?

"My lady hopes that the offer you brought earlier, *Monsieur* Charpentier, still stands. But that is not a condition. If God judges the King to be the victor, we are all at His Majesty's mercy, including my liege."

Lisbetta sat with her back upright, her hands in her lap, her eyes focused on Louis. Everyone else focused on her. Finally Charpentier spoke.

"You should not fight yourself, Your Majesty. You should have a champion."

"No champions," Lisbetta objected. "France against Alberensa. How else do we determine who is favored by the Lord"?

Louis looked to his mother, and then both pairs of eyes bored into Lisbetta, again. She remembered the eyes of Cardinal Donato, calculating, ever calculating.

Robert of Tourgéville spoke. "She cannot tie herself on, Heraldess. She must sit the animal on her own."

The Heraldess kept her eyes on the King as she answered. "Her feet will be lifted into the stirrups, that's all. Whether they stay there is up to God. And you, Your Majesty, you cannot just ride up while she sits there, blind, and push her off. It must be a joust, a full gallop, so that God can judge the winner."

"Beware of heretic witchcraft, Your Majesty," said the Bishop. "Or tricks. This Countess took the *Consolamentum*."

"My lady is weary of that nonsense, Bishop. It is a figment of Father Felipe's imagination. The Countess has never taken the Good Christian sacrament, ever. She is a faithful Catholic who is much burdened by your unjust excommunication." Lisbetta made a little motion with her hand. "You may send maids to watch my liege dress before the joust, Your Majesty. My lady proposes the day after tomorrow, so that a suit of armor can be tailored to fit her. A full truce, no fighting, no one moves position until the joust."

The King pondered only briefly.

"My lords, we face a costly siege here. If I can catch a blind and crippled woman as she gallops aimlessly around a field, catch her and push her off if she has not already fallen off, that siege will end. I will do it."

Felipe, the Bishop and the others muttered. The Count of Deauville spoke.

"Your Majesty, you cannot. You cannot take Alberensa by knocking a blind Albigensian harlot off her horse. This is a joke, an insult. Resume the battle and give me this Frozen Baroness of the Troubadours for the pleasure of my men."

Lisbetta's stomach tickled again, but differently, cold, with a lump. Her breasts tingled, remembering the fondling by Sir Robert's men. She tried to imagine how Andreva felt as Charles drove himself into her.

"Once they are finished, I will turn her over to Father Felipe's Inquisition, and the flames."

Keep your face calm, you are a lady, even if these French pigs will not acknowledge it.

The King looked at the Queen and back at the Count. The Queen looked at Lisbetta, but she saw only calculation, no mercy, in her royal eyes.

"My lord the Count of Deauville," the King said. "Would you prefer to save my honor by leading a charge this morning? If you attempt an escalade, we could find out how many of their catapults and trebuchets and arbalètes are aimed at the river wall. All of them, that's my guess, my lord Count."

"You Majesty…" the Count began.

"No, my lord, no more! This challenge will save many lives and much treasure. We need you, my lord of Deauville, we need Sir Robert, we need these men for bigger battles, to fight the treacherous English King Henry, the foul Holy Roman Emperor Frederick." The King was silent for a moment before he crossed himself. "If I am knocked from my horse by a woman in such wise, God must truly find me at fault with this war. Mother, what do you think"?

Mother was not sure.

"A woman with such spirit as this Iron Baroness would make an excellent vassal, Louis. And *Monsieur* Charpentier could warm up our frozen heretic here while he teaches her the tasks of a dutiful wife." Charpentier leered again, his best so far. "Still, I am not certain."

Lisbetta smiled at the Queen. "If I am wed to this Carpenter, Your Majesty, perhaps Count Theobald will sing of my passion as well as he does of yours."

Blanche's eyes flamed and her nostrils flared.

"Not if you have already been warmed by Father Felipe's flames"! Blanche turned towards her son. "You are right, my son. Let the joust take place. As the Abbot of Citeaux said before Beziers, the Lord will know his own"!

8

Giles' voice came from below. "A man grips the horse and controls it with his legs, Aggie. The stirrups let him rise up and fight while not losing his balance. How does it feel"?

How do you think it feels, husband? I can't grip and I can't rise up. My legs are like two strips of cloth hanging down, bouncing every time the horse takes a step.

"I'm going to turn him now, Aggie."

She felt the turn. She slipped again.

"Ah! No! No"!

Her hands found the pommel by luck just as she slid off sideways, one strip of cloth following the other, on the side away from Giles. The Countess hung with her elbows bent but the horse didn't like that, so he bucked and kicked while her heart raced. "Giles"! It was a shriek, a panicked cry. "Help me, Giles, help me"!

"Whoa, whoa." The horse dragged her forward, "Whoa, Vencidor, whoa." Vencidor's shoes clattered in the dark. "Push off him, Aggie, trust me, darling, push away and let go."

She pushed and her legs crumpled in the darkness. She waited for her rear to hit first and then she rolled to the side and put her hands over her head.

"Help, Giles, help"!

"Whoa, Vencidor, stop, stop now." Horseshoe against stone sounded close, too close.

"Giles, make him stop"!

He stopped.

"Agnes, Agnes." Giles was sitting her up, pulling her to her feet while he held her around the waist with a lovely strong arm. With his other hand he softly swept the tears and the…..dirt…..from her face. "Are you okay"?

"Yes. I'm sorry I behaved so cowardly. Lift me back on. We'll try again."

"You were right to be afraid, Aggie. It's too dangerous. You're falling off every time. You'll be hurt. Let's trust that Guilhelms will be ready for the joust. I'll tie you on so that you can practice. We only have two days, and you can't spend them falling off your mount." It was almost magic, the way he hoisted her up and set her in the saddle again. "Hold the pommel," and she felt him tying lines around her ankles and knees and waist. "Is that tight"?

"Yes."

"Aggie, darling, this is crazy. Let me fight the King's champion. I'm getting old, but I'm still damn good, sorry my lady, very good."

"Yes, and our Pious Blanche will bring forth someone who weighs as much as Vencidor, rides like the wind, and uses both lance and bow at the same time. She'll send you to meet Our Lord far earlier than I would like. Have faith in me, my love, and faith in God."

"You are fearless, Aggie."

"I'm scared to death, that's what I am. Let's try again."

All that is asked is that you fight as well you can until you no longer can, and then that you trust in Our Savior's merciful grace.

■ ■ ■

Father Duran read the Mass beautifully in the crowded chapel, but he read it to a distracted congregation. Even he had not centered himself properly in the Lord, and not only because he had given the Host, the Very Body of Jesus to the excommunicated Countess. The tension quieted even Madeleine and Hugh, sitting with their maids in the front row.

The Mass ended and Agnes crutched her way to the front. The Countess wore the embroidered blue silk tunic of her Service of Acknowledgment. On her head, the Coronet of Alberencidum. On her wrists, the bracelets of Baroness Ermessenda. A Saracen necklace of gold and precious stones. The ermine cloak of Angibert II. And her golden cross, the gift of Sir Martin.

Most likely, God and King Louis will be making you a commoner this morning, Agnes, but at least you will be a well-dressed commoner, for one day. Speak now to your congregation, to all these loyal people you have never seen, save your husband when he was still a sergeant, years ago.

"Mommy, will you give a long speech? Hugh is bored already."

Laughter erupted, a child breaking the tension. Agnes turned towards her children.

"Hugh. Mommy has to talk, Hugh. I hope you can sit still for a minute."

"Yesshh."

She turned back.

"My lords. My *Capitolum*. My husband. My friends. The Pope claims that we are heretics, that our lands are forfeit. The King claims that they are forfeit to him. We know their claims are false, absolutely false. Yet Louis is strong, too strong for us to stand alone. The Baron of Sarlant, my beloved husband Giles, has assured me that we can hold back the King this year. But what of next year? Or the year after"?

The Voice dominated the sacred space. Even Hugh was not squirming.

"I have prayed daily in this chapel. Prayed, and pondered the marvelous workings of God that made me your liege. My mother, the Countess Marguerite, was not expected to inherit Alberensa. Yet Count Jacme died without issue. Countess Marguerite died. My brother Count Hugh died. And so the rule of our County fell to a woman who can neither see nor walk."

A roar erupted, "God protect our Countess, Agnes"! She raised her hand to still the tumult.

"I grew up in a Frankish Crusader state, Tripoli, yet the blood of Provence and Languedoc is all that runs through me. Blagnac, near Toulouse. Ronzières, near Issoire. Montpelier. Aix. Alberensa. So it falls to me, a Frank from Outremer, to defend our beloved Lengadòc. Our *parainça*, our way of tolerance. Our acceptance of the heresy of the Good Christians. Our language, the songs of our troubadours, all of it is mine to defend."

It took Agnes a moment to calm her rising emotions.

"Sitting here, alone in my darkness, surrounded by this stained glass of my ancestors, I realized what God's plan for me must be. Our cause is just and the French cause is not. King Louis is devout. If Our Lord works a miracle for Alberensa, the King and his mother will accept it. Our County, our way of life in Languedoc, will be saved."

Again she paused, pushing back at the tears.

"And so at last I understood why Our Lord has left me blind and crippled. So that I could joust with Louis, and, if it is the Will of God, shove that arrogant Frenchman off his horse and save this County for our people"!

"Knock King Frog on his ass, Countess! Send that baby crying home to his Mommy's lap!"

"Thank you, Sir Bertrand. With God's help, I shall."

A gentle movement of her hand stilled the laughter.

"This decision is mine, entirely mine. I find it a great boon, a great gift, that you have accepted my wish. That you are willing to stake your lives and your fortunes and your honor on the outcome of this joust. I have prayed upon that, too, thanking Our Lord for your devoted loyalty. If through my sins I should falter in this combat, if we should lose our County, know that I will go to the flames ever thankful for your support and your love."

She stopped and made the sign of the Cross.

"Let us pray that God the Father, God the Son and God the Holy Spirit shines the light of His countenance upon us all, both this day and forevermore."

"God protect Agnes, Countess of Alberensa"!

■ ■ ■

Agnes made her way across her yard to the waiting carriage. She tucked her crutches under her arms.

"Lift the children up, Lissie-Bet." First Madeleine, her little feet dangling under her tunic. The Countess reached out, put her hands on her face and kissed her. Then Hugh, still light enough to be taken in her arms for a hug.

A hug that went on for a long time. Lisbetta watched the Countess fight her emotions, finally yielding her child back.

"Can we come, Mommy"?

"No, Maddie. Today is a day for grown-ups. Daddy and I will be back for dinner."

"After God knocks the Frog King on his ass, Mommy"?

"Exactly, precious, exactly."

Lisbetta helped her liege climb in, then climbed in after her, wearing her own dress of Alberensa blue, and her ruby ring, and her necklace, and her silver girdle. Lisbetta marveled at the calm on her lady's face. Her own fingers tingled and her stomach churned. Already she felt the heat of Felipe and the filthy touch of Charpentier.

No. Stay calm. Agnes will return to her children. Fulques and I shall wed, we shall.

"Open the gate for the Countess of Alberensa"!

The household cheered again as the Baron of Sarlant, with the coat of arms of the County on his tunic, led the column out of the yard. Riding by his side, Fulques carried the Alberensa guerdon. They led the procession along the Avenue of Our Lady. Ten men followed behind them, then Agnes's carriage and the wagons. Guilhelms drove the first, with Aenor alongside. The back held Agnes' saddle, and her armor, and the man's clothing she would wear under it for the joust. Tibaut rode alongside, bareback on Vencidor. A wagon with Anniken and Gracia followed, and a third with Peter and a bonesetter.

"The people are out, my lady, it's just that they're quiet." And then the cheers began.

"God Protect our Countess, Agnes"!

They heard the voices of Giles and Fulques, together, at the head of the column.

"God Protect Agnes, God Protect Alberensa"!

The crowd took up the chant.

"God Protect Agnes, God Protect Alberensa"! Agnes and Lisbetta rode through a continuous wave of sound.

"The children, Betta, have you…."

"Should God favor the King, my lady, Mabila and Docina will bring them to the Sisters of Charity. They will take Melisende and Isabèl Faure with them. All of them will be safe."

"If I take the King's offer, they will be…"

"Will they, my liege? Can we really trust that Bishop from Paris, that Preaching Friar? This joust protects your children too."

Agnes smiled, ever so slightly. "Thank you, Baroness."

They rode quietly through the cheers.

"The ladies of the Circle are in front of the Slingshot, Countess. They are bowing to their liege."

"Wave my arm out the window, Liss."

"Go with God, Agnes Alberensa," drifted in from the street. Agnes grinned and leaned back.

"I may indeed be Agnes Alberensa when this day is over, Lisbetta Deslegador." A pause. "Or I may be discussing my spinning with Julia Teissendièr, in Paradise." The carriage made the turn into the Compostela Road. "What kind of a day is it, Lissie? It feels cool."

"A little cool for the middle of June, my lady, yes, but the sun is out and the sky is blue. No haze, so it feels like you can almost touch the Sárdalo Pass. At least His Majesty won't get his britches wet when you dump him in the dirt."

"Thank you for that, Lisbet. And thank you for saving me, after Hugh died. I will never forget how you climbed into bed and held me."

"It worked for me once, too, Agnes Alberensa." Lisbetta took the Ring of State from her hand, reached out and let Agnes feel it. "This is your ring, my liege. Today you should wear it." Agnes slipped the ring over her finger as they approached the gate. A cheer went up from the soldiers. Like soldiers everywhere, they welcomed the end of a war, and today this war would end.

"Victory! Victory! Victory for Our Countess"!

9

The column rode up the highway towards Petrousset, through the French lines, beyond arrow range of the walls. They neared Dactalanne with the city still in sight behind them as they approached the lists.

"Lisbetta was right, Aenor," Guilhelms said. "They took her towards Petrousset. If the King is camped nearby, our house may still be undamaged."

Aenor snorted and waved her hands at the fields where the crops had been trampled into the mud by the French army.

"These poor farmers needed those crops for the winter. They don't care if Louis is their King or Agnes is their Countess." Her eyes blazed again at the travails of the serfs.

"They do care if they're Good Christians, my love. And you will care, too, if you find yourself with new employment, cleaning our house up for some Frenchman. Someone appointed by the King's brother, *Monsieur le Comte Jean Tristan d'Anjou et de Maine*." Guilhelms motioned towards the city. "No noble husbands for Ebel or Melita, either." Another snort, and he laughed. "You look lovely today, as always."

Aenor scowled. Guilhelms annoyed her with his ability to remind her of her weakness for nice clothes. Clothes that she had never owned until she met Hugh and Agnes. And she did fancy her daughters in nice clothes, too, and well-married.

"Here we are, Aenor."

The French soldiers had built the lists in a broad meadow at the top of a low hill. A solid circle of men, hundreds and hundreds, surrounded a shoulder-high fence two hundred paces long. Men-at-arms scoured the path on each side of the fence, searching out and filling in animal holes, pulling out rocks, shouting back and forth. Hooves pounded while horsemen rode back and forth along the trail, beating down the earth. Two tents with a canopy in between stood to the side of the lists. The French flag flew above one. No flag flew above the other.

"Fulques," Giles said, "Break off and inspect the work."

Agnes heard the sound of voices rise and then fall away as the Alberensa column passed through the French. Giles led the parade across the lists. A light breeze ruffled the pavilions and lifted the cloth on the table beneath the canopy.

"Halt"! The column stopped.

"We are here, my lady." Lisbetta kissed Agnes on the cheek, "God bless you, Countess." She opened the door, climbed out and helped her liege down.

The uneven ground made walking on her crutches difficult, but the Countess waved away any aid. Giles and Guilhelms walked on either side while Lisbetta whispered "left" and "right" from behind.

A thunder of hoofs stopped close at hand. "The lists are satisfactory, my lady Countess," Fulques announced. She nodded and crutched on.

The Countess stumbled her way into the canopy. The dozen French facing them watched with smiles, with smirks, with gloating. "We're here," Lisbetta whispered. She stopped, leaning on her crutches with her blue eyes gazing vacantly at some unseen place, perhaps in Outremer.

From the French side, Charpentier gazed back, joined by the Count of Deauville and Bishop Genet. Father Felipe exulted, barely able contain his own joy. Today, the Lord will avenge the Heretic Leper Boy's insult to the Holy Church. After the joust, after the King of France rules in Alberensa, I will lead an Inquisition. These two blue-silked Cathar witches will confess that they took the *Consolamentum* in the Sárdalo, recant and save their souls. Either that or be tied to the stake.

"Fulques," Lisbetta whispered, "that one-armed Baron and his son. They're the ones who murdered my family. The Black Friar is the one who spreads the false claim that that the Countess was in the mountains."

Fulques looked at the Épernays in their green tunics and triumphant grins. "'The false claim'? Steady, Spoiled. They are close to the King, or they wouldn't be here."

Charpentier drew himself to attention.

"His Majesty the King! Her Majesty the Queen Mother"!

Louis and Blanche appeared from within the royal tent. Louis wore the coat of arms of France on his tunic and his mother a tunic of white with a royal blue cloak. King and Queen paused to study their opponent as she leaned on her crutches. Blanche was as Lisbetta had described, Giles realized. Intense. Searching. And finally, satisfied.

"Please sit down, my lady the Countess of Alberensa. I'm honored that we meet at last." The King waited while Fulques and Giles seated their liege before sitting himself. "Is the agreement ready, Countess"?

"Yes, Your Majesty. The Baroness of Mayrènge has prepared it in accordance with your discussions two days ago." Lisbetta came forward with two parchments, placing them on the table.

"Bishop Genet, if you will," the King said.

The Parisian annoyed Agnes yet again. Did he serve the Holy Father in Alberensa or Queen Blanche in Paris?

Stop. Tomorrow. Discuss that tomorrow, if you are still Countess.

"They are as you agreed, Your Majesty," Genet said.

"Let us seal them."

The breeze rustled the parchment as Lisbetta guided Agnes' hand down to press her ring into the wax.

"The agreement is sealed," Charpentier proclaimed. "Prepare for the trial."

10

Two of Queen Blanche's maids followed Agnes and Lisbetta into the Alberensa tent. Anniken and Gracia stripped the Countess naked and removed her braces. Her small breasts embarrassed her again, but why she was thinking about that now, she didn't know.

Concentrate. And pray.

"Her Majesty." The French maids bowed low, faces in the dirt.

"Her Majesty the Queen has come to watch, my lady Countess."

"Thank you, Little Liss." She sat, naked on her stool, until hands lifted up her bony useless legs. Felt between them to be sure she was a woman. Rubbed her waist, her breasts, pressed against her eyes and ran fingers through her hair.

"What is it that you want, Agnes, that is not in the King's most generous offer? Perhaps if you spare him the shame of this joust, he will grant it and save you."

"I want to rule my County as my ancestors did, free and independent of any liege lord. That is not the King's most generous offer."

Agnes heard the murmuring, the rustling of the servants. She felt the Queen's hand on her cheek.

"This joust is foolishness, Countess. Look at your body. God decided against you years ago when He struck you down in Outremer."

"I would look at my body, Blanca, but I cannot see it."

Now French maids recoiled. Even Lisbetta put a warning hand on her shoulder. Agnes felt a swish of wind as the Queen moved towards the entrance to the tent.

"'The tongue is a fire,' Agnes, as Saint James said, 'a restless evil, full of deadly poison.' No man can tame it, but when this day is ended, the Lord Himself will give you cause to regret your insolence"!

"No man can tame it, but we are not men, are we, Majesty"? She heard the Queen stop. "What is your concern? That it is beneath a King to joust with a Count? That he will be laughed at for fighting me? He has agreed, Your Majesty."

"Yes, and I agreed, but now I am now convinced that my decision was too hasty, provoked, in fact, by insults from this wench of yours. My son's councilors are correct. He cannot win Alberensa this way. There is no honor in it. It will make the King seem weak. It will be no end of trouble for him."

"But you want Alberensa on your terms, and I will not yield it up on those terms. Provoked or not, you have agreed to win or lose Alberensa on my terms. Either that, or lose many men in storming my city."

Agnes felt the Queen walking back, walking close, standing over her.

"Appoint a champion, Agnes, and let my son appoint one, too. That will give honor to this trial by combat. That is what is done in these things."

The tent remained silent as the hand went to the mouth, and away.

"The King may appoint a champion, but I will fight his champion myself. It is God who will save me, Blanche, not my skill or my strength. I will trust in Him and not be afraid. He is my stronghold and my sure defense, and He will be my Savior."

■ ■ ■

Outside the pavilion, Baron Giles and Fulques watched carefully as Charles of Épernay knelt by the saddle. He fingered the blanket and studied Vencidor, the "Conqueror." Satisfied, he stood up.

"Saddle the horse."

Guilhelms laid the blanket over the animal, swung on the saddle and buckled it up while the French knight watched. "Steady, Vencidor." Queen Blanche marched from the pavilion, past the horse and into the King's tent. The two knights watched her pass as Guilhelms completed the saddling.

■ ■ ■

The French maids studied each item of clothing. They watched as Anniken and Gracia put it on. They bound Agnes' breasts and put on a gambeson over a linen cotte. Woolen hose. Chausses. Boots. Hauberk. Coif and helmet.

This is heavy, too heavy for a woman to walk in. You can't walk, Aggie, so that will be no problem.

"You are ready, my lady."

Agnes nodded. "It appears that your taunts about the crafts and Count Theobald had their intended result, Bet. You succeeded where many men have failed. You provoked Her Majesty into a decision that she now deeply regrets."

"We needed that decision, my lady. Perhaps I did give God a little help in working His miracle."

"The troubadours shall sing of you, Liss."

"If we are not roasted first, Aggie."

"Indeed."

Lisbetta opened the tent flap. "The Countess is ready"!

11

A hush fell as the Countess appeared in full armor with crutches under her arms. Murmuring began as she moved forward, flanked by Giles and Fulques. The complete absurdity of the contest became apparent as her guides repeatedly steered her and caught her from falling. A crippled and blind woman remained crippled and blind, even if protected by a full coat of mail.

"His Majesty"! Charpentier called.

Louis appeared from his tent with the arms of France on his tunic but without armor. Queen Blanche followed him and stepped to his side.

"The King fights without armor, my lady Countess," Giles said.

"The King is not fighting, Sir Giles. I have agreed to fight his champion instead."

"What"!

"Lisbet, sit with that traitorous Parisian bishop and change the agreement. Strike out the King's name and put in the name of his champion."

"Aggie, you can't....."

"Stop! It is in God's hands, Sir Giles, no matter whom I fight. Anniken. Gracia. My tunic."

The maids came forward and draped the garment over her hauberk. The sun gleamed off pure white linen, quartered by a red cross. Felipe stormed up, outraged.

"What insult is this, Your Majesties? This woman has been excommunicated! She cannot wear a cross"!

"Under that Sign," Giles said, "I fought for Christ in Outremer. As did my lady's brother, and her father, and Sir Julian of Blagnac who answered Pope Urban's call to free Jerusalem. My lady's grandfather wore this Cross when he died at Hattin. It is her right to wear the Crusader's cross. No sniveling Preaching Friar will deny her that right."

"Those were true Crusades, Your Majesties," *al-Zarqa'* blazed, "against Christ's real enemies, the Saracens." A rumble rose among the French. "I commend them to you. Our Christian brothers in Outremer are sorely pressed. Your murdering Épernays would do more good there than here."

Henri rushed forward, slamming his one hand down on the parchment, causing Lisbetta to start.

"Let me be your champion, Your Majesty! Let me quiet the insolent mouth of that heretic witch"!

Agnes laughed. "Is that you, Baron Henri? I cannot fight you, my lord. It would not be fair. You have but one arm."

Some laughter followed from the French, quickly suppressed. Giles decided that he must warn Fulques. These women of Ronzières had very sharp tongues.

Charles stepped up beside his father and bowed to the King. "Your Majesty, this joust is a farce. This heretic witch insults my father with impunity, for he cannot demand satisfaction. Let me be your champion, Your Majesty. I guarantee that my blow will send this imposter to join her ancestors in Outremer."

Giles stepped forward.

"You will strike that blow through me, you coward! The Baroness of Mayrènge says that you are very good at raping innocent girls, as you did to her sister just before you killed her! Let's see how well you do fighting someone who can fight back! You aren't half the man of the Saracens I've left on the ground"! He turned towards Lisbetta. "Baroness! Put in my name as champion for our liege"!

"Silence, my beloved Lord Sarlant, silence! I will not let you lower yourself to fight this coward! If the King wishes him for a champion, I will fight the murderer myself"!

Breezes blew and birds chirped and the tents ruffled in the silence that followed.

"Sir Charles," the King finally said, "I will accept your offer, for we must begin the joust while we still have a truce." He pushed his hand into the knight's stomach. "You will remember that you fight as my champion, my lord. When Our Lord has granted me the victory, you will leave the Countess where she lies. I will decide her fate."

"It shall be done as you command, Your Majesty."

Queen Blanche spoke, "Bishop Genet, your blessing, please."

Felipe protested, "You cannot bless the heretic! She has been excommunicated"!

Again the breezes and the birds and the ruffling. This time Agnes broke the silence.

"You should lift my excommunication, my lord Bishop. Otherwise if I prevail men will say that the Evil One defeated our Lord."

"I agree, Mother," the King replied. "I do not want to be responsible for sending the Countess to Hell if Charles kills her in this joust."

Genet stepped in front of Agnes. "In the name of the Holy Father, I lift the ban of excommunication from the Countess Agnes. She is restored to full communion with Christ's One Holy Catholic and Apostolic Church." The Bishop made the sign of the Cross as Felipe fumed.

Blanche stamped her foot, gently. "Are we now ready for your blessing, my lord Bishop"?

"Stand beside the Countess, my lord of Épernay."

Agnes felt Charles come close. Do not move. Do not flinch. Bow your head.

"We trust that the Lord our God will judge this combat fairly and award victory to the righteous fighter." Genet raised his hand. "O God, pardon and deliver these your servants from all their sins and bring them to everlasting life, through Jesus Christ our Lord, who lives and reigns with You and the Holy Spirit, One God, now and forever."

"Amen."

"My lord Henri of Épernay," the Queen said, "Watch as they lift the Countess to her horse."

"With your permission, Countess," Henri said, not waiting as he knelt down and ran his hand along the inside of her legs, studied her boots and the stirrups. Aenor smiled as she held Vencidor. She lifted her skirt ever so slightly, showing him her ankle, the lovely ankle that had cost him his arm. "Nothing, Your Majesty. Lift her on." He would give that insolent peasant to Charles once his son laid this Cathar Countess flat on the ground.

Aenor held the bit while Giles climbed onto the back of the horse, behind the saddle. Guilhelms and Fulques pushed Agnes up and Giles pulled her over, letting her legs dangle down the side. The two men fit her feet into the stirrups, very carefully. Guilhelms handed up shield and lance.

"The Countess of Alberensa is ready," Giles called.

"Countess," the Queen said, "do you wish to inspect Sir Charles's mount or armor"?

"Are you tying yourself to the horse, Sir Charles"?

"Roast in Hell, witch"!

"Perhaps I shall, but are you tying yourself to the horse"?

A bellow, "No, I am not"!

"I am satisfied, Your Majesty."

"Then the King of France is ready. Monsieur Charpentier, Lady Mayrènge, read the declaration."

The sun reached under the canopy, brightening their clothing, flashing off Lisbetta's jewels as the Frenchman began.

"Sir Charles of Épernay as champion to His Majesty the King and Her Lady the Countess Agnes of Alberensa shall make successive passes with the lance until one is unhorsed. If the other rider remains seated at the end of that pass, that rider shall be the victor. God Save the King."

"God Save the King"! the French shouted.

Lisbetta's turn. Her little trick of the heels made her taller than Charpentier, again. The herald felt the chill of *La Conglaçada* as she drew herself up, a princess. It had been a long time since she wore coarse-spun wool and played with Tibaut on a dirt floor.

"Countess, Sir Charles, take your positions, please. Signal when you are ready. Charge on the trumpet. God protect Agnes of Alberensa"!

The two parties separated, spreading out along the lists. Fulques offered Lisbetta his arm, but she preferred to draw herself closely against his side. The troubadours had not yet heard of the gallant soldier, but it would not be long before they sang of his warming powers. Assuming that The Frozen One was still a Baroness and that Fulques was still a soldier of Alberensa.

12

Charles rode quickly to his end of the lists and turned, waiting. His horse pawed at the dirt as he held up his lance. Giles held the reins of Vencidor as they rode slowly to their end, letting Agnes get the feel.

"It's working, Giles. The lodestone that Guilhelms sewed into the saddle is gripping the iron of the mail. It's positioned perfectly, all along my legs and underneath me. It's as though I'm glued on." Two more steps. "The stirrups, too. Sometimes the forging takes the drawing power from the lodestone, but not this time. My feet are fixed tight." Another step. "Thank God that Baron Henri did not get close enough to the horse with his mail."

"Sweetheart, forget this foolishness. You're going to get hurt. Let me fight that Charles. You will not lose your County, I swear it."

"We've discussed that. If I let you fight, Charles will be replaced by the youngest, strongest, fastest knight in their company." She reached back with her gauntlet to touch his face. "Stop interfering with my miracle, Giles, with God's plan for Alberensa."

"As you wish, my lady." They rode forward, three more steps.

"Giles, do you remember First Corinthians? 'Faith, hope, love abide, these three, but the greatest of these is love.' Kiss me, beloved, before you get down."

He leaned around and they kissed, full on the lips. The French whistled and cheered and laughed and called out her name. Giles waved at them as he jumped off, turned her horse down the lists, and moved it against the fence.

"Put down your visor." She did. "Position your shield." She did. "Good. Lower the lance." She did. "Good. Not too far back under your arm, yes, there, good." He handed up the reins so that she could hold them in her shield hand. "Do you have the reins? Can you feel the fence against your foot"?

She wiggled in the seat, testing. "Yes, and yes."

"The King would only aim for your shield to knock you off the horse, Aggie. Charles will aim for your head, to break your neck and kill you. Keep your shield high."

"Yes." More wiggling. "Where is the sun, husband"?

"More in his eyes than yours, beautiful."

"Give the signal, then, Giles my beloved. I'm ready."

She heard the grass swish against his boots as he stepped back. She found herself in the Cathedral again at her Acknowledgment, alone in the dark amidst thousands. Vencidor snorted and people murmured all around her, waiting. The breeze caressed her nose, the birds chirped and the sweet smell of freshly trampled flowers filled the air.

"Charles has motioned. I'm motioning now, my love."

Only a second, and then the trumpet sounded, a note, a higher note, the first note again, silence. Agnes spoke her mother's dying words, the last words of Christ on the Cross.

"Father, into thy hands I commit my spirit"!

The Countess tapped Vencidor on the shoulder with her shield. He started forward. She felt the fence against her leg and turned the reins right, making the animal stay tight against the wood. In a moment, a few steps, he got into the rhythm they had practiced, remembering to stay close to the lists.

"Good, Vencidor. Faster now."

Another tap, and the animal sped up to a trot, and a gallop.

Thanks be to God the lodestone is working it's working!

The sounds the sounds.

The crowd cheered all around her, calling her name, asking God to save the King. The birds disappeared, the wind on her face came from the speed, the loud hoofbeats of her horse assaulted her ears as she strained for the one sound she needed to hear.

Vencidor moved beneath her, holding to the lists, lifting, dropping. A sudden memory filled Agnes's mind, her sister Madeleine riding in front of her in the glade, looking back, yelling, smiling. Marguerite was screaming at the sisters to stop shrieking they were Ladies as they raced down the stream with their legs showing and their hair flowing and Agnes tried to follow her sister's movement in her mind, up, down, the lodestone keeping her on the saddle.

There, there, there's the sound! She guided her horse back against the fence. Hooves, the beat of Charles' horse. Drive all other sounds from your mind, the shouting, the cheering, the hooves of your own horse.

His horse, his horse, remember what it sounded like each time Giles warned of the coming collision.

Not loud enough
Good Vencidor good
Not yet
Wait
Steer in
Wait
In a moment
A moment
Madeleine looked back, grinned and pointed
NOW!

Agnes flipped up her lance and tossed it to Charles's side. She had but a second to grab the pommel and duck her head as she heard his shout and his curse and his lance glanced off her shoulder, hard but not hard enough. The crowd roared, cheered, shouting louder than anything she had ever heard.

Her shoulder shrieked as she held on and galloped past the end of the fence. Vencidor started turning now without the wall, but thank God he responded as she pulled back the reins.

"Vencidor, Vencidor, stop, stop." He slowed, stopped, snorted to clear his nostrils.

The pain mounted in her shoulder as she steadied her mount and waited for Giles to run up. Behind her, a horse was down, bellowing in agony, thrashing and kicking against the lists.

You are on your horse, Agnes. Sir Charles is not on his. Count Roland the Founder, your County has been saved through the Might, Majesty, Power and Dominion of the Eternal Triune God, may His Name be forever blessed!

Madeleine, Hugh. Daddy and I will be home for dinner, my darlings.

"Vencidor, you have served Alberensa well this day. I dub you Sir Vencidor." Don't take the chance of tapping his shoulders.

"Witchcraft"! surfaced from the cheering around the lists. "Heretic witchcraft"!

Someone was tugging at her, dragging her from the saddle. A strong yank overcame the draw of the lodestone. She thundered to the ground, on her bad shoulder.

"Whore of Satan"!

Charles of Épernay, Satan Himself, kicked her in the side, and again. He ripped her shield from her arm and tossed her onto her back. Suddenly she was being dragged along the ground by her legs.

"AAAAHHHH! Stop! Stop! My shoulder! My shoulder!"

Even that pain was less than the fear, the same fear that she felt in the cave in the Sárdalo, threatened and helpless.

Giles's voice sounded in the distance. "Let go of Aggie now or I'll kill you, you fucking rapist motherfucker"!

Her noble consort certainly remembered a few things from the barracks, although she had never heard them in their bedchamber. It was almost funny, through the unbelievable agony of being dragged on that shoulder. She could hear many men drawing close, more shouting.

"Your balls will be on my blade, asshole"! Fulques that time, as Épernay ripped her helmet off, and her coif. He was lifting her hauberk when suddenly there was a great crash and she was lying alone on her back while the sound of steel on steel began to ring out above her.

"Stop! I command it! Stop! Put up your swords. Unhand the Countess"!

"Giles," Agnes said, "if you're still alive, do as the King says."

The noise ceased, except for the baying horse. Someone was kneeling next to her, kissing her right hand, hurting her shoulder even more.

"Are you all right, my lady Countess"?

"Sir Charles may have broken my shoulder, Your Majesty. Pray tend to the horse first. I did not mean to cause it such injury."

"My lord of Deauville, please dispatch Épernay's mount. Lord Sarlant, do you need help in bringing your lady to her tent? Her right shoulder is badly injured. Sir Martin, that is your name, is it not, Martin of Ablois? Perhaps you could remove your steel from the throat of my champion, Martin."

"You are here, Sir Martin? After so many years, we meet again. Reach under my hauberk." Agnes grunted from her pain, but nothing happened. "Reach under, my lord. I am not endowed as Lady Mayrènge, so you will find a chest more like a man's. You will also find your cross, a gift I treasure greatly. With it, I fear, God has given me victory over your King. I hope His Majesty does not take offense."

"What we have seen today, my lady," the King answered, "is a miracle. It was the Will of God. I will give thanks to Him myself for your victory. I only regret that one so brave and so beautiful will never be my vassal."

Agnes thought to ask the boy king if he might regret that one so creative, so resourceful, so intelligent would never be his vassal. She remembered the restless evil tongue of Saint James and kept her peace.

13

Giles brought the bonesetter into Agnes's tent while she was changing. "Hmmm, this will hurt," and he swung her arm and squeezed her shoulder as she shrieked out at the shock of the pain. After which she could move her arm again, although it still hurt terribly.

The bonesetter left. Anniken and Gracia dressed her in her braces, her Alberensa silk, her jewelry, her coronet. When she left her tent, a roar went up, not only from Alberensa, but from the men of France.

"Sheyka al-Hadid"! the Albigensian Crusaders called, "Long Live *Sheyka al-Hadid"!*

With one shoulder injured, Agnes let Giles help her to the canopy. "Join us for a cup of wine, Countess. We would like this to be the start of a long friendship."

Agnes sat down across from the King of France and the Queen Mother. Anniken had fashioned a sling for her arm, and it helped, a little. Behind her, she knew, stood Giles, Fulques, Lisbetta, Guilhelms,

Aenor. Opposite her, all those Counts and nobles and men-at-arms. She doubted any of them were looking at Giles or Fulques or Guilhelms.

"I'm sorry about your arm, Countess."

"As am I, Majesty. I'm running out of parts to break, and I'm only twenty-eight."

She heard the Queen draw in her breath. "The Lord has proven me wrong today, Countess, but you should keep in mind the words of Saint James about the tongue."

"Yes, Your Majesty, you are right. It is a failing of which my husband reminds me constantly. I must work harder at it."

The King laughed, as did his court, except for the two Épernays.

"You are indeed the Iron Countess, my lady, as your troubadours say." She felt the King take her right hand, stop, and kiss her left instead. "Sir Ponset of Arguenos is in my company, my lady. I feel constrained not to hand him over to you."

"He is no longer 'of Arguenos,' Your Majesty. His felony bars him from any succession to the County. His fief is forfeit and his whole family banished. If he attempts to regain Arguenos, you must drive him away."

"As our agreement requires. What then"?

"He is young enough to make the pilgrimage. Send him to Outremer with his sons."

"It shall be done. What do you wish of these Épernays who refused to accept the judgment of God"?

"They have caused my County and my people grievous harm, Majesty, with their evil behavior. Strip them of Épernay and grant the fief to Sir Martin. He is a chivalrous knight, a friend of my husband and a friend of Alberensa."

"What of Henri"?

"He is too old for another pilgrimage to the Holy Land. He has already lost an arm for his sins. Let him end his days as a knight in service to Sir Martin."

"What of Charles"?

"He is not too old for a pilgrimage. Send him to join the Hospitallers at Krak de Chevaliers. The Christians are threatened in Outremer. His violent ways will be of use there. He may even repent of his evil behavior in the presence of such honorable men." The Countess paused, remembering. "One restriction only. He is never to attack the castle at Jabil al-Hadid. My nephew Baron Guilhabert rules there under the Saracens. I do not want him disturbed."

"So let it be done. Sir Charles, you will be gone from France within the week. We will hear from the Hospitallers that you have arrived in this sailing season. God grant you a safe journey to the Holy Land, my lord."

"What of this heretic bluebird, hugging and kissing this soldier in front of all"?

Be careful, Agnes, but be clever. "Father Felipe, you should heed Her Majesty's guidance concerning the tongue. I rule in Alberensa, not the Holy Father. You are welcome to preach against the heresy in my County, but you will cease from claiming that I took the *Consolamentum*. You will cease from attacking the Baroness of Mayrènge. If you persist in either, you will be banished." She let Felipe bluster for a moment. "The Baroness will be wed on the Feast Day of St John the Baptist this month. You are welcome to join us."

"So be it, then," the King said. "Cups for everyone. Let us lift them to the eternal friendship between Alberensa and France, sealed this day by Holy Writ of Our Lord and Savior Jesus Christ."

Agnes drank, without guilt. You tricked them with the lodestone. You tricked them by tossing away your lance, tripping his horse. Your victory is still a miracle. David has met Goliath and triumphed again.

■ ■ ■

The Countess fell asleep, despite the bumping, as the column made its way back to her city. More wine might ease the pain of her shoulder, but enough wine to dull it completely would leave her drunk. Lisbetta watched her sleep and thought of Fulques. Giles and Agnes, Fulques and Lisbetta, Madeleine and Hugh, six lives linked around one, for as long as they should live.

Guilhelms and Aenor and their children, they are linked too. After this battle, Guilhelms knows that he must accept a title. Only that will protect his furnace and his family beyond this generation. All the descendants of Esquiva of Foix had been lucky to hold to their possessions as commoners for as long as they had.

A shout went up as the carriage rode through the gates, a booming rush like The Pont when the workers charged the furnace. The war was over, Alberensa was victorious and their Countess was still alive.

"Close up the gates until the French leave," Giles called out.

The sound of her husband's voice woke Agnes up where the blast furnace had not. She was a little bleary-eyed as she leaned back, her face suddenly growing pale. And paler, and she broke out in a sweat.

"Lissie. The door, the door, open the door"!

"Giles! Aggie is sick, Giles"!

Even as Lisbetta reached for the door, she was too late. Agnes vomited red wine all over her lovely blue dress, and sprinkled Lisbetta's, and covered the floor of the carriage. The stench rose into the air, overpowering the perfume, making Lisbetta gag. Giles stood in the doorway, wiping her mouth with his tunic.

"Aggie! What's the matter? Is it the shoulder? Some other injury"?

A strange smile crossed the face of the Iron Baroness. Her blue eyes turned in the direction of his voice, and her answer was almost dreamlike.

"Not an injury, exactly, my beloved husband. It appears that once again we have mastered the getting." She retched, but nothing more came. She smiled as she remembered the feel of little Maddie's hands on her belly while she was pregnant with Hugh. This time, four little unseen hands would explore.

"You mean…"?

"I have not had my monthly time for over two months. I am with child, beloved, your child, our child. A child that will grow up in our County embraced in our love. Let us give thanks to the living God for such a great gift, forever and forevermore."

EPILOGUE

County of Alberensa
1 April 1260

Agnes rode in her dark up the Compostela Road. She sat the pillion as she had behind her brother, with her arms around her husband's waist, listening to the animal's hoofbeats against dirt and stone and the wood of the occasional bridge. Easier to ride a wagon down to Narbonne and take ship, but the Countess wished to leave over the Sárdalo Pass, the route that made her County wealthy, the route she took with Jamilla bint Hassan when they fetched her beloved cousin, the Baroness of Mayrènge.

Snow still covered *Lo Grandautar,* Giles said, but a warm March had cleared the Pass. Agnes felt the sun on her face and smelled the coming Spring in the moist soil beneath. When she first arrived in Alberensa, the damp of Languedoc reminded her of the glade with the pool in Jabil al-Hadid. Now whenever she rode up the canyon with Giles, the never-seen green of Alberensa would echo in her mind.

You ruled well in the years that followed your joust, Agnes, secure in the protection of the French crown. The iron flows from the banks of the Alberensa as it did from the Orontes, the pilgrims stream over the Pass and the land remains rich and fertile. Yet your finest prize, your greatest gift, are your three children, Madeleine and Hugh and Esther. In your condition, even one child would be a boon from Heaven, a true miracle unassisted by lodestone or lance-tossing trickery. The Lord has blessed you with three, all healthy, all still alive.

The horse clumped across a bridge in the company of a band of pilgrims. Giles tapped her hands, "How are you feeling, my Wise One"? By naming her *Agnes La Sabia,* the troubadours paid tribute to her skill in steering Alberensa through the constant threats. Pressure from Aragon. Pressure from England through Gascony. Subtle pressure from Louis and Blanche, masked as offers to send soldiers to protect the County from Aragon and England. Most of all, pressure from the relentless Inquisition. The Preaching Friars of Dominic de Guzmán terrorized all of Lengadòc. They held trials and pronounced anathema on the Good Christians, then gave them over to the secular authority to be burned at the stake.

"I should feel sadder than I do, Giles." Agnes fingered her cross, her gift from Baron Martin of Épernay, now long gone to meet their Savior. "There will be some happiness in this parting, and for that I give thanks to the Lord." She squeezed his waist. "It was time to leave. If we kept waiting for Rixenda to be without child, we'd never go."

"She blushes nicely every times she tells us, Aggie, while Hugh has a boastful gloat. Two sons and a daughter in five years and another on the way. Sir Laurent is as amazed at his daughter's fertility as we are."

"Our decision is for the best. To the Black Friars, I'm still the Blind Crippled Witch of Satan, the Heretic Leper Boy who took the *Consolamentum.* I must have taken the *Consolamentum*, they claim, because I refuse to burn heretics or even put them in the dungeon."

"What heretics"?

"None that we could find, anyway. The Preaching Friars managed to find many."

They rode a few steps in silence. "I will miss our grandchildren in the few years we have left, Giles, but Hugh needs us gone. The joust outside Dactalanne is already fading into the mists of time. It has become a ballad of the troubadours, the legend of *Sheyka al-Hadid*, not a fact."

"Yet like the Countess Harildis, Aggie, it is a fact."

"Yes, but when the King's son Philip succeeds him, he will find that fact conveniently not believable. Or if believable, not binding on him. It will fall to Hugh and Rixenda, to Maddie and her husband Fulques II of Arguenos, to Baron Tibaut of Pont de Molin to maneuver between the Church and Aragon and England and France to keep our County free."

The sighing of the breeze through the still-bare trees sounded pleasant but felt chilly as they climbed higher up the road. The rush of the tumbling Alberensa blended with the murmuring of the pilgrims around them. Agnes pushed back at her growing sadness, a sorrow that would sharpen to pain when they crested the Sárdalo and left their family forever.

"Do you ever wonder, Aggie, about the rule that family members cannot be forced into convents, into holy orders"? Giles, too, must have been thinking of the path behind and the path ahead, of Jabil al-Hadid.

"Jamilla and I discussed that. Let's begin with the ironworks on the Orontes. Do nobles own smelters, Giles"?

"No, my lady Countess, trade is beneath us."

"Exactly. Raymond did not ennoble Julian for throwing some Saracens off the wall of Hisn al-Akrad. Julian was a master of ironworking, a man who could free the metal from the rock. He was given his fief so that he could control the Iron Mountain for Raymond. 'Merchants with a Title,' that's what they called us."

"'*Julian de Blagnac,*' meaning 'from' Blagnac, not 'of' it. The same with *'Monica de Ronzières.'*"

"Exactly. Monica must have been 'Sister Barbara' at the Montjoix convent. That explains the inscription in the illustrated Bible at Jabil al-Hadid, 'Prepared with love for Sister Barbara, who nobly answered the Holy Father's call.' Monica broke her vows to marry Julian. How they met, that we'll never know."

"She was put in that convent against her will, why we'll never know."

"Exactly." Agnes leaned forward and kissed Giles's cheek. "Making commoners noble, that's what my family does, my love, starting with Julian and Monica themselves."

"Then me, then Lisbetta, the Baroness of Mayrènge, and then Fulques, the Baron of Arguenos."

Silence followed, the memory of the Baron, lost on King Louis's crusade a decade before. The King's plea for aid came while the Inquisition still raged across Lengadòc even after the mass burning at Montsegur.

"The Holy Church wonders," a graying Charpentier said when he brought the King's message from Paris, "How it is that convicted heretics in Alberensa are not put to the stake? His Majesty has defended your decision to have them work in your smelters, your mines, cutting wood from your forests. France benefits from Pont de Molin."

Agnes suspected that Blanche was behind the visit, another effort to trap her, to reverse the shame of the joust.

"Does His Majesty now suggest that I burn my heretics instead, *Monsieur*"?

"His Majesty suggests that you earn his support by answering his plea."

"Here am I," Fulques said, stepping forward, "Send me."

The Baron of Arguenos took one hundred men and set sail with the King from Aigas Mortas on the Mediterranean. Four years later, ten men returned with news that Fulques and the others had fallen in the disaster at Fariskur.

Within hours after the Fariskur survivors reached Alberensa, Bishop Felipe sent word from Our Lady of the Pyrenees that the Holy Inquisition sought to question the heretic Lisbetta Deslegador. Agnes could feel the tears on her friend's cheeks when she summoned her, tears for the loss of her husband added to the lingering sadness of two children lost to disease. She summoned her Seneschal.

"Peter, take Lisbetta's daughter Ermessenda to Arguenos immediately, to join her brother Fulques. He is now the Baron."

With her daughter dispatched, the Baroness of Mayrènge left for the mountains in haste, as the Israelites had done after the Passover, as she had done that Easter Sunday when she first taunted Felipe Vilalba. She was barely out of the castle when the Bishop of Alberensa arrived, together with two guards from the Cathedral.

"I have come to arrest the heretic Lisbetta Deslegador."

"Lady Mayrènge has left on a pilgrimage, my lord Bishop."

Felipe's face filled with rage. His eyes blazed. His gray head shook. "That is indeed a sudden decision, my lady"! The Countess shrugged her shoulders. "Where to"?

Agnes stood her ground, or rather sat it while her new secretary Lady Madeleine took notes at the little desk. "She said something about Egypt, to pray at the grave of her husband."

"Nonsense. She left for the mountains to join the other heretics."

"You know the way, my lord Bishop, if you wish to search for her."

"Her lands are forfeit for heresy."

"Then they are forfeit to me. If there is nothing more, Lady Madeleine will escort you to the door." She felt Maddie tremble, but only for a moment. Then she stood firm and tall with Lisbetta's little trick of the heels.

"This way, please, Bishop Felipe. My mother tires easily at her age and in her condition."

That hurt, since Agnes was only 49 at the time. Now she was 57. Today, with the emotion of the moment, she did feel old.

Fifty-seven, not so bad compared to Giles. He is nearly seventy. That is truly old, almost miraculous. Fortunately I remember only the vigorous man of his youth. My handsome sergeant with a wrinkled face and gray hair, I am glad I cannot see that.

"I remember crossing that last long bridge. Are we at the Shrine to Mary of Egypt"?

"Yes, and so is Lisbetta. She looks like Sister Ekaterina, wearing her *Parfait* robe like a nun's habit. Her hair is gray now, Aggie, like yours, like mine. Eight years eating only of water and wood has made her thin again, even after four children."

Giles lifted the Countess down so that the two women could embrace. A tearful reunion followed, even for the Baron of Sarlant. The pilgrims praying at the shrine watched the strange trio, wondered and passed on.

"I have missed you, Lisbetta, missed you so much. Maddie was a wonderful replacement, but a daughter is not the same as an old and true friend."

"Especially a replacement who longs to spend her days at Arguenos with her husband, not at her mother's side. You want me back, my lady Countess."

"Call me Aggie. In the Saracen lands, Baroness, our titles will mean nothing, so we should stop using them." They laughed. "I want you back so that I can rescue you while there is still time. Hugh will not be able to protect you once Philip is King."

"We're almost all gone anyway, my lady. I left three old people behind in the village, that's all. The Inquisition of the Black Friars has succeeded in destroying the Good Christians. I wonder if that fanatical Felipe ever asked himself if burning people at the stake was a Christian thing to do."

"Many times, I'm sure," Giles said. "The answer was always yes, to protect the Holy Church and the Christian faith from a dangerous heresy. He succeeded, but he destroyed the tolerance that was once a part of Lengadòc." Giles looked downhill. "There's another large group of pilgrims coming. We can fall in with them."

The knight lifted the *Parfait* to ride sideways in his saddle. He put Agnes back onto the pillion. She put her arms around Lisbetta as she once had around him, around Hugh, around her father Joscelin. Giles took the reins and prepared to lead their mount.

"It's Mary of Egypt's Holy Thursday this year, the first of April," Agnes said. "Hadassah's Holy Thursday, when threats drove out Angibert's brilliant Glassmaker. With all the threats against us, it is right that we leave on the same day. Please read the inscription, Lissie-Bet, one last time."

"Entreat me not to leave you or to return from following you. Where you die I will die, and there will I be buried."

"So shall it be, my friends. We will pass our remaining days in Jabil al-Hadid with Guilhabert and Jamilla. When our time is fulfilled, we will be buried with my brother at the end of the canyon. Our graves will be unmarked, for such is the Saracen way. No man will know where we are, but the Lord our Savior will surely know. His trumpet shall sound and we shall be raised. Our death shall be swallowed up in victory."

The Countess of Alberensa paused, filled with emotion.

"I shall stand again at the latter day upon the earth, and in this flesh shall I see God."

Made in the USA
Columbia, SC
02 November 2020